THE BLACKMOON SHARDS

BOOKS BY ELDON THOMPSON

the Legend of Asahiel
The Crimson Sword
The Obsidian Key
The Divine Talisman

Warder
The Ukinhan Wilds
The Blackmoon Shards
The Sundered Isle

WARDER

THE
BLACKMOON SHARDS

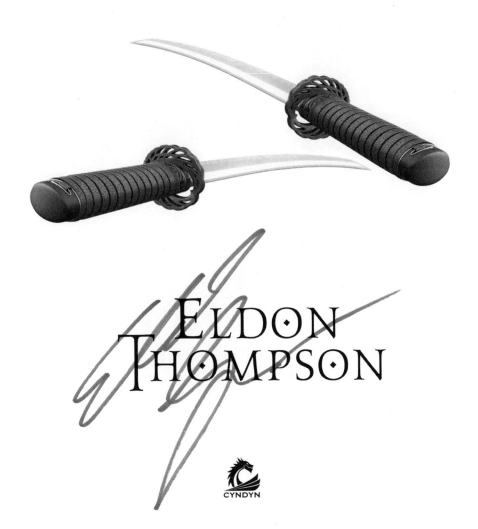

ELDON
THOMPSON

CYNDYN

THE BLACKMOON SHARDS
Copyright © 2018 by Eldon Thompson
All rights reserved

Cover illustration by Daren Horley
Addaranth map by Maxime Plasse

Library of Congress Control Number: 2018903352

ISBN 978-1-948825-01-6
Trade Hardcover – Limited Edition

Published by Cyndyn; Irvine, California
Printed in the United States of America

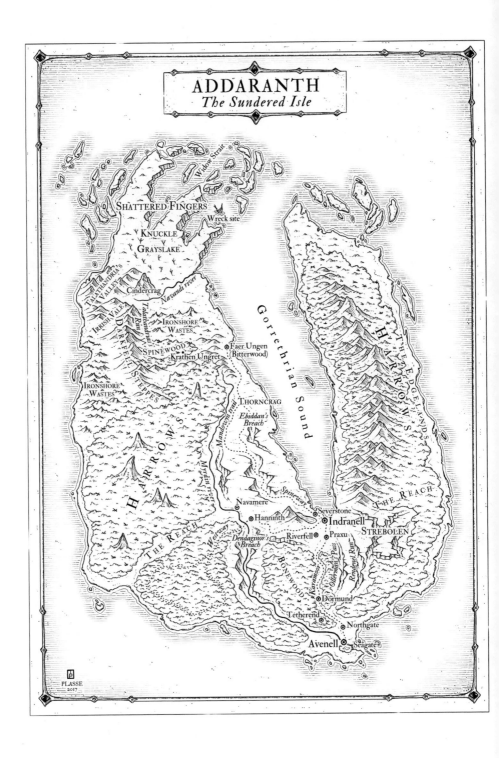

PROLOGUE

T HE SHRIKE PEERED BACK AT HIM with unmistakable bloodlust, its eye a crimson garnet burning with reflected torchlight and gleaming with primal hunger. Matching red markings painted its breast, its pinion feathers, the tips of its ashen talons and the scimitar curve of its ebony beak. Stark against an otherwise obsidian sheen, the vivid splashes of color seemed to pulse with the rapid ebb and flow of its breath. The magnificent raptor knew that it had once again served its purpose with unerring strength and efficiency. All that remained was to collect its reward.

The morgrats caged along the far wall of the rookery could sense it as well, mewling as they clambered anxiously about their kennel, fleshy forms writhing over and around one another in search of escape. Once plucked from their prison, the amphibious rodents would be given to make a mad dash down the broken hillside, racing to find a crack or crevice in the pitted slope in which to burrow their way to freedom—a jagged, coal-hued ground littered with the splintered bones of those who had made similar attempt before.

The only salvation lay in continued captivity.

"Well?" Temerius asked.

The harsh edge in his voice caused the shrike to rear back on its open perch, puffing in challenge. He might have reached out to stroke its nape or crop in reassurance, but not before the unsettled bird had sated its hunger. To do so sooner might cost him a finger.

Kriehl failed to respond. Sensing his hesitation, Temerius rounded with an asp-like turn, gaze kindling a fire of its own. Far below, the surf crashed against the razor-edged shoreline, echoing a dull roar while shooting skyward to form a briny, windborne spray that reached clear to their position near the open cave mouth.

He found the wizened shrikemaster hunched over his stone lectern, worrying still over the piece of lambskin the great bird had delivered. Rare, that it should take him so long to decipher an incoming dispatch. Perhaps his already compromised eyesight had finally failed him.

Nonetheless, he wisely spoke before being prompted again to do so. "Fell news, my lord."

Temerius grimaced. He had sensed as much the moment his lookout had alerted him to the shrike's imminent arrival. His intuition had formed at once a cold dread in the pit of his stomach that churned like rancid meat. He had not hastened from his ship's cabin in the cove below, abandoning Lehmyra's ebon-skinned warmth and braving the rookery's perilous stair in the dead of night, to hear a shriveled scow such as Kriehl prattle a general misgiving.

"Are you to determine for me now but the *nature* of this writ? Or is it within my province to know the content?"

The shrikemaster gave a cursory bow, gesturing vaguely for his liege captain's forgiveness. Too old to observe propriety, it seemed. Else too certain of the status he enjoyed as one of Grendavan's favorites. Temerius wondered briefly what that status might be worth if he were to pop Kriehl's remaining eye from that petulant, leather-wrapped skull of his.

Kriehl straightened. A laborious effort. As if encumbered suddenly by an invisible yoke draped over his bony shoulders. The seawind gusted, sending a shiver through his gnarled, whipcord frame. "We have been betrayed. Your great father is slain."

An abrupt tightness seized Temerius's chest, like an invisible fist clenched around his heart. His lungs fought the sudden pressure, while a gushing warmth flooded his veins. His mind filled with images of his not-too-distant boyhood, while his thoughts sputtered a denial that struggled desperately for release. But he found his tongue trapped behind gritted teeth, and the cords of his voice strung taut with pain and fury.

The lie echoed as he felt himself plummeting.

Your great father is slain.

"They bade him welcome, led him and his party into their cathedral, conducted the ceremony, and . . ."

The shrikemaster trailed off as Temerius strode forward, a swift, certain movement of unconscious command. He reached out as Kriehl withered in reflex, and snatched the lambskin writ from the interpreter's gnarled, age-spotted grasp.

He looked at the figures scrawled there, searching. Though he could not read them, he recognized the hand. Sabrynne. The Stormweaver. Which meant there could be no mistake, no error in the interpretation of events. Unless . . .

He whirled on the cringing Kriehl, who withdrew another step. The recently returned shrike let loose a shriek of impatience. The members of its cast, locked in their various cages around the limestone chamber, echoed in sharp chorus.

"You err, old man," he heard himself rasp. "The Pretender had neither the strength nor the will to oppose my father."

"'Twas not by his hand," Kriehl admitted. "An outlander. Some rogue assassin dredged up from foreign shores. Nara's doing, not Darr's. A mere youth, by the account you hold, but formidable, unpredictable, treacherous. 'Twas *his* hand that came to Nara's defense, *his* blade that—"

"Assassin." The word reverberated amid the pulse of hammer strokes raging in his skull. "A mere youth, you say." His gaze blurred as he strained to read the unfamiliar markings inked upon the lambskin, to decipher for himself the story they revealed. Liege captain, he was, of the *Kraken's Reach*. Chief steward of this outpost atoll, Rannuthrok—the Ravaged Maiden. Yet it was not given to him to know the arcane language by which a dispatch of this magnitude was communicated. That privilege belonged only to the Core—a handful of elevated shrikemasters and arc captains sworn to the Great Grendavan.

His father. His father could have read this. But not him. He had not yet earned the right to—

A drop of water hit the lambskin. *Not water,* he realized. A tear.

The neglected shrike squawked another reminder, its call filled this time with mockery.

Kriehl frowned a similar disapproval. "We foresaw this possibility. Your father, chief among all, understood that it—"

"This rogue. Assassin. Has he a name?"

"That and more. He has made off with the *Vengeance,* profaning its decks with a crew of the Pretender's landsnakes. He means to rescue Thane."

"His name."

The shrike squawked again, insistent, and again its surrounding cast carried the cry. The morgrats whimpered and writhed in their kennel. The patch-eyed Kriehl scowled. "Kronus, it is written there. Kylac Kronus."

"A name I shall carve in my bowsprit, once I have carved my father's in his flesh." He crumpled the lambskin in his fist, and turned back to tend to the shrike.

"That is not your reigning order," Kriehl argued, shuffling after him as if to retrieve the message. "Yours is to make for Pammelthrok."

There to join Arc Captains Irravius and Cortrus in the mobilization of an armada that would proceed upon command to the mouth of the Gorrethrian Sound. Temerius stopped as he came eye-to-eye once more with the starving shrike and its livid bloodlust. A mere candle now, compared to his own. "And these orders hail from whom, when our overlord, the Great Grendavan, is dead?"

Behind him, Kriehl stiffened at the derision in his tone. "'Ware your tongue, Temerius, and the treason it would sow. Your father may be gone, but this changes noth—"

"It changes everything," Temerius snapped, as the shrike's gaze pierced him. Softly, he repeated, "Everything."

He lashed out, gripping the shrike about the neck. The great seabird screeched, a shrill cry taken up by its cast. It thrashed and beat its powerful wings, and Temerius shook it in turn. While blood-dipped talons tore furrows in his forearm, he held fast, squeezing.

"My lord!" Kriehl gasped. "Temerius!"

The morgrats mewled and whined as if it were they being strangled. The meaty wings of the other shrikes slapped against the iron
bars of their cages. Far below, breaking waves surged and crashed,
bellowing their dull roar.

A sharp crack, and he felt the bones give beneath his jerking fist.
The shrike's head fell limp, even as its body shuddered through a final
series of violent convulsions. Its talons raked at him once, twice more,
then ceased to struggle. Triple eyelids sagged, half-drawn shutters
against the reflected torchlight.

Hoping the impertinent creature could yet feel a measure of pain,
Temerius shoved the lambskin dispatch clear down into its crop, drawing blood across his hand where it scraped against the shrike's beak.

"What have you done?" Kriehl asked breathlessly.

Temerius released the carcass, watching it tumble from its perch to
lie in a feathered heap upon the stone of the cavern floor. Its wizened
master rushed forward, stooping to cradle its broken form, while the
cries of its kin sang of fury and accusation.

"Fool!" Kriehl hissed. "This bird was worth more than mine own
life!"

Temerius Seahammer reached for the dagger sheathed at his waist—
a long, bone-handled blade of steel gifted him by his father. As dark
rivulets streamed from the riven flesh of his forearm, he wondered
if, with only one good eye, the shrikemaster of Rannuthrok could
see the flaming bloodthirst that consumed his own.

"To that," the captain growled, "we are agreed."

DARKNESS ENGULFED HER.

Her head spun. Her stomach churned. She clenched her eyes, her
jaw, gritting her teeth in a determined effort to hold the expulsive
forces in check. But the lightless void in which she found herself rose
and fell, rose and fell, rocking at the same time from side to side in
ceaseless rhythm. A roiling pressure mounted from within. Building . . . squeezing . . .

She lurched forward, vomiting in the blackness, cringing at the sound of her wretched heaving and the splash of half-digested food chunks spilling into the bilgewater at her feet. The stench of her own sickness washed over her, summoning another wave. She gave it vent, having no choice now, succumbing to her body's urgent need.

She gasped for breath before retching again, and again. When a subsequent spasm produced only empty sputtering, she spat and rolled back against the coarse-grained wall, gripping her knees in surrender and self-loathing, allowing her dizziness to take her.

To the depths, she hoped. *This entire cursed ship, and me with it.*

The mere thought ignited a fire in her belly, a coursing warmth set to greedily consume pain and weakness. Nara grimaced, shivering there in the dank blackness of the cramped bilge while scathed from within by the flames of self-reproach. A mere two days had they been at sea, by her estimation, though it felt like weeks, and may in truth have only been hours. Whichever, too soon to be praying for death or elsewise relinquishing commitment to her purpose.

Would you let them win? Would you see them go unpunished?

Their faces paraded through her mind's eye, as if to remind her of her course. Thane, her brother. Ulflund, her faithful shadow. Abinama, her love's light and devoted companion. Pain stabbed at her with the memory of each, and new faces emerged—vile, disgusting. Grendavan, the Grenarr overlord, dark and imposing as he leered at her from across the altar. Ledron, her father's mindless lapdog, expressionless and bull-headed in the execution of his assigned orders. And Kylac, the impertinent mercenary, so reckless and cocksure. Undaunted. Undisciplined. A marvel in action, true, but those actions had cost her everything.

Not everything, came the inner voice, as her brother's face pushed to the fore. A plea, it seemed, as she envisioned again his dismembered ring finger—presented to her in Wingport. If she would see him returned by the Grenarr unkilled, they had said, she must forfeit all resistance and return to Avenell to seal the accord with their hated enemies. This, she had done, never truly believing that it would come to pass as her father or Ledron had planned, knowing that her light roamed free, trusting that he would find a way to liberate her.

Her heart clenched in concert with her stomach. She bucked forward and offered another involuntary heave. Liberate her, he would have, save for Kylac. For it was the rogue alone that had made Abi wary. Barring his presence, her Ukinh love would have made short-enough work of Ledron's tattered company, likely before she had ever been led from Kuurian shores. She would have yet had a chance to put her request before the Imperial Council, to beseech her father's aged cousin, Emperor Derreg, for aid against the treacherous Grenarr. The voyage home, the trek across the Harrows, the confrontation within the Ukinhan birthing warrens—

None of it would have transpired.

Nara spat again and wiped her mouth with the back of her hand, permitting herself a voiceless, shuddering sob in the undulating void of her prison. Her broken thumb throbbed within its splint, an unnecessary reminder of the conflict in those subterranean caverns. Would that Abi had confronted Kylac sooner. Would that any number of the natural perils inhabiting the Ukinhan Wilds had done so for him. His very presence, shadowing hers, had kept a swarm of rival predators at bay. Kept her safe. But doing so had also served to shield Kylac from untold hazards, to make possible their continued trek, their pursuit underground in search of the lifesaving sageryst, into the domain of the merciless jaggeruunt . . .

Bilgewater soured by stomach fluids lapped at her feet as the ship continued to rise and fall in relentless rhythm. As unrelenting as the truth she kept fighting to deny. It stalked her even in her dreams, cold and implacable. He had claimed ignorance, the rogue, and genuine it seemed, not feigned. He had even tried to apologize, in his own rash and clumsy way. Far too little. Far too late. The attempt itself, though a blow to her enemies, had likely only made matters worse. While she might bear grudging respect for his refusal to cow to authority, and for his seemingly matchless skills, she could not abide his cavalier approach, or trust that he had truly taken her or Thane's interests to heart. A mercenary, for all his professed aims to set matters right. And even if he followed through in all that he claimed, achieved all that he intended, the most grievous harm inflicted upon her could not be undone.

Her precious Abinama would remain to her forever lost.

The ship rose beneath her, buoyed by a particularly large swell, increasing her lightheadedness. Her intestines knotted, but managed to hold onto whatever contents they had not already rejected. Vomit burned in her throat. She resisted the desire to quench the sensation, understanding that her freshwater supplies were limited. Only when convinced that her retching was finished would she wash the foul flavor from her mouth. Emptying her skins too soon would force her in search of more, greatly increasing the chances that she would be discovered. Be discovered too soon, and she was liable to be returned right back home to her father, who would no doubt shackle her in rusty irons, if need be, to prevent her from repeating this course.

She would have suspected him clever enough to do so before, had he not demonstrated elsewise. He had certainly kept a tight leash in the hours leading to her would-be wedding ceremony. But the chaos that had ensued, and the mad scramble with which the king and his inner circle had reacted afterward, had evidently chased such considerations from his mind. She had been all but forgotten, it seemed, once her protestations at being denied a berth aboard had been rejected. Shuttered in her chambers with a Blackfist to ward the door, cocooned in her own disappointment, had been caution enough, her father must have assumed.

The notion brought a smirk of grim pleasure to her lips, which even another abrupt heave from her stomach could not curtail. It wasn't the first time her royal father had underestimated her. Defying his refusal, she had stolen out the window and down into the bowels of the castle, there to treat with one who she believed would be sensitive to her wishes. He, too, had denied her at first, echoing many of the same driveling protests coughed up by the others, and adding to them the fear that his life would be forfeit should it be discovered that he willingly aided her in an act bordering on treason. But she knew that he himself had volunteered to join this mission solely out of his love for Thane, and that he had only done so to ensure to the best of his limited abilities that the endeavor met with success. For that, he would need all the help to be mustered. Once she had persuaded him of the value of having her present to oversee any negotiations with the Grenarr—and of vowing to carry the secret of his involvement in her stowaway effort to the grave—he had capitulated and reluctantly agreed to see her smuggled aboard.

A fact she now had ample cause to regret. She knew not how long she might have to endure these torturous conditions, secreted away in the deepest recesses of the ship's bowels, punished by thirst and hunger and seasickness. She knew not how long she *could*. Eventually, her presence would be discovered, or she would be forced to emerge of her own volition. But she had sworn to herself that it would not be until they had crossed a point of no return, when reversing along their own wake would no longer be a tenable option. Before then, she would accept whatever pain, whatever illness, whatever horrendous discomfort could inflict itself upon her. Recalling Abinama's face and the certain agony of his final moments, she determined that she would feast on rats and roaches if she had to, choke down vomit and bilgewater, shiver and soak amid the dank, briny darkness until her bones cracked and the skin sloughed from her feet, ere she yielded to her enemies.

She owed it to her brother, her people, her Ukinh consort. She would see Thane rescued, delivered from his abductors without further harm. She would see the Grenarr punished, their ill-begotten attempts to invade her homeland foiled. Kylac, mercenary and self-assumed warder, would be her weapon, a willing instrument used to achieve these ends.

And when he had, when her brother and her people were safe, she would see him flayed and gutted, obtaining her vengeance with the song of his screams in her ears, and the taste of his blood upon her lips.

1

THE WINDS HOWLED AND WHISTLED, tugging at Kylac as he scrambled amid the shrouds and ratlines, causing the strands to whip and twist. Circling gulls shrieked at him, as if questioning his purpose among them and eyeing him as a potential meal. An afternoon sun had burned away the morning's brume, so that rays unfiltered by cloud blinded him at certain angles. All while the *Vengeance* herself bucked and leaned, without pattern, without warning, as she rode the ocean's swells, sleek and strong, yet beholden still to the mercurial power of the sea.

Kylac welcomed the challenges, sure and swift as he played about the ship's higher elevations in a series of leaps and swings, climbs and drops. A spider, the crew called him, and not in any flattering way. He could feel the gaze of a man or two on him now. With awe they viewed him, but shaded by mistrust. It wasn't natural, athleticism such as his. Not for a man, anyway. Such speed, dexterity, and anticipation . . . the work of the ancient Breeders, perhaps, but not of the Fair Mother, Eriyah. Was it not possible, Kylac had teased, for some men to be blessed more than others? Endowed with abilities meant to inspire? The goad had won him only grumbles and scowls. Evidently, his own arsenal of skills lay beyond the glorious realm of divine favor, slipping somehow into the dark domain of magecraft.

Kylac couldn't speak to one or the other, and so let them cling to their superstitions. His only knowledge lay in the countless hours he'd spent—dating back to his earliest memories—in exercise such as this, intended to test and thereby develop the broad range of physical qualities a man possessed. Quickness, balance, agility . . . natural functions one and all. If racing along the main topgallant yard of a ship at sea, harried by wind and waves, distracted by hungry gulls and piercing shards of sunlight, seemed magical, so too did a toddler's first halting strides upon steady earth. An aberration he might be. But he'd done much more to hone his talents than stand around gawking at the movements of others.

Reaching the starboard end of the yard, he paused for but a breath before springing into the air, an overhead flip as the ship keeled to larboard beneath him. Leaning and straightening into a headfirst dive, he reached for the aftmost shroud line. Upon catching it, he swung back into the underside of the ratlines, where he proceeded to clamber skyward again, hanging precariously above the maindeck below.

As good a way as any to while away his time at sea, and better than most. Ledron had promptly sought to forbid the activity, of course, just as the Shadowguard captain had during their first voyage together—from the wharves of Wingport to the shores of Addaranth. For the damage Kylac might do to the rigging, the damage he might do to himself, and the distraction it served to his fellow crewmen. But this was a different mission than that had been, and Kylac far less concerned with giving offense.

For what offense could be greater than those he'd given already?

Even so, the royal guardian he'd privately nicknamed the Head had argued straightaway that he was wasting his strength, suggesting rather sternly that he would do better to remain well rested, should their enemies happen upon them. To which Kylac had reminded the Blackfist that leaving muscles to rot could bring about a lethargy every bit as dangerous as the fatigue he hoped to prevent. And while these acrobatics might appear exhausting, Kylac had assured the captain that they did nothing to diminish his appetite for swordplay. Not surprisingly, Ledron had opted to test that claim, approaching him later, unannounced, following an hour-long bout of scaling and tumbling amid the rigging. But a lengthy demonstration against rotating clutches of hand-picked soldiers—in which he'd delivered an array of bruises to serve lasting reminder—had proven sufficient to ease the Head's fears concerning his endurance.

As he neared the base of the crow's nest, he caught the present lookout, a Whitefist named Jahvid, peeking down at him over the rim. Kylac offered a wink, then freed a hand for a salute.

Jahvid frowned and withdrew.

It caused him to wonder again if his Addaran crewmates might view him differently if he were one of them, rather than an outlander spawned on foreign shores. Common enough, that a man should seek to vilify what he couldn't readily explain. A reflexive act, however irrational. But to be feared an enemy over something so capricious as a geographical boundary had always struck Kylac as flagrantly absurd.

At the apex of the rigging's underside, he reached back with his feet to grip the mast with his lower legs. He then released his hold on the shrouds, allowing his torso to swing down until he faced the decks, clinging upside down to the mast. He had in his time been hailed a hero, as well, he reminded himself as he shimmied down the massive spar, and found no better use for adulation than he had for derision. Being cast by others in either light or shadow had little enough effect on how he conducted himself.

Then why are you here? nagged an inner voice.

He paid it no heed.

All else aside, it would be disingenuous to suggest that Ledron and his assembled brood of Shadowguard, Seawatch, Stonewatch, and select stewards had been given no reason to mistrust him. He'd granted them no discourse, no warning, as to where his deeds would take them. Were it not for his self-assumed actions in—

"Kronus!" a voice barked from below.

As with most any shipboard shout, the cry became a lusty echo, passed along by bustling sailors and stationary lookouts accustomed to receiving and acknowledging orders. Though he'd heard it from the first, Kylac's name rang six more times from all four winds before he'd righted himself for a response.

"How mights I be o' service, Captain?" he hollered down at the deck.

The Head, it seemed, was in no mood for open conversation. Or mayhap he meant to spare himself the indignity of bellowing amid the wind, to compete with its fluttering roar and the indignant squawking of gulls. Whichever, his only answer was to raise the scroll clutched in his fist and shake it fiercely in unmistakable summons.

With a nod and a leap, Kylac caught the main topmast backstay and rode the line down to the deck.

Ledron scowled, unimpressed.

Kylac looked from the Head to Pevrick, the first mate beside him, whose slate-gray eyes never seemed to blink, even when raked by fervent winds. Leeches, Kylac had dubbed him privately, given the twin tattoos flanking his throat—symbols of an unfamiliar origin that could as easily have been a pair of crescent-bodied bloodsuckers gorging on the veins in his neck.

The mate's stone-faced expression offered nothing to becalm Ledron's ire.

"What grim news now, Captain?"

Ledron extended the scroll in hand like a butcher chopping meat. "See for yourself."

Kylac could have told him then, without looking, what the matter entailed. By the scroll itself and the leather-wrapped tube clutched by Pevrick, the truth appeared plain. Nonetheless, he accepted the item and slowly unfurled its contents, demonstrating an appropriate earnestness that he hoped might help to soothe the captain's fresh-brewed fury.

"Another chart," Kylac observed.

"And the logs to attend it," Ledron growled, gesturing at the scroll tube held by Leeches. "Discovered in a secret hollow belowdecks."

"I gather they speak a different tale than the first."

"And the second. According to these, our current heading will carry us more than a hundred leagues off course."

While sensitive to the captain's seething frustration, Kylac silently congratulated the Grenarr on the exhaustive nature of their deception. Three sets of navigational charts depicting the location of the Baravian Atolls, each inconsistent with the last. Further search was likely to produce more. He'd wagered as much the moment their navigation officer had happened upon the second set, discovered a day earlier, which contradicted the original. Since the first had been so prominently displayed, and the second painstakingly hidden, they'd quickly assumed the original charts to represent false information, and had adjusted course according to the second. Even so, they'd agreed as a precaution to scour the vessel for additional logs and charts, all the while hoping not to find any that might raise further question as to their heading.

Alas.

"So tell me," Ledron fumed. A sheen of sweat caused his shorn head to gleam in the sun. "Which are we to believe?"

It could be any one of them, or none. Else a combination of the three, mayhap, decrypted by means known only to the Grenarr. By that reckoning, the truth or a missing piece of it might lie in an altogether different scroll tube yet to be uncovered.

But the captain knew all this. They'd discussed the possibilities when the first secret set had been unearthed. He'd come to Kylac not for his assessment, but for his confession. They would hear it from his lips that he'd erred in assuming they might rely on the enemy's charts and logs to find the family of atolls on which Dethaniel was supposedly hidden. They wanted to taste his chagrin when he admitted the fallacy of supposing that the maps and schedules kept by the Grenarr would be the fastest, most trustworthy method of doing so. With the irreconcilable doubt cast by this latest discovery, were the navigational records aboard this stolen vessel of any use at all?

Fair questions, save for the fact that the shipboard accounts had only ever been one small piece of a larger puzzle.

"Have ya shown these yet to Tormitius?"

Ledron grimaced and crossed his arms over his chest, telling Kylac he had not.

"To what end?" Leeches groused on the captain's behalf. "I would sooner trust the adder to greet threat with its tail, rather than its fangs."

Another old argument, only loosely couched. When debate had first arisen as to whether they could trust the direction indicated by their maps, the first mate had belabored the possibility that the destination itself was suspect, as the information had been provided by Sabrynne, the Grenarr emissary to King Kendarrion's court. *If you would meet your doom, seek the prince among the Blackmoon Shards.* For all they knew, she'd pointed them along the wrong vane of the compass altogether.

Mayhap, though Kylac believed elsewise. He'd been the one to peer into Sabrynne's eyes, her life hanging in the balance, as she'd relayed the information. *If you would meet your doom . . .* A challenge it had been, a taunt to spur them headlong into perils from which she didn't believe they could escape. Her intent hadn't been to send them wandering aimlessly as the result of misdirection. In that desperate moment, she'd given rein to a much simpler, more primal need.

Revenge.

But Kylac hadn't disputed the matter then, and saw no cause to do so now. He might be wrong, and Pevrick right. Even were it elsewise, there remained the added fold layered upon them by the aged scholar of His Majesty's court who'd posited that the Blackmoon Shards referred to the Baravian Atolls. With none other to confirm or refute the information, the old cartographer had been able to collect payment without challenge. An easy wager. Should he prove mistaken, he could always beg ignorance later—assuming any of them returned to discredit his claim. As of yet, a mere suspicion, but even if Sabrynne had spoken true, it might be that their own man had led them astray, willfully or elsewise.

"I spoke with Tormitius just this morning," Ledron added, lest Pevrick's insinuation have been unclear. "As of yet, he is of no mien to assist us."

When an opponent had planted his shield before you, it was seldom fruitful to continue hammering head-on. Sensing already that victory in this argument would require a dismantling of defenses, Kylac set about a series of feints. "So we sticks to our course," he suggested, "until we strikes a marker that exposes it as false."

"A marker," Ledron echoed. The peak in his throat jabbed as he spoke. "When the nearest land-based artifact on any of these charts is two days hence."

"And the next a day beyond that," Leeches added.

"At such distances—and the overall range by which our target seems to be shifting—we could lose weeks chasing it back and forth," the captain clarified. As if his disgust were not already palpable, he slapped at the chart in Kylac's hand. "With only their lies to go by, we're as good as blind."

Would that they had maps of their own, the Head had lamented, drawn by a hand they could trust. But in sweeping the rival Grenarr from the shores of the Sundered Isle, the Addarans had become constrained to them. For the Grenarr hadn't died off upon their eviction, but had, over the pair of centuries that followed, managed to tame the seas, becoming masters of wind and sail, tide and swell. As vigorously as the Addarans defended the land did the Grenarr lay claim to the surrounding ocean, subsisting as pirates and marauders against which no Addaran vessel or fleet could stand. As a result of this bitter standoff, the Addarans' own sea charts were incomplete or contradictory, pieced together from a variety of expeditions forced to turn about or felled by attack—none extending more than a few days out. Of the location they sought, believed to lie a week or more to the east, they had but scraps of legend and hearsay, scarcely more substantial than myth.

"These charts tell us more than ya knows," Kylac claimed.

"Oh?" Pevrick pierced him with that unblinking gaze. "You've scarcely looked at it."

"It tells us our adversaries have something worth hiding." As captain and first mate shared a glance of irritation, Kylac pressed his point. "The larger question before us, 'til now, was not where these Blackmoon Shards are located, but if'n they exist at all. If'n their emissary lied to us—"

"To you," Ledron snarled in correction.

"If'n their emissary lied to *me*, Dethaniel could as easily be on another Grenarr ship. Or stashed away in pieces on this one. Or spread throughout the bellies of a school o' fish."

The Head clenched his jaw. "What's your meaning, Kronus?"

"Only that they's told us now, unshaded by doubt, that they's a homeland after a fashion, a geographical heart to their roving society."

"That's what you take from this?"

"Why else would they hold the prince there?"

Leeches shook his head, snickering his dissent. "The filthy tar-skins are known to lord over many atolls, flung near and far. Even if His Highness is where we've been led to believe he is, there's nothing to say this one boasts any particular significance."

Kylac hefted the map in his hand. "Then why go to such pains to hide its location?"

A broadside wave splashed against the ship, shooting misty spray over the bulwark while the *Vengeance* creaked and shuddered in protest. A passing gull shrieked. Both captain and first mate remained silent, however, as they struggled to determine if the conclusions Kylac had drawn could in any way be based on something more substantial than the wind from his lungs.

"An expansive leap," Ledron decided.

"Which changes nothing," Pevrick added, turning to address his captain. "Any significance portrayed in their charts might be feigned. Or historic in nature. If the Baravian Atolls are indeed where the Grenarr first found root when cast from Addaranth, it could be home to nothing more than an altar to whatever pagan gods the soulless devils have come to worship."

Ledron reached for the chart in Kylac's hands. The pitch and sway of the ship seemed to reflect his ongoing deliberations as he gave it another passing study, while a slow, helpless shake of his head bespoke his despair. "We've but ashes to feed on here," he reiterated at last, rolling it shut with an angry series of twists. "Even if you're right about the Shards, and His Highness is to be found there, we need something more to sustain our search."

And there it was, the argument Kylac had wanted the Head to make. Masking his satisfaction as Ledron brandished the scroll at him like a dagger, Kylac closed in for the decisive blow. "Indeed. Which is why I left us a witness. One I's not yet been permitted to question."

Again, the captain stiffened at the suggestion. "He tells us nothing."

"He tells *you* nothing. Mayhap I can cast a fresh light."

Pevrick scoffed. "That he might stoke the flames of our ignorance and confusion?"

"That we might has some interpretation as to their accounts."

"I've tortured a tar-skin or two in my time," Ledron confessed. "A vain effort."

"Torture?" Kylac asked. "Question, I say. He needn't necessarily answer to reveal what he knows."

Ledron glowered, but didn't immediately respond. Pevrick must have taken this to mean he was considering Kylac's request.

"He'll lie," the intractable mate insisted. "Either to divert us, or steer us into an ambush. Acting on his words can only work against us."

"There are ways o' sifting truth from falsehood," Kylac argued. "But far more difficult to do so without looking a man in the eye."

From Ledron, he sensed now a flicker of doubt absent before.

"Captain," Leeches snapped, in a tone that served to encapsulate his prior objections. Or mayhap he meant to remind the Head of some private argument they hadn't seen fit to share.

Ledron ground his teeth, reluctant to the end, but said finally, "Let us see."

2

THE CAPTAIN'S QUARTERS smelled of rich spices and old leather, foreign oils and exotic incense, crude beeswax and refined tallow, permeated by the tang of metals—iron, brass, copper, steel—and seasoned by the fragrance of various woods—teak, oak, cedar, mahogany. The resulting blend of multi-varied ingredients caught in Kylac's throat as he entered on Ledron's heels, hemmed by Pevrick at his back. Though denied access to the master cabin since before their departure, he recalled at once its overpowering taste.

Proceeding deeper, past the antechamber serving as a private navigation room, the pungent flavor thickened. As Kylac stepped past the inner sentry, vision adjusting to the curtained darkness in which these quarters were now kept, a new scent quickly emerged—the musk of a man too-long chained, reeking of sweat and filth, redolent of indignity.

Their captive had been shackled to the captain's impressive bed, Kylac saw, by virtue of irons anchored in the stern wall and threaded around the massive posts forming the bed's frame. The fetters were loose enough to allow him to sit upright, as he did now, but held him bound at the ankles and wrists. His body had been stripped save for a soiled loincloth, revealing bundles of lean muscle that clung to a thick-boned frame. Pearl-black skin, unwashed, gleamed faintly in the dim lamplight. Deprived and weakened he appeared, but unbruised, unbattered, save for a wound to his left foot, wrapped in a coarse dressing caked with three-day-old blood.

Kylac knew its age because he'd been the one to tie it there.

The prisoner scarcely raised his head, initially, glowering from beneath his chiseled brow with sullen boredom. Catching sight of Kylac, however, a fresh fury rippled through his body, and he sat up with sudden fervor, wincing at the chains that brushed against his wounded foot.

Defiant still, as Ledron had suggested.

A long, tense moment filled the richly scented air, as each party waited for the other to speak.

"You've brought your asp, I see," Tormitius growled—Tormitius Shorecleaver, as he was known among his people. He glared only at Kylac. "Afraid to bloody your own hands, are you, Captain?" His mocking tone made his use of the Head's rank an epithet.

Ledron flung the chart in hand at the shackled Grenarrian, striking him in the chest. He then took the scroll tube from Pevrick and tossed it with its sister documents at Tormitius's feet. "Your hidden logs," Ledron replied curtly. "Not so well hidden."

Tormitius broke stares with Kylac long enough to glance at the wood-and-leather housing of half-spilled animal skins. A smirk came to his black lips, and a measure of the tension drained from his body, replaced with cruel amusement. "This vexes you?"

"How many more will I find?"

"How thorough is your search?"

"I'll rend this tub to its ribs, if I must."

The Shorecleaver chuckled. "Please do, that I might introduce you to the lord of crabs, and watch him pare the scales from this one's flesh." His gaze again found Kylac's.

Kylac took that as invitation, brushing past captain and first mate to assume the fore. He felt both Ledron and Leeches stiffen at his presumption, and so gripped the polished, intricately carved board at the foot of the bed—hoping that keeping his hands within view might ease their discomfort.

"I's no great love o' ships," he confessed. "But I prefer those that float, yes?" He glanced back at Ledron—a quick, pacifying gesture that he hoped would purchase him a moment's time before their anger ran amok.

The captain folded his arms, his jaw clenched. His smoldering glare seemed to suggest that Kylac's moment would be brief.

"The asp hisses, and you, Captain, fall silent," Tormitius observed. While firing daggers at Kylac with his stare, it seemed the Grenarrian would not deign to address him directly. "Have you lost grip of your serpent's tail?"

"The captain is his own man," Kylac responded quickly, "as I am mine. It happens we share a common aim just now, as ya mights recall."

"Slaves, I see before me, to a pretender's bidding."

"Slaves," Kylac echoed. "Like those taken on one o' your raids, to be ferreted away on one o' the atolls ya call home."

The ship's former first mate—Great Grendavan's chief lieutenant—hefted his chin. "The Grenarr have no home but Grenah."

"The contents o' your hold, o' this very cabin, cry elsewise. Grains and vegetables, wines and spices, leather and weapons and woven rugs. Hardly fruits o' the sea."

"He admires our plunder, does he?"

"Plunder? Some. Mayhap most. But a mighty vessel such as this? Lashed together from more than foam and driftwood, I'll wager, and not upon the restless swells of a churning sea."

"No? Clever, this asp. Plain it is, why your pretend king should fund his services."

Pevrick turned to Ledron with an intolerant air. "Captain—"

"Fence as ya will," Kylac pressed. "A particular skill o' mine, as your former overlord could tells ya. Or any o' your shipmates—if'n they still had voice."

The defiance held, but only for a moment. As it crumbled beneath an avalanche of hatred, Tormitius seized the chart that lay upon his chest and whipped it at Kylac.

Kylac didn't flinch as it flapped and fell short of its mark, but leaned forward over the bed's footboard as it fluttered still. "The Blackmoon Shards."

A flicker of recognition as Tormitius looked away. "The what?"

"Has the captain not made mention?" A confirming glance caught Ledron's scowl and a barely perceptible head shake. "Our destination, we knows already. Courtesy o' one Sabrynne."

Another hesitation, before addressing him directly for the first time. "Betray her among the rest, did you?"

"Betrayed *us*, more like," Leeches grumbled.

Kylac cringed at the unnecessary intercession, but opted to build what he could upon it. "She lives, best as I know. And that was all her life cost her—the name o' Dethaniel's location."

A sense of relief, it might have been, that cooled the Shorecleaver's rage. Kylac couldn't say what to make of it. Mayhap the first mate and emissary had shared a more intimate relationship—be it familial, companionable, or even romantic. Or mayhap, given the slaughter of his crew, it reassured the Grenarrian to know that at least one of his kind had survived the wholesale bloodletting. Given more leash, Kylac might have rooted deeper for that kernel, but chose instead to mark it for future consideration.

"You know nothing," Tormitius insisted, a savage grin representing his renewed confidence. "Were it otherwise, you would not be here now."

"We's yet to see the Shards charted on any map," Kylac admitted. "And your various records would seem to reflect discord, confusion, or an active effort to muddle our path. Fair enough, save that the longer this venture drags, the longer ya stand to rot in these fetters."

The chief lieutenant loosed another throaty chuckle. "Then here shall I rot, come torture or death—as would any man of courage before betraying his kin."

Kylac shifted an elbow to brush open his cloak, revealing the leather-wrapped hilt of his slender longsword. "I's heard many a man sing o' courage before caressed by blade or flame. The tune changes."

"You frighten me, boy. See how I tremble?" The prisoner raised his manacled hands, holding them steady in the air.

"We waste our time, Captain," Pevrick groused.

"So many ways to loosen a man's tongue," Kylac offered idly. "Piercing, flaying, dismemberment . . . and here at sea, no one to hear him scream."

"Give me such voice, and my bellows shall draw my kinsmen like a shiver of sharks."

"Not if'n your tongue has—"

"Your kinsmen," Ledron echoed, stepping forward to intervene. "Landless. Leaderless. Your strength is admirable, but what will your death merit them?"

Tormitius shifted his glare, but swallowed his response.

"Why not claim your master's place?" Ledron asked. "Who better to rise to his seat? To negotiate on behalf of your people and lead them from this conflict to a higher ground?"

The Grenarrian scoffed. "My kinsmen boast more than a hundred great vessels, each of them ably captained—seven by Grendavan's own sons. A dozen arc captains. Twoscore liege captains. A minnow I am, by comparison. Inconsequential."

"You were Grendavan's first lieutenant," the Head reminded him, "aboard his flagship vessel. And you alone are here now, positioned to help us stem the bloodshed between our peoples."

A grim smile creased his black face. "And what manner of leader would I be, were my first act to jeopardize untold innocents to spare my own hide?"

"Not for yourself. For the future of your mighty ilk."

The smile soured. *Ya'd do better to insult him,* thought Kylac. False regard would win them nothing with this one.

"The Grenarr will hail a new kiros sooner than not," Tormitius vowed. "And he will be swift to rain vengeance upon Grenah's bespoiled shores."

"As they's been doing for, what, two centuries?" Kylac reminded him.

Whatever proclamations, coercions, and orchestrations, it all boiled down to the stalemate against the hated Addarans. Great Grendavan may have died, but would his plan to tip the scales in that interminable struggle have died with him? To personally set foot on enemy ground had constituted the ultimate risk—bespeaking foolish hope or outright desperation. Confident as the overlord had been in the deterrences established beforehand to safeguard himself and his company, he wouldn't have gone through with it had he beheld another choice.

"Your overlord saw a chance to make peace," Kylac continued while Tormitius seethed, "else gain an advantage over his enemy. He sought it urgently enough to die for it. I scarcely believe he or any to follow would relinquish the opportunity so easily."

"As long as Dethaniel lives," Ledron agreed, "you are in a position to barter. So let us do so now. Help me see to the prince's safe return, and you and yours will claim the land that was promised you—more, in fact, in reparation for the discourtesy shown you." At this, the Head turned toward Kylac with a slow, reproachful gaze.

Though he allowed the lure to twist for a moment, there in the pungent darkness of the master-cabin-turned-prisoner-suite, Tormitius refused to bite.

"Your half-formed asp slew my crew under a flag of truce—some in their hammocks—while at rest in your play-king's harbor. He slew my lord and master amid his marriage vows under the roof of your own cathedral, whereupon he slew my lord's entire retinue. You claim it a rogue decision, yet here he stands beside you, attending you—or you him—which suggests otherwise."

The Shorecleaver shook his large, black-skinned head, irons clanking as he leaned forward.

"As a rogue, or under the Pretender's secret order, it matters not. A horgworm he is, and I'm not fool enough to trust one who has already proven treacherous. Nor am I oblivious to the methods of interrogation, including this rudimentary threaten-and-caress routine you've taken three days to concoct. I swear now, lest I was vague before, that the most you will make of me will be shark bait, that you might feed your groping, maggot mouths."

His vibrant eyes, glossy amid the lamplit shadows, fixed Kylac in challenge.

"Whenever you summon the courage to do so, I'll be here."

3

THEY RECONVENED MOMENTS LATER in the ship's wheelhouse—in part, Kylac suspected, to spare the entire crew overhearing what promised to be an unpleasant discussion, judging by Ledron's stormy countenance. Awaiting them were the wiry, sharp-witted helmsman, Taeg, who wore his long gray mane in a tail at his back, and the more disciplined, deliberate-spoken second mate, Brenham, who served also as chief navigator. Heretofore, Kylac had seldom seen the pair of senior Whitefists apart.

The temperature climbed as Kylac entered and Ledron closed the wheelhouse door behind them. Mayhap it was the thick-paned glass that blocked the passing winds while permitting the heat of the sun's rays. Mayhap it was the fire of his shipmates' frustration boiling over.

"I gather it went well?" Taeg observed bluntly. Evidently, word of their visit to Tormitius's chambers had outpaced their arrival.

"I do believe we revealed more than we learned," Ledron grumbled, his gaze accusing.

Kylac shrugged the look aside. "Sometimes ya have to bait the hook. Sacrifice a herring or two for the true catch."

"Except you reeled in only seaweed and swordgrass," Pevrick scoffed.

Kylac turned eye to the first mate. "It might has helped had we presented a unified front, rather than the fractious derision ya seem so quick to unleash."

"His Highness would be safely delivered by now, were it not for you," Leeches spat. "It's because of you that we're out here, waiting for the sharks to find and devour us."

"We've agreed on that already," offered Brenham. His quiet, pensive tone was the kind that made one still and strain to hear, forcing a calming effect upon his listeners. "What I would know is, where do we go from here?"

As long as Tormitius was allowed to stonewall them, their options seemed limited. "Give me leave, and the Grenarrian will talk," Kylac assured them.

"A bold claim," Ledron argued, "but I say again, in my experience, the method you suggest is time-consuming at best."

"I speak not o' your experience, but mine."

"He might choose to die first, as he claims," Ledron pressed, as if deaf to Kylac's argument.

"Even if he speaks," Pevrick added, dredging up his original argument, "anything he reveals, openly or under coercion, is surely another lie meant to misdirect or betray us."

"A shame our rogue saw fit to kill off any other potential witnesses," Brenham agreed in that reflective manner of his. "We might have had another man's words to measure against this one's."

Kylac had considered that, of course. A rasher of enemy crewmen spared for questioning might indeed have helped to weed out lies and half-truths. But he hadn't wanted to risk leaving any Grenarr hands aboard to cause a stir before he could rescue Princess Denariel. Had he known Kendarrion's Shadowguard would be so thorough in their butchery of Grendavan's personal retinue, he might have reconsidered.

One or the other, it wasn't what truly hobbled them here.

"Would I be given any more leash with them than with Tormitius?" Kylac asked. "Or would our good captain choose to coddle them as he has Grendavan's first mate?"

Ledron's brow reddened with indignation. "Do not presume to—"

"Let us be honest, Captain, if'n only among ourselves. Ya could have commandeered the master cabin and consigned our captive to the hold. Ya could have let me question him from the first, rather than sheltering him the past three days. We needn't stand here bemoaning the loss o' potential witnesses if'n ya'd but lower your shield o' the one we have."

For a moment, Kylac thought Ledron meant to draw steel—an act that would force him to subdue the Head and almost assuredly all others present. Pevrick itched for it, given his coiled stance and the hand on his pommel. Brenham suspected it as well, raising his hands in a warding gesture meant to urge calm. Taeg had shifted left, as if to wisely seek shelter behind the great spokes of the ship's wheel.

But the captain surprised them all by bridling his fury and forgoing denial, loosing the truth through clenched teeth. "Dead or damaged, our prisoner loses value when the time comes to trade him for His Highness. Best to deliver him whole, if we wish to receive His Highness that way."

Firm as he'd been in his suspicions, it troubled Kylac that Ledron could be so naive. Did the captain truly believe, after recent escalations, that the Grenarr would be adequately appeased by such a trade? If Tormitius were in fact Grendavan's true heir, mayhap. Short of that, Kylac found it hard to see in their captive ample currency to buy back Kendarrion's son.

"A mite late for that," he said instead, "given they's already relieved Dethaniel o' one o' his royal fingers."

"For which you've already relieved their overlord of his life. Both parties are aggrieved. Someone has to be the first to set down the sword."

Kylac might have laughed. Whatever the outcome here, peace of the sort that Ledron alluded to was a fool's dream. He'd seen it firsthand at home in Partha, a nation that had been fighting battles on and off for centuries against Menzos, its secessionist neighbor to the north—a conflict momentarily resolved only because a larger conflict had overtaken it. If he held to nothing else, Kylac had been raised to believe that war of some kind was constant, immutable, inevitable. Resolve this particular set of grievances, and time would see a fresh one sprout or an old one flame anew.

His own plan was much simpler—and far more achievable.

"This is *my* voyage," he reminded the captain and his assembled lieutenants, "based on a promise I made to return a son to his father, a brother to his sister. I'll not see it sabotaged."

Ledron's blood appeared to curdle, a vein darkening at his reddened temple. "Your ship it may be, but you'll not sail her without a crew. These men labor to do so only insofar as your orders are in line with His Majesty's wishes—as determined by me."

Kylac took a measure of solace as he realized in that moment that Ledron's actions here didn't necessarily reflect personal belief, but merely a strict adherence to his liege's demands. Dangerous as it might be to enslave themselves to the desires of one who wasn't even here—one whose judgment had been severely impaired by emotional distress—better the distant fool than the one beside you. Their captain was irresponsibly dedicated, not daft.

A subtle difference, mayhap, but potentially crucial.

To Ledron's point, he could only offer silent concession. Kylac was no sailor. Were he the greatest seaman ever bred, however, he'd still not be able to wrestle a ship of this size by himself, making him beholden to the Head and his crew on that count. As he traded gazes with helmsman, navigator, and first mate—each more self-satisfied and scornful than the last—he wondered idly if he might have been better off executing some other plan. Could he have left Tormitius and his skeletal crew alone, let them try to make their escape once word of their overlord's demise reached them, and simply smuggled himself aboard the *Vengeance* as they embarked?

Mayhap. But that would have meant trusting Tormitius's small company to have successfully escaped Avenell's harbor, then trusted them to chart a course that would take him to Dethaniel. Upon freeing the prince, he'd have had to figure out how to sail from there to . . . wherever. No, he was better off acting as he had, relieving Tormitius's crewmen and replacing them with Kendarrion's, who—he still hoped—would prove more cooperative in this endeavor.

"Very well, Captain. And what might His Majesty suggest, were he here?"

The smugness of Ledron's lieutenants slipped. Pevrick scowled in narrow-minded anger. Brenham squinted and crossed his arms, putting one hand to his chin. Taeg massaged a knob on the ship's wheel and glanced at the others. He then shrugged and broke the deepening silence. "Loose and follow one of the shrikes, mayhap?"

Seven there were, in the ship's rookery—large, cruel-eyed raptors kept in cages that Kylac had felt it wise to leave undisturbed. He'd found them during his initial exploration of the *Vengeance*—back when she'd been tethered to Avenell's docks—upon venturing aboard to make silent study of those patrolling the vessel in Grendavan's absence. Only later had he learned of the great birds' purpose as carriers used to wing messages to home roosts hundreds of leagues distant—one of the principal means by which the Grenarr maintained their far-strung web of communications.

"Spitting in the wind," Brenham argued. "We've no way of knowing that the isle a particular bird returned to is the one we seek."

"Worse," Pevrick complained, "its arrival might serve to betray our position to any tar-skin pursuers."

"Attracting more o' the enemy could conceivably provide additional resources," Kylac pointed out. Glancing at Brenham, he added, "Potential witnesses, as it were."

Ledron glared, no doubt misliking his sardonic tone. "And might as easily result in an armada flocking down upon us."

"A strong eventuality in any case," said Taeg.

"Which only increases the deeper we sail into their waters," said Brenham.

"They'll track us down," Pevrick echoed. "And when they do, they'll take back their cursed ship and scour the decks with our blood."

Kylac snickered. "A marvel we remains afloat, weighed down with confidence such as yours. Mayhap we should just gives the ship back to . . ." He trailed off as the half-formed gibe twisted in his mind, abruptly taking shape as a plausible consideration.

"Yes?" Ledron prodded with a grunt. "If you would speak, give it voice."

Pevrick snorted. "Already he seeks to betray us."

"A mutiny, yes," Kylac explained, toying now with the exposed thread as a genuine course of action. "Feigning mercenary aims, I might depose the captain. Else you, my friend," he said to Ledron, redirecting, "already in disfavor with your king, could unite your crew against me. My bravado in this endeavor has proven false, ya says. I cannot lead ya to Dethaniel. And if'n I could, there's little reason to believes the Grenarr will honor the proposed exchange—leastwise not without hunting ya down immediately after."

"To what end?" asked Brenham, the first to recognize Kylac's earnestness.

"To curry favor with Tormitius before the Grenarr catch us. Offer him command, and let us see where the raider takes us."

The intervening silence was short-lived. Ledron was the first to balk at the desperate suggestion.

"To stage such an effort convincingly might necessitate the slaying of one or more crew members deemed expendable."

"Against what guarantee that he would lead us to His Highness?" asked Taeg.

"If given the wheel, I'd expect him more likely to steer us into an ambush," Brenham agreed, "his own life be damned."

"He would see us butchered or enslaved the moment he reunited with his people," insisted Pevrick.

Valid arguments, one and all. It was a breed of thinking Kylac cared little for, guessing at chances and possibilities, each as uncertain as the next. Woven like a tangle of serpents over and around one another, until likelihood and hopelessness could no longer be separated. While he seldom acted without purpose, he much preferred instinctive action—and any necessary reaction—to the paralyzing indecision wrought by boundless speculation.

"A drastic scheme," he admitted with a shrug. "Have we any other?"

Their tongues, viper-swift with criticism, recoiled from the invitation. For a moment, the only sounds were the skirling winds, the murmuring waves, the creaking ship, and the shouts of the men outside trimming her course.

"As long as we're spitting from the gallows," Taeg offered at last, "why not seek audience with the Sea Scribe?"

As suddenly as that, Kylac found himself relieved of the scowls and glares and furrowed brows of his shipmates, which redirected toward the helmsman. Taeg, his attention half-drawn by the task of steering the ship, was slow to acknowledge them.

"No more mad than the course *he* suggests," he claimed defensively. "Sea Scribe?" Kylac asked.

Once again, he served target to their ire. As if this newest proposal had been his to begin with.

"An ancient Elementer, by all accounts," Brenham explained. "Said to read the waves. To chart any landmass among them by some mystical means."

"Said also to be insane," Ledron grumbled. "To have sent as many ships to the depths as to the location for which they bartered."

"A relic of the ancient Mage Wars," Pevrick spat. "As treacherous and unpredictable as the Ukinha."

Taeg was unflappable. "If any other than the Grenarr would know of the Blackmoon Shards, it'd be him. And the isle he calls home is much nearer than the one we currently seek."

Another morbid, restless silence, as the ship's lieutenants traded wary glances. Kylac took it to mean they were considering it.

"Ya's heard my vote. But if'n we're not to make full use o' the resources at hand, seems sensible to me to seek another." When that drew only frowns and grimaces, he added, "What harm to ask?"

"A trek across known Grenarr sailing routes," Brenham cautioned.

"Another false lead," Pevrick groused.

"More time wasted," Ledron fumed. "His Highness may have little enough as is."

But the way in which the captain said it suggested to Kylac that, given the options they'd discussed, this latter seemed a safer wager. Silent alongside the others, he watched their appointed leader clench his jaw, grinding his teeth as if to make this foul-tasting decision easier to swallow.

Noting their anticipation, the Head looked up, regarding them with renewed disgust. "Have we no sounder advice, then?"

They looked to one another, to the world beyond the wheelhouse window, to the planks at their feet, and to their captain. The search proved fruitless.

"I'll give it thought," said Ledron, and turned heel toward the exit.

"Oh, and Captain," Kylac remembered.

The Head took pause as he slid the door open, ushering in a cool breeze and the unmuted song of wind, wave, and a gull's incessant shrieking.

"If'n ya mean to preserve our prisoner, ya might want to clean his wound and change that dressing, 'fore ya go giving him away to rot."

"Would that we could rid ourselves of you so easily," Pevrick muttered, bumping Kylac's shoulder on his own way out.

Kylac accepted the insult, as he accepted Ledron's ceaseless glare. When the pair had departed, he looked back at Brenham and Taeg. "My, but we's some tempers aboard."

He received only empty stares in response.

Hoping a pickled pear and a swig of ale might serve to flush the afternoon's taste from his mouth, Kylac left them behind. After? Mayhap a tightrope trot around the rim of the ship's gunwale, where he might consider leaping off and ridding himself of this cluster of fools.

"Is that it?" Kylac asked.

From the ship's bow, he could just make out a dark smudge on the forward horizon. At this distance, it might have been anything—or nothing. His eyes couldn't yet tell. But it wasn't his eyes that had first drawn him to it. An instinct much more primal, centered deep in his chest, had flared abruptly, to whisper now an ominous misgiving.

Orlin, sword raised before him, must have thought it a ploy. "You'll not bait me so easily." More humbly, he added, "Not again."

Kylac sheathed his blade, turning his back to the Blackfist as he moved to the bow rail. "There," he said, pointing in emphasis.

Maintaining a cautious distance, and keeping his weapon at the ready, Orlin joined him. "I see only waves."

And clear skies, the sun shining unfiltered among them. But the stain he'd spied at the farthest edge of the horizon continued to grow. "Something lies ahead," Kylac insisted.

"Could it be a Grenarr ship?"

"I think not. Whatever it is doesn't welcome our approach."

He felt the mistrust in Orlin's gaze as the Blackfist glanced at him. "A keen sense you have. Or perhaps a befouled ration of ale."

"The ale is foul regardless."

His companion snorted in amusement. "Bilgewater, to any but

a Whitefist."

Kylac thought to remind the man that it was the domain of the Seawatch they now sailed, and that its member Whitefists, however inferior by a Blackfist's reckoning, outnumbered the latter aboard their vessel by a count of ten to one. Though Ledron had requested more of his fellow Shadowguard, his rival within that order, Ruhklyn, had been at Kendarrion's elbow to remind the king that their ranks had been sorely depleted—in large part for having entrusted twoscore to accompany Ledron in pursuit of Denariel, none of whom had been with the captain upon his return. Ruhklyn had suggested instead a platoon of threescore Redfists to bolster a sailing crew of forty Whitefists, with just four Blackfists—including Ledron—to serve guidance. Rather than argue, the seething Head had quietly agreed to accomplish the task before him with whatever men His Majesty saw fit to grant him.

By Kylac's observations, however, the Whitefists were accustomed to the disdain leveled at them by their elitist brothers-in-arms, and bore it scant concern. Regardless, for all it might accomplish, now seemed a poor time to encourage discussion on the political discord between Addaran military divisions.

"Come," he urged instead. "Let's finish the session. See what more I might shows ya before it's too late."

They returned to their sparring, the Blackfist continuing to prove game on that count. Thus far, he'd been the only member of the crew to stow his pride long enough to seek lesson from the brash outlander. The others still found it easier to look down their collective noses at Kylac, suggesting that his weapons and fighting style were not suited to theirs, and would only teach them false habits. That they didn't care to discover the breadth of his knowledge—his ability and willingness to tailor specific forms and techniques to an individual's strengths and preferences—spoke further to their ignorance. But Kylac wasn't one to bestow his expertise upon those who didn't seek it. Were he entrusting his life to their martial skills, he might have pressed Ledron on the matter. Alas, his father had taught him long ago to trust no man's defense but his own. *An ally's blade is but another potential threat.*

Moments later, while in the midst of demonstrating a disarming method, Kylac heard the cry he'd been waiting for, ringing down from the crow's nest.

"Land ho!"

"Sharper eyes than yours, these Whitefists," Kylac observed, softening the insult with a good-natured smile.

Orlin stepped back and looked to the approaching horizon, squinting in apparent frustration. "A man should have *some* gift, I suppose."

Glancing astern, it became clear that a fresh fervor had taken hold of the ship's crew, sailors and officers bending to their tasks with renewed urgency and excitement. After six tense days at sea, the men were ready for a new outlook. Kylac wouldn't deny a small thrill of his own. Whatever awaited them on this enchanter's isle would seem preferable to the isolation and monotony of riding the waves.

That initial enthusiasm waned, however, as the Finch's Hour waxed on and the winds pushed them closer to their destination. The hailing of *land* may have been premature, for it seemed what they'd really happened upon was a thick pocket of mist, squatting unnaturally amid the glistening expanse of azure sky and cerulean seas. The larger it grew, the more foreboding it appeared, fostering a general sense of restlessness and apprehension amid those who'd initially cheered its arrival.

When it had become an ashen wall rising unbroken before them, completely obscuring whatever lay at its heart, the *Vengeance* herself hesitated, the order given to take in sails that brought her to a listless crawl. Kylac set his sights at that point on the wheelhouse, thinking it prudent to apprise himself of whatever command decisions were being made there.

"How do we know the tar-skins aren't waiting in ambush?" Pevrick was complaining, scratching at one of the tattoos on his neck as Kylac arrived.

"We don't," Brenham allowed.

Taeg acknowledged Kylac with a nod before adding his own assessment. "The Scribe and his native denizens have no greater love or disdain for the Grenarr than any other that might choose to comb the waters around their shores."

Ledron might have been a statue, his grim stare fixed upon the seemingly impenetrable cloud that had stolen their horizon. An eerie calm surrounded them, the unnatural stillness of the crew bespeaking a common reservation. Even to Kylac, the sun at their back seemed a tempting alternative.

"Ahead, Helmsman," the captain said at last. "Proceed with caution."

The Head departed without further assessment or explanation. First and second mates took to his heels, Pevrick glaring at Kylac on his way out, Brenham sparing an expressionless nod. Outside the wheelhouse, Leeches barked the orders that then echoed throughout the ship, executing her captain's command.

"Native denizens?" Kylac asked of Taeg when they were alone.

"The isle is said to have been inhabited prior to the Sea Scribe's arrival, by some savage breed of wild men who slew any who tried to land there before."

"And what? The Scribe tamed them?"

"There are tales that suggest as much. That they came to worship him in some way. Found his talents useful in deterring others." He gestured at the forward window. "As this fell gloom would indicate."

Even as he said it, that gloom enveloped them, eclipsing the light at their backs so that it became as dusk. A clammy chill came with it, though Kylac felt it again as less a physical sensation and more a preternatural warning. He crossed his arms, refusing to shiver.

"Others," he echoed. "Like the Grenarr. I thought they needed what land they could get. Limited to atolls, when here ya have what ya's called an isle. Is the Scribe so fearsome? The natives themselves?"

Taeg nodded. "Yes, and yes, though to what extent depends on the individual account and your tolerance for hearsay. I can tell you this for certain: There are those among the Grenarr—and those stripped off from them—who care not a whit for a magi's tricks, and would find it sport to engage with any pack of foes willing to meet them on open ground."

Unlike the Addarans, Kylac inferred, hiding behind their seawalls and range weapons. "Then what dissuades them?"

"The isle itself. Uninhabitable, most reports have it. With lowlands prone to sudden, violent tide swells that only the Scribe is able to predict or control—though others say he is the very cause. Flooding aside, most agree that the land's bounty is poisoned. Drinking its waters, or eating the plants and animals who do so, results in severe illness, culminating in madness or even death." Taeg eyed him head to foot. "I understand you have some experience with this on our own shores, from your time in the Harrows."

He did, and thereby found the proposed contagion easy enough to relate to. It wasn't an experience he had any desire to relive. "I presume the natives are spared this illness?"

"Or managed to adapt to it. By whatever means, they and the Scribe would seem to have a constitution that can tolerate the isle's pervasive toxins, or at least mitigate the harmful effects."

"One might think this would entice the Grenarr to give it a go themselves."

"And there are certainly stories alleging that one or another group did. Foolishly so. Taken as a whole, the isle's risks seem to outweigh its potential rewards."

And our *risks?* Kylac wondered, eying again the consuming mists— with a guilty twinge, now, for having encouraged this course. *Are they to meet with adequate reward?* "Has this isle a name?"

"Half a dozen I'm aware of. Nymar Gronin, our historians call her. Kallendrenthrok, to hear a Grenarrian speak of it. Mistwall, Rendtide, Dragon's Dome, Demon's Crown—those would be the more common, if unimaginative, that sailors bandy about. I've heard others, purportedly hailing from the natives themselves, but none I could comfortably pronounce."

"Mistwall would seem apt, for all that I can sees."

Taeg shrugged. "As it pleases you."

It might please me more to be elsewhere, thought Kylac. More and more, he missed his adventures on Pentania, fondly recalling the incredible challenges he'd faced upon chancing across Jarom and Allion in their quest for the mythical Sword of Asahiel—on the heels of which had arisen the terrible War of the Demon Queen. After, he'd left his homeland and his friends behind, seeking a measure of anonymity that would have been difficult to maintain on that island continent, and thinking it unlikely that there remained any trial upon those shores meriting his attention. Though he certainly hadn't expected to stumble across a conflict as violent, dreadful, or far-reaching in scope as that one—mayhap ever, in all the vast reaches of Eddaron—the often tedious nature of his travels since suggested at times that he could as well have remained in more familiar environs, amid friendlier faces.

But the past held no surprises for him, and so seldom held his interest. If not on his present mission, he would have doubtless stumbled upon another—marked, mayhap, by even greater uncertainty and even ruder companions. For all that one might yearn for better circumstances, there were always worse to be found.

"Thirty to starboard!" came the faint shout from an unseen lookout at the ship's bow.

"Thirty to starboard!" Pevrick boomed in relay, the first mate and his tattooed leeches lost to the mists amidships.

Garryn, a seaman posted outside the wheelhouse, thrust his face through the open side door. "Thirty to starboard, sir."

"Thirty degrees to starboard," Taeg acknowledged, turning the ship's wheel accordingly.

"Thirty to starboard, ho!" Garryn shouted back at his commanding officer.

The *Vengeance* veered. Moments later, a hulking cliffside emerged through the brume on their larboard side, bits of scrub brush clinging tenaciously to a craggy promontory that thrust out at them with threatening purpose. Sensing a similar weight from the other side, Kylac peered to starboard. Though faint with distance, a dark mass hemmed them in on that flank, as well. An inlet, he realized. A bay, mayhap. Else a river, strait, or sound. Knowing nothing of the isle's size or shape, he couldn't discern which, only that they'd happened upon an approach to the island within the mists.

"Well, lash me to the rudder," Taeg murmured in wonder.

"What is it?" Kylac asked.

"Take aim at the heart of the mists, the old mariners say, and the isle may receive you."

"That's what we seized upon here?"

"The charts in our possession mark a northern landing nearby, but they also suggest what legends do—that the isle is riddled throughout by a web of river tributaries, ever shifting according to tide and season. The Shrouded Skein, they call it, or the Splintered Stream, the Frayed Thread, the Unraveling River, the Forked—"

"A single name should suffice."

"The Skein, then. A tangle of waterways said to flow and vanish as they please. No matter our approach, I'd expected to spend hours raking the shoreline in search of a gateway such as this—particularly one broad and deep enough to accommodate this leviathan."

"Five to larboard, sir," Garryn relayed.

"Five to larboard," Taeg acknowledged.

"Five to larboard, ho!"

A lucky approach? Kylac couldn't quite bring himself to believe it. He eyed the closing banks of the inlet with suspicion. "Then we's no idea where this leads."

"None," Taeg agreed, flashing a fierce grin. "Trace the right path, and the Skein will carry you clear through the heart of the isle. It's one of the principal reasons a ship's captain might seek the Sea Scribe—to purchase a route that will grant him safe passage and a reprieve from Grenarr-infested waters."

"And the wrong path?" Kylac prompted.

"Might leave you wrecked or grounded. For hours, or forever. There are tales of men abandoning their vessels when supplies ran out and the waters still refused to flow. To end up at the mercy of the isle."

Kylac suppressed a smirk of his own, even as a familiar tingling flared at the base of his neck. The sense of an imminent challenge. A foray into the unknown. Mayhap all this time at sea had made him unduly cynical. The future was nothing if not possibility.

That belief cheered him even as the cliffs loomed nearer on either side, triggering his natural fear of confinement. "Would it not be wiser to tease our way forward with a longboat?"

"I'll not question the order, should the captain give it."

Shouts continued to echo from the bow as hazards were spotted, directions that led to further turns of the wheel and the rudder it controlled. The *Vengeance* responded swiftly and ably to the slightest caress, a deft bird, for all her size. Kylac had heard the crew marvel at her superiority—her sleek design and iron-skinned strength, bred of materials and techniques particular to the Grenarr. Even with precious little knowledge of the intricacies of seafaring vessels, it had been at once clear to him that this was a far more capable craft than the one that had carried him from Wingport, its creators true masters of their trade.

For which he now bore a newfound appreciation.

The sky brightened as the mists abruptly began to dissipate. From the wheelhouse, Kylac was able to make out the ship's foredecks, then the bow rail and jutting bowsprit. Beyond, the inlet on which they ran widened suddenly to starboard, carving into the western bank to form a harboring cove.

Where, amid the calm, clear waters, lay the half-drowned wrack of a burned-out ship, its charred masts reaching forth like skeletal fingers from their watery grave.

"There's an auspicious sign," Taeg muttered beside him.

A chill swept over the crew. Kylac felt it like an autumn breeze, recognizing the tang of fear and loathing that had spawned it. Understandable, given the legends of this place, and that none aboard knew enough to be able to dispel them. Yet Kylac had found the world to be fraught with sufficient perils without having to worry about the ghosts of those that *might* be.

As they came around the doomed ship, a crude wharf lashed together from driftwood fragments revealed itself, hugging the rugged shoreline. Almost at once, Pevrick's command rang out.

"Hard to starboard! Port maneuver!"

"Hard to starboard, sir. Port maneuver," Garryn repeated.

"Hard to starboard," Taeg echoed. "Bringing her in."

"As suitable a landing as any," Kylac presumed.

"First available," the helmsman admitted. "Captain's orders."

Given previously, then, and not within Kylac's hearing. An unnecessary reminder of his outsider status.

He glanced to the south, where the river proceeded inland, narrowing amid crooked banks that closed to either side, trimmed heavily with mangroves, moss-laden deadfall, and tufts of thorny growth mottled gray and brown. The uninviting appearance of that wetland corridor, along with the brackish stench of mold and decay wafting from its throat, caused Kylac to feel better about their chosen mooring ground.

As he looked back to it, he found a cluster of human forms approaching, descending a knoll overlooking the small cove. A receiving contingent, he supposed, though the bristling edges of their silhouettes, put forth by the sharpened spears and blades they carried, suggested they might be less than hospitable. Yet they issued no warning gestures, and hollered no threats. They simply strolled down the bank to spread out along the wharf, their ranks forming a wall of bodies stood comfortably at attention.

Though he couldn't yet make out a precise description, something in their proud bearing struck Kylac as distinctly familiar. Could it be? The possibility bloomed into a suspicion as the *Vengeance* banked fully to starboard, sliding unerringly toward the rudimentary wharf. As the light shifted, Kylac stepped around the helmsman, drifting toward the larboard window for a better view. He found the natives scantily dressed, their hairless, olive-hued skin adorned with little more than bands, scraps, and weaves of vine, leather, and thatch. Towering, thin-limbed warriors all, pierced and tattooed in a primitive fashion.

He smiled in recognition. "Well, that might explain their resistance to the isle's ills."

"How's that?" Taeg asked, gazing upon the assembled natives with a sour expression.

"They're not men at all. They're elves."

"Elves?"

Mookla'ayan, if he wasn't mistaken, though they might not call themselves such here, an ocean removed from those with whom he was familiar. When his view of the lowland shore and its assembled greeting party was obscured by the ship's towering hull, he excused himself from Taeg's presence, thinking to find out.

"Let's has a look then, shall we?"

The air upon the decks was thick with trepidation, the crewmen he happened past wearing furrowed brows and nervous gazes. Several made warding signs of a spiritual nature, or murmured prayers to the Fair Mother Eriyah beneath their breath. Now that they'd arrived, none appeared comfortable with the decision to come here, uncertain as to how their presence might be received by this alien breed.

Upon reaching the maindeck, he spied Ledron heading toward the larboard rail, flanked by Blackfists Orlin, Raithe, and Sanow. With no more noise than the captain's shadow, Kylac fell into step beside them. The Head scowled, opening his mouth with a ready admonition, but let it go unspoken. An acknowledgment, mayhap, that he knew no more about what they might encounter here than Kylac did.

Or mayhap he'd simply come to accept the futility of issuing the rogue orders.

"Square those shoulders, Captain. I's a measure of experience with these. Unless riled, most are not so fearsome as they look."

"Then I trust you'll do nothing to provoke them," Ledron replied sternly.

The *Vengeance* jerked slightly as she reached the end of her leash, as set by the length of anchor rope lowered to the harbor floor. Kylac wondered again that they hadn't anchored farther out and landed a party by way of longboat. Less risk to the ship, it would have been—though a greater risk, he supposed, to those who rowed ashore. Mayhap the captain had decided it better to show no hint of fear, or to intimidate the natives with the *Vengeance*'s sheer size. Regardless, a command decision that had already been made. And an acceptable one, given the reaction of the elves below, some of whom, positioned by notched pilings, appeared to be beckoning for the ship's mooring lines.

Ledron gave a nod, the order given to cast forth the ropes. The natives caught and took them up with practiced ease, looping them around their crude mooring posts. The last of the sails were furled, and the *Vengeance* listed to a halt, heaving gently in her makeshift berth.

Rather than lower a plank, Ledron signaled to an attending Whitefist to drop a ladder. As the seaman did so, the captain regarded Kylac and his trio of Shadowguard.

"We mirror our hosts," he said. "Hilts in plain view, but weapons sheathed. None draw unless I say."

He awaited no acknowledgment, clearly expecting the simple order to be followed without debate. Kylac let it stand. He saw nothing to be gained by informing the captain that, in a race to unsheathe weapons, few men stood chance against an elf. Better that they adhere to a nonviolent posture, as the Head proposed.

He thought to ask instead what plans had been made for the ship's command in the event of a prolonged absence, but decided that Ledron would have already shared such with him had the captain wished to. Or mayhap the Head had determined to see how their welcome transpired first. Whatever the case, Ledron wasted no time in stepping through a break in the gunwale and leading the descent.

Sanow went next, followed by Raithe and then Orlin. Kylac scurried after, observing as his feet touched down that the wharf had been fashioned not only from driftwood, but from bones.

Ledron and his fellow Shadowguard had realized this as well, judging by the way their gazes had become rooted upon their feet, and that none had yet taken more than a step from the ship's ladder. Kylac felt their alarm, though he didn't share it. A mere glance was enough to suggest that timber in this region—mayhap the entire isle—was scarce. What trees he could see appeared gnarled and scrawny. Whatever need these elves might feel to cow or dissuade potential visitors, it might simply be that bones were more readily available. Many of those at his feet, mortared together with mud and pitch, were too long or thick to be human, suggesting the remains of butchered animals. That he indeed recognized human fragments among them . . . well, that didn't necessarily portend ill will.

Not that it boded in their favor.

A sharp voice disrupted his musings. Kylac looked up to a native positioned centrally among their line, his terse speech marked by clicking teeth and curt gestures. Though familiar with similar patterns used by the Mookla'ayans on Pentanian shores, Kylac struggled to make sense of the elf's meaning.

Ledron traded uncertain glances with his fellow Shadowguard. "We seek one who calls himself the Sea Scribe."

The Mookla'ayans stared back, regarding the Head with stern faces and suspicious gazes. A moment later, the leader of their company, if that's what he was, repeated his initial greeting.

"Only one," Kylac interpreted.

"What?" Ledron asked.

Kylac chirped back at the elf before him, seeking clarification. He wasn't sure who he surprised more—the pack of natives, or the men at his shoulder. But it was the elven leader who recovered more quickly, to offer a brusque reply.

"Only one," Kylac repeated, with greater confidence this time. "Only one of us is permitted. They ask who it will be."

The Head balked. "How can you know this? You understand their gibberish?"

"Well enough," Kylac assured him. Seeing the native leader's scowl deepen, he added, "As they have a rudimentary understanding o' yours."

The Head reddened, but curtly bowed an apology. Kylac threw forth a hand to stop it, and quickly begged his own, verbal apology.

"Take care with your movements, Captain. Ya may offer insult ya don't intend."

"I mean no insult," Ledron grumbled. "How is it you're familiar with men such as . . . with them."

The native leader clucked and chirped, seeming to ask the same question. An ox, by Mookla'ayan standards, with bulbous shoulders and a thick neck. Kylac did his best to answer their host before responding to his ship's captain. "Elves, not men. Or so we call those, akin to these, who inhabit Pentanian shores."

"Creatures of legend," said Raithe. "Of myth."

"As some might say o' many o' the creatures inhabiting your own isle. Elves they are. Ancestors or cousins, mayhap, o' the Mookla'ayans I's known."

"Mookla . . . ?" Orlin attempted.

"Mookla'ayan. Though they don't seem to recognize the distinction."

"I care not what we call them," Ledron snapped, but mollified his expression when he caught Ox's disapproving reaction. "If you can in fact speak with them, perhaps you would be good enough to express our intent here."

"Our intent, they already know," Kylac replied. He spoke again to the elven commander, seeking confirmation of his understanding. According to the interpretable fragments gleaned in response, he was correct. "It's the only reason, he says, that anyone from . . . *beyond* . . . bothers to visit their isle."

"So? Will they permit us?"

"They will permit *one*, they say—our vessel's champion—to accompany them. I gather it's to limit the treachery we might commit on their soil."

"We have shown them no hostility," Ledron complained. "I should think that a small handful—"

A fierce outburst from Ox resulted in spears being raised by the elves down the line. Raithe and Sanow reached for their sword hilts in reflex. Kylac again had to intervene by raising his arms, hissing and chirping hurriedly to forestall further reaction.

"Begging pardon, Captain, as I'm interpreting what I can. But their demand seems as strict as it does simple. One among our crew may go with them, if'n we wish it. As a show o' faith."

"Faith? Whose faith? Ours alone, it would seem."

The native leader barked an earlier refrain.

"Our vessel's champion," Kylac repeated. "With your leave, I suggest that be me."

Ledron clenched his jaw in thought. "You lack the nautical knowledge we require. It was Taeg's idea to come here. He who best knows the lore of this isle. It may be that—"

"It may be that this Sea Scribe speaks only an Illian tongue, as these natives do. Taeg has informed me o' the isle's alleged origins, to the extent such tales might be useful. O' greater concern, I should think, would be one among us least likely to be waylaid."

If'n taken hostage, he might have added, but didn't want to risk undue offense to their hosts. Nor did he feel Ledron should need him to so clearly define their situation. Whatever reservations regarding Kylac's trustworthiness or capabilities, did the Head truly believe himself better suited to the task?

"I will—"

"Remain with the ship," Kylac encouraged him. "This was but a gallows wager, if'n I recall. Long as the ship and its former mate are intact, so is our mission. Would ya risk them to another's aims?"

Ledron chewed on that for a moment. As usual, he didn't appear to care for the taste of Kylac's words—or mayhap his tone. But the logic was sound. To have hope of defeating it, the captain would have to somehow argue that Kylac was critical to their quest to free

Dethaniel, and could therefore not be jeopardized. He didn't believe the Head capable of admitting as much.

"So be it," Ledron agreed. "You have until the Eagle's Hour. By sunset, you will find yourself aboard, else swimming after our wake."

The captain showed the natives his palms, then turned to reach for his ship's ladder. Sanow and Raithe were quick to follow. Orlin required a nod of reassurance from Kylac before climbing after.

When they'd gone, Kylac grunted and gestured at the native commander. *I am your humble guest.*

Ox's scowl radiated displeasure, but his nod and chirp promised safe conduct. A pair of Mookla'ayans took to Kylac's flanks, guiding him forward until he drew another pair front and back. Thus encircled, he found the leader's heels in marching up the knoll.

The remainder of the elves stood as they were, an armed wall along their wharf of bones, set to warily eye the crew of the *Vengeance*.

Whose members peered back at them in a mirror of mistrust.

5

His Mookla'ayan escort ring thickened as Kylac followed their leader from the cove, its ranks drawing natives from the brush on either side of the well-worn trail of mud and stone. Even sensing their presence, Kylac couldn't quite see them until they untwined themselves from the crooked boles, curtains of vines, or tufts of shrubbery amid which they hid. Once revealed, they fell into line without a word, attaching to those already surrounding him. Several regarded him in open appraisal, fierce expressions bespeaking disgust and curiosity in equal measure. But only a few struck a threatening posture, and if any truly wished him harm, he didn't sense it.

Still, their growing numbers, along with the plethora of weapons—stakes and spears, daggers and hand-axes—strapped to their lean limbs and finely muscled torsos, served sufficient reminder that they would brook no foolishness from their uninvited visitor. In all, their bearing suggested a people engaged in current or recent hostilities. It caused him to wonder if the Mookla'ayans on these shores suffered the same tribal division that they did in the jungles of Vosges, or if mayhap they'd suffered, as of late, some other assault on their native sovereignty. In his experience, a man or woman found to be inhospitable—be they human or elf—typically had reason to be.

They'd neglected to confiscate or ask that he shed his own weapons—

not even those hilts that protruded from his waist in plain view. A sign of good faith that Ledron had failed to credit them for. Else an indication of confidence in their ability to swiftly subdue a solitary intruder should he seek to raise arms against them.

He was given little to make of his surroundings, his view obscured by the wall of rangy bodies and the profusion of wild growth that lay beyond. So he eyed for a time the ground as it changed in composition—from stone, to clay, to soil carpeted with broken stalks, dead grass, and crushed thorns. The bare feet of those in front of him padded softly, painlessly, undeterred by pebble or twig while proceeding at a brisk pace over a gently rising elevation. Gentle by design, he saw, for the mostly smooth track wound back and forth amid an increasing number of fissures and gullies. Leave the designated path, and one would find the terrain far less friendly—steep and jagged and clogged with indiscriminate growth.

It was the sounds that first alerted him to the village outskirts, if village it might be called. Muted and indistinct, they nonetheless revealed to him the murmur of a general population engaged in various activities—the hammering of iron and chiseling of rocks, the thrashing and grinding of grains, the squawking and bleating of chickens and goats or whatever passed as such on this isle. Hard upon came the smells—of sweat and dung, of leather and salt, of bread and meat, of cookfire flame and hearthfire smoke. There were noises he couldn't place and scents he didn't recognize, but the bustle that lay ahead wouldn't so easily be masked.

Then the slope leveled off and the jungle growth peeled away, hacked or plucked or trampled at its edges. The trail broadened, emptying into a wide depression that spread for hundreds of paces over a broken plateau. Mookla'ayans filled the area, male and female, young and old, hunched over one task or another, else carrying their business from one place to the next. To Kylac's left, at the eastern edge of this central ground, stood a large pyramid structure, erected from great stone blocks piled atop one another in cairn-like fashion. At a glance, a tumbledown ruin that had no business standing. And yet, judging by the number of elves passing in and out of the torchlit opening at the base of its western face, the rugged mound served indeed as a viable structure—a fortress, mayhap, or temple stronghold.

Not surprisingly, it was toward this pyramid that they veered, keeping to the eastern fringe and away from the wattle-and-daub huts spread about in small clusters on the opposite side of the clearing. Kylac sensed a clutch of fresh gazes turn his way, reflecting mild curiosity. Some stretched after him like clinging cobwebs, but most broke away swiftly, finding focus elsewhere. Mayhap because they could see less of him than he could of them, concealed as he was by his warding contingent. Mayhap because his presence simply held no interest to them.

The pyramid loomed larger as they approached, its mouth much bigger than Kylac would have wagered from afar. Mookla'ayans milling about the entrance quickly formed an aisle for those escorting Kylac, whose pace didn't slow. A stone-paved trench sloped down toward the yawning mouth, where a pair of sentinels stood watch on either side, each in front of a tusklike pillar of lichen-covered stone. No words were exchanged, and neither sentinel blinked, as Kylac's party approached.

Into the breach he plunged.

A cold weight settled over Kylac's shoulders, this despite the flickering line of torches burning in sconces on either flank, warming the air. His lungs constricted, though his breath was remarkably clear of smoke, which seemed to funnel up through flues and chimneys built into the rock. Even with rough-hewn walls crammed with passing streams of elven bodies, a relatively clean and spacious corridor. He'd been in tighter confines, Kylac reminded himself, under far more threatening circumstances. And yet, his instinctive loathing of cramped spaces refused to attend him quietly, making its displeasure known.

Though smaller passages cut off to one side or another at irregular intervals, his escort seemed content with the main tunnel, which continued to burrow relentlessly eastward in a somewhat jagged line. Kylac tried not to guess at how many tons of rock had been laid overhead, or to imagine how the slightest tremor might bring it all down—without any regard whatsoever for all his finely honed talents. Instead, he reflexively counted his steps into what seemed now a fathomless warren, its inner depths smelling of mud and minerals, incense and oils, must and mold.

A break appeared ahead—another tusked opening warded by a pair of sentinels. A cavern, it seemed, or an arena of some sort, lit with the sun's rays from what must have been a large hole in the ceiling. The thought of entering the more spacious ground gave Kylac an itch of relief. Instead, Ox led their company to the right, to climb a broad flight of crudely hewn steps that narrowed at its apex. Kylac turned his head to find a similar stair behind them, ascending in the opposite direction. A nudge from one of the escorts behind him returned his focus to the path ahead.

Their path grew decidedly more complex after that, following a twisting series of stairs and passageways that seemed to bend and fold, climb and descend, in all directions, bypassing chambers large and small of indiscriminate purpose. Of some relief, in that it forced Kylac to concentrate more diligently on memorizing that course lest he find need to retrace it. Even as the walls closed in, forcing the elves at his flanks to fall back behind him, his nerves calmed, his mind consumed with more urgent purpose.

At last, they arrived at a chamber they deigned enter, somewhere near the pyramid's zenith, if Kylac wasn't hugely mistaken. Empty shafts in the slanted ceiling spilled pools of light upon the sanded stone floor. One of those pools lit an intricate mesh of polished wood that stood against the back wall. An altar, given the bowed form of the elven man kneeling before it.

Ox finally halted, with those accompanying him since the cove stopping alongside. A handful of Mookla'ayan sentries stood about the room, but, like those encountered earlier, made no move to recognize the contingent's arrival. For several moments, all was silent, the faint whispers of the outside world muted by heavy walls of stone.

Then the kneeling man stood, gesturing at the altar and at himself before turning to face those who'd entered his sanctum. As old an elf as Kylac had ever seen, given his slow, painful movements and the looseness of the wrinkled skin hanging from his gaunt limbs. Yet his eyes were bright amid the leathery parchment of his brow and cheeks, and he held his shoulders square and strong. Studs of animal bone pierced the rims of his ears and encircled the ridge of his head—not unlike the crown of sharpened stakes worn by Cwingen U'uyen of the Powaii, chieftain of that faraway clan.

The aged elf shuffled near. Reeking of mint and cloves, he initiated an exchange with Ox that confirmed Kylac's suspicions. Cloves was their chieftain, though the term they used was more familial, closer to *father* or *patriarch*. Mayhap because Ox, greeted as *blessed son*, was indeed the elder's direct offspring. Until given to observe other interactions, Kylac could only guess.

The two conversed a moment longer, with Ox referencing Kylac's shipmates held at bay in the cove below, their petition to treat with "the Keeper," and Kylac's unexpected grasp of their tongue. At this, the chieftain turned directly to Kylac, brandishing a warm, toothless smile.

"Rare," Cloves said, "skin pale. Slaves, yes?"

The words were broken, the accent thick and throaty. Nonetheless, it startled Kylac to hear Entien words spill from an elf's mouth. "Slaves?"

"To them of flesh black. Grenarr, they hail."

He recognized then the chieftain's confusion. Kylac knew not the numbers in which men set foot upon this isle, but given the dominion of the Grenarr in this region, those with skin like his likely did so only in irons, to serve or be sold like livestock.

"No," Kylac replied. "Freely, we come, to seeks knowledge that might lead us to a land the Grenarr call home."

Cloves took a moment to process the response, studying Kylac as if to discern any falsehood. "To see Sa'ahla, you follow, yes?"

THEY LEFT the temple stronghold along the same route by which they'd entered, weaving back through the tilting maze of stairs and corridors to emerge from the pyramid mouth at the foot of its west face. Kylac said nothing of his surprise upon exiting the structure. He'd anticipated finding the Sea Scribe housed in some other chamber within. Hence the danger of expectation, formed in this instance on cultural practices that had no relevance here. A suitable reminder to remain attentive and alert, ready to react rather than dictate—at least until he had a better sense of how this land and its native inhabitants functioned.

In any event, pleased he was to be rid of the pyramid's oppressive environs, breathing again the open air. Mayhap the Sea Scribe had no more love for such tight quarters than he.

They pressed westward from the pyramid's exit, traversing the clearing that would seem to serve as the village's heart. Chief Cloves led alongside Ox, flanked by a pair of personal warders who'd wordlessly shadowed his every stride since departing the temple sanctum. Kylac remained aback of them, at the center of his own escort ring, twenty elves strong.

Their passage drew little interest. Those Mookla'ayans who found themselves crossing their chieftain's path gestured respectfully, but not in any overtly submissive manner. Cloves in turn greeted his subjects with humble nods and courteous waves of his slightly tremulous hands. An elder to be revered more than a leader to be feared, Kylac decided, and one who strolled commonly among them.

At the clearing's western boundary, beyond the clusters of huts arrayed along its fringe, they seized upon a broad trail that wound down through the jungle growth. The village quieted, its restive sounds replaced by the calls of birds, chitter of insects, and ferreting of rodents rummaging through the brush. Father and son, if that's what they were, conversed privately, their words and gestures obscured. Though an outsider among a strange people in an unknown land, Kylac's misgivings receded.

Until a scream shattered the stillness.

A flock of birds erupted from a nearby tree, startled into flight. A squirrel scampered for the same cover they'd fled. Kylac tensed, palms itching for his sword hilts, as the echoes of the cry ratcheted up his spine. But it took him less than a heartbeat to realize that he was the only member of their company thus alarmed. Not one of his escorts had flinched; not one had broken stride. So he resisted the urge to draw weapon, opting for a facade of calm.

Cloves glanced back at him, proffering that warm smile.

Kylac was half wondering if he'd imagined it when the scream came again, shrill and quick. Another soon followed, a longer, deeper wail full of unbridled anguish. Kylac cringed, but guarded against reaction. The cries were human. They lay ahead, each nearer than the last. Whatever their source, his escorts weren't shying from it. They were guiding him toward it.

Though his legs urged him to spring forward, he couldn't do so without breaking past the natives' wall, and couldn't say how far he might make it once he did. So he continued to hold himself in check, the tiny hairs on his neck standing rigid, every nerve drawn taut, as they proceeded along the muddy trail, pursuing the string of human cries.

He smelled the first corpse before he saw it, and so had steeled himself for its appearance several moments before it came into view around a curving downslope—a charred husk draped in tattered strips of cloth, left to dangle from the twisted limbs of a skeletal shag tree. Its prominent display would indicate a victim of punishment, Kylac supposed, a warning put forth to dissuade others from committing similar crime. That, or ritualistic sacrifice, an offering to whatever god or gods lay claim to this people's fealty.

Mayhap a measure o' both, he thought, as they rounded the trail's bend, marching near enough to ascertain the damage inflicted upon the luckless soul. Grenarr, Kylac guessed, though it wasn't the man's skin that triggered this assumption, for that skin had been peeled completely from his body. Then the flesh beneath had been pared away in precise patches, tendons and ligaments detached at one end and left hanging from the other, bundles of muscle separated and fanned wide. It was this that Kylac had mistaken at a distance for tatters of garment—the very meat of the victim's naked body, strung out and blackened with fire almost beyond recognition. Only the length and thickness of his bones, along with the shape of his skull, characterized him as Grenarr.

Whatever he'd been, Kylac hoped he'd been killed long before he'd been so meticulously shredded.

Another agonized shriek upon the midmorning wind suggested

elsewise.

Additional corpses greeted him along the path, victims whose flesh had been removed, rib cages and abdomens emptied, and organs and musculature separated and draped amid the jungle brush in almost artistic fashion. Each looked less human than the last, more closely resembling some flowering undersea fan or other bizarre ocean growth. Kylac did his best to ignore the carnage, accepting it without reaction the way his attendants did. He'd seen bodies disassembled before, examined them piece by piece—for form and function—under the tutelage of Talonar's schoolmasters. Since earliest childhood memory, death had been the driving study of his life.

He'd just never witnessed a display quite so flagrant as this.

He heard murmurs now amid the screams, a soft hum that swelled and then subsided like shoreline tides. Observers, he supposed, bearing witness to the torture in progress. Kylac had a mind then and there to demand of the chieftain the purpose of this trek, lest they think him fool enough to willfully stroll his way into becoming their next victim. But an overriding sense urged him to maintain his composure, to endure their little show of cruelty and deny them the satisfaction of wringing from him the slightest measure of fear or disgust.

He'd counted more than twoscore Grenarr corpses, arrayed to either side of the ghastly corridor through which his escorts paraded him, before the trail opened onto a bowl-shaped glen serving as their sacrificial arena. At its center, a lone Mookla'ayan brandished a knife over the butchered but still squirming body of a sable-skinned man arched backward over a thick tree stump, arms and legs staked wide. A press of elves faced the executioner in quarter-moon formation, serving audience to his carefully orchestrated slaughter. With a chirp and a gesture, the executioner brought his blade low again, to slice at the victim's muscled forearm. The victim thrashed and wailed, the witnesses mumbled in unison, and the executioner came away with a flourish, raising a long strip of freshly flayed skin in triumph.

Spying their chieftain's approach, the pack of Mookla'ayans bearing witness cut their murmurs short. Alerted by their reactions, the executioner turned until he too faced the arrivals as they welcomed themselves into his glen. His teeth clicked together forcefully, his expression betraying fury at the interruption.

Esteemed father, he greeted with a hiss and a growl. *You honor us with your presence.*

Kylac wondered if he might have grossly misinterpreted the remark, given the anger that flashed in the executioner's eyes. The pinched brow and taut lips marked a seemingly universal sign of displeasure. And though he dipped a shoulder in proper respect, his opposite fist shook overhead, still holding the patch of skin.

But the chieftain took no offense, acknowledging the other with a benign nod. *Forgive me, blessed son. I bring outlander witness to marvel at your work.*

Or was it *cower*, rather than marvel? Though much might hinge on the precise meaning of this term or that, Kylac wasn't inclined to seek clarification. Rather, he held still and silent as Cloves gestured and drew Ox aside. The wall of escorts opened before Kylac, granting him an unobstructed view of the glen's proceedings—while yet walling off any easy escape.

A rat found aboard? the executioner asked, or something near it. His voice was husky, this butcher's, making his snarled words that much harder to comprehend.

Another visitor. Another ship. Another crew begging Sa'ahla's wisdom.

Kylac recalled the burned wrack they'd come upon in the cove. And this, he supposed, the remains of its crew.

Butcher clucked and pursed his lips, registering his own understanding. Tossing aside the flap of skin, he beckoned Kylac forward.

Kylac looked instead to the chieftain, Cloves, and the leader of his initial welcoming party, Ox.

"You see," said Cloves.

Butcher grunted an insistence. Kylac advanced, eyeing the hooks and barbs that adorned his flesh, and the thick smears of blood that painted his olive skin. He regarded Kylac with a wolfish sneer.

Fighting the urge to remove that sneer with a swipe of his blade, Kylac stepped toward the makeshift altar and the whimpering mass staked atop it. As if sensing his presence, the victim found the strength to raise his head. Though one eye had already been removed, the other fixed its reddened, tear-filled gaze on him.

"Help me," he whispered.

But it was too late for that. In addition to his eye, they'd already removed the meat from one arm, and had opened his viscera to the wind. His organs as yet remained intact, but a swarm of ants and beetles had been set to feast on them, worming over and around his entrails. Even if the insects could all be flushed free, there would be no sewing him up beyond infection's reach. One way or another, his death at this point promised to be painful. And while Kylac bristled at the brutality, there seemed too much to risk—and too little to gain—in granting the man the only mercy truly left to him.

"Help me!" the Grenarrian somehow found the strength to shout.

A handful of Mookla'ayans jeered his protests. Kylac cringed at the echoes—of their mockery, and of the plaintive cry—that reverberated within the arena, captured and magnified by the thick mesh of scraggly trees clawing skyward at the glen's perimeter.

Why am I to see this? Kylac asked of Cloves, as respectfully as he could manage.

"Thieves," the chieftain explained. "Sa'ahla. They take Sa'ahla." He turned his kindly smile upon the mewling Grenarrian. The expression now seemed anything but compassionate. "They try."

Sa'ahla. The Sea Scribe. Or the Keeper, as Ox had referred to him. The Grenarr whose butchered remains now decorated this stretch of jungle had attempted to abduct the Sea Scribe. At some point during the act, the Mookla'ayans had caught them.

And this the price.

Kylac gazed anew upon the whimpering Grenarrian. The doomed man's head lolled back, his lone eye searching the heavens for a mercy not to be found.

"Punished, all," the chieftain added needlessly, gesturing vaguely up the trail. "Only champion now."

Only their captain remains, Kylac interpreted. *And him not for long.* He wondered briefly how Taeg or Ledron or any of the others might have reacted to this scene. Might they have reveled in the fates of these, their hated adversaries? Or would they have succumbed to the indignation that hissed and churned deep within Kylac's stomach at such excessive cruelty?

And then he realized, as he should have from the first—as he *had*, he supposed, before permitting himself to be overwhelmed by the sights and smells of this atrocity. The derelict vessel left in the landing cove, which would have borne the Sea Scribe hence. The vivisected, insect-eaten remnants of the crew, left hanging so prominently amid the trees. Punishment, yes. But the true purpose of the display was to warn Kylac—or any other outsider who might have come along— against similar aim.

"I's not come intending to take Sa'ahla," Kylac assured the chieftain, and then again, chirping and gesturing in the Mookla'ayan version of the Illian tongue. *I have not come with the intent to take Sa'ahla. I would purchase a chart from him. A chart to a destination unknown. A rock upon the waves.*

Butcher clicked his teeth, nostrils flaring. Ox frowned and gestured his skepticism. Cloves smiled his peaceful, warm-hearted smile.

"You purchase," the chieftain said, "from us. Food. Weapons. We take, yes?"

In exchange for the chart, Kylac reiterated. *Sa'ahla maps our course, we barter price of goods. Coin, provisions—chickens, if it please you.*

You should give him to me now, Butcher growled at the chieftain. *The stink of treachery oozes from his marrow.*

Ox balked. *I swore him safe conduct.*

Cloves's bright eyes never left Kylac's face.

"Mother?" the Grenarrian captain asked of the midday sky. He wept, mumbling to some ghost beyond their vision, then bucked suddenly against the stakes pinning his wrists and ankles. "Mother!"

"We ask Sa'ahla," the chieftain decided. "His will answer you, yes?"

6

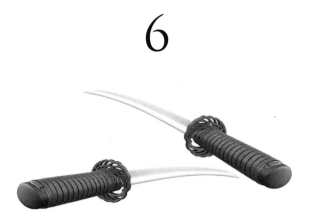

THE SCREAMS INTENSIFIED as Kylac departed the glen, as if Butcher meant to inflict additional punishment now for the unwelcome intrusion. Kylac had been unable to discern whom the sadistic executioner was more angry with—pale outlander or Mookla'ayan chieftain. Either way, it was the Grenarr captain beneath his knife who would now bear the brunt of that wrath.

Again Kylac swallowed his pointless urge to turn back and end the man's suffering. As easy as it seemed to judge the scene barbaric, it would be presumptive of him to take action against a people and practice he couldn't claim to fully understand—to interrupt a ritual that, for all he knew, might serve some greater, necessary purpose once carried through to completion. Cloves hadn't said as much, but mayhap the Mookla'ayan chieftain had shared with Kylac only what he believed the outlander could comprehend.

Justifying your cowardice? asked a bothersome inner voice. Truth unfettered, he'd made a conscious decision in that glen not to jeopardize the needs of his own mission and crew for the sake of a single stranger's anguish. He could seek now to rationalize his inaction, or simply acknowledge it and live with the bitter taste.

It wouldn't be his first brush with regret.

With footsteps made heavy by his nagging conscience, he nonetheless proceeded past the string of flesh-stripped corpses and on up the mudswept trail, led again by Cloves and Ox, encircled still by his native guard ring. When they'd returned to the plateau above, they crossed the village clearing as before and plunged again into the pyramid's depths. Within, they retraced much the same path, rooting through the structure's base before making a corkscrew ascent near its heart. This time, they bypassed the sanctum in which he'd met Cloves, climbing higher while veering north and then east. The tunneling passage ended in a final flight of steps that rose toward an opening in the stone ceiling. A clutch of nine sentinels warded the breach, each bristling with small, close-quarter knives and hand-staves.

The sentinels gestured respectfully toward their esteemed father, and greeted Ox with what surely passed for a salute. When the intent to enter had been acknowledged, a sentinel with eyes of amber reached for a pair of hemp-and-leather manacles hanging from a wall hook, and presented them to Kylac.

"You bind, yes?" Cloves explained.

Kylac knew better than to treat it as a question, or to balk at the suggestion. Though every inner sense screamed at the notion of willing captivity, he held forth his wrists. Amber-eyes tied the manacles firmly into place, lashing Kylac's hands together in front of him. Only then did the sentinels part ranks at the center, allowing their stoop-backed chieftain—attended by his personal guard—to slip past. The thick-shouldered Ox offered Kylac a stern expression in final warning, then guided him after.

Up through the breach they climbed, entering the chamber from the center of its floor. The space felt cramped at its corners, given the angled slope of the four walls that closed to a central peak overhead. All four walls also opened onto balconies, however—north, south, east, and west—so that the overall floor was much more spacious than unbroken walls would have allowed. Upon each balcony squatted a stone basin, intricately carved and pooled to the rim with water that gleamed with reflected sunlight. Packs of Mookla'ayan sentinels—six elves each—had arrayed themselves at the farthest edge of each balcony, dutifully facing in toward these basins. A far greater number than should be needed to protect one man, it seemed to

Kylac. Then again, if the legends Taeg had shared with him had been seeded from anything resembling truth, they weren't here to defend any ordinary man.

A storm cloud of a presence drew Kylac's gaze to a darkened recess in the chamber's northeast junction. Hunkered there amid a mound of casks and furs, the shadow of a form that might have been human peered out at the new arrivals with all the intensity of a cornered field mouse.

"Sa'ahla," Cloves greeted, peering about the room in search. "You come, yes?"

The shadow burrowed deeper into its corner, as if seeking escape through the very seams of the pyramid's stone. Ox's head turned toward the rustle of movement. Cloves's followed, unleashing his toothless grin. He clucked gently, a coaxing remark intended to put the shadow at ease.

"Away, Et'tanis," the shadow growled. "And your caller with you."

Instead, Cloves approached, beckoning Ox and Kylac to join him. *This posture suits you ill, mighty Sa'ahla. Have we ever given you cause to fear us?*

It wasn't quite fear that Kylac sensed. More a guarded fretfulness seasoned with suspicion. Directed not at the chieftain or his attendants, but unmistakably at Kylac, who felt it like a deep itch worming beneath his skin.

Your people have needs. Would you see them go untended?

The Sea Scribe's husky laugh gave vent to a hacking cough. "Our petty needs no longer have meaning. Not when we are set to be scraped from this rock like mud from underfoot."

Kylac had assumed that the biting tone and use of the Entien tongue had been for his sake. With this second outburst, however, he wondered whether it might also indicate an intentional act of disrespect toward the Mookla'ayan chieftain.

Cloves proceeded undeterred, shuffling right up to the edge of the casks and furs behind which the Sea Scribe sheltered. He then waded in among them, until his stooped head brushed against the angled ceiling. A stern tremor crept into his voice. His gestures became quick and sharp. *You will treat with him, yes?*

As if embarrassed to be admonished like a wayward child, the Sea Scribe leaned forward from where he sat cross-legged upon the floor, lifting his face into view. His features weren't elven, but human, if barely so. His sallow flesh, thin and veined and spotted with rash, stretched taut over high cheekbones and angled jawline, and dangled in withered folds about his throat. Chin, nose, and hairline all peaked toward the center, to form a piercing expression further accentuated by his sharply raked eyebrows. But it was the eyes themselves that most captured Kylac's interest. The ring of the left was a cobalt so bright as to be almost iridescent against the white globe, while the right resembled that of a shark—a solid black orb with just a hint of cloudiness at its center.

"I treat with whom I choose," Sa'ahla spat. "To the depths with this one."

"Our holds are well stocked," Kylac said, "our shipboard larder—"

"Food and trinkets. Did you not hear me, boy? They cannot help us here."

"And why not?"

The Sea Scribe shook his head, the loose folds of skin at his throat shaking like the wattles of a rooster. Fixing his shark's eye on Cloves, he resorted at last to the Mookla'ayan tongue. *Fool. His presence portends the very doom you refuse to recognize.*

Ox took a single, lunging step toward the hunkered Sea Scribe, his bare foot slapping against the stone in warning against further insolence. Sa'ahla flinched, but elsewise ignored the brawny elf, keeping his focus on Cloves—Et'tanis.

Though the chieftain's restraining chirp held Ox in check, his narrowed gaze gave his benign smile a malicious cast. *Would you have me surrender you to Chitral? He should be finished with the* akelma *by nightfall.*

Kylac had no reference for the term *akelma*. But he caught the sullen, cowed look that skimmed across Sa'ahla's features before the shadowed figure summoned a defiant grimace for the looming Ox. The disparity in his expressions told Kylac that the Sea Scribe bore a genuine fear toward this Chitral whom Et'tanis had mentioned—a fear he didn't bear for either of the elves pressing him now. That would make Chitral a third party to these proceedings. The executioner in the glen, mayhap. Or another of similar brutality.

Much clearer was Kylac's suspicion that Sa'ahla, the Sea Scribe, wasn't as revered by these Mookla'ayan natives as Taeg's report would have had him believe. A fresh survey of the chamber and its guards, given all that he'd heard, suggested to Kylac that the Sea Scribe resided here not under the natives' protection, but as their prisoner. A far different situation than he'd entered into, and one that he would have to unravel before proceeding.

What is this doom he speaks of? Kylac asked Et'tanis. The question drew an expression of surprise—though not necessarily approval—from Sa'ahla, as he revealed to the Sea Scribe his knowledge of the native language.

A senseless raving, the chieftain replied. *A nightmare spawned by a weary mind.*

Else a pretense, meant to disguise the shame of his failing powers, Ox suggested less kindly.

Might I hear it from him? Kylac inquired. *As he would recount it?*

Ox frowned intractably. Et'tanis, however, gestured his approval, waving at Sa'ahla in open invitation.

"I didn't sail here to brings you or your people harm," Kylac offered. A meager reassurance, even to his own ears, but a reasonable starting point, given the Sea Scribe's skittishness. When Sa'ahla remained silent, he asked again, more directly, "What is it ya fear?"

"You reek of dragon's blood," Sa'ahla croaked petulantly.

Kylac blinked, taken aback by the response, uncertain it had even been intended as an answer to his question. He thought to begin anew, undertaking a different approach, then decided abruptly to play along. "I didn't actually slay the beast."

The milky black eye fixed on him. "Not *on* you. *In* you."

He knew even less what to make of that. "Then it's dragons what got ya spooked?"

"Not dragons. Dragon. *The* Dragon. The Sleeper, the Watcher, the Dread Eye of the Deep. He stirs, and the oceans roil. Restless are the waves, signifying a catastrophic upheaval. For they shall rise as he wills, whipped into a fury to match his own. When unleashed, they will consume."

Kylac glanced at Cloves. Et'tanis. Chieftain of the Mookla'ayans native to this isle. He wondered now whether he should give more credence to the elf's assessment of Sa'ahla's demented condition.

"Et'tanis doesn't seem frightened."

"Et'tanis thinks me mad. Forannenuk"—he gestured at Ox—"would convince others that the unruly swells mean I am losing my ability to harness them. Old and frail, he calls me, as if bone and meat could have any such bearing on an Elementer's true strength. Chitral would take it even farther, believing he and his fellow priests might absorb my powers if they were to drink my blood and consume my flesh."

"Chitral angry," Cloves admitted. "But Chitral obey Et'tanis."

"For now," the Sea Scribe agreed ominously. "Et'tanis foolishly imagines he can restrain Chitral forever."

His insult of the chieftain drew another barking protest from Ox. This time, Sa'ahla expected it, and refused to cringe.

"I daresay ya's angered more than just Chitral," Kylac observed. "Mayhap I can helps ya calm 'em. What mights ya know about the Blackmoon Shards?"

The Sea Scribe chuckled, seizing the bait with a haughty sneer. "Haverstromme, the family is called. An archipelago to the east, formed in legend from the fallen pieces of a dead moon. When Gulgran collided with Razenrend and—"

"Can ya charts me a course?"

"I can. All it will cost you is your ship."

"I was led to believes we might purchase a map for—"

"For baubles and trinkets," Sa'ahla said. "Weapons and foodstuffs and glittering stones. You hear me not, boy. All shall be swept into the sea, along with our bloated, broken corpses, when the ocean scours this lowland isle bare. Better that you keep your meager belongings, and seek refuge aboard your ship, should you have any hope of outlasting the Dragon's wrath."

Kylac frowned. The waves had seemed placid enough upon his crew's arrival. But it wasn't the validity of the Sea Scribe's paranoia that troubled him. Rather, it was the light being shed upon the circumstances before him. *They take Sa'ahla,* Cloves had said. *They try.*

"The Grenarr," Kylac said, seeking clarification while hoping not to offend his attending host. "They tried to take you. At *your* request."

"I begged their aid in escaping these shores," Sa'ahla admitted. "Made a prisoner in my own temple for the attempt."

"Better than the fate o' your fellow conspirators."

"Their fate, I am certain to share, unless the ocean swallows us first." The Scribe thrust his hooded face forward, blue eye brighter for the dead orb beside it, the folds in his throat jiggling as he spoke. "I have pleaded with Et'tanis and any other who will listen. All are in peril. All should leave. For weeks they have ignored me. I see no honor in perishing beside them—not with the forewarning I have given."

"I see your predicament. I only—"

"No honor, and no cause. No cause to enrich them with all set soon to be flushed away. No cause to chart your course to Haverstromme with my own life made forfeit in the bargain. You would find your way? Help me find mine. If not, we shall meet again in the depths."

"And?" ledron asked, pressing for more.

Kylac shrugged, indicating his helplessness. "And he refused to engage further. Just withdrew like a peevish child. Et'tanis offered apology, but wouldn't coerce him from his stance."

"That's what you've got us paying for?" Pevrick balked. He gestured at the parade of supplies being carried from their larboard hold. Bolts of silk and rolls of leather. Bags of spices and sacks of grain. Braces of knives and bundles of spears. Barrels of mead and jars of olives. A crate of chickens and a tether of goats. A purse of gemstones and a chest of coins. These and a dozen other items brought forth by members of their crew—a fair sampling of just about every item aboard their ship—were scarcely touching the dock before a team of waiting elves snatched them up and hauled them inland. "Bloody shards, Captain. I'm putting a stop to this."

"I wouldn't," Kylac advised, as Pevrick strode from their place at the head of the ship's ramp to intercept a cask being ported by pock-faced Aramis.

At almost the same time, a knock-kneed Mookla'ayan oversee-ing the exchange at the foot of the ramp yelped a growling protest, drawing the attention of Ox and his heavily armed guard contingent, clustered alertly alongside Et'tanis just up the trail. Spying them as they adjusted grip on their weapons, Pevrick released Aramis and waved him along, then returned to Ledron and Kylac.

"Cowed by a pack of savages," the first mate muttered angrily. "Standing idle while they rob us blind."

"Ya might sees it as lightening our load," Kylac proposed. The *Vengeance* had been teeming with supplies upon her arrival at Avenell, the expectation of Great Grendavan and his shipmates being that they would begin settling their promised gift of land upon the northeast-ern peninsula of the Sundered Isle as soon as the Grenarr overlord's wedding to Princess Denariel had been consummated. Now that the ship belonged to His Majesty King Kendarrion, they had need for less than half of the hoard that had been packed into her hold—but hadn't known how much of it might prove useful in seeking to purchase Prince Dethaniel's safe release. Skeptical of its value on that count, Kylac was just as glad to be rid of the unnecessary weight. "We'll be much swifter when we resume course."

"Yet we continue to waste time here," Pevrick grumbled. To Ledron, he added, "A single volley from our shipboard ballistae should send these roaches skittering."

"Or have us clawing from the harbor under a Mookla'ayan swarm," Kylac cautioned. "Believe me, Captain. Better that we avoid their sting."

"I felt better when I believed these goods had bought us something in exchange," Ledron groused.

"We has the maps," Kylac reminded him.

"With no mention of our destination upon them," the Head snapped. "So you'll forgive me if I share Pevrick's frustration."

Kylac couldn't quite fault them there. Following the mostly fruitless audience with the Sea Scribe, Et'tanis had led him to a vault within their pyramid containing hundreds of ocean maps, loosing Kylac among them in hopes of doing barter despite Sa'ahla's refusal. When Kylac had asked if he might bring another ashore, someone better suited to selecting those maps that might prove useful, the chieftain had politely yet forcefully refused. So Kylac had pored through the flattened sheaves and piled scrolls as best he could for more than an hour, seeking some rhyme or reason to the order in which they'd been catalogued, while desperately hunting for some mention of either Haverstromme or the Blackmoon Shards. Having failed on both counts when Et'tanis had determined his time was up, he'd been compelled to grab the half dozen he'd set aside that at least appeared to contain Addaranth or Mistwall as a reference point.

It remained to be seen whether Brenham or Taeg or anyone else could make the slightest use of them. Now that Ledron and Pevrick had heard a more thorough recounting of Kylac's visit, captain and first mate seemed far less certain of that likelihood.

"We also has the new name to go by," Kylac said, unperturbed. Haverstromme. A name they might have easily overlooked during their earlier review of the Grenarr charts and logs, when their search had been focused on the Baravian Atolls.

"Provided by a madman," Pevrick snarled, "whose raving even these half-tamed savages won't tolerate."

"Then consider it a docking fee. A landing fee. A fee o' passage, or just a gesture o' goodwill. By any description, we're leaving peacefully, our ship and our crew intact. I recall no guarantee o' that upon our arrival."

"We're most likely in the same position as before, only poorer for the effort. So don't expect me to stand here while you congratulate yourself. Your pardon, Captain."

With a nod from Ledron, Pevrick took his leave, turning on a heel and tromping back into the depths of the open hold.

"It would've been better had you included us in the negotiations," the Head advised. "Only a desperate man counts a lack of loss as a gain."

"Desperate we are, if'n I'm not mistaken. We's not the time to wait around for the Scribe to has a change o' heart. And if'n we hoist anchor as is, we risk the same challenges as before."

Continuing as best they could, guessing at which course to take and exposing the falsehoods in the *Vengeance*'s charts and logs through slow, tedious exploration. Hoping to happen upon some new scrap of information should they fail to discern their path through trial and error. Wringing the knowledge needed from their prisoner, Tormitius—with or without Ledron's permission—else surrendering their quest altogether and turning sails toward home.

Off his lengthening silence, the Head asked, "Have you something else in mind?"

"I's been thinking on the word I gave Et'tanis," Kylac said, peering upon the chieftain's distant position, picturing in his mind the native's knowing gaze and charitable smile. "In Chitral's glen. Before he granted me audience with the Scribe."

"What word was that?"

"That I hadn't come with the intent to take Sa'ahla."

"True enough. What of it?"

"I don't recall saying I wouldn't."

7

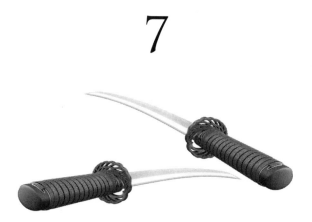

A WEB OF CLOUDS hung across night sky, filtering the light of moon and stars to leave the world draped in darkness. A matching brume lay thick upon the waters, drawn up like a curtain against their slow, steady approach. Padded oars dipped rhythmically into the black waves, pulling against the river's currents, angling their small craft toward what *had* been a deserted stretch of shoreline. Shrouded now by the misty void that had engulfed them, it might as easily be a gateway to the beyond.

At least one among their tiny crew seemed to believe as much. *A veil of ghosts,* Nadrum had muttered as the fog had coalesced around them. Forgetting his task for a moment, he'd drawn up his oar with one hand while flashing a warding gesture with the other. Jaleth, serving as coxswain, had hissed for silence, then motioned for a hard pull from the negligent oarsman to correct the hitch in their heading. Though stern and steadfast in his duty, he, too, betrayed nervousness. Observing from his seat at the bow, Kylac had watched the commanding Whitefist draw his cloak tighter with one hand while gripping a dagger hilt with the other, pale eyes roving as if wary of the mist taking corporeal form. Only Warmund, the crane-necked Whitefist whose comrades called him Worm, had guarded against reaction, remaining hunched over his larboard oar with the stubborn resignation of one who preferred not to witness death's approach.

Kylac might have offered a word of reassurance, pointing out that the thickening haze would serve them well as additional cover against any stray gazes. But a remark carried over open water to the shore beyond could only undermine their attempt at stealth. Seeing that his companions intended to carry out their task regardless of their reservations, he'd opted to remain silent.

With visibility reduced to no more than a pair of strokes in any direction, Kylac closed his eyes, withdrawing inward to where his less tangible senses drew focus. Whatever its source, the fog hid no discernible threat. He almost wished that it did, to better explain the tightness that had come to settle in his own chest ever since deciding upon this course hours earlier. When the last of their payment to the Mookla'ayan natives had been delivered, the crew of the *Vengeance* had raised anchor and slunk away, unsuccessful in their attempt to gain new direction from the Sea Scribe, but undamaged for the effort. Most aboard had been satisfied with the latter, content to escape the eerie island and its savage inhabitants unharmed. Only Pevrick had openly voiced displeasure with the outcome, continuing to grumble of supplies squandered and time wasted, advising that Ledron tighten his leash on Kylac and give ear instead to the able officers appointed by His Majesty, lest the next debacle cost them even more.

The petulant first mate was mollified not at all when he learned of Kylac's intent to return that very night to free the Sea Scribe and bring the purported Elementer aboard their vessel. If anything, his bitter anger intensified, as he set forth all of the many reasons it constituted a foolish risk. The Scribe might not go quietly. His tale might all be one big subterfuge—a trap to draw them in and this time confiscate their entire ship. Should they somehow manage to carry out the abduction attempt, would the madman prove in any way useful? Or would he become but one more errant cog set to lead them astray?

Ledron himself was not sold on the idea until Brenham, as chief navigator, had officially announced that he and his men had finished studying the maps Kylac had brought them, and had determined them to be of little aid. Even when referenced against the Grenarr maps in their possession, the effort had been like trying to force together pieces from mismatched puzzles. Nor had the term Haverstromme been found among any of the shipboard charts or logs already discovered. It was at that point that the Head had asked if, by himself, Kylac might truly bring the Sea Scribe to them. Though Leeches had scoffed at Kylac's ready assurance, the other senior officers had held conspicuously silent. In the end, Ledron had agreed to the attempt.

And Kylac had at once begun to feel as if it might well be a mistake.

A natural disquiet, he'd told himself, born of the increased expectation he'd taken on from the entire crew, and the uncertainty inherent in going about it. Even with the command given, it had taken hours to steer the ship at a creeping pace along the northern shore, then down a second, larger inland tributary, discovered well east of the prior inlet—as revealed on one of the maps that Kylac had procured. Like the first, they'd followed it south for some time, hoping not to come across any more docks or native settlements. It was decided that, if discovered, they would claim they were endeavoring to save time and avoid any prowling Grenarr ships by cutting through the island itself by way of the watery warren that was the Shrouded Skein.

Kylac had worried that Et'tanis and his clansmen would see right through the excuse, given that he'd made no mention of such goal earlier. But loosing his tongue on that count might have only persuaded their captain to sail on to a more distant point, or to surrender the incursion attempt altogether. He required access at a location within reasonable proximity of Sa'ahla's pyramid, yet remote and inaccessible enough to discourage a possible sighting by the natives. Reservations notwithstanding, with all that they could read from the map, this particular tributary had seemed their most promising road.

With night's cloak and the island's mists as their allies, they'd sailed down to a highland spur that, according to Brenham, lay almost due east of the native village—at a distance of roughly three leagues. There, they'd dropped anchor in the middle of the channel and lowered a shore boat into the waters below, with Jaleth, Nadrum, and Worm drawing the choice assignment of ferrying Kylac to his drop point. Having come this far without incident, and rid himself momentarily of Pevrick's ceaseless discontent, he might have hoped that his unknown apprehension would have bled away.

Mayhap ghosts ruled these mists after all.

He sensed the oncoming shore by its looming mass and by the soft slap of the river waves sweeping and churning along its base. He counted six more strokes, then nodded at Jaleth, who in turn motioned for Nadrum and Worm to ease up. Kylac twisted in his seat to face fore, gaze searching. The river carried them onward, its smoothly running surface masking a deceptive strength. The low-hanging brume shifted and swirled, like gossamer curtains rustled by a hint of breeze.

A spur of doubt caused Kylac to wonder if they might have missed their mark—before the curtains abruptly parted, pierced by a thrusting jag in the cliff's base. He heard Jaleth gasp and curse, then felt the tug of oars squaring in the water, checking their approach. The river carried them anyway. Kylac reared back, bracing as the prow of their little shore boat rammed up against the wet limestone with an abrasive thud, catching long enough for the stern to swing downriver. Nadrum nearly lost his oar, but managed to recover and help Worm steer them to a halt broadside within a small recess formed by the jag, just large enough to serve cove to their tiny vessel.

It wasn't the drop point they'd targeted by spyglass from the *Vengeance*, but Kylac couldn't say as to whether they'd ended up north or south of their chosen landing, and wasn't inclined to go combing up and down the shore in search of it. Peering up at the bluff before him, he came to a decision in hopes of forestalling unnecessary debate.

"This will do," he whispered.

Nadrum gaped as he gazed skyward up the height of the cliff. Worm raised an eyebrow in surprise. Jaleth frowned, recognizing as Kylac had that this marked a slight shift in their plans. When the coxswain opened his mouth, Kylac anticipated an objection to spill forth.

"It's your neck," the Whitefist agreed instead. "You'd have us anchor here, then?"

"While I disembark," Kylac clarified, shedding his outer cloak and stashing it in the locker of his bow seat. "Then proceed south until ya finds a more welcoming slope for our return."

"The Thrush's Hour," Jaleth added. Not a question, a warning. Hitch in plans or no, he would grant no more time than originally allotted.

Kylac bowed a quick nod, then checked the blades sheathed across his back. With all secure, he positioned himself atop the boat's gunwale and sighted a knob of rock protruding from the cliff's face. An uncertain wager, given the unknown composition of the stone. Based on their minor collision, the erosion at the cliff's base would seem to indicate untold centuries of the river's chewing assault on an iron shore. But it might as easily suggest earthen materials incessantly crumbling at the water's merest brush. If that knob were to break free . . .

With the night already almost half gone, Kylac was short on hours. Nor did he care to grapple upside down amid lower reaches made slick by the river's slapping spray. He'd likely take far greater risks before the night was done. This first leap, he would take on chance.

He sprang, catching the knob in both hands. Loose grit sprinkled around his face, but the rock itself held. He drew himself up, catching smaller crags with his toes. Sturdy limestone, as he'd hoped. With that lone, minor concession to good fortune, he aimed higher, feeling as much as eyeing his way skyward, forging a path through instinct and determination. Crags, cracks, niches—he found and used them all. He felt the gazes of his shipmates clinging to him, silently urging him on. Doubtless, a lookout or two aboard the *Vengeance* sought to mark his passage as well, though they would be unable to do so unless the fog dissipated—hopefully meaning that no Mookla'ayans who might happen to be patrolling along this branch of the Skein would be able to spy *them* in return.

His passage slowed as he neared the upper third of the cliff, where the base of bedrock gave way to softer layers of clay and sandstone. Here, he had to check his holds more carefully, respecting not only the treacherous nature of the land, but the greater plunge that now awaited him should he make a mistake. In some patches, he was able to seize upon exposed roots that had managed to snake down from somewhere above. Across other, more barren stretches, he resorted to the pair of scaling knives sheathed at his belt. Twice, his grip betrayed him, sending loose chunks spinning toward the water below. Each time, he cringed at the throaty splash as it plunked into the river—better as it was than raining down upon his comrades to elicit a clattering or howl. On neither occasion, however, did he let it threaten his overall perch or cripple his conviction. Had his struggles drawn attention, he would simply need to reach the top all the sooner.

His single-minded persistence rewarded him moments later, the jungle spilling a tangle of thick vines out over the cliff's lip as if in gracious recognition of his effort. Scrambling over the ledge with a windlike rustle, he rolled into a crouch and let his senses go to work, seeking out the potential for any threat. His uneasiness remained, carried up from below—telling him that the greater danger yet lay ahead.

But it hadn't come to ambush him here. The jungle slumbered restlessly, a cacophony of chittering and warbling and flapping and rustling, but of small creatures only, on about their nightly tasks. Nothing threatened him from amid the profuse tangle of growth—nothing more than serpents and insects, anyway. Mayhap a poisonous lizard or venomous toad, but even these, he told himself, were most likely to withdraw at his approach. He couldn't let such dissuade him tonight.

He held still a moment longer, then took an angle and set off through the trees, slinking stealthily at first, but soon gaining confidence and hastening his stride. With three leagues to cover, he faced an inland jog of an hour and a half—if not longer, given the uncertain terrain. Seeing as he needed to run that distance twice in order to return by the appointed hour—on the way back, with the elderly Sea Scribe in tow—he had little time to spare for even the most practical hesitation.

Slipping westward amid the tufts and walls of wild growth, he pressed deeper into the night-cloaked jungle, until it had swallowed him whole.

His heart thrummed gamely in his chest, a slight sheen of sweat coating his skin, when the peak of the pyramid at last came to view. Kylac slowed, shifting from gentle breeze to silent shadow. A small spike of adrenaline coursed through his well-warmed limbs, registering at the nape of his neck as a tingling anticipation.

He'd made good time through the jungle, its vegetation abundant, yet not so dense as to arrest his passage. Nor had he happened across elf or beast to give him pause. He'd drawn attention from the wildlife, to be sure, the eyes of raptors and feral predators that had sized him up as potential prey—but nothing large or swift or desperate enough to challenge him. He'd crossed the western river fork that flowed past the Mookla'ayan harbor without wetting his feet, at a southern narrows choked with boulders and deadfall. It all boded well for the return trek. Assuming, of course, that the next phase met with similar success.

The pyramid vanished again, for a time, its blocky heights screened by a mesh of upthrust boles and interwoven branches laden with broad, serrated leaves. It was enough for Kylac to know it lay near, his sense of direction sufficient to track the structure unerringly now that he'd glimpsed it. A smaller target, on the move, might have required a further measure of concentration. But a massive mound of stone? From here, he could reach it blindfolded.

So he held focus on his more immediate surroundings, his eyes, ears, and preternatural senses probing for any sign of Mookla'ayan patrol. Though he'd seen little upon his earlier visit to suggest the natives had reason to ward the outer boundaries beyond their village proper, he'd seen nothing to convince him they didn't, either. If not watchmen, then hunters set forth to capture nocturnal game. Unlikely as it might be for quarry of significant size to roam so close to an established settlement, wiser he would be while upon this strange island to curtail his assumptions. If not hunters, it might be a pack of moon worshippers he encountered, or children undertaking an adventure, or illicit lovers seeking a moment of stolen intimacy. For the half dozen scenarios he could imagine and the countless others he couldn't, better that he avoid them all.

Invisibly he crept, from shadow to shadow, over and along animal trails and Mookla'ayan pathways, forging the most direct route whenever possible, making subtle deviations when it wasn't. He did so effortlessly, having practiced the art of stealth since his earliest memory.

A short life, some might argue, given that he remained three weeks shy of his seventeenth spring. Nonetheless, the force of routine made it more natural for him to tread unnoticed than it would have been to make his presence known.

For all his skills, his mysterious reservations continued to twist in his gut, an internal caution he'd been unable to escape. Something about this venture wasn't right. He knew it in his bones. He just didn't know what. And until the source of his discomfort revealed itself, he would suffer its vexing protests as he might a bothersome fly or a pebble in his boot.

He'd wondered if it might stem not from any outward threat, but from a disturbance more intrinsic in nature. More than once since he'd begun this task, he'd questioned its validity. *I's not come intending to take Sa'ahla.* And at the time, he hadn't. Yet now he had. Did that make his earlier declaration to Et'tanis a lie?

It seemed not, but lay close enough to scratch at his conscience. Precisely why he'd learned to avoid making statements that he would later be compelled to adhere to. Raised from birth to give little credence to stark moral concepts of good and evil, he'd come to believe that a man's only compass of genuine truth was to match his own words to his own deeds, no matter how they might be judged by another. Personal integrity. The principal touchstone by which he allowed himself to be guided, in a life often devoid of mercy or fairness. It troubled him to think he might be violating his tonight.

The foliage thinned as he neared the jungle's fringe, the pyramid's east slope a towering black wall beyond the loose screen of stunted trees and scraggly growth that edged the clearing. Kylac paused, senses tasting of the emptiness beyond. The dim glow of flickering firelight emerged from a handful of ducts spaced about the pyramid's stepstone heights. He watched a bird swoop down from the north to alight briefly on a stone lip before darting eastward overhead. He sensed the subtle movement of elves nearby, though he couldn't quite hear or smell them. Mayhap sentinels, mayhap villagers. Whichever, on the far side of the structure. In all, he found the immediate area remarkably quiet, its inhabitants either too still or too distant to draw notice. He'd expected a greater level of activity, given the nocturnal habits of the Mookla'ayans he'd known back in Vosges.

Reminding him yet again that he'd left Pentania behind long ago.

He slid forward at a crouch, gliding past the last of the bowed trees and grasping groundcover, leaking into the open. With the nearest wall of the pyramid as his target, he sped into a dash, a gray wisp amid the cloud-shrouded darkness. The night took no notice. Forty paces flew underfoot, the base of the pyramid looming before him. He didn't slow as it came within reach, but launched himself with a running leap, planting his second foot against the wall's skin and springing skyward, gaining just enough lift to grasp the top ledge with his outstretched palms. A quick pull and push brought the rest of his body after, until he'd come to rest atop the stone lip, pressed against the pyramid's second layer.

He scurried at once toward the structure's southeast corner, padding softly along the weathered stone, searching as he went for any indication of discovery. He heard no threatening shouts, no cries of alarm. Just the ceaseless chitter of insects, the whisper of swirling breezes, the shriek of a prowling nightbird. The thrashing of leaves as something fled through the distant brush. Nothing to suggest his presence here had drawn any interest.

At the corner, he peered around to the pyramid's southern face, scanning the earth beneath it. He spied no guard lines, no native patrols. Discomfort plucked at the cords in his stomach, giving them another twist. He told himself that the lack of an external sweep meant anything and nothing. Mayhap Et'tanis's people abandoned their temple stronghold at night, no matter what the fires flickering from within would seem to suggest. Mayhap they settled for warding only the entrance, open to the west and beyond his present view. Mayhap dozens of native sentries had retreated inside, to ward its tunneling passageways from within. It had been a hive of activity during the day, teeming like an anthill. The same might be true now.

Given more time, he might well have preferred to make a full circuit of his own around the perimeter, to see what possibilities could be confirmed or eliminated before pressing further. But he'd known from the outset that this wouldn't be possible. Rather than concern himself with the lack of native defenses, he would have to count himself fortunate, remain vigilant, and continue along the most direct route he could think of to reach Sa'ahla, trusting that the Sea Scribe would be of use in guiding their swiftest, safest departure.

Clinging to the pyramid's corner so that he could duck to either the east or south side as needed, Kylac continued his climb. The blocks were of a height to prevent him from simply reaching up and pulling himself from one ledge to the next, but were cracked and pitted and overgrown with crusty patches of lichen that offered him all the grip he required. Steadily, methodically, he worked his way up the successive layers, avoiding the ducts and fissures aglow with firelight, working toward the balcony openings at its apex. Exposed as he was, better this approach than seeking to navigate the labyrinth of stairs and corridors within.

He could not, of course, be sure that the Sea Scribe's captors were still holding him in that central chamber above. But he had no reason to think they might have moved him, either. The Elementer had certainly seemed entrenched in his space earlier. Though, it might only have been Kylac's unwelcome presence that had made him adopt such a turtlelike posture.

Just one of many variables he was contending with this night, none of which altered the measure of need. With so little known, he simply had to rely on guesses and instincts, and adapt as required.

Doing so made him feel alive.

As he neared the top, his ears detected a dull roar. Muted by distance, it sounded at first like ocean waves butting rhythmically against a smooth shoreline. But the only waves within range that he was aware of were those of the river and harbor, neither of which he should have been able to hear this far inland. The wind, then, swelling in strength as it sped through some duct or fissure. Yet, if that were so, should he not have been able to feel its stirring brush?

When he paused to see what he could determine of the sound's source, it faded, subsiding beneath the range of his hearing. He held still a moment longer, then continued on his way. The sound came again, and this time he paused sooner. Again, he failed to make sense of it. An unfamiliar animal, mayhap. Or the midnight rousing of a land unknown.

Upon reaching the level of the balconies near the summit, Kylac shifted eastward again. Though he didn't suppose it made much difference which opening he entered, the east would put him closer than the south to Sa'ahla's earlier location in the northeast corner. Should one of the chamber sentries attempt to kill or injure the Sea Scribe to prevent his escape, Kylac would be better positioned to minimize any potential damage to his prize.

Torches ensconced just within the chamber lit the sides of the opening. Kylac crept to the wall's edge, taking care not to cast a shadow inside. With a steady hand, he slid a slender shortsword from its sheath on his back. The leather-bound haft felt soothing to flesh made raw from climbing. Or mayhap it was merely his anticipation of the weapon's blade being put to use.

He listened for a moment to his own eager heartbeat, striving to detect a snore, a shift, a shuffle—anything to indicate the placement and status of the chamber's occupants. Save for the crackle of the torch, the room offered only silence in reply.

Kylac curled around the wall's edge, his blade held behind him to hide any reflection, his free hand ready to grab a throwing knife, the torch, or another weapon as needed. He needn't have bothered. Neither sentries nor Sa'ahla reacted to his arrival. Neither weapons nor netting flew at him. No other trap was sprung.

The chamber before him lay empty.

8

Kʏʟᴀᴄ ᴄᴜʀsᴇᴅ ʙᴇɴᴇᴀᴛʜ ʜɪs ʙʀᴇᴀᴛʜ. His gaze swept the room a second time, probing the angled recesses of its sloped corners, seeking any hint of movement. There were few hiding places amid the meager collection of pedestals, casks, and sculpted trinkets. It didn't take him long to confirm his initial assessment.

Sa'ahla no longer resided here.

Even though he'd anticipated the possibility, Kylac felt a stab of frustration. He didn't have time to go skulking through the lower chambers and corridors of the temple—or worse, through the outlying village and jungle—in search. This was to have been a snatch-and-vanish, the odds of success already piled against him. With the Sea Scribe not to be found . . .

His options rolled through his mind, none of them appealing. The only logical course was to surrender. To take the few hours of darkness remaining to him and return to the riverside promontory beneath which he would find Jaleth and the others waiting. Elsewise, he risked stranding himself on this island—a doomed land, if Sa'ahla's ravings could in any way be taken for truth. He'd be forced to subsist in secrecy among the natives, awaiting the arrival of another vessel to which he could attach himself, then owing to the mercy of whatever objective its crew had undertaken. A better situation than the *Vengeance*, mayhap. But any hope of making good on his word to retrieve Prince Dethaniel would be—

The dispiriting thought was brushed aside by a sudden murmur not unlike ocean waves. The same sound he'd heard earlier, only clearer, more sharp and insistent. Kylac looked to the west balcony, the noise clearly rising from that direction. Sheathing his shortsword, he rushed across the chamber for a better view, chasing the sound as it ebbed again from hearing.

He restrained himself at the inner wall of the opening, wary of the balcony itself and its increased exposure. Despite the somewhat limited vantage, he saw clearly the collection of huts spread forth at the pyramid's base, and the pathways that snaked through them, wending into the jungle beyond. A twinge of suspicion raked upward along his spine, coming to rest in the nape of his neck. Short of an actual thought, but a kernel of instinct close enough to raise his hopes. Somewhere out there, something was taking place. Something . . .

He scanned the dark for the telltale glow of firelight, but didn't see any. But then, he wouldn't, he realized, recalling belatedly that Cwingen U'uyen and his fellow Mookla'ayans back in Vosges saw as clearly in darkness as they did in daylight. The spread of torches in and around their temple stronghold had led him astray on that count. Likely, they served some ceremonial purpose rather than a functional one. He would need the sound to—

As if summoned by his need, it flared again. This time, he pinpointed it easily, to the west and slightly north, mayhap half a mile distant. *The glen,* he thought. Chitral's glen, wherein Et'tanis had shown him the Grenarr captain being butchered. At almost the same time, he recognized the mysterious murmur for what it was—a cadre of voices raised as one. A communal response of some kind. Mayhap a cheer.

Kylac felt the slow smile that spread across his face this time as the sound faded. It contained no mirth, for his intuition told him that the relentless misgivings associated with this mission hadn't yet been satisfied. Whatever its precise nature, the event unfolding in that jungle glen would not be to his advantage. If anything, it constituted a warning, a premonition of further adversity.

But at least he knew where he must go from here.

The doubts in his stomach reared, countering with a final objection. It wasn't too late to turn back now. A far wiser choice, they seemed to hiss. Dethaniel might already be lost. Those relying on Kylac to help save the prince might forever despise him for it, but his own welfare would be better served by abandoning this venture and seeking another—the mad Scribe and whatever they might gain from him be damned.

Safer, sure. And dreadfully dull.

Spurred by a fresh sense of urgency, he withdrew to the east balcony at the rear of the chamber, crawled back outside, and began backtracking along his path of ascent. Though any other face of the pyramid might have granted him a better view of events, it would also be more likely to place him within eyeshot of a wandering native. Had this been a human village, he would have gladly taken the risk, confident in his ability to elude detection. Mookla'ayans, however, were far keener in their senses.

He completed his descent within moments, touching down at the southeast corner of the pyramid's base. No sooner had his feet struck earth than he rounded the structure to the north. He might have returned to the jungle east, to round south and then north amid its camouflaging foliage, encircling the village clearing and surrounding huts without ever emerging onto open ground. But that would have been a long, circuitous route across unfamiliar ground, costing him more time than he cared to spend. North and west would be much faster in terms of distance, and would require that he cross into the open only upon traversing the trail leading to the harbor. If he couldn't manage that, well, then there wasn't much hope for the rest of what he'd come here to accomplish.

Into the northern jungle he sped, slipping among the boughs and leaves, just a stray gust amid the brume. He felt the scrabbling retreat of rodents, the clinging curiosity of insects, and the sharp gazes of birds and reptiles far more circumspect in their appraisal. He breezed over and around sinkholes, deadfalls, and would-be snares formed by vines, roots, and other tripping groundcover. His heart beat comfortably, his pulse a light throbbing in his ears.

He paused as the trail took shape through the filter of growth ahead. Empty, it seemed. Quiet.

He cut across its well-traveled surface, on the balls of his feet, scarcely leaving a toeprint to mark his passing. On the far side, he scrambled up a grass-lined embankment and plunged through a hedge of ferns. He heard no pursuit, and didn't wait for one to form, slowing just enough to confirm his new heading—almost due west along a thickly wooded downslope. The larger trees—and more specifically, their roots—did him service by holding the ground together despite the steep grade. Spongy earth cushioned his footfalls. Nonetheless, he fully recognized that one errant step, or a single wayward lean, could send him tumbling or skidding. A balance it would be, a blend of speed and stealth and caution.

And luck, of course. Only a vain fool would discount entirely the ever-present role of blind fortune.

The glen called to him from below, its murmurs grown louder and more frequent. Not a cheer. More a solemn acknowledgment. An individual's loud, punctuating cry preceded each surging echo. The Butcher, Chitral. It wasn't the voice Kylac recognized so much as the cruelty in its tone. Scenting blood on the wind, he tried not to imagine the ritual being performed—or the Sea Scribe as its victim.

His throat tightened. His stomach clenched. Stealth and caution slipped a notch, making way for haste.

His descent leveled off, the slope flattening near its base. Recalling the layout of the Butcher's glen, Kylac veered slightly south, easing pace as he made his final approach. The path brought him to a squat ridge, mayhap twelve heads in height, overlooking Chitral's shoulder. A hedge of tall, spearlike leaves, stirred by the wind and layered in thick rows, parted before him like silken folds, masking his movements. Kylac dropped to his belly regardless, lest he reveal himself to some stray eye amid the crowd of observers.

Through the final row of stalks, the glen came into view. He was immediately glad of his approach angle, for the crescent-shaped gallery of onlookers to which Chitral played had tripled in size from that seen earlier, its members forced into the jungle backdrop along the bowl's rim. Their attention seemed rooted squarely on the Butcher, many of them swaying and humming as Chitral yelped and danced though an array of movements that alternated between savage and sinuous. A wall of warrior sentries stood between audience and executioner, their broad backs to whatever slaughter was taking place. Blocked by Chitral's form, Kylac could see the leg of a body staked over the tree stump at the glen's center, painted with rivulets of blood. His pulse quickened.

The Butcher shifted, revealing the victim's face.

Et'tanis.

Warring reactions pierced Kylac's chest like fire and ice—a warm rush of relief, and a cold stab of regret. He recalled Sa'ahla's warning concerning Chitral's ambition, and the barely bridled animosity with which the Butcher had regarded the elderly chieftain during their earlier confrontation. Regrettably, Kylac didn't think it coincidence that whatever betrayal or uprising had taken place had been initiated so soon after his own visit. The sting of guilt wouldn't hear elsewise. He thought of the kindly demeanor Et'tanis had exhibited toward his clansmen, and the polite reverence afforded him in return. Now, those same clansmen and kinfolk bore unflinching witness to the elder's torture.

So much for respect. Or even civility.

It all brought a dangerous stirring to Kylac's veins, the urge to unleash his blades and teach them a lesson or two about the use of force against those less capable. He looked for Ox, and spotted him by his massive shoulders amid the line of warrior guardsmen. Ox and Chitral. If he could but face those two, he might comfortably bid Et'tanis a peaceful departure.

But a calmer, more rational instinct held him fast. He'd heard no screams, no cries upon his approach. This told him that Et'tanis wasn't in pain. Mayhap he'd died earlier, and the ceremony unfolding now was but a Mookla'ayan form of farewell. Mayhap he'd offered himself up in sacrifice. Kylac couldn't yet know what had happened. Not with any certainty that would merit action here and now, where the result would only be the deaths of myriad more natives and mayhap his own. Sa'ahla. Sa'ahla might yet be found. An insult his abduction might be to Et'tanis's memory. But it might also be the best revenge

Kylac could bring against the chieftain's suspected betrayers.

And yet, as he searched the glen anew, he saw no sign of the Sea Scribe. What was it Sa'ahla had claimed? That Chitral meant to absorb his powers by consuming the Elementer's flesh. That only Et'tanis stood in the way—and wouldn't be able to do so forever. With the chieftain dead or overthrown, might Chitral's adherents have gotten to the Sea Scribe already? Kylac refused to believe so, for it would mean he'd already failed. Could that be what the roiling in his gut had been seeking to tell him?

Then his gaze snagged upon a pair of stone-faced Mookla'ayan sentinels posted side by side in the deep curve of the glen's north-west bend. Crowded by observers and draped by reaching tufts of leaves, only their cool vigilance caused them to stand out amid the press. Behind them, a narrow trail that he'd had no cause to notice earlier—just a sliver of an opening into the jungle. Possibly nothing. But then, why would they be warding it?

Having nothing better to go on, Kylac fell back through the brush and circled around the back of the glen's rim, keeping deep enough to avoid those shoved to the rear of the gallery. Chitral's fierce cries raked his spine, while the steady responses of the Mookla'ayan people curdled his blood, all the more chilling for their lack of emotion. That small voice of self-preservation had returned, seeking to turn him around, insisting that he make for the *Vengeance* with all haste. To silence it, Kylac summoned an image of Pevrick. Even if all that remained of the Scribe was a bucket of entrails, he wasn't about to face the first mate empty-handed.

He found the ribbon trail behind the sentinels, picking it up where it snaked across a stream before descending along a natural stair formed of exposed tree roots interlaced with packed dirt. While skirting its path, he ran afoul of tightly grown hedges of thorns and nettles. They clutched at the loose folds of his tunic and breeches, clawing him as he passed. Kylac looked to reroute, but the jungle here seemed overtaken by them. Opting for a more expedient course, he surrendered to chance and took to the trail itself, crouching low, a slender dagger in hand.

He stole along the narrow path until it opened onto a small clearing

ringed by a horseshoe brook and dominated by a ring-shaped paddock further divided into stalls. A sacrificial staging area. Fronting
the paddock, a lean-to structure with a thatched canopy and a carpet
of broken bones underfoot. Amid the bones, a broad stump like the
one in the glen above.

Lashed to a pair of posts that had him kneeling atop the stump
with arms spread wide, Sa'ahla.

The Sea Scribe saw him at once, pinning him with that strange
black orb, as if he'd known all along that Kylac was coming. A heartbeat later, the pair of Mookla'ayans tending to the Elementer turned.
Kylac's dagger hit one in the throat. The other managed only a hiss
of surprise before a slender longsword pierced him through the heart.
A shortsword bit upward through the jawbone of the first, twisting
into his brain to finish what the dagger strike had started. A tug
freed the blade. A spinning slash with the same weapon claimed the
second elf's head.

Matching mortars and pestles fell with the bodies, spilling a black
paste with which the Mookla'ayans had been painting strange symbols
across Sa'ahla's naked arms and chest. *Acolytes,* thought Kylac, paying
little heed to the defiant thrashings of their stubborn corpses. He
snatched his longsword from the still-beating heart of the second to
fall. With primary blade in his right hand and secondary blade in his
left, he stepped forward to face the Sea Scribe.

The Elementer flinched at Kylac's approach. Bound and gagged
and stripped save for a loincloth, he bore almost no resemblance to
the tightly bundled creature Kylac had met earlier, wedged into that
crevice of his temple chamber. His right shoulder was drawn tight
against his neck, severely knotted and riddled with moles. His hair,
peppered in color, appeared strikingly coarse and spiked in all directions—like a fledgling coral formation. His emaciated torso looked
to be little more than an empty ribcage, overstretched by flesh so
pallid as to reveal the entire network of veins beneath. His knees and
elbows were too swollen for his lean limbs, his fingers and toes too
far splayed. It struck Kylac that if there was anything to be gained
from devouring him, it was most likely a savage stomach illness.

A resonant swell from the gallery above reminded Kylac of his purpose.

His swords swept out, one to each side, severing the ropes that held the Elementer in position. Sa'ahla winced until he realized what Kylac had done, then reached for the gag and yanked it from his mouth.

"We've little time," the Scribe wheezed. "Et'tanis will be dead soon."

"He's been silent for some time."

"Dead, I said." Sa'ahla struggled to his feet, turning at once toward a sort of workbench, where lay a pile of garments. "They drugged him with numbing compounds. It must be chafing Chitral to have afforded him such mercy, but the clan would surely have risen against him had he not."

Kylac watched the Elementer root through the garments, tossing aside those that had been cut into unwearable shreds. "Did they numb you as well?"

Sa'ahla scoffed, even as he settled finally on a torn travel cloak and wrestled his arms into its sleeves. "Chitral claimed it would despoil my blood, weakening the power to be gained upon drinking it."

Kylac breathed a small sigh of relief, having feared for a moment that he would be forced to haul the aged fellow the three leagues or so to freedom. "You know why I's come?"

"I believe I made my conditions plain." He finished fighting with his robe and turned back toward Kylac, casting about as if in sudden concern. "Where are your companions?"

"Companions?" Kylac smiled, hefting his blades. "These are my only companions."

The Scribe scowled. "How do you mean for us to escape, without at least a diversion?"

"Quietly, if'n ya can manage it."

"Your vessel is in the harbor?"

"The river. A fork three leagues to the east. If'n you're ready, I suggest we—"

"Three leagues?" Sa'ahala balked, then cursed and muttered in what might have been a foreign tongue. "Fool. They'll run us down within a mile."

"A risk already settled upon." *Ungrateful wretch.* "Given the circumstances, your options appear limited. Do ya desire passage off this rock, or not?"

The Scribe regarded him with that cold, black eye—a withering stare if ever Kylac had seen one. "East, you say? How far from the mouth?"

"Four leagues. Just south of the Jenovian Spur, as it was marked on your chart."

Sa'ahla worked his jaw back and forth, thoughts grinding with his teeth in a very Ledron-like manner.

"We're wasting—"

"Can you swim?"

The abruptness of the question and the intensity with which it was asked caused Kylac to hesitate. He blinked at the strange old man, trying to discern where the query was leading.

"Bury me in sand. Can you swim?"

"I can," Kylac replied defensively.

The Elementer revealed a half smile of chipped, jagged teeth. The dead eye took on a gleaming cast. "And for how long can you do so underwater?"

"At best? Three minutes, I'll say."

Sa'ahla turned his gaze to the west, sniffing the wind. The half-crazed smile slipped a bit. "Come. There may be a way."

They departed north through the back of the staging area before veering—not to the east, but the west. The Scribe didn't say why, and Kylac didn't ask. Though he thought to point out that the *Vengeance* was anchored in the opposite direction, he felt certain he'd made that plain already, and that only insult could result if he sought to correct his strange companion on something so basic as points of the compass. Their lives hung in the balance, sure. But this was Sa'ahla's island, and it was Sa'ahla whose principal skill was mapmaking, no less. Kylac decided, therefore, to show a little trust.

He tried not to cringe at the loud, reckless path that the Elementer beat through the brush. While speed might count for more than silence at this point, Kylac was reluctant to assume that every clansman on this island was gathered now in Chitral's glen. Should even a single Mookla'ayan happen upon them, he might well be forced to slay the man—or woman—before they could raise an alarm. Capable he most surely was of doing so. Contrary to what the bodies of the acolytes back in the staging area might suggest, however, he hadn't come here to slaughter a bunch of innocent elves.

Despite the whipping, snapping, plodding noises of the Scribe's passage, Kylac kept an ear tuned to events in the glen, marking the ebb and flow of Chitral's killing ritual. It faded quickly, muted by the thickening mesh of jungle woodland rising between them. Comforting, it might have been, save that he didn't truly believe the natives would be so easily eluded—and that Mookla'ayans as he knew them typically hunted silently. If he couldn't hear them, they might have already taken up the pursuit. And it would be that much harder to track their movements.

They'd covered nearly eight hundred paces when a new sound arose ahead—a rough gurgling that quickly resolved into rushing waters. The volume and intensity seemed to multiply with every stride. A waterfall, mayhap? The itch in the back of his mind that wondered what the Scribe had planned grew more insistent.

For all his crooked frame and age-worn joints, Sa'ahla proved surprisingly spry, loping along for another hundred strides over uneven terrain before staggering to an abrupt halt. At first, Kylac thought the old man had pulled up lame. But when he hurried forward to assist, the Elementer brushed aside his concern with an indignant shove and irritable grunt. Breathless, Sa'ahla gestured at a ravine hollow a few steps ahead.

Kylac slipped forward to investigate. Not just a hollow, he realized, but a sinkhole, deep and broad as it cut across the ground like a jagged streak of lightning. A subterranean river filled its depths, surging through the earth beneath their heels, at a drop of roughly forty feet. Surging eastward, Kylac noted, and a spike of fear lanced through him like a sudden chill.

"Four minutes, must we starve our lungs," the Scribe explained as he came hobbling up, "before escaping at another portal farther east."

"Portal? Another sinkhole, ya mean."

"Swift. Silent. The perfect escape."

Kylac checked the Elementer's visage to determine if he was serious.

A thick sweat had pooled on his brow and gathered in the loose folds of his neck. But there was no sign of bluff. No hint of jest. "Three minutes, I said. The longest I's held my breath."

The Scribe replied adamantly. "Four buys escape. Three, a lung-strangling death."

The roar of waters consumed now all but the sharpest calls of the surrounding jungle—a shrill, ceaseless chirping and brief, raucous screeching being the only other sounds to reach Kylac's ears. *A lung-strangling death.* This, along with his inherent distaste for confined spaces, made the course Sa'ahla suggested nothing less than horrifying.

And then it struck him. Here it was, the source of his persistent misgivings. Some innate sense had known it would come to this. A swim through the blackness, traveling beneath the earth to some distant point that might or might not deliver them as the Sea Scribe claimed. Would it not be better to tackle an overland route? To trust in his blades should the bloodthirsty Chitral and his fellow natives discover them? Of what use would all of his finely honed skills be below, in the drowning dark?

A strange trumpeting knifed through the throaty roar of the sunken river, followed by the squalling of what might have been horns. For only an instant did Kylac wonder what sort of creature made such a noise. By the time his gaze sought and found Sa'ahla's, he knew.

"We are discovered," the Scribe confirmed. "We do this, or we join Et'tanis."

A voice from deep inside reared up to challenge the claim. Sa'ahla might have to do this, but he did not. They could each go their separate ways and seek to meet at the river. He'd given the Scribe clear enough directions to find them. Of course, they very likely wouldn't arrive at the same time. One or the other would get there first, and then . . . what, ensure he waited for the other? For how long? With what degree of certainty that the other would arrive at all?

The surest way to convey the Sea Scribe safely was to remain at his side and deliver him personally. Anything less would be to risk fell possibilities too numerous to count.

But that wasn't enough to decide it. What truly maddened Kylac was the understanding that those inner voices of doubt and justification were bred from a single seed—fear. Looking up, he realized that Sa'ahla recognized it—even with that peculiar, sightless eye of his. It was enough to stir Kylac's blood, to remind him that he'd always been one to face his fears, not cringe from them.

"Show me," he said.

The Scribe didn't disappoint. With his cloak tied fast about his waist, he pressed the fingertips of either hand together, muttered some form of invocation, then dove into the sinkhole, striking the waters headfirst and vanishing beneath their torrential rush.

Had he any gods to pray to, Kylac might have done so. As he did not, he bonded his blades to their scabbards and crept to the precipice of the sinkhole's upper rim. With a final, sweeping look at the jungle around him, he drew the deepest breath he could summon, and dove.

9

COLD, CRUSHING BLACKNESS gripped Kylac as he plunged into the river's depths. The water seized him, its raging current yanking him downward and sucking him swiftly beneath the earth. He counted to three before opening his eyes, afraid of what he might see.

Nothing. Not a hint of light to illuminate his path. His body rotated, twisted and spun by the powerful flow. For a heartbeat, a gray haze. He reached for it, only to watch it retreat from his outstretched hand. The sinkhole, he realized. The breach through which he'd entered this underwater tube of rock. The haze vanished, eclipsed by a darkness both sudden and absolute. As if a hood had been dropped over his head. Like a man condemned.

He blinked against the scratching waters, but elsewise kept his eyes open, waiting for his vision to adjust. But there was nothing to adjust *to*. Not a sliver of light to lend even the barest clarity or definition. His heart beat with reflexive panic. How could he have agreed to this? How could he have willfully taken that final, foolish leap?

Whatever the answer, his choice couldn't be unmade. There was no swimming against this torrent. He could only go forward, riding its flow, trusting that it would spit him out again on the other side of oblivion.

He reached out again, kicking instinctively as he rolled and tumbled through the void. His hand scraped against glasslike stone—a tunnel wall worn smooth. He tried again, in another direction. And then another, seeking some pocket of air, enough to at least orient himself within this hellish womb. But his efforts proved fruitless, vain. Until a thrust of water sought to invade his nostrils, telling him that some form of gravity was still in play. He used it to right himself, so that he could at least face his fate head-on, reclaiming some small measure of control.

A churning laughter seemed to mock his ridiculous determination. This gush had been at work for centuries, eons, eating away at earth and stone, chewing holes in the very foundation of the world. What did he, a mere animal, think he might do to overcome its immutable grasp?

Surrendering to blindness, he closed his eyes, withdrawing from the physical world in a desperate attempt to dispel such thoughts—to relax and seek a point of mental focus that would distract him from the pressure building already on his lungs. How long had it been? A minute? Two? Likely a mere fraction of that. If he couldn't take rein of his terror, he stood no chance of surviving.

More easily imagined than accomplished.

He tried a methodical approach, working through a mental list of all he'd learned in terms of clinging to a single breath. Unfortunately, most involved routine, physical exercises that, in addition to reducing excess weight, served over time to increase the capacity of a man's lungs. There were other techniques, performed immediately prior to a dive, that he hadn't had time for, such as the rhythmic expulsion of low-quality air and the splashing of cold water on his face to slow his heart rate. All that truly remained to him was to exhale in only slow, small increments, and to refrain from swallowing as fatigue set in.

And to relax, of course. He had yet to relax.

He tried counting, wishing he could in some way correlate the numbers with the pace of his progress. The river was certainly bearing him along much more swiftly than he could have run—a blessing, that. But thoughts of speed and numbers only served to remind him of the one that mattered. Four minutes, the Scribe had said. Anything less . . .

The notion snagged against some corner of his mind. Could Sa'ahla have misestimated the distance and duration of this course? At once a hope and a fear. It might be shorter—but it might also be longer. Might his guide have willfully betrayed him? Tricked him into taking a suicidal plunge? He'd watched the Scribe leap in ahead of him, had he not? But then, an Elementer he was rumored to be. Aggethrehn. The ancient sect of magi whose obsession and power had lain in harnessing and controlling the natural elements by mystical means. For all Kylac knew, Sa'ahla could breathe underwater, where he himself could not.

Or might the Scribe be but a mad old codger who believed himself capable of powers lost to his kind in the great conflagration of the Mage Wars a millennium earlier?

Try as he might to dispel them, the dark doubts chipped away at Kylac's resolve. In response, his muscles screamed at him to swim faster, defying the knowledge that any exertion would only increase his need for breath. *Let the river do the work,* he begged them, as they tugged at his mental leash. Like hounds near the end of a hunt, close enough to smell the fox's fear.

He continued to wrestle with them as he was swept along, battling the unfamiliar strain. It wasn't just his muscles rebelling against him now, but his inner organs, contracting as if gripped in a merciless fist. He allowed a touch of air to leak from his lips, then immediately regretted its loss. He hadn't enough left. Despite feeling that his lungs were about to burst, he should have held onto it awhile longer. If even just another ten heartbeats. Another five.

A dizziness crept into his skull, which gave way to a pulsing ache. He couldn't help but wonder what his life's work would amount to should he succumb now. The peoples of Pentania would still owe him their lives, he supposed. To a degree. He hadn't actually slain the dragon Killangrathor, but in summoning the courage to confront the beast as he'd been instructed, the dragonspawn had been eradicated. And while it had been Torin who ultimately defeated the Demon Queen Spithaera, he'd never have had the opportunity to do so had he not met up with Kylac during his search for the fabled Crimson Sword. The Sword itself might never have been found, remaining instead for all eternity beneath the creature-infested ruins of Thrak-Symbos.

Despite these seeming triumphs, it was his failures that pushed to the fore, crowding all else aside. Denariel. He'd wronged her, though he hadn't meant to. In his haste to put Pentania behind him and strike forth on a new adventure, he'd joined an expedition he hadn't fully understood, allowing himself to be misled by Ledron and his fellow Shadowguard concerning their purpose. He'd returned her to her father, but had won no gratitude in doing so. She blamed him for the death of the ravening mutant that had pursued them across the Ukinhan Wilds, and though he viewed events somewhat differently than she, he couldn't deny the role he'd played. Amends, if any could be had, were to have come in the form of her brother's liberation from the Grenarr.

But that couldn't happen now. Not as a result of *his* efforts, anyway. The boastful assurances he'd given both her and her father tasted now like ashes in his mouth. Shards, he wasn't even going to make good on his promise to return Sa'ahla to the *Vengeance*, which meant that Pevrick and Ledron and anyone else whose objections he'd shot down would forever remember him as a braggart whose unfounded pride had doomed not just himself, but them alongside.

He expelled another bite of breath, and again hated himself for doing so. His lungs, half full, felt as if they were turning inside out. Instinctively seeking escape, his thoughts receded further into the past, to his formative years at Talonar, his father's battle academy. So vividly he remembered the various halls and courtyards wherein he'd trained and studied. The porcupine tree, with its myriad branches and rungs. The balance-defying tangleweb, with its ever-shifting maze of tightrope pathways, swinging beams, and hinged trapdoors amid gaping pits and pools. The combat arena, with its sanded, bloodstained flagstones. He saw Briallen, crouched upon that deadly ground with her bucket and sponge, scrubbing. Scrubbing . . .

He shied from her ghost, only to be greeted by others. His father Rohn, with that critical, stone-crushing glare, his loathing of human-kind carved upon his face. Xarius, Kylac's principal rival, though twelve years his senior. How many countless hours had they spent honing their skills against each other? Kylac had won the majority of

those contests, including their sole confrontation outside Talonar—
when it had truly mattered. Having believed that another reckoning
was inevitable, he somehow felt cheated now, knowing he would
never face the assassin again. He wasn't certain yet that he'd exacted
the proper vengeance. Had he been wrong to let Xarius live? Rohn?
His own culpability had spawned a mercy toward them that they
probably hadn't earned. How much suffering had been inflicted upon
others as a result of that choice?

With the notion of suffering came the face of the first man he'd
killed. And then the second. He'd come to regret in some ways the
former, but, years later, still savored the latter. After that, a cascade
of others had followed. Some deserving, some not. But a life's outcome wasn't always determined by its merit, no matter how much he
might want to believe elsewise. It led him to wonder, was his own
imminent death warranted, considering his life's deeds? Or was this
a colder, crueler end than he had earned?

And who was to judge?

A small part of him vaguely recognized the delirium that had overtaken him. Select memories flashed before his mind's eye, brought on
by a sort of dementia reminiscent of that experienced just two weeks
ago, in the Ukinhan birthing warren amid the Harrows of Addaranth.
Though he recognized it, he wasn't able to prevent it. The parade
of images flooded through him, near-death visions spawned in this
instance by his addled, breath-deprived mind. Most, he recognized
from his past. Those he couldn't place, he assumed stemmed from
events forgotten. Still others—most others—couldn't have happened
as he remembered them, or seemed to belong to a future he would
never know. His friend Torin as a bitter old man. His enemy Xarius
become a faceless form that faded and coalesced like smoke. A young
woman of breathtaking beauty, whose enchanting smile warmed his
chest even as she plunged a dagger into his gut.

The girl's grin became Briallen's, fair locks and flawless skin giving
way to Brie's dark hair and freckled cheeks. This time, he refrained
from pushing her away. Brie, his childhood friend. He couldn't tell
if she was welcoming him or mocking him. Mayhap a bit of both.
She extended a hand, and he reached forth to take it. He wondered

abruptly if he'd already died, somehow drowning without realizing it. Seeing Brie again, he decided it didn't matter.

Before their fingers could touch, the pitch of the river's rumble changed, alerting him to a change in the terrain ahead. A breach. The portal, as Sa'ahla had called it. He wasn't dead. He was almost there.

As if seized by a divergent current, Brie sped away from him, her smile fading. Kylac stretched after her, to grasp at only darkness. His lungs spasmed, gulping reflexively. His eyes opened. The water stung them. His gaze found nothing.

Then, a faint graying of the dark. The gray brightened, a soft gathering of twilight, like the first blush of dawn. A globe it formed. The flow carried him toward it. The globe expanded, stretching open as if to engulf him . . .

The globe burst, resolving abruptly into glorious starlight, hazy and shimmering as if hidden behind a veil. The river roared as it popped him free. Already near the surface, Kylac kicked toward the stars. An instinctive act, for he no longer remembered why he needed them, understanding only that he did.

His head punched through the veil, and his lungs recalled what he did not, drawing a glorious, life-saving gulp of air. He bobbed down beneath the surface, then up again, spewing water, inhaling a second time. A wracking heat burned through him, bearing with it a flush of awareness.

Four minutes. *Four buys escape.*

He caught a glimpse of the old man ahead of him. Sa'ahla. He was kicking to the side, reaching for an outcrop of stone. Despite the great gash in the earth overhead, Kylac realized abruptly that the river didn't empty here, but plunged underground again, mayhap a hundred strokes ahead. The Scribe hadn't mentioned how they would exit. Or if he had, Kylac couldn't seem to recall it. As far as he knew, this could be his only chance to escape this liquid tomb.

Desperately, he redirected his efforts, thrashing no longer upward, but sideways, toward the craggy outcrop. Sa'ahla was pulling himself free, sodden cloak dragging against him. The treacherous river tugged at Kylac, refusing to let go. He cursed now its rushing speed, while still straining for the spur of embankment. The cave mouth beyond loomed larger, devouring the crushing flow of waters within its ravenous gullet, bellowing a ceaseless thirst.

Even as he fought, Kylac recognized his weakened state. His legs felt like lead anchors, his arms like bricks. Though he kicked and pulled, he couldn't seem to propel himself toward his goal. It was close. Painfully, tantalizingly close. But as he lurched forward with one final, frantic reach, he felt the tug of the current he'd been riding and knew his efforts had fallen just short.

The hand that slapped across his wrist was cold and clammy. But its grip was fast and strong, securing his body even as the river grabbed his legs and drew them toward the breach—as if it didn't care whether it ripped him in two, content to take some piece of him. The Scribe proved equally stubborn, leaving Kylac to hang there in a moment of pulse-pounding uncertainty, his back twisted, his shoulder wrenched in its socket, waiting to see how it would all end.

While clinging to his wrist with that bone-crushing grip, the crouching Elementer reached his free hand into the waters. Abruptly, the river relented, its currents redirecting, loosening its pull. With surprising strength, Sa'ahla stood, hauling Kylac onto the rocky out-crop. The river returned with renewed force, more insistent than before, but could only yank at his feet.

It seemed he wasn't going to drown this night after all.

For a long moment, he lay there, heart racing, lungs heaving, the truth of his salvation the only thought he could keep in his aching head. His gaze lay riveted upon the cave mouth, eyeing the waters being sucked down its throat, listening to its growling song of what might have been.

"Where does it go?" he heard himself ask.

"Below," Sa'ahla replied. Though the Sea Scribe, too, seemed content to rest, he spoke evenly, his breathing unchallenged. "Hundreds of fathoms it delves, over several leagues, before emerging at the island's base on the ocean floor."

Kylac imagined the worming, subterranean passage as described, and his breathless, ragdoll body caught within it. "Ya neglected to mention that."

"It was the only way."

Kylac nodded, lacking the energy to argue, and deciding that, in retrospect, it hardly mattered. "Ya saved my life."

"As you saved mine. For how long remains to be seen." The Scribe stood then from the rock on which he sat, turning toward a steep gouge in the sinkhole's side, through which a narrow rockslide offered egress to the surface.

Remembering the natives, Kylac took to his feet. As he looked up at Sa'ahla's scrabbling form, however, he wondered if it might be something other than the Mookla'ayan pursuit that the Elementer referred to. For he suddenly recalled the initial moments of their earlier introduction. The Scribe's cowering stance. The cryptic talk of dragons. Of Mistwall's imminent demise.

He followed his companion up the trail of fallen stones, regaining a sense of freedom and confidence with each nimble stride—notwithstanding the painful shards taken root in his skull. The cloud cover from earlier had dissipated, allowing the blessed, untrammeled light of moon and stars to illuminate their ascent. Near the top, he slipped ahead to scale a small escarpment before reaching down with a length of vine taken from the jungle to help Sa'ahla do the same. As he assisted the Sea Scribe in cresting the rim, Kylac became aware of a piercing uproar, just barely audible over the river's din.

"Their search widens," Kylac announced, attuning his ears to the ongoing alarm. "But the pursuit is yet a scattered one. How far to the ship?"

"Half a league. We'll reach it if we do not tarry."

With that, the Scribe set off to the east at a brisk trot. Kylac followed, glancing skyward in an attempt to gauge the hour. Their river passage had cut more than an hour off their return, leaving them ample time now to reach their boat before its scheduled departure. But he saw little enough to be gained in saying so. Let Sa'ahla's fear of the natives drive his pace, as there was no guarantee Kylac's skittish boatmates had given him the full amount of time offered.

However close it promised to be, he liked their chances. For all that could yet go wrong, it felt like the worst lay behind them. Though his head and lungs still ached and his wet breeches chafed as he ran, Kylac felt the smile of relief that spread across his face as he sped into the jungle, reciting the singular thought he always had whenever fortune favored him. A sardonic mantra his cheerless, faithless father had often muttered as a concession to blind fate.

Not even the gods can resist my charm.

10

"Gods curse you," Jaleth growled, as Nadrum and Warmund squared their oars and the prow of the small rowboat bit into the gravelly shore. "How many of those savages give chase?"

The cries of the natives were nearly on top of them, an indignant, confused tone having given way to a howling excitement and the promise of retribution. So much for hunting quietly. The possibility of a silent vanguard notwithstanding, their pursuers were clearly more interested in intimidation than surprise.

"Be pleased we arrived early," Kylac replied.

"Bloody maggots," Jaleth cursed, letting Kylac know he was in no mood for japes. Yet there was a touch of relief in the coxswain's voice as he added, "I very nearly left you to rot. If the captain calls for a flogging, it'll be your skin, not mine."

Kylac bowed his acceptance, holding the prow steady as Sa'ahla stepped aboard. His shipmates eyed the Elementer warily, shifting to give him more room. The Sea Scribe cared not, else pretended not to notice, seating himself on the bow bench without a word or gesture of greeting. "Come," he urged Kylac instead.

Kylac required no further invitation. Much sooner than he would have liked, the elves had tracked down their scent. The lead he and Sa'ahla enjoyed had enabled them to outpace the pursuit, but by a thinner margin than he would have wagered. A sliver of alarm had pierced his stomach when he'd reached the river, only to see their shore boat stroking hard away from them, halfway home to the anchored *Vengeance*. Fortunately, a shrill whistle had been sufficient to draw their attention and, after a moment's hesitation, to turn them back around.

While the boat had approached, Kylac and Sa'ahla had descended the bank along a far tamer slope than the bluff from which Kylac had disembarked, bringing them to a more accessible landing—as he'd hoped and instructed. With the night's fog thinning beneath a vibrant moon and stars, Jaleth's crew had found them and directed their craft accordingly.

"Whenever the itch strikes ya," Kylac encouraged as he slipped aboard.

Nadrum regarded him with suspicion. Mistrustful of the unlikely swiftness of Kylac's return, mayhap. Unnerved like Jaleth by the intensity of the growing commotion. He made certain Kylac knew it. "The Scribe, you were to bring. Not the entire festering clan."

Kylac shrugged. "Row quickly, then."

They did so without further complaint, rounding swiftly and dipping to the brutal pace that Jaleth set for them. Nadrum stole glances over his shoulder at the Scribe as they went, as if fearing some form of betrayal. Warmund chose to focus on his oar, seeming more concerned with the cloud of gulls that shrieked at them from overhead as if to give away their position. Jaleth, seated astern, seemed to be urgently measuring the distance to the *Vengeance*, his brow furrowed with concern.

Kylac, alongside Sa'ahla, searched the ridgeline abandoned in their wake. As of yet, no Mookla'ayans had entered view, despite the skirling furor raining down from those heights. He didn't foresee the natives leaping into the river and swimming after, and none who did would be able to scale the *Vengeance*'s sleek hull. A small sigh of satisfaction escaped his lips. Escape was at hand, the Sea Scribe now a member of their company. His night's incursion had been a success. Near drowning notwithstanding, should Prince Dethaniel's rescue unravel as smoothly, he would consider them fortunate.

They reached the *Vengeance* within a quarter-mark, a full three hours before daybreak. While Worm used his oar to steady their small craft upon the river's smoothly churning waters, Jaleth and Nadrum took hold of the dangling falls waiting to retrieve them. It was then that the pursuing Mookla'ayans reached the edge of the bluff, a scattering of individual forms joined by others until they'd formed a ragged wall. There they danced, baying and yowling, brandishing their blades and cudgels. Threads of them spilled down from the ridge in thin lines, descending along narrow pathways to reach the river's banks. A handful even waded out into the waters, until swallowed to their necks. But there they stopped, chirping shrill curses, seeming to understand the futility of venturing any further.

"They say I've betrayed them," Sa'ahla muttered. "Countless warnings, I gave. It is they who refused to heed."

Kylac glanced at the Sea Scribe, to find his grim features etched with guilt. Even while disavowing responsibility, it was clear he felt an obligation to this people. "Are they truly doomed, as you say?"

The Scribe faced him, seeming to focus through the milky black orb of his dead eye. "Nothing is certain, save that the Dragon stirs and the oceans roil at his unrest. I know not what may sate him. Perhaps you do?"

Kylac felt a jolt as the falls drew taut and their shore boat was hoisted from the water, to begin its creaking ascent. He held the Scribe's gaze as the craft inched skyward, wondering what it was the supposed mage believed he knew. *Not on you. In you,* the Elementer had said when raving of dragon's blood. Recalling it now, it seemed to him as absurd and insignificant as it had from the first.

"I know little o' dragons," Kylac said, "and less o' the sea. But I'd be happy to learn whatever ya might teach, if'n it'd help in discovering the Blackmoon Shards."

The Scribe searched him a moment longer, good eye twitching, dead eye unblinking, as if to discern anything Kylac might be hiding. If there, then it was hidden also from Kylac himself.

"The blindness of youth," Sa'ahla mumbled, looking back at those he'd abandoned. Those clamoring for his return. It was left for Kylac to guess as to whether the Elementer's words referred to him or the

Mookla'ayans—or both.

Their bumpy, skyward ride came to a jarring halt as the shore boat reached the top of its davits. There it remained, hanging off the starboard side, while members of the ship's crew flocked to the rail, to form a wall that struck Kylac as more defensive than welcoming. Ledron himself, flanked by senior officers Pevrick and Brenham, anchored the receiving line.

"Is this him?" the captain asked, glaring at Sa'ahla with distaste. The question, addressed to no one in particular, threatened to hang in the wind.

"He's the only one the rogue brought us," Jaleth answered.

"He's not one of the natives," Brenham observed. "I'd say that makes him a candidate."

"Sa'ahla," said Kylac, "if'n ya require presentation. The so-called Sea Scribe."

The Elementer cleared his throat with a hacking cough. "Ithrimir, my mother named me, of the Savaliol Jessath. Sa'ahla was given me by them." A jerk of his head indicated the distant ridgeline and its swarm of Mookla'ayans.

"Is that him that stinks?" Pevrick asked.

Kylac frowned. "Might be your own." He hopped from the boat, stepping smoothly on the rail before dropping to the deck. Half of the men forming the receiving contingent withdrew a pace to give him room. The other half reached for their hilts. Kylac snapped a glare at Ledron. "What? Ya mean now to refuse us?"

"I mean not to endanger this crew any more than I must. What evidence do you have that he is who he claims?"

Kylac searched the nearby faces. The helmsman was missing. "Mayhap ya should fetch Taeg, then, that he might confirm."

"Taeg has no physical description to measure against. I would have our guest tell me now, where are the Blackmoon Shards?"

"Ya can't be serious."

"The Shards. Heading and distance. If he can't tell us that, I see no use for him aboard this ship."

"And if I tell you?" Sa'ahla growled, slipping a glare of his own toward Kylac. "Of what use shall you determine me then?"

In the intervening silence between challenges, the disparate howls of the natives melded together, reined in to become an organized chant of shrill protest. Kylac didn't have to see Chitral to sense the Butcher's influence among them.

"Listen to them," Kylac suggested. "They want him back. We stand here brewing long enough, they may just decide to chance an assault."

"Let them. Tell me what I would hear, or *I* may just decide to make it easy for them."

Kylac felt his patience slipping. "Ya sent me to fetch him. Here he is."

"I sent you to fetch information, not stowaways."

"That wasn't my understanding."

"If he can't tell us—"

"Ya can't verify anything he says here in any case," Kylac snapped. "And sending him back is a death sentence."

"It is *our* deaths that concern me," Ledron countered, though his conviction in the argument seemed to be slipping. As if it had been another's to begin with. A gambit this was. A probing to see what more they might gain while lessening their risk.

"Should he prove a liar or charlatan," Kylac offered, "I'll cast him overboard myself."

"And yourself with him," Pevrick grumbled.

"And myself with him," Kylac agreed, though the look he gave Leeches was made to promise that, should it come to it, he wouldn't be parting the *Vengeance* without bidding her first mate a final farewell. "Now may we board, Captain? Or are we to sails the rest o' the way with a pack o' angry elves clinging to our rudder?"

Ledron considered for a moment, chewing on his own teeth. Pevrick kept glaring at Kylac, refusing to back down, making it clear that if it were *his* decision, he'd sooner cut the lines and feed the entire shore boat along with its crew to the river depths. It wasn't going to happen that way, and they both knew it. Leaving Kylac all the more irritated by the senseless posturing.

"North or south?" the Head asked finally, meeting the Sea Scribe's ravaged gaze.

"The Moravial runs both ways, Captain, depending on the tide's flow."

"I'm asking which will carry us faster to the Shards. If you would leave this island behind, surely you can give us our initial heading."

The Scribe's good eye blinked. His dead, black one did not. "North."

Ledron held his gaze a moment longer, then leaned toward Pevrick. "Make ready to depart."

"Ready to depart!" Pevrick bellowed. "Coming about!"

Waiting until the echoes had died, Ledron added quietly, "Let them aboard."

Leeches practically snarled at the decision, but his shipmates snapped to obey. Ropes hummed and whistled through squeaking pulleys, reeling the shore boat in toward the ship's deck. Half a dozen hands seemed to reach for it at once—bracing, tightening, fastening. Kylac stepped aside to let them work, but remained close enough to intervene should the need arise. A fair number of crewmen eyed Sa'ahla—or Ithrimir, now—with obvious distaste. Kylac could practically smell their pungent superstitions. Meanwhile, the Mookla'ayans continued to carry on at the shoreline, their communal song taking on a mewling tone that seemed to beg redress.

"Too late now," the Scribe muttered, shaking his head as he peered back at them.

"Come," said Kylac, extending him a hand when it became clear the others were waiting on him to disembark. The Elementer spared it a withering glance, then stepped from the boat on his own. As he had when boarding the shore boat, he ignored the glares, whispers, and expressions of disgust that greeted him, betraying little concern for what these men thought of him. Whatever his conflict of emotions, he seemed neither frightened nor excited, merely doing what he must.

"Shadowguard," Ledron snapped.

Raithe and Sanow stepped in to flank the Sea Scribe. Kylac slid forward to join them, claiming a spot within the pool of predawn shadow at Ithrimir's back. The Blackfists glanced at him, Sanow warily, Raithe with a flicker of annoyance. Kylac eyed each man with a thin, tight smile. The kind meant to remind them they were all comrades here. And that, should they forget it, he could slay them both before they freed their blades.

Ledron's deepening scowl suggested an acknowledgment of that message. For half a heartbeat, Kylac thought the captain meant to address the challenge openly.

Good sense prevailed. "Bring him."

Pevrick and Brenham fell in bestride the Head as he marched aft. Ithrimir and those attending him followed without complaint. The remainder of the crew dispersed like crabs after a feast, scuttling off in separate directions, each to his own corner of the ship. The keening from the shore grew more strident.

To no one's surprise, Ledron stopped when he reached the wheel-house, and motioned for those trailing him to enter. Taeg awaited them within.

"Back the way we came, eh?" the helmsman asked, as they filed inside. His gaze, like so many before, snagged upon the Sea Scribe, to take in the Elementer's bizarre appearance. The damp robe that hung from his bones like thick-bladed seaweed. The crooked shoulders, the spiked coral hair, the sallow skin, the milky black eye. Taeg's reaction was difficult to read. He seemed startled and amused at the same time—as if surprised to discover that the mythical figure were somehow precisely what he'd envisioned.

The Head entered after the rest of the company and closed the door. "Lash him to the chart table."

Pevrick sneered. The Blackfists, Raithe and Sanow, glanced at each other and then at Kylac. Kylac failed to completely bridle his surprise.

"Uh, Captain, I believe we just—"

"Would you prefer I offer him my quarters? If you'll recall, I surrendered them already."

"I'd prefer he receive some basic courtesy. I'm not sure why—"

"A fair offer I extend him. Draft us a chart to our destination, or remain bound to the wheelhouse, to offer course correction as needed."

"He's not your prisoner," Kylac protested, no longer certain the Head was merely posturing.

"I am the captain of this vessel, Kronus, and I tire of reminding you. Should he prove to be with us, and not just using us, we will treat him in kind. Until then, he remains here, for our sake, and for his."

Kylac might have pressed the argument but for Ledron's tone—no longer sharp, but dulled by the weariness he professed. Mayhap the Head had a valid argument. It might not be prudent—for any number of reasons—to set the Scribe loose to wander among these crewmen who harbored such fear and mistrust. Had Kylac merely been blinded by the life debt he felt he owed Ithrimir for saving him from drowning?

"Lash me to the rudder if it please you, Captain," Ithrimir agreed, extending his wrists. "Just bear us from this rock and to the open sea before it's too late."

Raithe reached for a coil of rope hung from a leather loop tacked into the cabin's rear wall. Sanow, with another wary glance at Kylac, moved to assist. While Kylac looked to the Scribe in apology, he did nothing to stop them. Ithrimir met his gaze only briefly before directing it outward through the forward window, suggesting neither forgiveness, nor accusation.

Before the bindings had been fully knotted, Taeg turned the wheel. The *Vengeance* responded, spinning to larboard with the Skein's northbound current. The same waters that had helped carry them inland hours earlier would now bear them out again. And the winds, of course. Weaker here within the river channel—and blowing just now, it seemed, in an opposing, southwesterly direction—yet gathered and guided by sail and spar to push them along the desired course.

A minor magic all its own.

When the ship's newest guest had been suitably leashed, Ledron addressed him like a wayward child. "When you have something you would share, with me or my navigator, I'll be most anxious to hear it." To Raithe and Sanow, he said, "To your stations." He reserved a final summons for Pevrick. "Lieutenant."

Leeches followed him to the door, a smug grin tugging at his ears. Raithe and Sanow had already exited, while Brenham had moved to stand between Taeg and Ithrimir.

"Permission to remain, Captain?" Kylac asked.

Pevrick's grin was eclipsed by his ever-ready scowl. Ledron's frown had never left.

"Free him without my leave," the Head warned, "and I'll feed him to the sharks."

Kylac bowed his head in a promise of cooperation, suppressing at
the same time a smirk of his own. This was the game they played,
he and the captain—Kylac serving reminder of his prowess through
feigned servility, Ledron couching his pleas within threats he knew
he couldn't keep. At least, he believed it to be a game. The captain
could be so convincing that, at times, Kylac wondered if he alone
was playing.

The starboard door remained open upon Ledron's departure, permitting a gust of wind to swirl about the wheelhouse. It carried with
it a briny scent, a dusting of sandstone, and the cries of Ithrimir's
Mookla'ayan people, swollen into a fiendish caterwaul.

"Shards, but they carry on," Taeg observed. "I daresay they're
hesitant to see you leave."

Ithrimir ignored the feeble jape, choosing to stare out the window
at the low-hanging moon.

"Will they pursue us?" Brenham asked. "Have they the means?"

"Too late now," Ithrimir replied, echoing his earlier refrain.

Brenham and Taeg shared a bemused look, seeming to ask—each
the other—whether the Scribe's response constituted an answer.

"If'n they could, they'd has done so already," Kylac assured the pair.

Navigator and helmsmen turned their attention to Kylac as if
noticing him for the first time. "A bit wet around the gills," Taeg
noted. "Boat didn't suit you?"

If only to drown out the elves' ceaseless lament, Kylac related then
the details of his incursion. He did so in a prompt, matter-of-fact
tone, his limited practice as a storyteller making it all sound painfully
mundane. He checked for Ithrimir's reactions often, pausing whenever he thought the Scribe might care to take up the oration. But the
Elementer said nothing, and gave no visible sign to whatever he might
be feeling, leaving it to Kylac to share the tale as best he could. Even
when questioned about certain occurrences—such as the means by
which he'd known the course and length of that subterranean torrent,
or how he'd managed to wrest Kylac from its gushing waters—the
Scribe remained dismissive or altogether silent, lost in the privacy of
his thoughts, dealing with the memories or whatever else in his own
way. Mayhap he wasn't yet ready to address it. Mayhap he never would.

"But you *can* tell us where we're going, yes?" Brenham prodded when it was done.

The winds blew, and the silence lengthened, as the ship tacked amid the cresting swells of the waning tideflow. Kylac had all but surrendered any hope of an answer when the Scribe muttered softly to himself, then louder to them.

"I will guide you to Haverstromme, as agreed. Though many a man among you will wish I had not."

"Men wish and maidens dream," Kylac recited, "and in the end, only worms pay heed."

Taeg regarded him with a raised eyebrow. "A lullaby?"

"Just something my father used to say." He shrugged dismissively. "He used to say a lot o' things."

"Ah, well, if that's the game, allow me to regale you."

The unabashed helmsman proceeded to do just that, unleashing upon them a deluge of paternal lessons received and summarily ignored as a child. The mischief and consequences that invariably resulted were by turns humorous and frightening in context. Kylac couldn't quite determine if even half of the stories might be true, but decided that, if not, Taeg was a great and worthy liar who'd earned his attention all the same.

Curtains of fog rose and fell around them as one tale led to the next and the *Vengeance* carved her way northward along the Shrouded Skein. The river Moravial, Ithrimir had called it, though Kylac knew not if that applied to the entire network of waterways, or just this particular thread. He hesitated to ask, for fear of unnecessary confusion. Whichever, the cries of Chitral and his clansmen could no longer be heard, save as a lingering echo that scraped at the back of Kylac's skull. To help silence their ghosts, Kylac continued to encourage Taeg in his various recountings. The helmsman required very little urging. A small laugh here or there, or an occasional, pause-filling response such as *ya can't be serious* or *you're fortunate to be alive* or *and what did your father has to say about that?* seemed sufficient to fan the wind in his lungs.

Brenham was not so easily engaged, making no attempt to interject, and proving reserved or reflective with responses to any questions or invitations that Kylac directed his way. Mayhap he was accustomed to such spirited rants from his comrade, and knew better than to involve himself. Mayhap he'd heard all of these anecdotes before, and could no longer summon interest in them. When he did comment, with a word of challenge or skepticism tossed in here or there, it was generally witty and well-timed, albeit uttered without a hint of a smile. Whatever the remark or its intent, invariably Taeg would seize upon it, and off his tongue would wag again, with even greater enthusiasm than before.

For three hours, Kylac listened to this, marking the lack of visible reaction in the Sea Scribe, who simply stood there, bound to his table, gazing out upon the wafting layers of mist. His only other interaction—his only acknowledgment of their noisome existence—came when they reached the northern mouth of the river, upon which he interrupted Taeg with a single word.

"East."

"Say again?" Taeg asked.

Ithrimir ignored him.

"East, he says," Kylac offered, searching the Scribe for further confirmation.

Brenham nodded.

"East it is," the helmsman agreed.

He turned the wheel, and a relay of calls went out. Within moments, they were speeding toward the dawning sun—swathed as it was in a haze of fog—as if to pin the flaming orb upon their bowsprit. For several moments, no one spoke, with Brenham consulting a chart that he spread across the table in front of Ithrimir. The navigator glanced at the Sea Scribe as he pinned the map in place, but, noting the Elementer's stormy expression, didn't invite his opinion.

With the *Vengeance* at last putting some real distance between her stern and the Butcher-led natives of Mistwall, Kylac felt a weight slip from his shoulders that he hadn't realized he'd been carrying. The island still loomed to starboard, its north shore a broken collection of jagged rises and steep wedges, with loose monoliths scattered about the fronting waters like crumbs from a giant's table. It would follow them for some time, according to the maps, all of it pitted and salt-stained and capped with tenacious patches of sparse, stunted growth. But its inhabitants could no longer haunt them. Its perils no longer threatened.

As if attuned to his unchained spirits, the veils of mist began to thin, burned into wisps by the still-rising sun. Taeg recalled a tale involving himself and a miller's unruly wife. While lewd for his tastes, Kylac laughed all the same where the helmsman expected him to, and found himself smirking throughout.

His mirth only faded when he chanced to peer out the larboard door, glimpsing far to the north a trio of specks on that distant horizon.

"What is it?" Taeg asked as Kylac drifted past him, angling for a better look.

While too small and dark to reveal anything in detail, the kick inside Kylac's chest told him all he needed to know. Three ships, bearing down on them, rank with vicious intent. The lookouts had yet to spy them, which meant mayhap that those ships hadn't spied *them*, either. But Kylac knew the voice inside himself well enough to listen when it chimed with danger.

"We'd best fetch the captain," he said. "I do believe the Grenarr has found us."

11

"REAVER CLASS," LEDRON CONFIRMED, peering through his spyglass. "Shepherding two Prowlers."

Pevrick cursed and gripped the rail. Brenham frowned, crossing his arms, one hand climbing to brace his chin. Throughout the ship, crewmen angled and squinted for a better view, as dread and rumor eddied among them. Kylac measured the various reactions, sensing the weight of their concern, as the *Vengeance* heeled against the waves, scuffing eastward against an erratic wind. The word heard most often echoed his own assumption.

Grenarr.

Ledron lowered his spyglass long enough to wipe its lens before raising it again with an air of desperate hope. His chief officers surveyed and hoped alongside. But the distant specks looked to Kylac the same as they had a moment before. The hope around him curdled, giving rise to fear, anger, and bitter resignation.

"We've the shore in backdrop," Brenham observed. "Might be they haven't spotted us yet."

Pevrick snorted, his reply acrid. "Whatever camouflage, it won't hold."

"We could seek shelter behind rock or cove," the second mate reasoned. "Hide until we can determine their course."

"Hide? This behemoth?" Leeches scoffed. "And when they spy her jutting hindquarters, we'll be pinned against the shore."

"They've spotted us already," the captain interjected. "I'll not believe their eyes are duller than ours."

Their lookout had called it down within heartbeats of Kylac's own sighting. *Ships to larboard.* Ledron and Pevrick had emerged promptly from the captain's quarters to see for themselves, while word rippled amid the decks and spars and rigging. Kylac and Brenham had met them on the command deck, leaving Ithrimir in the wheelhouse with Taeg. It had taken only moments for shipwide fears to be realized.

"Why not meet them head-on?" Kylac asked.

Pevrick sneered at his apparent idiocy. "Three ships to one?"

"Are we not the superior vessel?"

"Without reserves," Ledron reminded him. "They can afford the casualties we cannot."

Kylac conceded the point. Though he might easily fend off a circle of enemies afoot, a different matter it would be to scurry from one end of the *Vengeance* to the next, seeking to sweep aside missiles or boarders. Ledron knew his skills. If the Head felt them insufficient to defend vessel or crew against a crippling wound, Kylac would respect his opinion.

Yet it had been made clear that surrender wasn't an option. Kylac wondered where that left them.

"Permission to crack the whip, sir," Pevrick requested.

Ledron grunted. "Bloody palms, Lieutenant, or their blood on the decks."

The first mate took his scowl and stormed forward, bellowing the captain's message.

"Where are the isle's mists when we need them?" Brenham wondered aloud.

Kylac felt an invisible tug that drew his gaze toward the wheelhouse. Through the salt-stained glass, he eyed the Sea Scribe. "A fair question. Shall we go and ask?"

He turned and led the way, knowing that any further discussion as to heading would necessarily involve their helmsman on duty and he whom they'd brought aboard to be their principal navigator. It would make no sense for Ledron or his second mate not to follow.

"Merely a murder of crows?" Taeg presumed, greeting their arrival with a half-hearted jest. But as Brenham delivered the news, Kylac watched the helmsman's brow twist with consternation. "They knew we were coming."

Brenham nodded, his expression sober.

"Because?" Kylac prompted.

"Because Prowlers should be out prowling," Taeg answered, "not clinging to a Reaver's skirts."

"Easy enough to guess we might seek the Sea Scribe," Ledron growled dismissively. "Can we outpace them?"

Taeg gazed aloft, bright eyes calculating as they played about the rigging. "We've the larger sheets, and more of them. Steady push from the stern, I'd like our chances."

"In these winds?" the captain clarified.

The helmsman shook his head, gray mane rustling against his shoulders. "To be seen. But they can shift sail faster than we can."

Through the forward window, Kylac watched Pevrick and those he commanded shove and heave and scurry about as if in defiance of that wager—swinging booms, tugging lines, trimming or loosing sail as needed to bend the wind to their will. The silence within the wheelhouse, however, seemed to indicate a more somber expectation.

"Can we not turn?" Kylac asked. "Put the wind at our backs as ya suggest?"

"A difference there is between unfavorable and unsteady," Taeg explained. "We let winds as fickle as these push us around, we'll be sailing in circles."

"We've enemies north *and* south," Ledron grumbled. "And no better chance of fleeing westward than committing to our easterly course. You came to inquire about some form of cover?"

Kylac turned toward Ithrimir, conspicuously silent where he stood bound to the chart table. "A curtain o' fog might be o' use, if'n ya's some power to raise it."

The Scribe's good eye twitched, but surrendered nothing in terms of emotion. "From my sanctum. Not from here."

That he would claim control of the mists at all caught Kylac by surprise. He recalled the Elementer's chamber at the peak of the pyramid, with its wells of water set at each point of the compass, and reconsidered the moment in which Ithrimir—Sa'ahla then—had, with a submerged touch, freed him from the torrential pull of the river at the close of their subterranean escape. He'd just about decided that the latter might owe as much or more to his delirium at the time as to the involvement of some mysticism. For all that he'd seen and experienced of creatures and forces most men would describe as magical, such simplistic explanations struck him as primitive, defying credence. Was it truly possible that the Scribe's powers comprised more than legend and sleight of hand?

"Is there anything to increase the distance between our vessel and theirs?" Kylac asked.

"The winds could favor," Ithrimir allowed, without conviction.

Ledron's gaze darkened, brows knifing inward over eyes made hollow by lack of sleep. He regarded Kylac sourly, as if this failing were somehow his responsibility, then stalked from the wheelhouse. Pausing just beyond the door, he commanded, "Give her spurs, Helmsman," before turning to lend his voice to the furor on the foredecks.

"Dare I ask to lend a hand?" Kylac asked of those who remained.

Brenham eyed him curiously. "Captain seems to let you tread where you please."

"Not suggesting he could stop me. Just wondering where I might be o' best use." *Or cause the least trouble,* he thought. By now, he felt he'd learned enough to be more help than hindrance if asked to hoist a sail, swing a boom, or belay a line, so long as a shipmate stood by to direct him in what was needed. Yet he also remained keenly aware of the crew's general perception of him, and worried his presence might disrupt their rhythm or outlook. The very fact that Ledron hadn't invited him to join the effort seemed to imply it better that he keep from sight.

"Your man isn't going anywhere," Taeg said, nodding toward Ithrimir. "If that's your concern."

It wasn't. With the Grenarr upon them, there would be no more room for error—making their need for the Sea Scribe that much greater. Whatever their superstitions, his fellow crewmen were almost certain to turn to the Elementer if matters became desperate, thereby assuring his safety in the interim. Nothing inspired faith like a crisis.

No, Kylac's concern just now lay in the gnawing irritation of his own helplessness—an almost constant companion since setting sail, yet one he still grappled with. A struggle at hand, and no clear way to affect it. It left him feeling raw and itchy, anxious for some form of release.

"Suppose I should be glad enough to stay out o' the spray," he murmured.

Taeg glanced at an uncaring Brenham. "As you will."

Kylac stepped over to stand beside Ithrimir at the chart table. The Sea Scribe didn't acknowledge him, shark's eye unblinking as it stared out the forward window—far beyond their prow, to some other time and place. Physically, the Elementer had been tied to the wheelhouse. As to his mind, well, that may have been lost long before he'd boarded. Kylac could only hope that, should they be needed, his strange companion would be able to summon whatever faculties might prove useful.

As apart from one another as men could be in such close quarters, Kylac stood there with the supposed mage, the pensive second mate, and the uncouth helmsman, riding the steep climbs and sudden drops of their rugged course through the seas. Despite the mad urgency that had gripped the ship, theirs was a chamber of calm. Taeg took to whistling a carefree tune, as if untroubled by their circumstances. Brenham busied himself stepping back and forth between the open larboard door and a charting table on that side of the wheel, peering out through his spyglass, then returning to scratch notations and lines in apparent measurement. He worked studiously, but without anxiety, as if tracking the movements of some harmless oddity rather than a pack of predators seeking to wring the blood from their corpses. Kylac resisted the urge to ask him what, if anything, he'd been able to determine, assuming that Brenham would share word with them—or at least with Taeg—when he had something to report. Resolving to be patient, he similarly resisted the urge to engage Ithrimir as to any other options they might have, or to request that Taeg cease his discordant warbling. Should the warning in his senses manage to overtake them, he would have ample opportunity to loose his frustrations.

For a time, his sight warred with his instincts, seeking to imply that his fears might be wrong. To his naked eye, the enemy vessels remained but small blots on the horizon, hazy and nonthreatening amid the flare of the rising sun. Given the extreme challenges of the mission and the fretful dispositions of those around him, it had been easy to assume the worst. Mayhap he'd done so hastily, attuned less to the reality of the situation and more to the crew's grim perception of it.

But it was his sight that ultimately proved flawed. Glancing frequently to larboard, he found the Grenarr ships evidencing little change. So he began forcing his attentions elsewhere for longer spans. He tracked the calls and responses of his fellow crewmen, reconciling their actions with the response of the *Vengeance*, to increase his understanding of the means of her control. He eyed the craggy shore as it stretched along their starboard side, chewed and chiseled by wind and wave, but broken only by narrow fissures and shallow inlets. He studied a chart of that same coastline—one of those purchased from the Sea Scribe's vaults with Et'tanis's permission—and discovered a remarkably accurate depiction of Mistwall's scarred features, from the capes and coves of its mainland to the scattering of salt-stained, scrub-encrusted monoliths obstructing its base. Thus distracted, it was some time—mayhap a quarter-mark of the sun—before he turned eye again to the trio of ships to the north.

To find them more than doubled in size.

He looked at Brenham, steady and detached in his ongoing observations, and at Taeg, who continued to whistle while making adjustments to the wheel. With neither deigning to mention the obvious, Kylac decided to do so.

"At what point do we cease running and talk tactics?"

Brenham cocked his head, his expression one of boredom. His eyes, however, never left his parchment. "There are no tactics, outnumbered as we are."

"They'll sink us," Taeg agreed. "Else disable us. I'm thinking the latter, that they might reclaim their ship—and collect as many slaves as possible."

"We'd do better to scuttle her ourselves," Brenham observed flatly.

"Set a fire in her hull and ram her into the sharpest rock we can find."

Ithrimir perked, drawn from his reverie. "And leave our bodies strewn upon the shore? To be gathered by the Ladrakari?"

Brenham frowned as if perplexed by the term. He quickly shrugged it aside. "Whatever your fear, better that than fall prey to a vengeful liege captain."

Ithrimir appeared ready to protest, but clamped his mouth shut and settled for an angry glare instead. Kylac was half tempted to convey the Elementer's argument for him. Presuming Ladrakari to be the name of Et'tanis's Mookla'ayan clan, he could remind the impassive second mate of the part of his incursion in which Chitral had planned to artfully dissect the disgraced Sea Scribe fiber by fiber in order to spin a web from his ligaments, tendons, and other tissues—without numbing agent of any kind. Try as they might, could any Grenarr captain match such cruelty?

Apart from that, Kylac had witnessed firsthand a shipwreck the likes of which Brenham described, and harbored no great desire to experience another.

"Put me aboard this so-called Reaver," Kylac suggested, "and I'll see to it she's piloted only by ghosts."

Taeg vented a burst of laughter.

"Ya think I jest?"

"As a seaman, I've heard some outlandish boasts in my day. But that there would be the most absurd by a leviathan's length."

"Would you have us fire you over there with a ballista?" Brenham asked dryly. "Or just drop you in the sea and hope they decide to take the time to fish you out?"

"As I'm the one who slew their overlord," Kylac said, "I doubt they'd be satisfied to let me drown."

"Best try the ballista," Taeg said. "Put him close enough, they'll have a chance, at least, to snag him before the sharks do."

"And after you've singlehandedly slain seventy-five tar-skins in close quarters," Brenham allowed, "you'll, what? Swim on over to take down each Prowler in turn?"

"Mayhap they'll come to me. Else flee back to their usual hunting grounds."

Brenham and Taeg shared a look of profound amusement.

"Should I fetch the captain? Might just buy y'all the time ya needs to escape."

"Or nothing more than a rogue in ribbons," said Taeg. "Let it go."

"It is certain they will overtake us?" asked Ithrimir. The force of his tone, along with the abruptness of it, sapped the others of their mirth.

"At their current rate of gain, somewhere around here," Brenham answered, pointing to his chart.

The Sea Scribe scowled and gave a slight tug on his bindings, prompting the second mate to bring his chart to the starboard table. There, Brenham pointed again at the approximate intercept point, east of their position along the island's north shore.

"When?"

"An hour. Perhaps more, perhaps less. The blow from the north is strengthening, aiding them southward while we fight not to be raked against the shore."

The Scribe seemed to be only half listening, focusing on the chart with his one-eyed gaze. "We should make for the Moravial," he determined.

"Turn back?" Taeg balked, looking to Brenham for help.

The second mate shook his head. "There isn't time. Swing west, we might buy ourselves another hour. But they'll still run us down well short of the river's mouth."

"I speak not of its mouth, but its gullet." The Scribe stabbed at the chart with a gnarled, clawlike finger. "The Trellong," he explained, pointing to a coastline inlet that opened onto a ribbon of a river. "We enter here, to the east. A winding, shallow tributary, it may work to our advantage."

"How?" asked Taeg. "They're adjusting sail and channeling the wind faster than we are, as I believe one of us predicted."

"The tide is retreating. But if the waters favor, they may yet bear us over a northern chokepoint, here." His nail indicated a convergence of the Trellong's banks, a stretch or two inland. "Our pursuers, still trailing, should arrive too late."

"Stranding them until the tide rises again," Brenham observed.

"While we trace the Trellong westward until it feeds into the

Moravial, here."

Kylac studied the chart. "And then what?" he asked. Turn north once they reached the Moravial—which he understood now to be the backbone of the Shrouded Skein—and they would essentially have sailed a full circle, with the Grenarr likely waiting to trap them again—having probably summoned reinforcements. But the only alternative . . . "South would run us through the heart o' the island. Assuming ya can guide us, would we be safe from your Ladrakari?"

Ithrimir's grim visage didn't inspire confidence. "Clinging to the river's channels, we might hope."

If successful, they would have built a significant lead upon the pursuing Grenarr, else forced their enemies to circumnavigate the entire island in order to find the *Vengeance* as she exited the Skein amid Mistwall's southern reaches. The plan appeared tempting on paper. Plans on paper often did.

"And should we fail to clear the chokepoint?" Taeg asked.

Ithrimir didn't answer. He didn't have to. They'd be landlocked. At a dead end. Caught by the Grenarr—and quite possibly a hornet's nest of furious Mookla'ayans, if Chitral's clansmen were in any way marking the *Vengeance*'s path of retreat.

Kylac's gaze drifted to larboard, to mark the position of their pursuers. Brenham and Taeg, he noticed, did the same. He wondered if they were judging as he was—that an immediate threat generally outweighed a potential peril.

He allowed them a moment to deliberate. They seemed to do so without either man opening his mouth, old friends able to think through each other's thoughts. It was Taeg who finally translated for the rest of them, turning to Kylac to say, "*Now* you should fetch the captain."

A FOGBANK marked the entrance to the Trellong, a stray patch of erstwhile mist snagged by the jutting spurs of headland flanking the river's mouth. Out of place, it seemed, with the land to either side lit clearly by the morning sun. A gateway then, thought Kylac. A ghostly curtain drawn across the threshold of the portal they must pass through. He sensed the reluctance and heard the murmurs of the crewmen who regarded it an ill omen. While he didn't share their superstitions, he couldn't quite fault them their misgivings.

But any chance at hesitation had passed. Having seen for himself the rate at which their enemies were closing on the *Vengeance*'s rudder, Ledron had quickly agreed to chance the Sea Scribe's proposed river route. He'd done so through clenched jaw, while Pevrick cursed the time they themselves had lost by not sailing south along the Moravial to begin with. Kylac couldn't have said which frustrated the Head more—the first mate's futile gripe, or the meat of truth behind it.

"Should we be slowing?" Taeg asked, the wall of fog seeming to thicken at their approach.

The Sea Scribe shook his head. "The knave's tide draws nigh. We dare not a timid approach."

Nor did they have much distance left to surrender to the trailing Grenarr. Kylac had gazed upon them moments ago from the stern-castle. No more than a mile back. Near enough for him to make out the echo of lusty shouts and the frenetic movement of their crews. The larger ship—the one Ledron had dubbed a Reaver—led the pair of smaller Prowlers by half a length, one to each side. When the Reaver had angled just so, Kylac had been able to spy the large flag whipping in the wind atop her mainmast. A great red hammer upon a field of black. The standard differed from the shark's fin brought down from the *Vengeance* when they'd assumed her command—and from the flaming eye on one Prowler and the spear-and-trident on the other—telling him that each Grenarr ship flew its own. He'd tried to ask Ledron if the symbol told them anything about their particular pursuer, but the captain had waved the matter aside as a pointless irritation. Known or unknown, he'd growled, one tar-skin was as vile as the next.

"How certain are you of what lies beyond that veil?" Brenham inquired of Ithrimir, echoing Taeg's concern. "We race in blind, it may be the Grenarr are left sifting through our splinters."

"It is not we who will be blind," the Elementer murmured.

Helmsman and navigator looked at Kylac as if expecting some form of assistance. *He's your dog,* their expressions seemed to say. Not without irony, given Taeg's role in directing them to the Sea Scribe to begin with. But Kylac just shrugged and smirked reassuringly. Running short of options, they had to lay their faith somewhere. As of yet, the Elementer had done little—if anything—to merit their mistrust.

Kylac couldn't deny a twinge of nervousness, however, as they accelerated toward the looming mist wall, with nothing but jagged rocks visible to either side. So slow, their pace had seemed out upon the waves—crawling, it felt, from those seeking to run them aground. Bearing down now on the mass of earth before them, it seemed as though the surf—ebbing as it was—had joined with the wind to hurtle them landward. Just another quirk of perception, he knew. But his logical understanding failed to make the illusion seem any less real.

"Well," said Taeg, with an edge of forced cheer, "if we *are* to mince ourselves upon the shore, our friends stand to do the same."

Indeed, upon last check, the Reaver and her escorts didn't appear to be shying from the hunt. They continued to breathe down the *Vengeance's* rudder at full sail, as if maddened by the scent of their quarry so near at hand. Even if the retreating tide weren't a concern, the enemy would cut them no slack in this chase. A legitimate fear thus compelled Ledron and his Addaran crew to maintain their maximum pace. Fear, and a palpable pride. For if the hated Grenarr were willing to sail headlong toward a stony landmass at full speed, who were they, chosen of their king, to shirk from the same?

Waves surged against the limestone shore, breaking against rocks in furious geysers of spray. Where blanketed by the mists, however, the same breakers were devoured, as if sucked up by some monstrous gullet. Kylac stepped through the starboard door, emerging from the wheelhouse for a better look. Though not the keenest vantage point, he could see the white foam crests that formed and reformed at the base of the fogbank, the waters wrestling against an opposing force . . . yet one that differed from the sheer, fortified earthworks that flanked the eerie pocket. As to the precise nature of the terrain beyond the fog, he could only hazard a guess. But the mouth of the river, he told himself, was there.

Or mayhap he was only urging it to be so.

Throughout the ship, men braced for impact, seizing whatever beams or lines or netting lay at hand, hunkering low and leaning aft if their position permitted it. A deck forward and below, Ledron took hold of the starboard rail. The lanky Sanow, spotted nearby, all but disappeared when he lay back against a mast. Pevrick leaned over to clutch a capstan. High above, Jahvid hunkered in the crow's nest, ducking beneath its rim. Their reactions had Kylac reaching instinctively for the wheelhouse doorframe with his left hand. He became aware of it when he felt Ithrimir staring at him. As he met the Elementer's harsh gaze, he released his grip and offered a trusting nod.

Their bowsprit pierced the mist, disappearing from view. The prow was engulfed next, followed by the foredecks, until Kylac could no longer see them. The fog raced amidships, claiming the main-deck . . . and then he too was inside it, brushed by a chill cloud of droplets, a smell like buttonwood swamp and jungle decay invading his nostrils. He closed his eyes, then realized there was no need. He was blind already.

The winds, so lusty before, died suddenly to a whisper. An unnatural stillness overtook them. Kylac heard a few whimpers, and a smattering of groans. He felt the sails flagging, falling limp. They hadn't crashed. But would they suddenly be becalmed?

He felt a momentary flutter of panic, and turned to face aft, hands itching for his sword hilts as he half expected the Grenarr to come crashing in upon their stern. If so, it would be they who were caught off guard, not he.

Then the *Vengeance*'s momentum carried her through. Whatever had caused the pocket of deadness, her sleek black bulk slipped past, presumably unscathed. The winds gathered anew, softly at first, then with greater zeal. The fog astern lay unbroken, but as Kylac faced forward again, he found the mists ahead thinning into layers. A vague outline of the Trellong came to view, creeping landward before them, its calmly retreating waters hemmed by wide banks east and west upon either side of the ship.

As the Sea Scribe had promised.

A faint cheer gave way to a hearty one as the haze continued to peel back in dissolving streamers and those aboard realized they were safe. The celebration was short-lived. At a sharp bark from Ledron, Pevrick's voice boomed, urging sailors to their tasks, reminding them that their flight wasn't yet ended. The call promptly triggered a cascade of shouts and a flurry of responses that restored movement throughout the vessel.

And the race began anew.

12

As THE THICKER MISTS BLED AWAY, the tenor of the chase altered. Gone were the endless, windswept seas, where even a mammoth vessel such as the *Vengeance* was but a grain of sand upon a vast beach. Where there was scant danger of an errant swing or pull from which they couldn't recover. Gazing ahead, it was immediately clear that the Trellong would grant them no such leeway. Her wide banks were little more than a stone's throw from either rail, armored with crags of reef and half-submerged boulders, with fallen trees and splintered stumps angled outward like sharpened palings at the base of a fortified wall. Presuming that a central channel ran somewhere along its basin, it lay hidden beneath the darkness of the river's surface and the lingering remnants of fog. Tough as the Grenarr may have built the *Vengeance* to be, they could ill afford to have her bouncing from bank to bank, or dragging keel along whatever hazards littered the Trellong's floor.

"Veer to larboard," Ithrimir said.

Brenham and Taeg regarded him in surprise. "River bends to starboard," Taeg replied in confusion. "Why would we—"

"Now, Helmsman."

Taeg frowned, but gave a turn of the wheel. The rudder engaged, shifting them against the approaching bend. Kylac ventured to the starboard rail and peered over the side—where he could just make out, beneath darkly glistening waters, the even darker shadow of a knifing protrusion of rocks. It reached for them like a lunging spear point . . .

But the bow swung wide, evading its reach. It settled for grazing against their side just below the waterline, scraping a thin line of barnacles from those clinging to their hull.

Cries and murmurs passed throughout the ship, in delayed reaction to the abrupt turn and gentle collision. Kylac caught Pevrick, down on the maindeck, twisting toward the wheelhouse, his expression obscured by distance, but radiating irritation.

"To starboard," Ithrimir directed.

This time, Taeg didn't hesitate, bringing the wheel back to realign them with the river's snaking bend. An instinctive course correction. But the helmsman must have also felt the shudder of the ship resulting from their brush against the submerged shore, and surely realized that—whatever the nature of the obstacle—the damage would have been worse had he failed to heed the Scribe's instruction.

Though she responded more quickly than Kylac might have believed possible of a ship her size, the aft portion of the *Vengeance*'s larboard side bumped softly against the western shore as she straightened, jostling a few hands and drawing a smattering of grunts and groans.

"Take hold, mates," Taeg mumbled. "She looks to give a rough ride."

"All the rougher, should you question my directives," Ithrimir replied.

Brenham's eyelids fluttered, as if to blink away what he was witnessing. "You knew that reef was there?"

The question went unanswered as gazes shifted to meet Pevrick, the first mate bounding up the starboard ladder to the wheel deck, thrusting angrily past Kylac to bark at Taeg. "Keep to the channel," he ordered. "She's hard enough to control without you swinging her hither and yon."

"He'll veer as I say," Ithrimir snapped.

Leeches gaped. "What?"

"This is *my* island," the Elementer reminded them. "Every bar and spit, every channel and every cove. Heed me not," he added, as the first mate seemed about to regain control of his tongue, "and your bones will join its list of hazards."

Pevrick's face boiled with indignation. He stepped forward, fists flexing, to thrust his nose within an inch of Ithrimir's. "Hear this, sniveling wretch. This is *my* ship. And I'll be sucking swells before—"

The *Vengeance* herself stole his outburst, jarring and stuttering over a rocky shallows, triggering a chain of dismayed outcries. A tense silence ensued. Like the first breath after a cut, when waiting to bleed.

Once convinced they'd escaped catastrophic injury, Kylac looked to draw Pevrick's attention. "Ya had your word, Lieutenant. Now I suggest ya leave these lads to their work."

A telltale tightening of the muscles in Leeches's neck preceded the spinning fist that came flying at Kylac's face. Kylac waited for it, then sidestepped the blow and reached up to arrest the elbow that followed. A twist and a shove pinned the arm forcefully behind the first mate's back, and had his bearded face kissing the outer wall of the wheelhouse.

"No shame in being frightened," Kylac whispered smoothly, calmly, in the sailor's ear, "but it'd be best for all, I'm thinking, if'n ya return to your station."

Pevrick hissed and sputtered, barely able to speak through the hold at his back and the rage in his throat. "I'm going to fillet you like a carp and weave an anchor line with your entrails."

"In due course, I'm sure. Until then—"

"Kronus!" Ledron barked, as he climbed the nearest deck ladder. "Release that officer before I order an arrow through your throat."

"Test me," Kylac warned Pevrick quietly, "and I'll have ya over this rail, begging us to come about and fetch ya. I wonder how that might end?"

"Kronus!"

Kylac gave Leeches a nudge in final warning. Even so, he fully expected an attack as the misguided fool whirled about. He was already mentally preparing himself for the stuttering tirade that Ledron was sure to unleash once he'd relieved them of the petulant first mate for once and all. But Pevrick surprised him by leaning back against the wall, massaging his wounded arm and smirking coldly as the Head arrived with fellow Blackfists Raithe and Sanow on his heels.

"Bloody maggots," Ledron griped. "If mercy should spare us, I'll be shrouding each of your corpses in the other's flayed skin."

"Permission to detain a mutineer, Captain."

Ledron struck his first mate in his tender arm. "Curse you, Pevrick. Who is the man here, and who the child? Get back to your post before I detain *you*."

Leeches put forth an indignant expression. "Captain, he assaulted—"

The Head put his back to Kylac, walling him off while permitting Raithe and Sanow a clear path to Pevrick. "Return him to his command, or pitch him overboard. I've no time for this folly."

The first mate opened his mouth as if to renew his objection, but managed abruptly to control his rage and snap a furious salute instead. As Raithe reached for him, he swatted the Blackfist's hand away, cast a single vengeful glance in Kylac's direction, and then stormed down the ladder that would return him to the foredecks.

Ledron watched him go, then spun to address Kylac. Before he could do so, a call echoed down from the crow's nest.

"Ship astern!"

Through the veil of mist at the river's mouth surged the first of the Grenarr vessels—the Reaver, bloody hammer sigil fluttering on its field of black, its figurehead a beaked kraken riding a knot of tentacles, two of which speared forward ahead of the rest. The pair of Prowlers emerged a moment later, side by side a ship's length astern of their leader. Standing to starboard of the wheelhouse as the *Vengeance* curled westward, Kylac had an unobstructed view of their pursuers, who'd cut through the mists—as *they* had—under full sail. Any aboard who'd hoped the Grenarr might balk at carrying the chase inland would be regretting that foolish optimism now as it soured in their stomachs. Not only had the enemy pierced the fogbank, but they were still gaining.

"They'll not be able to surround us, at least," Kylac observed. "If'n we can find a narrows, we's a better chance now o' holding them off."

"Our aft ballista will have greater range than theirs," Raithe agreed after a moment's hesitation. "Should they continue to close—"

"A spear or two will not deter them," Ledron snapped. "Nor would I trade shots at their bow for those on our rudder."

Sanow sided with his captain. "Unless we're trapped, we'd do better to conserve our ammunition."

"Assemble a squad of Redfists upon the sterncastle," Ledron ordered Raithe. "To engage only on my command." He turned to Kylac. "Stand with them, if it's a fight you crave. But strike another of my men, and I swear by my mother's teeth, you'll be fighting the crews of four ships, not three."

Despite the tension gripping his jaw and shoulders, the emotion in Ledron's gaze was closer to that of sadness than fury. Before Kylac could speak to it, the Head turned on a heel and trudged forward again toward the maindeck, drawing Sanow with him. Kylac felt a stab of sympathy for the beleaguered captain—burdened with the same doubts and challenges shared by the rest of them, but saddled also with the incalculable weight of responsibility and expectation governing this desperate enterprise. For all that he yearned to set right concerning his involvement in these matters, Kylac remained an outsider. If it all fell to shards around him . . . well, he would accept his mistakes and try not to repeat them as he moved on with his life's endeavors. For Ledron, there was only success or disgrace. Kylac half wished for some way of relieving the Head of a measure of his stresses—of reassuring the Shadowguard captain that he was, in fact, committed to the cause, and not willfully seeking to complicate matters. Alas, if he hadn't convinced Ledron of that by now, he wasn't liable to soon do so.

For now, then, he would simply follow orders.

He proceeded astern, climbing the poop deck to stand at the taffrail, availing himself a clearer view of their enemy. It told him little he didn't already know, and nothing of apparent use. The Reaver looked to be but a smaller version of the *Vengeance*—three masts instead of four, with a leaner girth and shorter frame. Elsewise, she bore the same sharp styling as the Great Grendavan's former flagship, raked and bristling like a sleek black beetle. From what he could see of them, the trailing Prowlers were but smaller cousins still, limited to two masts, but no less menacing in appearance. If the Reaver truly bore seventy-five crewmen as Brenham had suggested, he could count on each of the Prowlers carrying another fifty.

Nearly two hundred foes. Should he be forced to do battle, the river's low waters would lap the banks crimson when he was done.

Raithe and his squad of Redfists came thudding up the ladders to join him. Kylac sensed their anxiety. These were Stonewatch, not Seawatch, brought aboard not as sailors, but foot soldiers. If matters continued to unravel, they would finally be called upon to earn their berth. Like him, many were excited by the prospect. But terror tinged their eagerness. He smelled it in the sweat captured within their tunics, and saw it in their involuntary fidgeting. Where one man drummed his fingers against the pommel of his sword, another rubbed his bow or stroked the fletching of an arrow. All the while, they peered intently through the trailers of mist behind them—those that clung to their pursuers like wisps of cobwebs—as if all that stood between them and battle was the tenuous strength of those delicate strands.

"'Hold them craven nips, a'cling to the scag's shanks," jeered a Redfist at Kylac's elbow. Creyl. The one man aboard with an accent— dialect, rather—stranger than Kylac's. Though he claimed to have been born on Addaranth, his parents had hailed from Sekulon before putting down in a remote patch of the frontier region known as the Reach—that no-man's-land serving border between the northern-most lands settled by the Addarans and the southern stretches of the Ukinhan Wilds. An outlander himself, really, he'd likely have been disdained as such, were it not for the blend of fear and admiration afforded those who spent the better part of their lives amid the savage terrors of the so-called Harrows.

"Bleed the bitch, nips'll round un spur, tah?" Creyl added, grinning proudly through his crooked teeth. He didn't seem to care that his breath reeked of smoke and vinegar, or that less than half of his comrades could fully understand him. He didn't seem to care about much of anything. Touched with a madness typical of the half-wild, it was said, but fiercely loyal to whoever held his leash. *Ask him to dive overboard and wrestle a shark,* Orlin had insisted when describing him to Kylac, *and he'll do so.*

Or, like any feral creature, decide to tear your face off in your sleep, Kylac had thought.

That suspicion echoed anew as he nodded an acknowledgment at the fleck-eyed soldier, if only in hopes of redirecting that half-crazed gaze and vinegar-laden breath. Having spent a fair stretch himself once among a band of Sekulonian refugees, Kylac had interpreted Creyl's words without difficulty. Take down the Reaver, and the Prowlers were liable to turn about and flee. But Kylac remembered well the reaction of Brenham and Taeg when he'd suggested as much. Though he had no wish to start a debate, Creyl's prediction struck him as only so much bluster.

The *Vengeance* veered abruptly. Kylac recognized why when, a moment later, a nest of deadfall clawed at them from just below the waterline. He watched with renewed interest as it fell behind and lay waiting instead for their pursuers. The Reaver, however, avoided it in turn, with the Prowlers trailing accordingly. Kylac thought it unlikely they'd spotted the hazard themselves. If asked to lay wager, he'd have said they were simply mimicking the *Vengeance*'s maneuvers. The realization sapped a measure of the confidence he'd felt upon gaining the river, where wind-wrangling had become less critical than knowledge of the river's hidden obstacles. The Grenarr would require no such knowledge as long as they kept their quarry in sight. Mark and trace the path taken by the *Vengeance*, and they would be safe.

He considered relaying his observations to the wheelhouse, before realizing how elementary they must seem to experienced seamen. Doubtless, Ithrimir and Brenham and Taeg understood already how best to evade those who followed—if even possible. It might depend entirely, as the Sea Scribe had predicted, on gaining the chokepoint in time.

South they sailed, in general heading, while skirting from one bank to the next, drifting, heeling, or listing as needed to safely follow the fickle course of the Trellong as it meandered through the wetland shallows. Reefs, sandbars, and deadfall scratched at them with increasing frequency as the waters continued to ebb, exposing more of the natural litter around the river's bed. Amid it all, the Grenarr ships continued to gain, giving chase with seeming abandon, anxious to bring the pursuit to an end. The lusty shouts and deprecating calls that mocked their escape attempt grew in volume and intensity as the gap between parties shrank. It wasn't enough that the treacherous, ship-thieving Addarans were to be caught and tortured and killed. In the interim, there was humiliation to be reaped.

The river's bed flattened. Even from high atop the poop deck, Kylac could see the sand and grass at its bottom, and wondered that their rudder wasn't dragging already through the muck. Deeper than she looked, mayhap, but deep also was the *Vengeance*'s draft—at least compared to that of their enemies. Once they started dragging . . .

The Reaver's captain must have sensed the same. As the waters widened over the shallow expanse, the Prowlers dug in their heels and surged forward, summoned up alongside their commander. Preparations atop the forecastle of all three included the loading of deck ballistae. If there'd been any question about the willingness of the Grenarr to fire upon their own flagship, it seemed set to be answered.

A bump jarred their starboard side. Kylac looked down to where the dark hump of a large sandbar lurked beneath the water at their stern, to the left of their passing rudder from his aft-facing view. He instinctively wondered what fell hazard must lie on the opposite bank, for Ithrimir to have directed them so close to this one. Unless Taeg at the helm or Pevrick's crew at the sails had made a mistake. Improbable, Kylac felt, given the sureness with which they'd guided the great vessel thus far. More likely, they were simply running out of options.

Or so he believed, until he searched the waters to larboard and spied no visible hazards. Which meant either the Scribe knew of one hidden from the rest of them, or . . .

Kylac looked up again as the trio of enemy ships steered to starboard. With the Reaver's prow driving a wedge down the center of the *Vengeance*'s wake, the Prowler on her starboard side—the vessel flying the flaming eye—was nudged nearer the bank. And nearer . . . Until, as Kylac could have predicted, a string of alarms resounded from her forward spotters—echoed by those positioned starboard aboard the Reaver—as the sandbar was sighted.

The cries spawned a frantic attempt to redirect. But, even for the nimble Prowler, it was too late. Her prow rammed into the bar with a grit-filled moan, lurching skyward and listing to larboard. Shouts of surprise spawned anger and dismay, the Reaver slowing as she scraped against the submerged spit, the Prowler of the flaming eye skidding to a beached halt.

As abruptly as that, the enemy was two to their one.

The gathered Redfists cheered. Kylac was more circumspect, smirking at Ithrimir's cleverness, but doubting the same trick would pay twice.

He should have given more credit to the Scribe and those carrying out his directives. Not more than a quarter mile farther on, amid a grating, cracking yelp, the remaining Prowler—of the spear and trident—dragged its keel against a submerged reef. The hazard knocked it off course, driving it against the Reaver's larboard flank. Hulls groaned and screeched where they scraped against each other. It should never have happened—*would* never have happened if the Reaver's commander had allowed the attending Prowler to fall back. But fearlessness had given way to recklessness, and exacted its toll.

Alas, it proved too much to hope that either vessel be stalled. The Reaver slipped past the stumbling Prowler, powering forward with only a scar of splinters to mark the raking collision. The Prowler herself, while staggered, recovered quickly, choosing this time to trace the path of her master's rudder. By the time she regained her speed, she'd fallen a good five or six lengths behind the Reaver. But by no means had she been eliminated from the hunt.

"The odds favor us now," Raithe observed.

"We should hit them before they regain their stride," another among them agreed.

"Shards un splinters," yapped Creyl, his meaning plain.

Kylac turned his head, gazing forward, wondering if the ship's officers were of any mind to make such a call. He spied nothing to indicate as much. As he was about to return his focus aft, however, he caught sight of Ithrimir exiting the wheelhouse, his hands bound before him, Brenham escorting him by the elbow.

"Your pardon, sirs," Kylac said, as he squirmed through those assembled at his back. Extricating himself from their formation, he

sprinted forward, catching up with Ithrimir and Brenham upon the
maindeck.

"Change o' plan?" he asked in greeting.

"Our chokepoint," Brenham replied, pointing inland. "He claims
we won't make it."

Kylac followed the second mate's outstretched finger. There, beyond
a final gauntlet of exposed rocks and crags and sand-heaped bars, lay
a hump of land at which the river's banks converged. At a distance, a
gateway that indeed appeared too narrow and shallow to cross. "And?"

"Take me to the waterline," Ithrimir snapped, "and we'll see."

Something in the Elementer's visage reminded Kylac of his narrow
escape from the subterranean river torrent. All at once, he knew what
the Scribe intended.

"What is this?" Pevrick demanded as he spied their approach.

As soon as the first mate turned, however, Ledron caught his
arm and thrust him back toward his present duty, turning himself
to address them.

"We need to drop a shore boat," Brenham explained to their captain.

"A ladder would be quicker," said Kylac.

Ledron squinted and clenched his jaw. "Thinking to abandon us?"

"To save us, Captain," Ithrimir growled, thrusting forth his bound
hands. "If it pleases."

If the Head's expression was one of pleasure, it matched the same
bitter grimace he'd worn since the moment in which Kylac had
met him. Nonetheless, he eyed the Scribe's bindings before nodding
permissively. "Free him."

When Brenham advanced to pick at the knot, Kylac intervened.
"Permit me."

With the flash of a dagger, the severed ropes fell free.

"Ladder!" Ledron barked.

Warmund, the nearest deckhand, tossed a string of wooden rungs
over the starboard side. Ithrimir practically dove after it. The swiftness
of his movement seemed to renew an instinctive fear that he meant to
desert them. Both Brenham and Worm reached for him as if to arrest
his descent. Only, Kylac was two steps quicker than both, lunging in
to forestall their efforts and allow the Scribe to scramble over the rail.

"A moment," Kylac urged them. "Ya'll see."

A knotting in his stomach made him second-guess his own assumption that Ithrimir could be trusted. He reminded himself that the Scribe had little to gain by forsaking them now, unless the Elementer meant to beg passage of their Grenarr pursuers. A possibility, mayhap, but there seemed little point in speculating when all would play out quickly enough.

The ropes of the ladder squeaked and groaned as Ithrimir scurried down to the waterline. When confident that the others had surrendered to curiosity, Kylac allowed them to approach, and turned with them to peer over the rail.

Together, they marked the final reaches of the Scribe's descent. As he neared the bottom, the *Vengeance* gave a sudden jolt that nearly threw him from his perch. A rock or bole, clipping the ship from the other side. Somehow, the aged Elementer managed to maintain his grasp on the ladder with one hand, and to swiftly regain a rung with one foot. On the deck above, eyes shifted toward the wheelhouse as if pleading for their helmsman to hold her steady, then shifted forward to see what other hazards might lie in her path.

"Mother's mercy," Ledron muttered.

The chokepoint seemed to race toward them, spurs of earth jutting at each other like an insect's pincers. Gazes fell again toward the Scribe. Kylac could sense the pleading this time that accompanied them, unsure how much of it was his own. Ithrimir stood crouched now upon the lowest rung that remained above the water, left arm wrapped in the rope to secure his hold, right hand dipping into the river. The latter hand skipped against waters grown nearly still, the swiftness of the *Vengeance*'s passage transferring to them a speed and strength that slapped back as if to repel his touch. But Ithrimir held tight, even as the ladder bumped and twisted against the hull, thrusting deep to carve a furrow in the Trellong's skin. His head lowered as if in prayer.

Nothing happened.

The winds sweeping the deck shrieked fiendishly as the men surrounding Kylac held their collective breath. The tide was too far gone. Beyond the chokepoint, the waters appeared deep and broad, but those spanning its threshold seemed a mere trickle compared to the breadth of the *Vengeance's* great prow. They were deceiving themselves if they thought they could climb that jagged hump of earth. They were fools to believe they might escape.

"Brace for impact!" Pevrick bellowed, and the call echoed throughout the ship.

Kylac felt those around him seeking what purchase they could. He crouched in his stance, preparing to be launched forward when the ship ran aground. The impending collision would send him rolling—given their speed, probably clear to the stumpdeck at the base of the forecastle.

Their keel touched against the river's bed, vibrating as it scraped along the layers of sand and stones and silt. Still the chokepoint rose before them, climbing . . . narrowing . . . Kylac glanced at Ledron, to find the captain wincing.

A fresh churning filled Kylac's ears. Abruptly, the scratching beneath them stopped, their hull lifting free. The churning grew louder, building to a crescendo. The ship angled higher in response. Gazing from the side of the ship forward to the base of her prow, Kylac saw layered waves cresting beneath her, rising as a singular swell, bearing her up . . . up . . .

The chokepoint loomed before them, and the *Vengeance* shuddered as she reached it. *Too little,* Kylac thought. *Too late.*

Impossibly, the sudden swell hefted them higher still—and, with a sudden heave, carried them through. The *Vengeance* moaned as bed and banks clutched at her, clawing at the base of her hull, seeking to snag her like the closing jaws of a huntsman's trap. But it was those teeth that were too little, too late, with the rush of foaming waters boosting the intrepid vessel over the land's snare and into the placid depths of the waters pooled beyond.

Gazes shifted astern. The Reaver seemed all but affixed to their rudder, and Kylac felt with a crushing sense of certainty that she would follow them through.

But as the swell that had hefted them clear receded, it did so in a powerful rush—ripping outward with the strength of a thief's tide. The Reaver slowed, faltered, fighting suddenly for ground like a climber scrabbling against a breaking avalanche.

Though it seemed for a moment as if she might surge clear, that slight, backward slip proved sufficient to steal her footing. With a grinding crash, the banks took hold of her body, pincers closing. She skidded forward, but only by a quarter length.

And like that, she was caught.

13

KYLAC PEERED BACK at the grounded Reaver like the crewmen around him, in a momentary haze of wonder and disbelief. Though he'd watched her succumb to the retreating tide, he half expected her to grind her way up and over those pinching landmasses formed by the Trellong's banks, so determined had she been—and so close—to catching them. Even now, the shouts that echoed from her decks rang with resolve. Even now, she refused to quit.

Then he remembered Ithrimir, and peeked out over the rail. The Sea Scribe hung there at the base of the ladder, dangling from its ropes with all the strength of a baitworm on a hook. It struck Kylac that, whatever the source of the Elementer's mystical energy, it must have required a tremendous amount to summon and control the river as he had. Mayhap he'd given too much.

The concern was interrupted by a change in the Reaver's cries, stubbornness at last giving way to fury. One among her voices peaked above the rest, a wordless trumpeting fueled by anguish. It silenced all other shouts, all other sounds, subsiding only to rise again, louder than before. Three times it resonated upon the wind, part shriek, part roar, driving birds from the trees and riverside rodents into their muddy dens. As if seeking like a roll of thunder to rend the very air.

Only when it had finally died did realization set in. The *Vengeance* was safe. Bereft of the waters needed to carry her beyond the choke-point, the pursuing Reaver was trapped, shrinking by the moment, of no further concern—for a time, at least—to those sailing the glassy waters on the southern side of that elevated narrows.

Cheers took spark among the *Vengeance*'s crew, swelling in strength as they rolled across her decks and up into her rigging, to form at last a united cry of relief. A smattering of jeers for the Grenarr slipped in, adding depth and tone to the celebration. This time, no one tried to stop them. Pevrick flashed a crude gesture toward the enemy and barked insult. Even Ledron wore what might have been a wry grin. All aboard seemed to be enjoying the moment, while the spear-and-trident Prowler drew up behind her stranded companion like a cub slinking near to check on its wounded mother.

Kylac checked again on Ithrimir, and was relieved himself to find the Sea Scribe slowly climbing the ladder. Whatever trauma the mad mage had suffered, it would appear it wasn't lethal.

As he reached the top, Kylac extended him a hand. The Scribe glowered, but accepted it, as if too weary to resist. By the time Kylac had helped him over the rail, the ship's crew was in full chorus, crow-ing a bawdy tune about a fishmonger and his daughter and the clever silverfin who stole a worm and a kiss and swam away.

Ledron approached. "How much time have we won ourselves?" he asked of Ithrimir.

The Scribe flashed him a withering glare. *We?* his arched brow seemed to ask.

The captain didn't flinch. "The fortune *I* know is fickle in her favors, and the knave's tide has bought us only so many hours. One? Two?"

His cheerlessness cast a pall that swiftly stole the smiles from those around him. Though the general fervor of the crew continued else-where upon the ship, Pevrick and Brenham stepped closer to attend their captain's concerns.

Ithrimir regarded their expectant gazes with a sour face and a vague gesture toward the sluggish waters beneath their bow. "She won't need a king's tide to make it through, if that's what you sug-gest. Should she remain there, straining at her leash . . ." He glanced skyward, tilting his good eye toward the sun. "Call it one and a half."

"What measure of lead will that grant us?"

"Enough to reach the Moravial, I should think."

"You should think?" Pevrick scoffed, then snorted and shook his head.

"The Trellong is not without say in this," Ithrimir cautioned.

Ledron's brow furrowed. "Meaning what?"

"Meaning we've been lucky thus far," Leeches interpreted. "He pretends to guide us, but is no better than some vagabond charlatan traveling from hamlet to hamlet with his sack of tricks. Yet we put him at the wheel and—"

"Your objections are noted, Lieutenant," Ledron said.

Pevrick spat. "I'll see them noted in the log. On the cursed dreg of a chance we ever see home again to suffer royal review."

The first mate had the decency to keep his voice low, but it must have become apparent to the rest of the crew that the huddle of captain and senior officers was not a congratulatory affair. Upon her decks and throughout her rigging, the celebration of the *Vengeance's* crew softened prematurely, song and praises giving way to murmurs of curiosity.

"In the log," Ledron agreed, with a dangerous glint in his eye. "Until then, you'll convince me that you're the man to milk this wind for all she's worth, or I'll find me the man aboard who is."

Leeches glowered, then offered a salute. "As you command, Captain."

He turned on his heel and stormed to a forward position, hurling shouts at those given to suffer his leadership. Behind him, it was Ledron's turn to shake his head, while watching the insolent first mate depart. Weariness, disbelief, frustration—a safe wager, any combination of the three.

Mayhap Ledron perceived the thought, or sensed the sympathy that accompanied it, for he swiftly spun back to the rest of them with an authoritative frown. "I see two navigators before me, and a pilot with none. To your posts, if I can trouble you, sirs."

Brenham nodded smartly. Ithrimir only glared with that ravaged half-gaze, his dead eye seeing everything and nothing, and giving no hint as to any feeling he might have toward Ledron's sarcasm. Kylac was inclined to remark upon the Head's attitude with a harmless jest, but supposed the captain might not recognize it as harmless. So he, too, remained silent.

Ledron dismissed them by stepping away from their huddle, heading forward to wherever he felt most inclined—likely in some futile attempt to escape the madness by which he'd come to be surrounded. Brenham was the first to turn aft, with a gesture inviting Ithrimir to precede him in their return to the wheelhouse. The Scribe obliged him. Kylac took to the Elementer's heels, with the second mate taking to his.

They'd covered all of three paces when a mighty shriek split the air, shrill and challenging, like a heavy blade screeching against plate armor. Kylac's gaze snapped skyward, instinctively tracing the unfamiliar sound to its source. Necks craned around him, hands rising to shield against the sun's glare.

High above, to the north, an obsidian stain appeared against the cloudless blue, whipping and flailing, unfurling like a black satin cloak caught in an angry wind.

With a pair of flaps, the form seemed to straighten and level out. A streak of crimson flashed amid the obsidian sheen. It shrieked again, angry, indignant, gaining speed in its approach.

Kylac finally recognized it, barely a breath before Jahvid called out from the crow's nest.

"Shrike!"

"Archers!" Pevrick bellowed.

A flurry of fresh movement rippled throughout the ship, as men scrambled to lay hold of their ranged weapons. Longbows and crossbows, quivers and bandoliers, were drawn from lockers or snatched from hooks. Several had them close at hand, having scarcely stepped down from battle posts taken up as the Grenarr had closed upon them. Within a few breaths, the first scattered volley was away.

The shrike greeted the loose, spear-tipped cloud with a defiant, ear-splitting shriek. Rather than shy from the missiles, it tucked its massive wings against its body and dove headlong in among them, thinning into the spaces between shafts, speeding through.

"Again!" Pevrick shouted. "Loose at will!"

"Bring it down!" Ledron barked. Half encouragement, half plea.

The mighty seabird swept directly overhead, low enough to rake the *Vengeance*'s mast tips with its pinion feathers, had it sought to do so. Jahvid ducked reflexively, covering his ears against yet another piercing cry. Others clinging to the spars or ratlines amid the highest reaches of the ship similarly cringed or cowered, seeking shelter where none could be found, retreating within themselves as if certain the shrike had come to snatch them from their perch. Weapons were fumbled, shafts dropped. Bolts and arrows whisked skyward in a haphazard rain, many fired so hastily as to be without aim.

Kylac had the sense that it might not have mattered. The bird, fearless and majestic, flew past the projectiles as it might a cloud of gnats. Though some looked to pass near enough to graze the creature, none pierced it. From the foremast, it dove deckward, a missile itself taking aim at their forecastle. When it appeared as though it might ram directly into the bow rail, it hitched upward and then fired forward as if from a catapult, streaking past their bowsprit and winging south. A final barrage of arrows chased after it, but by then the shrike was moving too fast, and elevating too quickly. The shafts that pursued it arced or lanced gamely depending on the line of sight, but in the end crashed feebly into the river or surrounding wetland.

The great bird continued on, winging southward from their position, a final, furious cry mocking their efforts.

An awed hush fell over the ship, with crew cursing or murmuring or just staring after the shrike in fretful denial.

"Shards!" Pevrick cursed. "Bloody, festering . . ." He turned to find Ledron and stormed toward the captain's position.

Brenham, Kylac noted, had turned to do the same, so Kylac took it upon himself to rejoin the officers' debate. Ithrimir followed, albeit more hesitantly, as if he cared nothing for what further arguments they might have for one another, but felt it his place to stand by Kylac.

"By the time we regain the central river," Pevrick fumed, "that feathered dragon will be halfway to the nearest Grenarr atoll."

"Might be it broke tether," Brenham offered, clearly seeking to temper the first mate's fears. "That Reaver at our back did not run aground lightly."

Leeches spat. "You jest or dream."

"If the rookery had suffered damage," Ledron agreed, "likely more than one would have flown free." The Head ground his teeth as if chewing gravel.

"Safer to assume the bird bears word," Kylac gleaned. "Possibly fetching reinforcements."

Ithrimir scoffed. "Possibly?"

His mocking interjection drew the captain's ire. "It hardly matters. We're at this point committed to our course, are we not?"

"The Trellong will bear us to the Moravial," Ithrimir confirmed. "To sail north again, or south, shall depend upon the captain's bidding."

"North, we step back into the snare we just escaped," Pevrick snarled.

"Mayhap not," Kylac remarked, "if'n those who found us there remain committed to chasing our rudder."

"If they're sending messages south, they'll be sending them north, as well," Brenham advised. "If they've not already."

"South," Pevrick snarled, as if neither man had interjected, "and we're liable to find them waiting there, as well. We're trapped."

"Have you a recommendation?" Ledron asked irritably. "Or is your aim merely to recite known hazards?"

"Were this ship under my command—a Whitefist's command—and not that of some pampered nobleman's buttocks-scrubbing shadow—"

"Belay that remark, Lieutenant. If we're indeed doomed, as you suggest, the loss of a mate or two costs me nothing."

And there at last, while Leeches stood silent and seething, the source of his near-constant rage lay exposed. Or leastwise a critical measure of it. Kylac hadn't seen it before, given his limited familiarity with the intricacies of the Addaran military. But he saw it now. Pevrick might have been named Ledron's first mate on this voyage, but the Head was a captain of the Shadowguard—a royal guardian, not a seaman. Leeches, most likely a ship's captain himself, had been asked to relinquish a rank in order to serve one in the role who, by his estimation, lacked the integral knowledge and experience to properly execute it.

As decisions were made that he disagreed with, and circumstances deteriorated, the easier it was in Pevrick's mind to heap blame at the feet of their unqualified leader.

"The bird may fail to reach its nesting ground," said Brenham, his hopeful words and calming tone an obvious attempt to alleviate the brewing tension. To the collection of doubtful expressions, he added, "Or its home roost may be distant enough that we can be gone and out to sea by the time the Grenarr mobilize a response. For that matter," he pressed, "we don't know that any will heed the call. With Grendavan slain, who can say where the allegiances of his lesser captains lie?"

"We could argue the length of the day what little we know," Ledron determined. "True from the outset. The only choice I see is to stand together or unravel."

The captain gestured toward the ship around them, calling attention to the packs of sailors and soldiers perched or standing about in mostly silent confusion, the way men accustomed to following orders did when awaiting a new command born of dissension.

"I invite opinion," Ledron went on, directing his words chiefly at Pevrick. "But I seek solutions, not hazards, as I am keenly aware of the latter."

The first mate's seething gave way to sulking. It lasted all of a heartbeat before he turned to bay at his layabout crew. "To work, maggots! I gave no order to stand by!"

With the men set to scurrying, Leeches turned back to face Ledron. "It is the ship's captain who must make the call," he said, firing an expression of disgust toward Ithrimir, "no matter who he chooses to consult."

Absolving himself of responsibility, Kylac realized. Covet as he might the captain's chair, he wasn't about to lay claim to the rank in the midst of a no-win situation.

Ledron met the challenge squarely. "How far to the nearest Grenarr atoll," he asked of the Sea Scribe, "if following the path of that bird?"

Ithrimir cocked his head, squinting out across the southern expanse of stagnant riverlands over which the shrike had flown. "Farengthrok, by their name. A day's sail, or near enough."

"And how far to exit your Moravial, and this forsaken isle, at her southern mouth?"

"A day's sail. Or near enough."

The captain permitted a heavy silence, but refused to let it linger. "South, then. Less likely to be warded than the north."

Inspiring choice, Kylac thought, but left it unsaid.

Once again, it was Pevrick who first broke their huddle, venturing forward to seek escape from the unknown in the more certain routine of his duties. As the other members began to disperse, Kylac turned aft, spotting Taeg's face in the wheelhouse window. Abruptly, he recalled a claim the helmsman had made, back when the Grenarr had first been spotted.

They knew we were coming.

Kylac halted. It wasn't a suspicion, exactly, that arrested his stride. Merely a nibble of instinct that spawned a question worth asking. But he hesitated to do so here and now. No reason to trigger a false alarm. Not when the evidence, be it for or against, could be found so close at hand.

"Captain," he said, "mights I trouble ya for a private word?"

Ledron eyed him with suspicion of his own. But at least the weariness Kylac had observed earlier was gone. Whatever else the enemy pursuit and Pevrick's challenge had done, it had stoked the captain's ire and strengthened his ironclad resolve. "We've time on our hands," he finally agreed.

"Belowdecks, if'n ya'll permit it."

Brenham paused. Ledron's gaze soured, but he nodded, first to Kylac, then to his second mate. "Return our guest to the wheelhouse, if you would."

The chief navigator bowed, a slight dip of his head. "Come," he said simply to Ithrimir.

The Sea Scribe regarded Kylac, a question in his gaze that went unspoken. Without argument, he carried on alongside Brenham, leaving Kylac to guide Ledron to the nearest hatch.

Into the heart of the *Vengeance* they proceeded, where musty smells and the crushing nearness of close walls and narrow passageways lay claim over fresh air and the liberating expansiveness of the outdoors. Kylac suffered it as he seldom did, curiosity outweighing his aversion to tight spaces. *A mere jaunt,* he told himself, *and then we'll know.*

He could feel Ledron's desire to say something. A question to address his own curiosity, mayhap, or a remark on how rarely he saw Kylac venture beneath the ship's skin. Kylac knew not how apparent his phobia might have been to the captain. He had the impression Ledron kept many of his observations to himself, as befitting a soldier trained to catalog potential disadvantages in any rival or foe.

They encountered few crewmen belowdecks. With nearly all hands having been summoned for battle, only those limited to steward functions—purser, porters, cooks—had been excused from reporting topside. Even those sailors and soldiers who'd been relieved required an unwinding of taut nerves before retiring to their berths. A ghost ship, she might have been, were it not for the constant echo of those clattering about abovedecks.

Amid those knocks and thuds and other reverberations, an anxious chittering arose ahead of them as they proceeded aft. It grew louder as they approached the stern of the ship on her starboard side, nearing the door to the rookery. As he reached the portal, Kylac took pause, glancing over his shoulder at Ledron while the strange birdsong—a chorus of restless chirping and fluttering—continued.

"I's not heard them carry on like this," he admitted.

"It's said they seldom do, when caged," Ledron replied. "The call of the other is likely what has them riled."

"Ah," said Kylac. That would have been his guess, too—with a side wager that he simply hadn't spent time enough among them to know. But he'd also been taught that another's assessment was more reliable when invited openly, without the taint of presentiment.

Ledron frowned impatiently. "What is it you would—"

Kylac opened the door. A stale gust greeted him. The ship's rookery was an expansive cabin, by shipboard standards, stretching the full length of the stern in which it was housed, two decks below the captain's quarters. Large patches of its aft and side walls were comprised of latticework, allowing fresh air to circulate throughout. But no wind could completely drive out the smell of so many birds of a sea shrike's size—their bodies, their droppings, their barrels of feed—housed in such an enclosure.

He hadn't known what sort of greeting to expect, but was surprised by the instant hush that fell over the assorted raptors, hung in their various cages throughout the cabin. He couldn't know what that said about their perception of him, but he supposed it wasn't flattering. Mayhap it was just the malicious cruelty reflected in their gimlet eyes, or the blood-tipped color of their beaks, but he earnestly believed that, given the chance, they would peck him to shreds merely for the pleasure of scattering his entrails.

Yet it wasn't their smell that concerned him just now. Nor their sounds. Nor even their perceived malevolence, be it innate or inculcated. So he curtailed his thoughts and impressions long enough to execute a far simpler study.

A physical tally.

At a glance, the numbers appeared in order. Twelve cages, each of them occupied. But an instinctive urging caused him to look closer. And there it was, the confirmation he'd come to find. Even then, he took a moment to be sure, to work through any feasible alternatives to the sinking truth he was about to suggest.

"Have our cooks requested permission to serve shrike?"

Ledron grunted in surprise, as if finding the notion absurd. "Of course not." His mien darkened. "What are you on about?"

"Not to present another hazard, Captain. But I do believe we's a mole among us."

14

"Mole?" ledron replied, brow furrowing in surprise. "What makes you say so?"

Kylac gestured toward the array of captive birds. "We're missing a shrike of our own."

The captain's gaze traced the motion. His scowl deepened. "The cages are full."

"The largest, there in the center. It held three birds, not two."

"Might you have miscounted?"

But Kylac was certain. "Summon your quartermaster. His logs will attest. Nineteen birds when we left port. Eighteen now."

Ledron approached the cage in question, a heaviness in his stride that hadn't been evident a moment before. Daylight mingled with shadow in patches across his face, filtered by the latticed panels in the wall of the hull. Where caught by the crimson-and-garnet eyes of the great shrikes marking his advance, the light glinted red.

"If so," the captain allowed after a moment's study, "perhaps it was consumed by its own brood."

"Bones and all?" Kylac asked dubiously. "Without talon or feather to mark the carcass?"

"It doesn't have to mean there's a traitor aboard."

"I swept the ship myself, before we'd taken possession. I left no

Grenarr save Tormitius, and him bound."

"Meaning any tar-skins who *did* escape notice are accountable to you."

"Meaning we's brought along ourselves one or more in service to the enemy."

Ledron's jaw clenched until Kylac feared his teeth might shatter. "Impossible. I personally approved every man admitted aboard."

"Impossible? Then tells me, how did the Grenarr happen to be waiting for us as we set sail from the Scribe's island?"

The captain hesitated in his answer, belatedly realizing that Kylac referred not to the bird that had just escaped their arrows, but one set free much earlier in their voyage. "Chance, likely as not. Doubtless, they've been sweeping the seas for us since we embarked. And who knows what information they had from the outset? Your actions against them had all the stealth of a rutting walrus. And Avenell, as you were warned, is riddled with informants."

And not just Grenarr secreted away among them, Kylac had since learned, but Addarans given sway to their cause. Some for coin, some for blackmail, some for the lives of kinsmen held hostage by Grenarr raiders. Even the most loyal mother or father could be persuaded to commit treason when a child's life depended on a marauder's enduring mercy—as borne out, said many, by the capitulation of Kendarrion, their very king, in response to the abduction of his royal son.

"Yet none in Avenell knew then that we'd be visiting Mistwall," Kylac argued, "as even we didn't."

Ledron scoffed. "Easy enough to anticipate. They must have known we'd find their conflicting charts. And might have justly believed that Tormitius would never willingly aid us."

"Or is it possible," Kylac suggested, "that someone alerted them from this very chamber as to our intent and location?" He waved casually toward the shuttered portal in the aft wall—the opening through which the carrier birds were given release as occasion arose.

Ledron glanced at the portal, then at the nearest shrike eyeing him with hate and hunger through the iron bars of its prison. "Foolish a man would be to withdraw one of these raptors. And from the master cage where three roost?"

"A fair point—for those of us not given to know how to handle the creatures. But can ya truly claim that none aboard possesses that talent?"

The captain folded his arms defensively, his staunch refusal etched plainly in the creases of his face. "If they'd known where we could be found, they'd have assembled an armada, rather than the small pack we stumbled across."

"Another reasonable wager. 'Less the rest are simply too far out. Are ya prepared to risk the entire mission on it?"

The Head opened his mouth, but closed it without responding. From across the cabin, one of the smaller, solitary shrikes issued a hacking cough, which it cleared with a shrill squawk.

Kylac smirked. "Then what says we cease speculating among ourselves, and sees what our esteemed guest has to say about it?"

THE SHIP'S MASTER CABIN lay as dark and pungent as Kylac had remembered it. Still chained abed, Tormitius Shorecleaver had gone unwashed, unaired, for days now since their prior meeting. It appeared the dressing on his foot had been changed, as Kylac had suggested. But the cleanliness and vanities of the *Vengeance*'s former first mate had elsewise gone unattended, given the bristle of beard upon his jaw, the ridge of hair sprouted round his head, and the rank smell of his oily, bedridden hide.

Nonetheless, he greeted them with a smile.

"The charmer and his asp. How fare we in our voyage? Tell me I dreamed it, but I heard a commotion."

The strength of his voice told Kylac he'd been well fed, well watered. Unless their mere visit had somehow invigorated him. Regardless, the seething fury they'd met with before had clearly been supplanted by some form of snide delight.

Ledron answered it with a glare. Kylac respected the resulting silence, awaiting the captain's lead. But when the quiet gave way at last to a sidelong glance, he seized upon the opening.

"We ran afoul o' your friends," he admitted. "A small pack. Seems they were expecting us."

"Oh? Then the hunt is on, and soon finished."

"Not so soon, I fear. They's been waylaid by a knave's tide, to await the pleasure o' the king's return."

The Shorecleaver grimaced, but his narrowed gaze couldn't shade the gleam in his eyes. "Might I inquire as to their standards?"

"What difference?" Ledron snapped.

"Perhaps none. Perhaps all."

Kylac determined not to let the other rattle them, but to meet smugness with confidence. "A pair o' Prowlers, clearly o' no consequence." He approached the bed, to seat himself at its base. With that casual display of insolence, he watched the cords in Tormitius's neck tighten, the shark's fin tattoo on the side of his throat flexing in response. "The Reaver that led them flew a crimson hammer."

The Shorecleaver's rage gave way to a broad grin of pleasure unfeigned. "Temerius Seahammer."

"Seahammer? A proud name," Kylac permitted. "But o' what repute?"

"You slew his father."

"I's slain many a father."

"In the midst of his wedding vows."

His enemy meant it as a punch in the gut. Kylac accepted the blow, swallowing it like a piece of gristle. "Ah. One o' Grendavan's pups?"

"The youngest, but the most headstrong," Tormitius replied. "Most beloved, and loving in turn."

Ledron scoffed. "Somehow a vile notion, spilling from your black lips."

The Shorecleaver spared the captain a piercing glance. "He has ranged far from his typical hunting grounds. Be assured, it is retribution he seeks. If you think an opposing tide will in any regard slow Temerius, you—"

"Temerius, Tormitius . . . filth, by any name," Ledron interrupted. "How did they happen to find us?"

Kylac wondered briefly at the intensity of the Head's ire. During their earlier interrogation, Ledron had been quick to bridle Kylac's threats and seek to placate the prisoner. Now, it was almost as if they'd exchanged roles, with Kylac thinking he might have to restrain or ask the captain to excuse himself in order to finish the conversation. Mayhap now was his chance to seek Ledron's permission to bring a blade into the discussion.

The Shorecleaver chuckled, his mirth resonating a perceived advantage. His eyes, glimmering until now with sadistic amusement, took on a calculating cast. "You claim not to know? A fine act, Captain," he said, infecting the title with his contempt. "I wonder, at times, just how long you'll be able to maintain it."

Kylac glanced at Ledron, spying the confusion that rooted suddenly in the captain's visage. The Head caught his look, but turned hurriedly back to their prisoner.

"What act?" Kylac asked.

The laughter spilled again, from deeper in Tormitius's chest. "The asp has teeth, yet dances to the charmer's song, never questioning its master's aims."

"You would belay us with riddles now?" Ledron grumbled.

Kylac smiled. "Did I fail to speak plain before? I serve no man's bidding but my own."

"Do you, now?" Tormitius licked the corner of his mouth. "A crown prince abducted from his father's court, by an enemy that can scarcely set foot on the Pretender's stolen soil. Have you asked yourself, asp, how that could be? Not without aid from within the royal house, I'd wager." His penetrating gaze shifted pointedly to Ledron. "One called to serve at the most intimate level. Close to the prince himself, perhaps?"

Kylac followed Tormitius's gaze, to find the Head's face growing flush. Anger? Embarrassment? Whichever, the captain covered it with a huffing laugh of his own. "You would implicate *me* in your scheme? Unwise, I should think, when I'm the one holding our asp by the tail. Barring that, you'd not long go unharmed."

"And why?" the Shorecleaver teased. "*Why* keep me unharmed?" He shook his broad head dismissively. "My place is with my crew," he declared. "Dead I am, or shall soon be." His shackles clinked as he hunched forward slightly, addressing Kylac. "Be they *his* threats or yours, I care not. But snake charming is a fascinating dance. As anyone, I've a curiosity as to how long the serpent suffers darkness beneath the master's lid."

Ledron fumed. It seemed he was on the verge of sputtering a denial when he glanced over to meet Kylac's questioning gaze. Jaw clenching, he gripped the pommel of his sword and growled, "I've heard enough."

With heavy stride, he marched from the cabin.

Kylac hesitated, itchy fingers playing about the butt of his own slender longsword. He wondered again if this wasn't the opportunity he'd been seeking to pry a little deeper into their prisoner's mind—forcibly if need be.

"The captain himself betrayed our position. That's what ya'd have me believe?"

Tormitius reared, sucking from his nose. A breath later, Kylac slipped aside to avoid the mouthful of phlegm launched his way.

"Believe what you wish. The Seahammer has your scent. A bloody pulp you'll be when mashed beneath his boot."

He reclined, corded muscles falling slack. Finished, it would seem, though his eyes continued to burn while his chest heaved gently.

For a moment, Kylac considered pressing the matter. But he could foresee little to be gleaned without risking Ledron's ire. Conceding to the Shorecleaver's silence, Kylac stepped from the darkness.

Feeling the cruel sting of his adversary's smirk like whips upon his back.

THE CAPTAIN, he was pleased to discover, hadn't gone far. Kylac found him on the deck just outside the master cabin, peering out over the starboard rail upon a gray, wetland wilderness riddled with stunted trees and shrouded in moth-eaten mists.

"Is it true?" Kylac asked bluntly. "Has ya got a role here hidden from the rest of us?"

Ledron's glare might have melted iron. "If I were his ally, why

PC

would he expose me to you?"

Kylac shrugged. "Mayhap he seeks a partnership more to his liking. Yours has him rotting away in fetters, to die o' bed sores."

"A clumsy effort to sow doubt among us," Ledron claimed.

Kylac was reluctant to believe elsewise. The intimation that Ledron could have aided the Grenarr in Dethaniel's capture suggested a deeply rooted deceit he didn't care to contemplate—a web of subterfuge too intricate to unravel. Even if he managed to cut his way through the lies, he'd likely regret whatever resided at its heart.

Apart from that, there'd been dozens of guardians, soldiers, and servants in service to Kendarrion's royal household. A near limitless flock of potential traitors in this conflict.

No, he'd determined even before exiting the master cabin that Tormitius was simply playing games, seeking to make him question his own footing—the only real means by which the Grenarrian might lash out and seek some measure of revenge against him. Had Ledron indeed betrayed them, he wouldn't likely have welcomed Kylac to question the Shorecleaver about it.

And yet, instincts notwithstanding, it would be imprudent of him not to broach the possibility their enemy had raised. For, whatever the motive, it wouldn't be the first time the captain had played him false.

"What?" Ledron demanded, as if offended by Kylac's deliberations. "His Highness was Ulflund's charge at the time of his abduction."

"With yourself, it seems, among those to benefit from the erstwhile captain's resulting disfavor."

The Head purpled with indignation. "I have ever served my king with fidelity and fervor."

"Back home, mayhap," Kylac allowed, and watched the captain squint with rising fury. "But out here? A lad might wonder, might ya's taken to heart my notion o' mutiny?"

"Mutiny?"

"A gambit I proposed, before we made for Mistwall."

Ledron turned, crossing his arms as if to sheathe his clenched fists.

"As I sees it, ya's little to gain on this voyage, and everything to lose. Short o' returning His Highness unharmed, your king won't thank you. Even *that* might fail to win ya back his good graces. Might be there's more in it for ya to sell us to the Grenarr."

"A suicidal folly. They'd sooner see me braised in acid, or spitted on a harpoon and slowly roasted over a small flame."

"An obvious risk," Kylac agreed. "And yet, ya knows enough about your people's ways and workings to be o' significant value should ya defect. The Grenarr would stand to gain more if'n they refrained from slaying ya out o' hand. Might be you're wagering on it."

The captain held his gaze as the river winds gusted by them, eyes flashing with defiance. "I am here at His Majesty's service," he claimed. "I needn't defend my honor against a tar-skin's accusations, or explain myself to some cheap, lordless rogue."

Kylac chose to overlook the growing clumsiness of the captain's protestations, and the nervous hitch that had entered into his voice. Though either might indicate a lie, they might as easily stem from having to defend against false accusation. "Not as yet, mayhap," he conceded. "But we's tread this path before. Should I find ya's tried to blind me again, ya'll wish ya hadn't."

"Spare me your threats and suspicions. We can bandy both until the oceans dry, but doing so will merit us nothing. I am innocent."

Kylac wanted to accept that. He'd voiced his concerns primarily to observe the Head's reaction to them. And yet . . . "Then answer me my spawning question. Allowing for now that it was neither you nor I, who among us might have reason to empower the enemy?"

"None," Ledron answered flatly.

"Who has access to our prisoner? Had occasion to lend ear to a bribe?"

"None who would have succumbed."

"You're certain? How well can ya knows each member o' your crew? Has none a potential obligation to the Grenarr? Or grievance against the Addarans? A history o' mercenary tendencies, mayhap?"

"I tell you, I considered all of that before allowing each aboard—with yourself looking on, as I recall."

"Without exception?"

Ledron steamed, though he seemed as amused now as he did angry, made indignant by Kylac's stubborn string of impertinent questions, but also finding them bizarre. "Believe it or not," he remarked at last,

"I am no fool. To know and command men is my lifelong expertise."

"Ya mistake my meaning, Captain. I mean not to question your judgment, but to ask, might there be any aboard ya *can't* account for?"

The Head's bewilderment spawned a withering stare. "A stowaway? But you've already insisted—"

"Sir!"

They turned as one to face the interruption. Pevrick stalked toward them, positioned now at the top of the nearest deck ladder, his bearded face flushed with urgency. Or mayhap the crimson color about his neck owed to the leeches at his throat having recently engorged on his fathomless bitterness. Attending him was the pock-faced Whitefist, Aramis, who wore an ashen expression.

"Yes, Lieutenant?" Ledron permitted. His quick pardon of the disruption told Kylac that he'd had his fill of their own, futile conversation, and was anxious to end it.

Leeches offered no apology. He glanced back at Aramis, then forward again, his brow knotting sternly. "Sir, we have a problem."

15

A SHIVER THREATENED TO BREAK across Kylac's shoulders as he stood there in the bowels of the forward hold, water pooled to his ankles, the weight of the entire ship seeming to press upon him. Before him, Ledron bent with Pevrick over a gash in the hull, through which the river sprayed lustily. A small breach, it seemed to Kylac. No more than a hand in length along a buckled seam in the prow. Nonetheless, the Head regarded it gravely in the light of his lantern.

"This is the larger of the two we've found," Leeches informed the captain. "Rehm and Tareth continue to search for others—with no knowing how many lay hidden beneath the waters at our feet."

"I reported it immediately, sir," added Aramis, the shadowy light deepening the pockmarks scarring his cheeks.

"I've set Jaleth to task on a fothering sail," said Pevrick. "I trust the captain won't begrudge me the liberty."

"What's the flow rate?" Ledron asked.

"Sixteen buckets a minute. Nearly a full barrel, sir."

"Assessment?"

"We've only the rate of this breach. Without knowing how many cousins it may have, we can only guess as to—"

"So guess, Lieutenant."

"Nine hours before we founder."

Kylac felt a stab of surprise, while Ledron balked at the first mate's reckoning. "We've a hundred hands aboard this vessel. If set to bailing—"

"From this depth? Line up every man we've got, we manage maybe eight buckets a minute. Thirty barrels an hour, sir. Against sixty."

Kylac saw no reason to question the numbers. What difference, nine hours or ninety, when they likely had weeks of sailing left ahead of them? Observing again the near panic in Aramis's face, his own surprise edged toward alarm. Difficult it was to imagine that such a minor nick could take them down. But he wasn't going to wager elsewise against sailors as experienced as these.

"Set every Redfist to bailing," Ledron commanded stubbornly. "Every Whitefist not manning a sheet or line is to assist as you deem fit. Hauling, patching, bracing—whatever techniques, I want this leak stemmed. First priority, Lieutenant."

"Aye, Captain," Leeches groused. He turned and slogged aft through the slow-rising waters, brushing past Kylac without apology. Beckoning curtly for Aramis to follow, he ascended the nearest ladder, murmuring beneath his breath.

"Is it so severe?" Kylac asked Ledron when they were alone.

"Must have split when grinding through that chokepoint," the captain muttered.

Or at any one of several points en route. To Kylac's recollection, they'd grated past a handful of reefs and ridges, mayhap more, while racing along the hazard-strewn Trellong. He'd assumed the *Vengeance* could suffer the resulting scrapes and bruises, given all the talk among her crew of the impregnable nature of Grenarr vessels. Only as compared to Addaran ships, it would seem. Now, when they depended on it, the enemy's strength had failed them.

"How might I be of aid?" Kylac asked.

"Fetch a bucket," Ledron grumbled.

Kylac obeyed, snatching the one set upon a rib to one side of the deceptively dangerous fissure. He dipped it beneath the pooled waters, tugged it free, and trudged toward the ladder.

"Leave it, Kronus. It's six decks to topside. To buy us a few heartbeats."

"Might be one'll make the difference. And I'm headed up anyway."

A task it was, scaling half a dozen ladders with the bucket in hand, growing heavier with each level climbed along a switchback course. But he completed it, if only for the example he hoped it would set. After just the one trip, however, he understood better the futility of the effort. Nearly two minutes it had taken him to complete his ascent, with a good fifth of the bucket's contents sloshing free along the way. His shoulders, arms, and hands had burned with unfamiliar fatigue by the time he'd reached the rail. Barely a cupful, it had seemed, when heaved over the side, to make but a paltry splash against the river's surface.

There had to be a better way.

Garryn, posted again as relay man beside the wheelhouse, must have agreed. "Might we shift tack?" the Whitefist asked of Taeg as Kylac entered. "Heel clear?"

Taeg gestured at the narrow river snaking out before them. "She gives me only so much room to roam."

"The open sea would avail us nothing," said Brenham, as he picked through sheaves of drawings that detailed layers and sections of the ship's structure. "The breach is too far below the waterline, if Erresh reported true."

Garryn swallowed thickly, his face pale.

"Ya's heard, then," Kylac surmised. He'd expected as much, given the general alert. The decks echoed and swarmed with activity, word and instructions spreading like wildfire, drawing men from the heights and funneling them belowdecks. Everywhere, Redfists and Whitefists alike were abandoning their posts and patrols, individuals forming into packs, assembling to confront the new threat. "How much do ya knows?"

"Enough," Brenham grunted, gathering up his armload of diagrams. "But if you'll kindly make way, I mean to know more."

Kylac stepped clear to let the second mate through. Watching him go, Kylac asked of Taeg, "Does he fancy himself a shipwright, too?"

"Best we've got."

"Aboard, ya means."

"Or anywhere on Addaranth."

"Ah." Kylac was duly impressed. Seaman *and* architect. Similar disciplines, he knew. Impossible it would be to claim expertise in one and not know something of the other. But he hadn't imagined that King Kendarrion's best navigator might also be His Majesty's best ship builder—both sacrificed to this folly of a mission.

"You saw the leak yourself?" Taeg asked him.

"One o' them. A scratch, looked to me."

"None bigger than a finger will be patched without brace. And if there are others . . ."

The helmsman surrendered the thought to their imaginations. The silence it spawned among them went unchallenged, until Ithrimir said, "Twelve to starboard."

As Taeg nudged the wheel, Kylac noted with a slight flare of irritation that the Sea Scribe had been bound again to the chart table. "With all respect to these lads, I'm wagering *you* could tells us more o' what we face below."

Ithrimir tugged gently at his bindings. "Not from here. And not without risking further damage in my absence."

"From anything our spotters won't see?" Taeg asked. To the Scribe's glare, he added, "Not saying I won't miss your company. Just that, if we're indeed set to founder, I'd like to know all we can while there's time yet to do something about it."

A fair argument. Nonetheless, they remained for several minutes more, allowing for the Elementer to guide them past a nasty chunk of razor-edged shoal—upthrust like a hedge of spears from the island's foundation to penetrate the Trellong's channel beneath its dark surface. Once that particular hazard had been cleared, Ithrimir agreed to momentarily defer his navigational duties to Garryn and those in his relay chain, stretching forward to the team of spotters perched around their bow. Long enough to follow Kylac back down into the *Vengeance*'s bowels to examine her bleeding.

"Seven breaches, not four," the Scribe determined. He knelt amid a flooded section of the forward hold, both fists thrust into the calf-deep waters. His eyes were closed, his brow furrowed. "Rents along either side of the forward keel, another amidships. We've half the time your captain believes we do."

"You're certain?"

Ithrimir's eyes opened, blinking in irritation. "You seek my counsel only to refute it?"

"No," said Kylac, "I only . . ."

He hesitated, marking the efforts around them. Dutiful Redfists sloshed back and forth, passing along buckets full of water, as quickly as they could manage. Hooked ropes lowered from hatches above hastened the ascent of these containers deck by deck as compared to Kylac's climb via ladder, but by heartbeats only—and still without any direct path skyward. Other hands busied themselves stuffing the visible cracks with tar-sopped padding, seeking to secure the messy plugs by nailing them over with timber. A near pointless endeavor, from what Kylac could see, as the water simply spurted free around the boards' edges. Longer boards braced against bulkheads appeared more effective in holding the patches in place, but only marginally. Though the crew fought gamely, Kylac held little doubt that theirs was a stalling tactic, at best.

"Can ya do nothing to repel the flow?" he asked. "Or leastwise slow it?"

The Scribe's irritation deepened, though it struck Kylac as less an outward anger and more a self-assumed frustration. "Momentarily. To claim a few breaths, perhaps. Only the greatest Aggethrehn of ages past might have—"

"Kronus!" Ledron shouted from across the hold. "What's he doing down here?"

Ithrimir rose beside Kylac as the captain waded near. Those crewmen distracted by the Head's ire were quick to refocus when confronted by his glare. Even as they worked, however, their gazes stretched after him like clinging webs.

"I don't recall according him free range of this vessel," Ledron growled as he came upon them.

"For once, Pevrick's assessment proves brighter than warranted," Kylac explained. "We's four hours or five, not nine."

The Head bit short whatever he'd been about to say. "We're thrumming a sail now. When drawn into place—"

"Your efforts are admirable, Captain," Ithrimir allowed. "They are also arrogant and futile. Haul and brace and fother until your limbs tear free—the waters will not be denied."

"To work, maggots!" Pevrick roared at Ledron's back, telling Kylac that the bailing crews were still struggling to maintain focus while drawn to their captain's discussion with the strange Elementer in their midst.

"What choice have we?" the Head hissed.

"We dare not head to sea with the ship thus hobbled," Ithrimir replied. "At some point between here and there, we must beach ourselves in order to effect a more thorough repair."

"The Grenarr will be on our heels," Ledron reminded him.

"And the Ladrakari may be tracking us, waiting for us to expose ourselves," Ithrimir added. "You asked your choice, Captain. I give it to you. Risk attack from one or both, else ride this tub to the depths."

"Have you a location in mind?" Ledron asked through clenched teeth. "One that might permit repair while hiding us from our pursuers?"

"We must clear the Trellong first. The Moravial will afford greater cover. Forks through which to evade those at our tail. Mists and jungle to shelter us from Chitral's view."

Chitral. Kylac recalled the relief he'd felt upon believing that the Butcher and his Mookla'ayan clansmen would no longer serve threat. Alas.

"Can we make it?" the Head demanded flatly.

Ithrimir let his gaze play about the hold, as if measuring the activity of the crew. "See that your men do not flag in their labors," he said at last. "If there is chance to be had, I will find it."

Kylac spent the next two hours striving alongside Jaleth and fully a quarter of the men aboard to finish preparing the fothering sail—a tedious, sticky affair that consisted of stitching rope-yarns and tar-sopped oakum to a spare mainsail. While Whitefists executed and oversaw most of the effort, a smattering of Redfists, a pair of Black-fists, and even a handful of stewards were recruited to the task. Kylac found himself toiling for the greater part alongside a purser named Brohn and the ship's chief cook, Aythef, by turns picking apart old cordage or threading the resulting fibers into place. Though discussion proved minimal in deference to a common sense of urgency, Kylac learned that both Brohn and Aythef had served similar roles in the royal household prior to being assigned to this voyage—the former for seven years, the latter for nine.

"Quiet, the king's palace must be," Kylac remarked upon hearing the news, wondering how easy Kendarrion found it to replace such longstanding servants.

No sooner had their task been completed than Kylac and the stewards were brushed aside. In their stead, a dozen experienced Whitefists labored to draw the massive sheet under the bottom of the *Vengeance* along her keel, in desperate hope of using the pressure of the incoming waters to force the thrummed canvas into the largest of the cracks taking them down at the head. Ithrimir attended the effort, to ensure proper placement. When finally the sail had been secured, the exhausted crewmen, their tarred fingers raw and aching, congratulated one another on a job well done, then ventured below— those permitted—to see what their exertions had won them.

Kylac was among those disappointed at the sight.

Despite all their efforts—the hauling, the patching, the shifting of stores farther aft in an effort to raise the bow or at least maintain balance—the river continued to overtake them. Weary bailers had been pushed amidships by the rising flood, where they waded to and fro through knee-high waters. Forward of that, the level had risen to chest depth at the bow. With all breaches now under water, there was no immediate way to perceive what effect their fothering might have had. Nadrum had been set to counting the rate at which the invading river claimed successive marks scratched on a bulkhead. Those at rest between bailing shifts awaited his revised assessment as they might a magistrate's sentencing.

"Two minutes," the seaman called out, voice tinged with unexpected surprise.

His listeners responded in kind, perking hopefully, passing the measurement along the bucket line with a whisper of wary excitement.

"Two minutes, twenty-four seconds," Nadrum called moments later, this time with greater confidence.

A muted sense of triumph began to build throughout the sinking hold. Kylac inserted himself within the line, doing what he could to spur the enthusiasm. At three minutes and twelve seconds, it sparked an infectious surge of energy and a foreman's calls to "dig faster, boys!" At four minutes and twenty-three seconds, the cabin rang with an outright cheer.

A chant went up, the crew calling for five minutes. The next mark fell short, however, by eleven seconds. The one after, by seven. Whatever difference made, it had clearly stalled. But they'd bought themselves time. Kylac learned from the crewman feeding him buckets that, prior to his arrival, Nadrum had been calling out flood marks at ninety-second intervals. They'd improved upon that more than three times over. A minor victory, at least. With fortune's favor, a turning point in the war.

He remained in the hold—upon what seemed the front line of defense—for another hour and a half, outlasting the initial rotation and carrying on through two more. He did so in an ongoing effort to incite by his example the energies of those around him, as much as for the scant difference his position in the bucket line made. He finally took pause only when Brohn, the purser with whom he'd worked to pick oakum and thrum sail, sought him out with a summons from the captain.

"He awaits you in the wheelhouse."

Kylac nodded, passed one last bucket from Seius to Sethric, clapped the latter Redfist on his weary shoulder, and headed topside.

Itching along the way for an opportunity to more meaningfully combat their predicament.

The sunlight of early afternoon was momentarily blinding when compared to the darkness of the hold, sharp as daggers where it reflected off the surface of the Trellong. The river continued to unfold lazily before them along its slow, meandering path, its outward calm betraying no sign of the assault it waged against them below. A glimmer of somewhat greater intensity burned at the distant edge of its farthest visible bend. Mayhap the Moravial, coming at last into view. Mayhap only a trick of the light.

All three senior officers—Ledron, Pevrick, Brenham—awaited him in the wheelhouse, along with Taeg, Ithrimir, and the captain's favored Blackfists—Raithe and Sanow.

"Ya sent for me?"

Leeches dismissed himself with a grunt through the opposite door. If unexpected, none seemed troubled by it. At his back, Ledron regarded Kylac with an abiding frown. "Seems you may finally have a chance to earn your berth."

Kylac ignored the insinuation that he'd done nothing to earn it thus far, interested only in the captain's proposition. "Oh?"

"I'm told we'll reach the Moravial within the hour. If we can manage to keep our nose out of the mud, we'll be turning south as planned. An hour farther on, we hope to set her down, somewhere along here." Ledron pointed to a chart of the branching waterways of the Shrouded Skein—or the Moravial, as they seemed to all be calling it now—while casting a glance toward Ithrimir. When the Scribe offered no response, he proceeded. "At that point, we'll be launching three separate landing parties, six men each. Raithe will lead one, Sanow another. Can I entrust the third to you?"

"What is it we'll be seeking?" Kylac asked. If the captain was forming landing parties, it meant they were to go in search of something. If separate parties were being deployed, it meant he didn't quite know where to look.

The Head's stark expression did nothing to congratulate Kylac on his reasoning. "A tree."

Kylac arched a brow in question.

"Its sap, rather. To facilitate the necessary repairs."

"Any particular breed?"

"The grompike. Though absent from many shores, and rare on most others, our esteemed Scribe claims we might find a copse or two near to where we plan to put aground. We'll send with you a man who can identify it."

"And this sap is special because . . . ?"

"You don't just tack boards to the outer hull of a Grenarr ship," Brenham explained. "The wood is too hard. And most pitch and tar won't effectively adhere to it. Only sap from the grompike will serve as the putty that will plug our gashes and allow what timber and shavings we can gather to take hold."

"I see. And with that, we'll once again be watertight?"

"Fifteen to larboard," Ithrimir instructed Taeg, river guide and helmsman still quietly concentrating on the more immediate task.

"It will remain a patch," Brenham advised. "We don't have time to properly prepare and treat replacement planks. Nor, in truth, have we ever been able to adequately duplicate the processes used by the Grenarr to do so—key to why their vessels are stronger than ours. But the grompike's sap should at least allow us to create a more effective bung."

Should, Kylac noted. Not *will.* And yet, the mission sounded more promising than bailing or picking or thrumming—or sanding, sawing, spreading sap, or whatever else might be required in a ship's repair. If nothing else, it would afford him another chance to stretch his legs.

Nonetheless, expediency compelled him to ask, "The Grenarr don't keep a supply o' this rarity aboard?"

"It hardens once bled from a living branch or bole," Brenham replied, "and is thereafter unusable. The samples you return must be fresh."

"Understood. Anything else I must know?"

"Final instructions will be given once your parties have been formed," said Ledron. "Raithe and Sanow will help to select your company's members. If there's a man aboard you care to have at your side, you're welcome to select him, subject to my approval."

The very notion triggered a recollection of their earlier discussion, in which Kylac had tried to persuade the captain that one or more of their fellow crewmen was in fact a Grenarr informant. He couldn't say whether Ledron had intended to dredge the matter up—suggesting mayhap that the Head had come around to accepting the possibility—or if it had bloomed within his mind of its own volition. Either way, it occurred to Kylac that this new task might afford him an opportunity to pry a little deeper along that vein.

He offered only a crisp nod in reply. Perils and complications notwithstanding, the matter seemed simple enough. "Square those shoulders, Captain. Needs doing, we'll sees it done."

16

"Tah?"

Kylac held up alongside the others in his party. Four heads turned toward Creyl, who peered back at them expectantly. Only Kylac maintained his focus on their jungle surroundings, wary of distraction.

Aythef glanced at him before shuffling forward through the deepening dusk. The chief cook approached the half-wild Creyl as he might a feral dog, his nervousness tinged with fear. To be fair, Creyl's mad grin wasn't exactly a reassurance against attack.

"Well?" Talon prompted as Aythef bent to examine the leaves that Creyl had discovered.

Aythef shook his head. "No," he said, speaking to Creyl as if admonishing a child. "Its leaves will have three points, not four, with serrations at the edge. And the trunk will be less gnarled, more tubular, at its roots."

Creyl's expression sharpened dangerously, flecked eyes gleaming in the fading light.

"But a fair sighting," Aythef added quickly, shedding all exasperation from his tone. "The general shape is certainly the same."

Creyl tore the leaf in question from its stem, crumpling it and tossing it to the earth. The others sagged with disappointment. Ebens, dubbed Pommel by his fellow Redfists on account of his broad shoulders and polished head, flexed his interlaced fingers until they popped. Marrun, nicknamed Stumps for his undeniably short legs, spat a mouthful of juice from the ever-present wad of fig leaves stuffed in his lower lip. Talon abruptly considered the brush around them, as if suddenly concerned that some enemy might have stolen upon them while his attention had been diverted. Kylac couldn't have said if the latter was the soldier's given name, or a moniker assigned on account of his narrow, sharply hooked nose.

"It's nearing dusk," Pommel observed. "We should be heading back."

"And trust one o' the other parties to better luck?" Kylac asked. He clicked his tongue reprovingly. "What happens if'n all return empty-handed?"

"Captain said to be back before dark," Stumps reminded him.

"With the grompike," Kylac said. "Not much cause in returning without it."

Ledron had in fact stood firm on both counts, tacitly ignoring the possibility of failure. Kylac had taken that to mean that each company's appointed leader was to determine on his own the preferred course should discovery of the required tree prove elusive.

"Roam un rove, then," Creyl grumbled, turning from his discovery to retake the point.

Kylac awaited objection from the others, be it the trio of Stone-watch or the nervous cook. Stumps looked to his comrades for support. Pommel evaded by wrenching at the waist, once to each side, releasing a pair of audible snaps from his spine. With a tilt of his neck, Talon deflected the unspoken question to Kylac. Aythef saw none of it, busy breathing a sigh of relief as the space between himself and Creyl increased with the latter's steady departure.

Kylac winked. "A bit farther, eh?"

He slipped forward, a whisper amid the clinging groundcover, leaving it to those who accompanied him to choose for themselves whether to follow. He considered calling Creyl back, lest the half-wild Redfist stray too far ahead, but saw little reason to rein the other in. Even if the tangle thickened to the point of blocking Kylac's vision, it wasn't as if any of them could wander far enough afield to escape his awareness of their positions. He'd known upon requesting Creyl's assignment that the soldier would be the one most likely to strain at the leash. He intended to make use of that enthusiasm, not bridle it.

Talon and Pommel fell into stride almost at once—the former to his right, the latter to his left—staggered upon his flanks a few paces back. Stumps lingered momentarily, his gaze rooted upon the direction from which they'd come. Then he, too, turned to follow.

Only Aythef remained where he'd been standing, forward of their position, beside Creyl's latest false find. His attention was drawn by Kylac's approach. Kylac spared him a brief, encouraging smile. Aythef's mouth twisted sourly in response. Still sore at having been selected to come in the first place, mayhap. But the chief cook had been one of only five men culled from among their crew who claimed to be able to identify the grompike. Two of the others had been Brenham, who'd remained with the *Vengeance* to oversee her repair effort, and Ithrimir, whom Ledron had determined should remain tethered to the ship, as well. As a result, the timorous cook's only real choice had been to join Kylac's party or that of either Raithe or Sanow. As Aythef had stood there, undecided, shunned by both Blackfists and still seeking to persuade their captain that his presence wasn't truly necessary, Kylac had welcomed him, and the matter was settled.

By then, Kylac had ceased being overly selective. Despite the captain's promise to take any requests into consideration, the Head had denied him his first choice, Orlin, due to a desire to keep another Blackfist beside himself in rearguard. Ledron had then proceeded to deny him any with whom he was more familiar—the staunch Warmund, the sharp-eyed Jahvid, or even the somewhat skittish Nadrum. It had come to where Kylac had ceased presenting names and simply asked the captain whom he might suggest. Mayhap these were men whom Ledron suspected of uncertain loyalties. Mayhap it was only the Head plying him with petty games.

Whichever, he'd dutifully accepted those presented him—Pommel, Stumps, and Talon—before requesting Creyl. To his surprise, the captain hadn't balked, but instead shrugged an assent. Kylac had immediately wondered then if it were an unwise choice, but hadn't cared to back down. Once Aythef had been assigned, their company was set.

Soon after, they'd reached the Moravial, proceeding south but half an hour before veering from the main channel to follow a smaller tributary tucked away along the river's western shore. Given the thickly overgrown appearance of the narrow corridor, Kylac hadn't been certain the *Vengeance* would even fit. But Ithrimir had been adamant, and once again proved correct in his assessment.

The great ship had been dragging heavily at the nose by then, leading to a greater number of murmurs as to the wisdom of continuing. Better to put aground at once, many had suggested, rather than wait until she wedged herself face-first into the bottom of the river, to leave them stranded amid some sucking lowland mire. For a time, Ledron had given ear to those voices, allowing them to run unchecked. When all, it seemed, who shared that view had cast their lot, the captain had rebuked them with such force that Kylac believed he'd never truly been considering their opinion, only seeking to measure the number of dissenters aboard.

Ultimately, they'd beached the *Vengeance* upon a spit of land cushioned more by sand than by mud, connected to the western shore by a long, slender causeway of charcoal-colored limestone and packed, rust-tinged clay. Heaps of driftwood lay gathered in the southern crook of the sandbar like bones discarded at a feast, while a forest peppered with hardwoods and evergreens crested the attached overlook. Timber aplenty with which to, first, raise the ship off her forward keel, and second, prepare the planks and braces they would use to properly patch her compromised hull.

All save the grompike.

No sooner had the ship been brought to rest than the three separate parties had set forth as planned. Raithe had been given first choice of direction and headed inland due west. Sanow had then elected the southwesterly track, leaving Kylac's company to venture northwestward. Back toward the primary Ladrakari settlement, Kylac had observed silently. Judging by the expressions of his comrades, he'd not been the only one to make note. None had mentioned it openly, however. Mayhap hoping that enough leagues lay between this location and that to protect them. Mayhap fearful that, by mentioning it, they would make the possibility of running into Chitral or his clansmen more likely.

Of Kylac's companions, only Creyl, then as now, had seemed entirely undaunted, quickly assuming the point without being asked, behaving as though the mission to locate the rare sap were a prize hunt to be won. The vast bulk of the *Vengeance*'s crew had scarcely begun the work of felling trees or scavenging driftwood before the half-wild Redfist had led them into the jungle, pressing through the tangle until all but the echoes of their crew's labors—carried out as noiselessly as possible—were obscured.

Since then, they'd faced a ceaseless progression of trees and under-brush woven together in no discernible pattern. Hale and hearty overarching growth presented in equal measure to wilting leaves, rotting boles, and stunted deadwood. From one patch to the next, it was difficult to tell whether the dying vegetation was choking out the living, or if it was the living that had sprouted triumphantly from the compost of the dead. By turns, the groundcover lay sparse, allowing smooth passage over barren stretches of stone, or surged up to form hedges so tall and thick and tightly wound as to resemble an unbreachable wall. While confident that his own blades could have easily cleaved these stalks, and pressed by the accompanying Red-fists to do so, Kylac had instead bade them circumvent the barriers whenever possible, reminding them that the quieter they were, the safer they would remain.

Another intersected their path now, a great profusion of vines and brambles grown over and around the skeletal remains of a fallen granitewood, its rotted trunk riven with ants and beetles and other insects hunkered from view in cool, shaded patches, but whose pres-ence—and venoms—Kylac could smell. As he came upon the shaggy deadfall, Creyl ventured westward, upslope, deeper into the jungle and toward the tree's massive nest of upturned roots. Kylac followed, and the others followed him. He had no better compass than the half-wild Redfist. Ithrimir had provided them general directions only, along with a handful of clues concerning the type of environment the grompike preferred. A higher, drier elevation for one. A thicker bedding of soil, for another. But there was nothing in particular to suggest that this rise would keep climbing, or that it wouldn't just lead to a bald protrusion of stone. One companion's guess would have been as likely as the next.

An unfamiliar cry stuttered through the brush, a guttural growl that had the outlying members of the company closing ranks and reaching for their sword hilts. Ahead, Creyl stopped, peering westward over the fallen granitewood, crouched and ready. Should a threat present itself, Kylac couldn't have predicted whether the Redfist would launch himself against it, or wait for his companions to do so. Tough, he had to be, to have survived a life within the savage borderlands of the Reach. But *dead* he'd be if he hadn't learned at least some semblance of respect and caution.

Kylac continued forward, maintaining his steady pace, exuding an air of confidence to which he had no particular claim while within this unknown territory. But he knew the others looked to him as to how they should respond, and wanted them to feel as though all was in hand. And he believed that it was. After all, he'd faced down demons and even a dragon. Whatever stalked these wilds, chances were it would be of a far tamer variety than some of those creatures he'd vanquished before, and therefore foolish to show itself.

Mayhap this creature sensed as much, or hadn't been interested in them at all, for several moments passed in which the bestial sound failed to manifest a second time, giving way to the steadier, more rhythmic undertones of the jungle's song—buzzing insects, chirping birds, chittering rodents.

"How far do you intend we stray?" Aythef asked as he ventured nearer to Kylac. The cook's labored breathing, coupled with the softness of his lean limbs and the paunch at his belly, suggested mayhap that he was ill-accustomed to trekking about forested hill-sides. "Marrun may have the right of it. What if the other parties have returned with the sap, and wait now on our return?"

"The repairs'll take half the night, regardless. They'll not likely depart without us, if'n that's your concern."

"You don't know that."

Kylac considered arguing, then shrugged. "I suppose not. But what sense in worrying over a challenge that may never manifest?"

"To prepare for the chance that it might. To avoid making a foolish decision."

A fanciful notion, to Kylac's thinking. People spent so much time puzzling through the potential hazards of their lives, guessing at consequences and trying to avoid those they deemed unpleasant. Of what help was that when events took unexpected form? All at once, one was left as unprepared as if they'd never wasted time considering it. Or worse, startled into paralysis by mismatched expectation, else committed to a course from which it would be too late to redirect. Anticipation paid its occasional reward. But better to react, Kylac had found, than to follow some strict, preconceived path through an inconstant, duplicitous world.

"Every decision carries the potential for foolishness," he said. "Ya might sidestep chance here or there, but there's no outwitting it."

Aythef frowned, his youthful brow creasing with annoyance. "Is that how you justify your recklessness? Jeopardizing the lives of those around you?"

Kylac stifled a laugh. "Been eavesdropping on your captain, has ya?"

"The men all talk of it. How we wouldn't be here, were it not for you. How we *shouldn't*."

That again. Kylac had seen it in their gazes, where he hadn't heard it in their whispers. But he wasn't about to let it trouble him, thinking it now, as then, a byproduct of their shared uncertainty, their common fear. He'd known even before foiling the accord between Kendarrion and Grendavan that his deeds would be judged harshly by some—justifiably so. But he'd also spent enough hours among the people of Avenell, those outside Kendarrion's court, to know that not all held Prince Dethaniel's life sacred enough to buy it back in ransom. For every man who named Kylac meddler, enemy, rakehell, there were many others, back on Addaranth, who praised his courage and defiance. While their stake in these matters might seem less immediate, who was to say that theirs was not the more defensible view?

"Tell me," Kylac said softly, his greater senses still attuned to their surroundings, "is there any among the crew who bears standard on the matter?"

"What matter?"

"My, shall we say, *unwelcome* involvement."

"A common account, I said."

"From the outset? As I know them, sailors and soldiers are prone to debate, if'n only to combat boredom. Was there none who first fanned the flames against me?"

Aythef seemed to withdraw, taking a step away from him while glancing around at the loose circle of their comrades. "Why ask me this?"

"You're the chief cook. Beloved of every man aboard. Privy to discussion, mayhap, that others aren't, be it direct or indirect."

"Not, why *me*. Why the question? Would you think to use me to eliminate your enemies?"

Kylac glanced over with an arched brow. Enemies, was it? Doubters, he'd have said. Naysayers. But outright enemies? "Is the attitude against me so strong? Who were the first to raise it? Or the most vehement?"

"His Majesty cursed your meddling from the outset, given whispers within the palace. These men are sworn to him. Yet you expect some would question his wisdom? Take *your* side?"

"Not *my* side. The side o' resistance. The side that wouldn't so readily cow to an enemy's treachery."

Aythef snorted. "What would *you* know of it? Acting on raw whim and half-baked instinct?"

Where before he'd felt the reproachful cook was simply sore at having been dragged from the relative safety of the *Vengeance*, Kylac wondered now whether his young companion harbored some deeper bitterness. For he seemed on the edge of a sterner, more personal rebuke, fueled by something other than hearsay. "Is there more I should learn o' the matter?"

Aythef's gaze speared him momentarily, hot as a poker, before shattering in a burst of mirthless laughter. "How could you presume elsewise?" With Kylac waiting on him to say more, he shook his head. "I'm given to trust in those who command me. Safer I'd feel if you could say the same."

Kylac frowned, pitying the lad his servant's mentality, while at the same time frustrated by his recalcitrance. He had half a mind to etch it out for the lad on a slate—his suspicion that the Grenarr had an informant among them, for which he could use another pair of eyes and ears in order to ferret the individual—or individuals—out. As chief cook, Aythef had access to almost every man aboard at one time or another. And he knew more about each of them, in all likelihood, than Kylac would be able to discern before whoever it was could enact some further act of betrayal or sabotage.

At the same time, he could scarcely fault the lad his criticisms. To his eyes, Kylac had done nothing to warrant trust—while steeped from the outset in negative rumor. Mayhap, before this voyage was ended, Kylac would find a way to win among these skeptical crewmen an ally or two. But it didn't seem likely to happen now.

Would that it might before it was too late.

They journeyed until the close of the Crow's Hour and on through the Cardinal's, pressing through nightfall and the darkness that descended with it. Debate was raised again by Stumps as to when, exactly, they might surrender their search and turn back toward the *Vengeance*. Were they to beat their way through the unfamiliar brush all night? How were they to find in the deep dark what they'd been unable to spy in the daylight?

But the complaints were mostly strengthless, half-muttered grievances when set against the eager determination exhibited by Kylac and Creyl, and the noncommittal stance of Talon and Pommel. Even Aythef's support for Stumps's pleas was only loosely given, as if he understood the odds arrayed against him. The paths before them were sufficiently visible, illuminated by a cloudless wash of moonlight bolstered by the glow of a myriad stars. Though loosely filtered by the jungle canopy, and dimmed occasionally by passing curtains of brume, the night's silver radiance shone bright enough. And the surrounding creatures continued to prove more wary than curious. Save for stubborn swarms of insects, the native wildlife allowed them to pass unhindered. Unless Pommel and Talon were to tire of the quest and tip the scales toward opposition, there was no real impetus to turn back. Even if the latter were to happen, Kylac had already determined to invite those with flagging hearts to seek their own return, to explain to their captain their failure.

Fortunately, it didn't came to that. Though Stumps sulked and Aythef brooded, both matched pace dutifully enough, keeping the company intact for the moment in which Pommel called out abruptly for them to hold.

"I may have something," he said. The others stood patiently while the Redfist thrashed his way through a hedge of gnarled bushes to their left, then pushed through a veil of mossy vines. He disappeared from view, only to whoop with triumph a moment later. "Our march is ended, mates!"

Kylac caught the various reactions of his comrades—Creyl's scowl, Stumps's doubt, Aythef's hope. Then, all three were rushing after Pommel, beating a trail through the tall brush. Talon waited on a gesture from Kylac before he, too, followed.

When gathered again, it indeed appeared that their search had concluded. Within a copse of fir, alder, and fire poplar sprouted a pair of trunks with a tubular root base, such as Aythef had described. From these boles, amid a twining of interspersed limbs, branched those with broad, three-pointed leaves, thickly veined and serrated along the edges. Kylac felt a knot of certainty bloom in his stomach. Unless they'd been misled, this was the tree they'd been seeking.

"Grompike," Aythef confirmed. "Two, in fact."

Talon whistled, a congratulatory tone. Pommel grinned, while Stumps sighed in apparent relief. Only Creyl seemed disappointed, glaring and frowning as if he'd been cheated of his prize. "Fool's fortune," he groused. "Who ya done buggering, eh?"

Pommel just smiled all the broader, then withdrew the axe strapped to his back. "Clear me some room then, *tah?*"

Aythef stumbled back as the other Redfists—Creyl, Stumps, and Talon—unsheathed their own axes and set about chopping through the shielding tangle to have at the grompikes in the center. A noisome affair it soon became, made louder by the lively banter between soldiers—a flurry of challenges and insults, each coming faster than the next.

"Must they make such a din about it?" Aythef asked Kylac, his own voice low as he cast about at the fluttering of displaced creatures and the scattered echoes that rippled outward, conveyed endlessly, it seemed, from one attending tree to the next.

Kylac had considered it already. But as it seemed unlikely they'd be able to complete the task quietly, given all the hacking, snapping, and cracking involved, he'd decided they might as well focus on doing it quickly. "Let's not *sap* their enthusiasm, eh?"

Aythef's scowl deepened, mouth twisting in disapproval of either Kylac's decision, or his fool-worthy wordplay. More likely a dash of both.

"As much as we can carry," Kylac reminded Stumps as the Red-fist deposited at their feet the first branch severed from the pair of grompikes. That had been Ledron's order. A sensible one, given that they knew not how many of the parties who'd gone in search would prove successful, how much of the sap could be harvested from the samples returned, or how much would be required overall for their repairs.

"We?" Stumps grunted dryly in response. He turned away without explanation. Kylac required none. So long as the soldier completed the assigned task, Kylac would gladly suffer whatever disrespect was deemed warranted.

Without being asked, Creyl clambered up the trunks to gain access to the higher branches. Undaunted no matter how precarious his perch, he labored dutifully to clear out some of the heartier limbs, if not necessarily the thickest. They still had miles to march with their growing bounty in tow. While felling the trees at their base might have provided the greatest yield, little good it would do them—or the grompikes—if they chopped down pieces too unwieldy to transport.

While the half-wild Redfist worked from above, the others toiled below, hacking at the lower limbs and clearing from the tangled copse those that were shed. When it came time for Talon and Pommel to shorten some of the longer branches into more manageable segments, Aythef stepped forward to assist by bracing one end or the other. The cook then helped to strip away some of the twigs and leaves, as adept at the task as if he were shucking corn or plucking a chicken.

Kylac stood silent and watchful as the others labored, accepting the pointed stares leveled at him from time to time, not bothering to explain that his aloofness owed not to laziness, but to vigilance against

the arrival of anyone or anything that might threaten their efforts.
With the bulk of the company preoccupied, it seemed prudent that
at least one of them remain at full alert, ready to rise to their defense.
He'd begun to sense that they weren't alone, though he preferred not
to alarm anyone by articulating as much. Especially when the source
of the warning sensation wasn't yet clear to him. He hadn't seen, heard,
or smelled the approach of anything intending them harm. But that
was the itch he now felt worming up from inside.

An itch he knew better than to ignore.

"Looks to me just about enough, lads," he decided moments later,
seeing the heap of grompike branches grow and feeling the mounting
pressure of whatever unknown entity stalked them. "Let's sweep it up."

The soldiers obeyed, Creyl descending from the nest of twining
tree limbs to help the others gather and finish stripping the last of the
hewn branches. The effort required only a few moments more—a
final separation of prepared pieces from the discards, the former neatly
stacked, the latter heaped to one side or strewn about the work area.

They next set about dividing the piled branches into smaller bundles, and lashing these together with rope. When each man had
gathered a bundle and hefted it over one shoulder, Kylac did the
same—only to present his to Stumps.

"Do you mean not to dirty your hands at all?" the Redfist asked,
flushing indignantly.

"Take it," Kylac urged. "Then fumble it and chase it to the ground."

"What? Why would I—"

Kylac half tossed the bundle onto the Redfist's free shoulder.
Stumps endeavored to catch it, only to unbalance himself and his
existing load in the process.

"Of all the bloody . . ." the soldier grumbled as he dropped both
and bent after them in reflex.

Narrowly avoiding the javelin that hurtled from out of the jungle
to skim his back.

Kylac was already moving, using the staged distraction to draw a
throwing knife and hurl it in the direction from which the missile
had flown. He heard it stick into a body too fleshy to be wood, and
took grim satisfaction in the accompanying shriek of pained surprise.

There was no time to savor the fortune of the strike, for the victim's companions burst then from the wall of vegetation, with a chorus of howls that drowned out that of their wounded comrade. Mookla'ayan hunters, as might have been expected. Whether hailing from Chitral's village or some other habitation scarcely seemed to matter. Whether dispatched with the express purpose of tracking those who'd abducted Sa'ahla, or simply a stray party in search of game, counted for little more. Whatever, they clearly hadn't come extending an offer of friendship.

Kylac accepted this while darting behind the nearest trunk—a rough-skinned conifer—and drawing his swords. The shorter in his left hand, the longer in his right. Each slender and lightweight and slightly curved. Single-edged like a saber, but with a small, disc-shaped crosspiece he'd fashioned himself, and a blade that had never been nicked. Stronger than any known ore, any known metal, forged or shaped by human hand.

And, in his hands, far deadlier.

Kylac brought them to bear in a pair of twirling arcs as he came around the trunk to flank the charging elves, intercepting their van-guard. The foremost hunters were still focused on Stumps and the rest of the small company of intruders, most of whom still clung to their bundles of grompike wood in openmouthed shock. If any of the attackers had seen Kylac spin aside, they certainly weren't prepared for his sudden, unheralded return. The Mookla'ayan serving point scarcely had time to turn his head before a slashing strike swiped it from his shoulders.

The trailing elves scattered like a school of fish, darting around him in sudden bursts of redirection. For half a heartbeat, Kylac feared he would have to run down each separately in order to engage them. But as quickly as they'd peeled off to one flank or the other, the Mookla'ayans spun back, closing round the immediate threat as they might a larger predator, bringing their superior numbers to bear in a concerted effort to kill him quickly.

Precisely as he wished.

Nine in all, he observed instinctively. He couldn't have easily counted them any other way, given the swiftness of their movements—their

lunging legs, thrusting arms, stabbing javelins. In all, a vortex of
sharpened stakes. A raking, piercing tempest from which there should
have been no escape.

But Kylac wasn't seeking escape. With a sensation like liquid fire
igniting his veins, he went to work. His swords spun like the blades
of a windmill, fanning near and wide to block or swat aside the
weapons that reached for him. Where intercepted by a blade's edge,
the heads of his assailants' javelins fell away, the hafts sliced clean
through like soft fruit. At the same time, his body shifted amid the
storm like that of a serpent—coiling, arcing, leaping, weaving from
harm's way with a swiftness that others had called inhuman.

Human or not, the elves couldn't touch him, and he began to
lash out in response. Before they understood the danger they'd so
heedlessly rushed into, three of the nine were dead or dying, pierced
or gashed or spurting their life's blood from the stumps of severed
limbs. A tenth—the initial javelin-thrower—stumbled into view,
clutching at the handle of the knife protruding from his ribs. He did
so only to watch two more of his companions fall, and then another
pair after that. Kylac wasn't discerning. He countered against what
was exposed and whittled it down, be it crude weapon, rigid bone, or
supple flesh. Wasting no movement, he scored a block or a hit with
every swat, slice, or jab. Strings of blood filled the air, while streams
and puddles fed the earth.

Shrieks and screams echoed through the night.

It ended so swiftly that none had the presence of mind to withdraw—to consider fleeing or to direct their attacks toward one or
more of Kylac's companions instead. Elves they were, swifter than
most men, but their decision to burst into that narrow grove of jungle,
seeking to catch the intruders unaware, was the last they would ever
consciously make.

Their dying was completely involuntary.

When the last of the nine fell from his swords, Kylac cast about
the circle with an air of regret. It felt a cruelty, to have slain them all.
But reaction and instinct had left little choice. Though he searched
for one whose wounds might not be immediately mortal, he knew
already, upon replaying the carnage in his mind, what he would find.

While a few gasped desperately or reached out in plaintive denial, none had sufficient voice to beg quarter or spit curses or answer questions, their throats slashed or their lungs punctured or their spines severed. Most had suffered some combination of the three.

In final hope, he turned toward the javelin-thrower, only to find the elf facedown in a patch of blood-spattered leaves and thorny groundcover.

Amid the smell of blood and entrails and loosened bowels, Kylac looked back to his comrades. A wide-eyed daze had overcome them, freezing them in place. Most had managed no more than to drop their bundles and fall back in a protective crouch. Creyl was the only one who'd freed a blade, though he looked at it now as if uncertain where it had come from, or what he might do with it. Aythef bent over to retch at his own feet.

"Shards," Talon gasped.

Pommel tried to speak, fighting through the lump in his throat to summon words on the second attempt. Even then, little more than a hoarse croak. "Who . . . ? Where did they . . . ?"

"I doubts they're hunting alone," Kylac replied. The Mookla'ayans were only scantily clad, so he used his own cloak to wipe his blades clean. He fetched his throwing knife, the body of the javelin-thrower twitching in protest. "Would seem wise that we hurry."

His companions stared dumbly, still stricken by what they'd witnessed. Kylac had seen such expressions before, and knew them to serve no useful purpose. "Wits, lads. Let's move."

He stepped toward them to demonstrate how, helping to retrieve the discarded bundles of grompike limbs. As Stumps was the nearest, he was the first to be loaded up again.

"With your leave, might be best I remain unencumbered," Kylac suggested, offering the Redfist the second bundle that he'd previously sought to reject.

Stumps nodded mutely as he accepted the burden, shouldering it without complaint.

17

A ROSY TWILIGHT SUFFUSED the prevailing mist, the first faint blush of predawn rays lending color if not clarity to the protrusion of land on which the wounded *Vengeance* remained at rest. Echoes of the crew's activity filled Kylac's ears, a dull clamor of scraping saws and pounding hammers, crackling flames and popping branches, humming ropes and squeaking pulleys, tramping feet and grumbled commands. Taken together, they comprised an unnatural tone overlaying the soft lapping of the Moravial's slow-rising waters, the croaking of frogs and toads along the river's banks, and the fading cries of nightbirds and other nocturnal predators looking to complete their business amid the forested heights to the west. Similarly, the alien odors of sap, tar, ash, and wood shavings mingled with the brackish smell of the river and the pungent scents of the land—of fresh growth and rotting timbers, of blooming flowers and moldering underbrush. For hours now, the two had clashed—sounds and scents both manmade and natural—until merging into one, a sensory blend comprised of elements that *belonged*.

Kylac cared only for those that didn't.

He was seated on a flat boulder, chipped and jagged about the edges, but worn smooth upon its table-top surface. The stone slab lay situated amid a scattering of others a hundred paces inland, just above the sand line that divided the lower reaches of the peninsula from the more rugged elevations bridging to the island proper. A great causeway, had there been keep or holdfast at its summit. Lacking that, just a finger of earth by which their enemies might descend upon them—those who hunted them by land, at least.

Those were the ones Kylac had been set to warn against. Other lookouts, Whitefists, had been posted along the river's banks or aloft aboard the ship to warn of discovery by the Grenarr. Unless an alarm sounded on that front, Kylac's charge was to ignore the waterways and monitor the jungle, on the chance that Chitral or his Ladrakari clansmen happened to find them first.

His small shore party had encountered no further packs or patrols as they'd made their return. The expectation that they might had been sufficient to silence his comrades, even when the shock of the natives' attack had thawed and some had sought to remark on the awe and horror inherent in what they'd witnessed. Having no desire to speak of his ruthless—however necessary—response, Kylac had curtailed their comments and questions with a simple reminder that the danger of another assault would remain until they were safely aboard their ship, sailing clear once more of Mistwall's shoreline. Until then, best that they remain quiet and alert.

That threat had only served, however, while his companions traipsed through the jungle, laden with their parcels of grompike branches, casting wary glances into the surrounding foliage and flinching at every small flutter or cry. Upon their unmolested return to the *Vengeance*, the tale had spread like ale from an overturned barrel, flooding through the ranks of the crew, seeping into every ear. The resulting curiosity had run unchecked, reactions ranging from compliments and praise to skepticism and a deepening mistrust. Whichever way one skewed, most wanted to know more—about his training, his blades, his background. Some urged him to demonstrate, either to justify their disbelief, else expose and demystify these pre-ternatural skills. Though they'd witnessed him at play throughout the ship, exercising acrobatics and, to a lesser degree, practicing with his swords, his slaughter of the natives as described by their fellow crewmen bespoke another variety of talent altogether. What was he, some breed of sorcerer?

It had taken Pevrick, with Ledron's backing, to disperse those hounding him, setting them to one task or another relating to the repair of the *Vengeance*, or ordering them to stand down and take rest until it became their turn to contribute. Both Raithe's company and Sanow's had already returned, having met with some small success, so the effort to heat the gathered grompike limbs and thereby withdraw the tree's blood was under way. Given the meager amount of saplings scraped up between the two, and with Kylac's party so late in reporting, there'd been discussion about sending them both out again. With Kylac's arrival and the relative bounty his company had managed to reap, those efforts were put aside. But there was still much to be done, and time didn't favor them.

So Ledron had taken the further step of isolating Kylac from the rest of the crew, setting him upon his inland watch post, where the ongoing murmurs concerning him were of minimal hindrance. Had Kylac believed the decision was made for his benefit, he might have thanked the captain for doing so.

Roughly six hours had passed since, with Ledron only once sending a man, Simalen, to relieve him. Kylac had politely declined, assuring the veteran Redfist that he was awake and alert and better suited than any other to his appointed task. Simalen had eyed him doubtfully, but stopped short of challenge, glancing up at the distant ridge of jungle before grunting in response that he would go back and see what the captain had to say about it. Unless Kylac had missed his guess, the Redfist had been all too happy to turn about. Certainly, the fact that he hadn't returned suggested that neither the soldier nor his acting captain cared enough to debate the matter.

The night's chill lingered now as it had then, deepened by a dampness in the air, brought on by the thickening brume. It never truly grew cold in this region of the world, insofar as Kylac had experienced, but there remained something about the absence of the sun, so bright and blistering during the day, that sapped the warmth from his skin. Or mayhap it was again only the brush of the mist, clammy and invasive, that clutched at his clothes and his flesh as if seeking to weigh him down, reluctant to let him leave.

His senses tightened, triggered by an approach at his back. He felt it first as a tingling in his blood, the detection of a solitary strand unraveling from the web of activity at the tip of the peninsula, reaching toward him. He didn't bother to turn, for the advance was distant yet, and of no threat. He nonetheless surrendered his reflections, releasing them like trailers of smoke, closing his eyes and narrowing his focus.

A moment later, his ears confirmed it. Booted footsteps belonging to a lone man, borne by a measured pace neither hurried nor stealthy, just steady with purpose. The weight of the gait, the length of stride, became familiar.

"How fare we, Captain?" he asked in greeting, still without turning, when the Head had come to within a dozen paces.

Ledron evinced no surprise at Kylac's ability to identify him sight unseen. By now, he knew to expect as much. "We've plugged the forward gash as best we can. Still need time for it to set. Which it seems we'll have, because the damage to the keel is worse than we believed."

Forcing them to dig deeper to clean out the wounds. That would explain the ongoing ruckus, much of which should have subsided by now. Kylac nodded an acknowledgment, then slid over to make room should the captain wish to sit beside him.

Ledron ignored the gesture, crossing his arms and peering up at the rising slope.

"How's our Scribe?" Kylac asked.

"Keeping out of sight, per my request."

Despite all the commotion regarding his brief skirmish in the woods, Kylac had neither seen nor heard from Ithrimir on the matter, the Elementer keeping—or kept—from view during his return and subsequent watch assignment. Whichever, be it late or soon, he would have to face the Sea Scribe concerning the slaughter of his former subjects. Something about that reckoning had touched upon Kylac's nerves—a tinge of regret made worse by the stir that had resulted. While he felt no particular shame, he didn't want Ithrimir believing he'd taken any sort of pleasure in his actions, either. For some reason, not knowing how the Scribe might feel about it had caused him to wish he could reconcile matters sooner rather than later.

"No sign o' Grenarr, I gather."

Ledron grunted and shook his head. In turn, Kylac said nothing for a moment, uncertain yet of the captain's purpose in coming to see him, only knowing that it hadn't likely been to enjoy his company or to be plied with questions. Mayhap, if left unprodded, the Head would come around to revealing his intent.

"The woods are quiet?" Ledron asked finally.

As quiet as could be, with all the splitting, cracking, and sanding of planks that echoed across the open expanse of the peninsula's length. But Kylac sensed that the Head needed to hear something somewhat more reassuring. "The elves are busy elsewhere, it seems."

He waited through another prolonged silence. Mayhap the captain required further prodding after all. Kylac decided to cease fencing and call the other out. "Ya might as easily has sent a herald to request report."

Ledron rubbed a hand over his bald pate, fringed now with a gray-blond stubble matching that which had sprouted from his chin. His eyes had grown increasingly dark and hollowed, presumably from a lack of sleep during their voyage. Scarcely given a chance to recover from their ordeal in trekking across the Harrows before undertaking this mission, it seemed a marvel he remained upright at all.

"I've had available hands scouring the vessel in your absence," the captain confessed finally, in a tone heavy with reluctance. "They've produced no evidence of stowaways."

Ah. So it's the mole what's got ya troubled. Kylac withheld reply, waiting for Ledron to find his gaze. When finally their eyes met, he shrugged. "A prudent gesture. But don't let it trouble ya. The mole was merely a notion. Our pursuers might has happened upon us by some other means."

The response was intended to be soothing, but seemed to have the opposite effect on Ledron, whose brow and stance tightened with anger. "Adamant you were before. Enough to accuse even me, as I recall."

"Would ya confess to the role?"

The captain's cheeks reddened. "This remains a game to you, does it?"

"It's all a game, my friend. Our dogged pursuit o' whims and fancies . . . mere posturing until the darkness comes calling."

"Spare me your aimless worldviews. Some of us are given to a greater purpose."

"Inflicted with a greater sense o' self-importance, ya mean," Kylac replied, then hurried to stave off the next rebuke. "However ya describes it, I understand your seriousness, Captain, and respect your dedication. Has I not shed blood enough to convince ya o' mine?"

"The only blood you shed is that of others. And you seem to do so as it pleases you, none other."

An unfair assessment, but Kylac saw nothing to be gained in debating the matter. He didn't require Ledron's approval to do what he believed he must. "If'n suffering is the sole measure o' dedication, I'll admit, I . . ."

He dismissed the thought as the scent reached his nose, a distinctive musk blown down from the heights. Faint, distant, yet unmistakable.

"What is it?" Ledron asked, head turning so that his gaze chased inland after Kylac's.

"Finish your repairs, Captain. Time runs dry."

"The savages?" The Head's voice knotted with tension and denial.

"In force, by the smell of it."

"Too soon," Ledron hissed through gritted teeth. "Shove off now, we'll go straight to the bottom of the channel."

And yet, the river's waters were retreating again, having cycled through a midnight knave's tide and a predawn king's tide. Should they fail to slide free of their makeshift dry dock now . . . "If'n we don't leave soon, we'll has to hold off half a day for the tide to reverse course and carry us clear."

Ledron murmured a string of curses beneath his breath. "I hear nothing. How close are they?"

"The breeze isn't that strong. Within a league, I'd wager. At best, half an hour away."

"How many men would you need to stall them?"

Kylac considered the thread of broken earth between themselves and the mainland. Narrow, but widening with the ebbing tideflow. "It wouldn't take but a score to build a two-deep phalanx there,"

Kylac replied, indicating a thin, crooked hump some ninety paces west of their position. "Might stopper 'em there for a half-mark, if'n they number less than a hundred. More than that will overrun us without breaking stride."

"We could erect a barricade—"

"None that the receding waters won't expose at the flanks. And not one high enough to deter a Mookla'ayan hunter." Kylac faced the Head squarely. "I'll gives ya an hour, Captain. Aim for more, and we'll be hunkered behind the ship's bulwark like a castle parapet, defending the vessel herself from siege."

Ledron's clenched jaw worked from side to side, teeth grinding. "An hour, you say."

"We don't leave by then, we may not leave at all."

Ledron's jaw hinged open, then snapped shut without speaking. Rounding abruptly, the captain stormed east again, back toward the ship, his stride lengthening, his pace this time hurried and angry. Kylac did nothing to stop him, his own attentions focused westward, to discern what he could of the approaching natives. A handful of desperate options flashed through his mind: silencing themselves in the hope that the Ladrakari would be unable to so easily locate them, forming one or more diversionary packs in an effort to fragment and draw away the gathered pursuit, or mustering a larger force and setting forth to ambush their adversaries further inland.

But each alternative seemed less plausible than the last, with more to be lost than could possibly be gained. The natives would find the ship, if they hadn't already. A battle at this point was unavoidable. Better to keep their own strength intact, and to avoid the woodland domain with which the elves were more familiar, more adept. A defensive line at a chokepoint, out in the open, where they might hope to throttle whatever numbers the elves brought to bear . . . Buying what time they could for the captain and his crew to expedite their repair work and launch clear of their grounding point . . .

Of the available strategies, it was the only sensible one left to them.

Bolstered by his reasoning, Kylac accepted the chill warning building in his stomach and set forward at a comfortable trot, to gain the inland rise on which he would make his stand.

Wondering idly if chance might have it be his last.

18

Twenty minutes later, the natives found them.

The dawning sun had scarcely crested the horizon, its golden hues spilling across the peninsula in a warm wash, etching patterns through the darkness until only a tattered shroud of shadows remained. Kylac watched his own appear on the ground at his feet, a caricature tall and lean, emerging from that of a hedgerow of jagged spikes cast by their driftwood barricade and the spears and halberds of the soldiers clustered around him. Not a moment later, he sensed a subtle tremor in the earth, heard the shriek and flutter of displaced wildlife on the wooded ridgeline, and watched solitary birds flock as one from the ragged line of trees.

"Positions, lads," Kylac bade them.

Even given to expect the natives' arrival, the soldiers come to stand with him peered up in doubt or surprise. Most were still gathering rocks or dragging driftwood trunks, piling them onto the makeshift wall. Kylac himself stood atop the barrier, guiding a twisted log into place. A feeble cordon, but it would have to do.

Sooner than he'd hoped, their time had run out.

A fierce cry trumpeted this fact as the Ladrakari vanguard burst from the tree line, screaming like hawks as their prey came to view. A loose, jagged front they formed, stretching some twenty, thirty, forty paces from north flank to south. The length of spread didn't bode well. As more and more elves emerged from the jungle to fill the gaps between flanks, Kylac's fears were confirmed. This was no small hunting party, but a relative battalion by Mookla'ayan standards, come to reclaim that which the thieving outlanders had taken from them, and, in doing so, massacre them for their trouble.

Witnessing the growing horde with their own eyes, Redfists and Blackfists alike dropped their stones and branches and scurried into place behind the wall, taking up shields and weapons as they fell into formation. Ten abreast in each of two lines, forward and rear. Concentrated to either side in a reverse wedge.

"Mother embrace us," Talon whispered, with an eye to the heavens and a prayerful warding gesture.

Standing centrally among them, Kylac glanced reflexively skyward. Seeing no help descending from that quarter, he drew his blades. "Archers," he called to the squad of bowmen, ten strong, backing up their phalanx. "Let's not be stingy with those arrows."

Jaleth, the Whitefist sent to serve as squad commander, nodded resolutely. His face, however, was as pale as the gloves his order's members wore on ceremonial occasions. Kylac recalled how the sailor, serving as coxswain during his mission to free the Sea Scribe, had initially ordered him abandoned—only to dutifully return when summoned. He wondered which might happen here.

Farther east, upon the sandbar at the foot of the peninsula, shouts of alarm rang about the beached *Vengeance*, sending those tending to her into a renewed frenzy. Kylac could only hope that Ledron had taken his warning seriously, and that the crew was on pace to embark within the hour. If not, then his purpose here, however well served, would only delay the inevitable.

The elven screams had swelled into a bestial howl that echoed across the surrounding riverlands. The far-ranging din triggered in Kylac the hope that the Grenarr presumed to be hunting them were well south by now, lost amid the maze of tributaries comprising the Shrouded Skein, unable to hear or retrace the sound. He didn't care to consider how they might raise a defense if trapped between their enemies.

Distant concerns, he reminded himself, compared to that streaming down upon his position now. He took a rough count as to the number of elves brought to bear. Twoscore, threescore, four. Mayhap a fifth. Already near the maximum he'd told Ledron they might be able to withstand, with more still trailing from the woods in reserve. He sensed their indignation and fury, and the bloodthirsty excitement at having cornered their prey. He sensed, too, the fear and gut-wrenching nervousness of the much smaller company of men around him.

"Trust in your assignments, lads," Kylac urged. "Ya need worry only about the enemy in front o' ya. The men beside ya will do the same."

"We know our work," Raithe barked crossly. "Don't we, men?"

His challenging holler was met with a half-hearted cheer. *Not against elves, ya don't,* Kylac thought, but withheld the disparaging notion, hoping they might prove him wrong. He glanced around at their faces, the soldiers chosen for this task. A score in all, only half of whom he'd spent any measurable time with. "Pommel" Ebens and "Stumps" Marrun. The beak-nosed Talon and the half-wild Creyl. The quartet of "Rags," "Lisp," "Mutton," and "Graves," engaged, it had seemed, in a perpetual game of knucklebones since setting forth from Avenell. And Orlin, his sometime training partner and pupil, the only other Blackfist beside Raithe to join them.

The remainder were familiar to him by one feature or another while met in passing aboard the ship, else recognizable from a reference given by one of their comrades. The squint-eyed Andrel, said to strike true with a spear, and the thick-limbed Moh, said to be stout with a shield. Quiet Ysander claimed a heavy hand with his pole-axe, while boisterous Drewes staked claim to having survived no fewer than seven groll attacks during an event dubbed the Season of the Swarm, at the edge of the Ukinhan Wilds a decade past. Turrech, Wooton, Jethmus—capable all, they and the rest, for Ledron to have entrusted them with this assignment. Else deemed expendable to the larger effort to rescue Dethaniel, and thus sent forth as frontline fodder. Kylac might not know which until it was too late.

But then, his dependence on them stretched only so far with regard to their aims here. His own life, as always, rested firmly in his own hands.

He shook those hands to loosen his grip on his sword hilts, closing his eyes while breathing deep of the brackish air. In doing so, he reached out for the familiar, unseen energies of the natural world around him, seeking their rhythm and meshing with their flow. Finding the calm amid the chaos. The resultant tingling surged up his spine and spilled out through his shoulders, rushing down toward the tips of his fingers and back again, a welcome wash that crackled in his veins like caged lightning . . .

He opened his eyes as the leading Ladrakari converged, funneled by the narrowing peninsula into a tight knot of screaming forms. Lithe and agile, they flowed into the shallow ravine at the base of the stone-and-driftwood barricade and came bounding up the other side, spear tips leading as they scrambled up and over the defensive wall.

A curtain of arrows greeted them, fired at close range, piercing them with sufficient force to fling them back or knock them aside. Others were caught upon the spears and pikes braced in welcome. In a sudden reversal of pitch and tone, howls of bloodlust gave way to shrieks of pain, fury transformed abruptly into dismay.

But the next wave crested immediately on the heels of the first, fresh elves clawing past their wounded kin before Addaran blades could be withdrawn from the still-thrashing bodies. Trained to work in tandem, the secondary line of defenders pushed forward to absorb the new rush while their comrades finished their killing business, the converging sides of their open wedge herding the attackers toward the center like a closing trap.

Where Kylac waited.

At the heart of the melee, he churned like a maelstrom, whipping and fanning his blades in ceaseless arcs and sudden thrusts. The Mookla'ayans wore no armor, simplifying his work. Soft leather and sinewy flesh parted beneath his swords' edges like overripe fruit. Even their thin bones, given a clean stroke, offered only perfunctory resistance. Seldom did it come to that, as Kylac directed his strikes at joints and tendons and vital organs, maiming and disabling if not killing, often with a single hack or stab.

He left it to his comrades to finish off the wounded, reaching forward and from side to side to meet and dispatch the new arrivals.

He'd warned the men to give him room to play, lest they fall within his reach. There wasn't a one of them he'd spare if it meant compromising their overall position. While most had scowled or snickered at the threat, they seemed now to be taking the caution to heart.

Within moments, he'd settled into a smooth rhythm of advance and withdraw, whirring and lunging as needed to maintain the slaughter. While some bodies were dragged away, others began to pile at his feet, some sightless, some squirming, some seeking even in their critical condition to lash out at him or his companions. Kylac ended or disrupted those efforts as he did all others, relying on instinct as much as his physical senses, acting and reacting as it seemed best in and between each heartbeat that pulsed in his chest.

On less favorable ground, the defensive effort would have been short-lived. But the thin breadth of the earthen corridor, the height and unevenness of their bulwark, the steady barrage of friendly arrows, and Kylac's acumen all worked in their favor. The elves couldn't have known what they were truly up against, and in their haste had yet to come to terms with it. That they kept hurling themselves at him bespoke a savage frenzy or foolish desperation, either of which played into his hands.

Then Pommel went down beside him, a Ladrakari spear tip ripping through his throat in a ghastly eruption of blood and severed tissue. At almost the same time, Drewes tripped over an elf's corpse, pitching sidelong into Turrech's back so that both tumbled askew. Before Turrech could recover, a wounded Mookla'ayan buried a curved blade through the side of his heart, spitting a vile curse even while choking on a mouthful of blood.

Kylac veered from the frontline long enough to save Drewes and restore order behind him, then surged ahead to cut down a concerted rush made by four elves. A fifth leaped clear over his head, only to be intercepted by the tandem of Ysander and Moh. The ground, however, was fast becoming untenable, heaped and blood-slicked. Even Kylac was becoming hard-pressed to find clear footing amid the carnage.

Despite their initial success, mere minutes had passed when their flanks were breached. Both at once, by design or misfortune. The Redfists positioned there held only momentarily before being

overwhelmed. With Kylac's aid, Orlin and Andrel recovered quickly
to the north, lunging forward to repel the overeager attackers. To the
south, however, Rags took a spear in the stomach that, when pulled
free, brought with it a squirming tangle of entrails. Raithe froze at
the sight, just long enough to miss the enemy stroke that disabled
his sword arm before a Mookla'ayan longknife plunged through his
eye socket clear to the hilt.

With that, the southern flank crumbled, soldiers stumbling back in
instinctive despair as a line of attackers flooded through the resulting
breach. Kylac spun in that direction, but as soon as he did so, the
north opened up again, a clutch of elves dragging Andrel down as
a pincushion. Orlin retaliated with a vengeful charge, only to be
received as if by a pack of wolves, summarily tugged and torn and
carved into pieces.

"Fall back!" Kylac shouted, even as he himself advanced, a funnel
cloud of razored edges seeking to suck all enemies toward him.

It proved effective, if overly so. The Ladrakari converged on him
from three sides, cresting the bulwark and skirting its ragged edges.
Kylac was forced to accelerate in response, his movements little more
than a blur. There he held, a moment, two, three, with the weight
of the press closing round like a noose.

When he, too, felt near to being overwhelmed, he tore free in a
whirling flourish that sent shards of spears, strings of blood, and slivers
of bone spinning through the air. He rolled back, trusting that his
men had done the same. A pair—Mutton and Graves—were racing
for the *Vengeance* at full sprint. Lisp hobbled along in their wake. The
rest of the survivors had the sense to retreat in a more controlled
manner, fighting their pursuers in rearguard formation, successful
thus far only in that Kylac had drawn the bulk of the enemy, and that
Jaleth's squad of archers, while also in retreat, worked to maintain
their barrage.

One of those shots became an errant missile that grazed Kylac's
side, nearly taking his liver. He hissed in frustration while watching
the arrow skip off a rock and careen uselessly into the air as a wall of
elves re-formed on the near side of the bottleneck and came pouring
after him in pursuit.

Kylac dashed forward again to meet them, fearless, seeking to disrupt their flow. The frontline elves slowed in response, having seen enough by now to be wary of him. They held up to receive him, shying back from his spinning blades. He took advantage of that hesitation to drive in among them. When their numbers grew and their resolve stiffened, he carved clear to one side, mowing down weapons and limbs, veering toward a stack of boulders. He sprang atop the rocks, drawing a line of elves after him, then leapt to safety before the others could surround the ground below, using the stones as a momentary barrier to shield his escape.

By then, he'd caught sight of the frantic progress being made about the *Vengeance*, her crew disassembling the timber-and-driftwood cradle that had been erected to help heft her bow clear of the water-line, hoisting sheets and elsewise laboring to prepare her departure. He wondered how much time she still required in order to sail clear, given the distance between the ship and those who would tear her asunder.

More, he decided.

So he endeavored to provide it, dancing a treacherous, zigzag path of retreat down along the neck of the peninsula, drawing as many elves as he could with himself as a lure. Not all followed, but those who beat a more direct path toward the *Vengeance* were limited in number and felled by arrows fired from the withdrawing squad of bowmen or those stationed aboard the ship. Kylac concerned himself only with those he could, by turns harrying and harried, using the landscape to his advantage. Where rocks or rents channeled the pursuit into narrow lines, he paused to engage his adversaries in smaller packs. When in danger of being overrun, he withdrew and sprinted for the next stretch of defensible ground.

Exhilaration from the ongoing challenge offset any threat of weariness—that and the certain knowledge that if he were to falter, his death would be swift and without mercy. The savage frustration and almost feral fury emanating from his opponents assured him of that. How many of them had he killed? How many crying out to be avenged?

The hailstorm of arrows intensified as he neared the ship. The humming of bows, the whistle of passing shafts, the thwack or clatter of arrowheads striking bodies or bouncing off stone. Most sang over his head, aimed at his pursuers, but whenever he closed with the enemy, he invariably found himself ducking or dodging some fool comrade's overzealous fire. Grateful he was that this particular clan of Mookla'ayans seemed not to possess or utilize bows, blowguns, or other range weapons of their own, else this strategy might never have had a chance. As it was, he'd feel favored were he to escape this engagement without one or more feathered shafts protruding from his back.

And yet, he couldn't deny the effectiveness of the thickening volleys in stemming the rush of elven pursuers, thinning the ranks of those who slipped through. Critical when he heard the telltale groan of the *Vengeance* as she grated over sand and log, easing aft into the river. A glance revealed that the crew hadn't been disabling the forward cradle, but levering it higher, to help ease the massive ship backward, off the bar. Great sails captured the wind, billowing in reverse. Whole or not, the vessel would soon be embarking.

With or without him.

A game of measurement it became, between himself and the enemy, the enemy and the ship, the ship and the shore. Arrive too soon, and they'd be repelling elves as if beating ants out of an infested cloak. Too late, and . . . well, he'd be hauled back to their hill in pieces, delivered whole to Chitral, else swimming after his shipmates in a desperate pursuit of his own.

Thus he gauged his continuing retreat. Though instinct would have him err on the side of self-preservation, he tamped down that urge in order to purchase more time than he thought he needed. Given the relentless press of his enemies, he resisted turning to look behind him toward river and ship. Fortunately, in addition to the shouts and sounds at his back, he had the heightened urgency exhibited by the elves facing him to serve as clues. As the *Vengeance* continued to slide free of the sandbar, their cries and contortions and movements reflected their overarching desire to reach her, even if it meant for-saking their attack on him.

When that shift in his enemies' focus led to an almost all-out sprint to bypass him, and with the widening ground that leveled out toward the foot of the peninsula making it easier for them to do so, Kylac knew he had no further choice. Cutting down the last few that pressed him, he turned and joined the footrace. There was no catching the elves in front of him. Their strides were too long, their pace too swift. But with their sole remaining intent being to reach the ship, he might at least hope to catch a rope or ladder as they did.

His legs burned with a pleasing blood rush as they carried him onward. Arrows rained, but loosely, and to little effect. While slowing or dropping the elves they struck, most of the tips pierced only sand, the pursuers thin and nimble and agile enough to avoid being hit.

The *Vengeance* was almost fully clear. The last of her shore handlers and members of Kylac's rearguard were leaping onto the ladders and knotted lines strung out over the bow. Many shouted for support from their comrades above, sensing the savages treading on their heels. They were right to fear, as some of the nearest elves closed the distance, leaping up with the grace and dexterity of giant hunting cats, slicing the men free and taking hold of the lines for themselves.

Kylac foresaw what came next. Shouts rang out from the decks, and the lowest man on each line put knife to rope, sawing frantically. In some cases, the lowest man wasn't fast enough, overwhelmed by the elves scrabbling up from below. As some lines grew heavy with enemies, and the crewmen above realized just how quickly these natives could scale the ropes and rungs, the effort at severing the lines ran farther up, above the heads—despite frantic protest—of some of the crew still endeavoring to climb up from below.

A great fear it bespoke, Kylac thought, to sacrifice their own in order to avoid a handful of elves scrabbling aboard—enemies they should be able to dispatch abovedecks. He wondered if a common order had been given to do so, or if the act was but the result of panic on the part of a few hands. One or the other, his own fate was about to be determined.

He sheathed his swords as he sped across the final stretch of sand, taking aim at one of the last accessible lines on the starboard side—a trailing length of knotted rope typically used to take depth measurements. Two of his men were on it, near the top, climbing as quickly as they could. A Mookla'ayan native was even now leaping to catch it. Kylac drew a dagger as he bounded in pursuit, his paces slowed by the give of the drying sands. But there was no turning back, no other choice but to dig deep and jump . . .

He sliced at another elf leaping for the same strand at almost the same time. When the Mookla'ayan caught the rope, it did so without the fingers on one hand, sabotaging its grip and leaving it to pinwheel into the river's waters.

Its shriek drew the attention of the clansman already clinging to the line, but by the time this other turned to look down, it was too late to defend against the same blade piercing it through the back of a knee. The leg gave in response, and Kylac had to tighten his own, one-handed grip on the rope as the elf skidded down beside him, his enemy's involuntary struggles threatening to tear him loose in the bargain. But Kylac still had a blade in his free hand, while the Ladrakari warrior could only shriek his rage. A quick slash to the throat ended that threat.

Kylac clung to his perch, until one trailing elf and then another found and caught the line beneath him. Without hesitation, he severed the rope just below the knot to which he clung with his left hand. The weighted end fell away with a splash.

He looked skyward to see if any above meant to trim the line farther up. Sure enough, he found Creyl peering down at him from over the rail, a bloody dagger pressed against the braided cord.

Then the half-wild Redfist flashed his feral smile, and Kylac took it to mean he was safe. Hoping he wasn't mistaken, he sheathed his own blade, reached up to secure his hold on the truncated line, and resumed his climb.

19

Hand over hand, with the cries of battle still screeching around him, Kylac ascended the knotted line to reach the ship's rail. Creyl, mad grin in place, reached for him in welcome. Though he required no assistance, and found the other's amusement vaguely disturbing, Kylac saw no cause to offend. So he took the Redfist's gloved hand, allowing himself to be half pulled over the rail and onto the deck.

"Done bleed un run, t'ain't a scratch," Creyl remarked enthusiastically.

Kylac nodded, sweeping a glance past the soldier to confirm that the ship's deck was clear of enemies. Though it had cost them a handful of their own crewmembers in the process, not a single elf had managed to scale rope or ladder before the line had been severed. Below, a gathering horde of Ladrakari spilled from the edge of the sandbar, wading out into the river's waters, but could only scream and yelp in frustration as the ship drifted backward, once again leaving them and their shores behind.

Kylac's gaze drifted inland, tracing the long line of dead and dying whose maimed and mutilated forms littered the lower length of the peninsula. As expected, the carnage lay thickest at the earthen bottleneck where he and his company had made their initial stand. Dozens, scores, laid out in a gruesome swath of gut-churning slaughter. Already, gulls and other seabirds were descending to peck at the corpses, laying claim to the fresh remains, squawking and squabbling despite the plentiful bounty.

Unavoidable. But then, why didn't he feel better about it?

"There's a fight the bards won't have to embellish," observed Talon, sweating and breathless as he came to stand at Kylac's elbow.

Kylac spared the soldier a noncommittal grunt. Mayhap it was only the odors of blood and bowels, salt and sweat, smoke and tar—combined with the gentle rocking of the ship—that caused his stomach to hint of queasiness. Or mayhap it was his distaste for the cheers and jeers swelling around him, those of shipmates who felt the need to celebrate their narrow escape and mock the natives' failure—again—to bring them to heel. In all, a subdued reaction compared to last time, sapped of energy by those who remained silent—who understood just how close they'd come to being overrun, or who remembered the companions they'd lost in the process. And yet, less grating it would have been to Kylac's ears had more shared the latter view.

Countering that, remarkable it was they'd lost so few. He turned eye again to the bustling deck to take stock of those returned from the cordon. Most bore minor wounds, but none had been disabled. That left only the dead as casualties. A pair of Shadowguard in Orlin and Raithe, for which Ledron wouldn't thank him, given that they represented half of the total Blackfists aboard. Of the Stonewatch, Andrel, Rags, Turrech, and Pommel—plus the handful who'd been brought down or sacrificed while trying to board. Just two felled for every score of the enemy slain, had Kylac been forced to lay wager. If not a sense of triumph, he should at least be able to find some measure of solace.

Alas, with the indignant cries of the natives and the shrieks of scavenging birds piercing his ears, all he felt was an abiding disgust.

He glanced toward the wheelhouse and there spied the stern visage of Ithrimir, bound again to the starboard chart table, beside Taeg at the helm. Though the distance was too great to divine the Elementer's expression, Kylac sensed a thorny disapproval. At the overall situation, mayhap, though he couldn't help but wonder if the Scribe's reaction were more accusatory, and aimed at Kylac in particular.

Determined to find out, to face the Elementer and come to some reconciliation of views, he turned from Talon and Creyl and strode wordlessly aft, leaving them and the other surviving rearguard defensemen to congratulate one another on their relative success. An organized chaos reigned across the deck and aloft, as sailors shifted booms, loosened or tightened lines, and elsewise performed the work to arrest the ship's rearward momentum and direct her forward once more. While the Whitefists labored, the majority of Redfists persisted in lining the rails, stacked more thickly along the starboard side, to ward off any effort the natives might try to mount against them. As the Ladrakari were mostly helpless on that front, and too wise to spend themselves so foolishly, the soldiers were chiefly relegated to mimicking the elves' cries or elsewise hurling taunts or invectives—as if there were any useful cause to do so. Here and there, an archer loosed arrows into the native throng, cheered by his comrades when the bolt struck home, else mocked for his errant aim. A sport it had become, no more.

"Might want to save some o' them shafts," Kylac advised as he passed one such cluster. The opposite of what he'd suggested earlier. But then, their lives had depended on it before, where now they didn't.

The soldiers' laughter and smiles faded, but only momentarily, resurfacing in his wake along with murmurs of confusion or challenge. He chose to ignore these, unaffected by their toothless scorn, and pressed on.

He'd reached the ladder to the wheel deck when a shout rang from the crow's nest. "Enemy afore!"

Kylac twisted to look back over his shoulder, peering forward through a faint screen of gathering mist. Most aboard did the same, heads turning, necks craning, in reaction to the lookout's cry. The ship had only scarcely started in that direction, but other than a few maddened elves giving chase along the shoreline, the enemy was falling behind. What possible threat . . . ?

He spied it at once, a fresh swarm of bodies spilling from a forested ridge mayhap a mile ahead. Mookla'ayans, racing toward a promontory jutting from the western shore. A promontory the *Vengeance* would have to skirt, Kylac realized, judging by the narrow breadth of the channel formed there by a similar horn of cliffs encroaching from the east. A land bridge it might have been, in ages past. Broken now, but of a height and reach that made it clear, with a twinge of foreboding, what their enemies intended.

The abrupt withering of dozens of voices told him that others recognized the danger, too, the resultant hush reflective of a grim understanding.

"Stations!" Pevrick hollered near the foredeck.

The alarm echoed, spawning secondary directives from unit commanders and a flurry of movement as the soldiers and sailors aboard reorganized themselves in streaming packs and clusters.

Abandoning his desired visit with the Sea Scribe, Kylac wheeled about and carved his own path across the decks, slipping through the throng to where Pevrick and Ledron conferred atop the forecastle. Had any consideration been given to reversing the ship's direction or seeking another route, it had been abandoned quickly in favor of an all-out sprint. Sensible enough, given that the tributary they sailed wasn't wide enough to allow a behemoth like the *Vengeance* to come about. And drifting backward was a slow, tedious affair that would cost them precious hours while retracing miles of river. At full sail, she might just be fast enough to clear the cliff-flanked narrows before the bulk of the natives could reach it.

The conference ended before Kylac could join it. As he dashed up the steps of the starboard ladder, Pevrick was sliding down the steps on the opposite side, bellowing urgent commands to those wrangling lines and wrestling knots—wringing what speed they could from the ship's sails. Ledron, meanwhile, had turned to Sanow, gesturing forcefully, presumably instructing the lanky Blackfist as to the preferred positions of their fighting men.

Kylac arrived as Sanow departed with his orders. "What say ya, Captain?"

Ledron failed to respond. His gaze lay fixed upon the western ridgeline, tracking the natives' progress as they raced for the promontory. A thickening veil of mist lent their movements a ghostly quality well suited to their bloodthirsty wailing. The combined tone resonated abruptly with Kylac's earlier misgivings, striking a chord of realization. It wasn't the unfortunate slaughter of so many natives

that truly troubled him, nor even his shipmates' cavalier response to
it. Merely an instinctive sense, unbidden and deep-seated, that they
hadn't escaped their pursuers yet.

Beside him, the Head grunted finally through gritted teeth. "I
trust those blades of yours still have their edge."

"Forge fresh," Kylac assured him.

Shouts rang. Sails strained. The *Vengeance*'s cutwater sliced like a
razor through the river's still surface. Measuring their pace against
that of the natives, Kylac quickly saw, as Ledron's words suggested,
that it wouldn't be enough. Already, the first few elves serving point
had reached the promontory's edge, where they brandished their
blades and spears while howling in challenge.

Ten, fifteen, a score . . . the number of natives awaiting them
continued to grow. But there was no turning back. Kylac sensed only
willful determination from Ledron beside him. Most aboard shared
the captain's stubbornness, spawning an overwhelming wave of sol-
dierly daring that crested at Kylac's back. The rest—the handful of
crewmen scattered here or there who lacked their comrades' foolish
enthusiasm—were borne upon the zealous tide like bits of flotsam.

Archers at the rail and leashed to platforms amid the spars nocked
arrows to their bows. Soldiers concentrated on the starboard side
hefted their blades while shaking or stretching the tightness from
their limbs. Some grunted or growled or laughed, to bolster their
courage or that of their brothers-in-arms. Even without their cries,
Kylac could taste their anticipation, in response to that of the natives,
fueling the impending clash.

"Draw!" a voice boomed as the promontory came within range.
Other voices echoed the call, giving rise to the telltale squeak of
flexing bows. Unnecessary chatter subsided, making way for a shared
breathlessness.

"Loose!"

The reverberating command spawned a rain of iron-tipped missiles
that whistled through the air like a cloud of stinging insects. The
thickening cluster of elves writhed in response, dodging or falling
as the barbs descended. But the yelps of pain could not overcome
the cries of defiance. Nor did the damage sustained deter those

Mookla'ayans still racing to join their warrior clansmen. If anything, their strides lengthened.

A second volley followed the first, and then a third. After that, the bowmen along the rail fell back, making room for the swordsmen and pikemen to step forward. A squad joined Kylac atop the forecastle as the distance between ship and jutting rock closed to within a few strides, some forming a wall at his back, triggering in him a twinge of confinement. On both sides, amid ally and enemy alike, weapons lifted, as did voices, screaming a common madness.

A hail of native javelins filled the air in lethal welcome. For all their bluster, Redfists cringed or dodged or fell back as the shafts struck home, piercing their flesh or that of their comrades. Kylac himself had to duck as one of the weapons sailed toward his face. Stumps, positioned too closely behind him, was slower to respond, and caught the missile through the throat. Glancing back, Kylac watched the Redfist cough and sputter his last, blood mixing with the dark juices of chewed fig leaves that sprayed from his mouth, eyes bulging in denial.

He had no time to give the soldier's struggle further thought, for the elves were spilling then into the ship, leaping from their stony perch to pour down upon the clustered defenders. Perched at the bow, Kylac engaged the first few to do so, receiving them with slashing motions so as not to weigh down his blades, ending their fight almost before it could begin.

But others followed, all along the starboard side as the *Vengeance* made her pass. One after another, in startling numbers, Ladrakari cascaded onto the decks like a cresting storm swell, sidestepping or springing over their fallen clansmen to join those ahead of them. Given the speed of the ship's passing, not all were able to do so, trailing too far behind or inhibited by the narrowness of the ledge from which they made their mad leap. But the *Vengeance* was a large ship, more than seventy paces in length. As Kylac peered aft, he saw that more natives than he'd have wagered possible had hurdled or elsewise breached the defensive line by the time her stern had slipped by.

Even then, some elves chanced the leap, fueled by their frenzy, only to plummet to the river below. Others hurled their spears and javelins, shrieking their hatred or screaming encouragement to those clansmen who'd managed to succeed where they'd failed.

Those who now swarmed the ship, bringing the battle to her decks.

Slicing past walls of defenders, they overwhelmed their human counterparts with speed and agility. Within heartbeats, lines of elves were sprinting inward, carving or weaving through reserve soldiers and bowmen to assault the sailors manning the cordage. A sudden certainty knotted in Kylac's stomach. Of only secondary concern were the ship's men-at-arms, he realized, watching more and more natives bypass the outer ranks. First and foremost, they meant to disable the vessel and thus prevent its escape.

"Bring them down!" Ledron roared, a general plea as nimble Mookla'ayan bodies began scrabbling up the spars and ratlines, hacking at the *Vengeance* herself. He, too, must have recognized what the natives intended.

Yet could do little about it.

With ruthless efficiency, they tore at the rigging—severing shrouds, rending sails, hacking at stays—clearly seeking to cripple the ship in whatever way they could. Meanwhile, Kylac's determination to thwart the enemy effort was inhibited by the press of soldiers and sailors streaming aft. Better had his fellow crewmen simply cleared a path. As matters stood, he found himself limited in where and how he could bring his blades to bear, forced to slip and lunge amid a stampede of shipmates caught up in a suddenly frenetic melee.

Weaving through a sea of thrashing limbs and contorted faces, he nonetheless squirmed past allies and cut past enemies, inching aft toward the heart of the maindeck. Though he gave necessary focus to one step, one slide, one dash at a time, a part of him feared for Ithrimir and Taeg in the wheelhouse. He couldn't see them through the intervening chaos, but believed instinctively that the elves would seek to commandeer the wheel, thinking to steer the ship aground, where their fellow clansmen, many of whom still raced alongshore, might come to bolster their attack.

Driven by that suspicion, he shifted aim, worrying not so much about hewing down every native whose path he might cross, but driving onward, leaving much of the residual killing to his shipmates while he concentrated on gaining ground. That the natives seemed more concerned with harming the ship than its crew worked to the Addarans' advantage, as far fewer men were falling than would have had the Ladrakari been targeting them specifically. Between their superior numbers, the enclosed fighting ground, and the enemy's distraction with its sabotage effort, Kylac's allies were slowly but steadily reclaiming control of their vessel.

Past the mainmast he flew—beheading a shrieking elf who warded its base—neglecting those clansmen scurrying up its length. It rankled him to bypass the latter, but to chase them all would have him running in circles. Like roaches the Ladrakari had become, skittering everywhere he looked, indiscriminate in the damage they inflicted. An infestation from which the *Vengeance* wouldn't quickly recover. But before he could concern himself with her recovery, he had to rid her of their plague—the most vital areas first. While the mainmast might be her backbone, the wheel was her heart.

Trusting that a sufficient measure of the Redfists who followed him would make the climb in his stead, he pressed on. Edging to starboard, where the fighting lay thickest, he mowed his way across the maindeck, slashing through thin-limbed, olive-skinned bodies like stalks of wheat, doing what he could to affect the battle's tide while plowing aft with single-minded focus. As feared, the wheel deck was under siege, with just a small knot of soldiers fighting back against the bristling mass of natives seeking to force their way into the wheelhouse. Incensed, the enemy had become, if not by the proximity of the ship's wheel, then by the sight or smell of the Sea Scribe—their Sa'ahla—hunkered just beyond the barred doorway amid a pair of inner warders. Two major objectives, so near at hand, seemed to have stirred them into a foaming frenzy.

A sheet cut from the jiggermast was set to flapping and fluttering in the wind before flying free completely. High-pitched elven voices cheered the victory. At that moment, a clutch of attackers scrambled up and over the roof of the wheelhouse, skittering to the larboard entry. Defenders shouted an alarm to the trio staged upon that side, but the cries were quickly engulfed by the general furor, leaving the soldiers no true warning.

One—the Redfist Drewes—happened to look up as the first of the elves fell upon him, narrowly dodging the spearpoint that would have pierced the back of his neck. But his forward lunge carried him away from the doorway, where he was separated from his companions by the descending attackers. The remaining two—Graves and Lisp—fell back against the closed door, shields raised to help block the entry. Given the sudden press against them, neither likely saw the excess elves who set immediately upon Drewes, hamstringing him before slashing at him in a rabid pack and finally hurling his screaming remains over the ship's rail.

Kylac abruptly redirected from starboard to larboard, bounding up the wheel deck stair to scatter the pack that had slain Drewes and tear into those assailing Graves and Lisp. He was too late to save the latter, who doubled over when a spear found his knee and promptly suffered a flurry of knives to his exposed back. But Graves, hunkered behind his shield, was spared as the remaining Ladrakari were compelled to turn at Kylac's approach—only to be cut down in a whirlwind of dicing blades.

Four more elves spilled down from the roof, and died for their effort. Blades still in hand, Kylac sprang then from a waist-high locker bolted to the outside of the wheelhouse to reach the roof himself. There, he swept aside a pair of hesitant stragglers before racing across and dropping down amid those Mookla'ayans clustered on the other side. Like most of those before, they refused to flee, allowing him to make short work of them—relieving the battle-weary shipmates still standing barrier.

Among them, a bloodied and winded Pevrick.

The first mate assessed the carnage around them, as if startled by the battle's sudden ebb. His awed expression twisted angrily, however, the moment he found Kylac's gaze.

"Hold here," Kylac directed, before the lieutenant could find his voice. Whatever response Leeches might have summoned, Kylac had more critical matters to attend.

He continued aft to the command deck and poop deck, racing headlong as before into the thickest concentrations of enemies he could find, carving a path for his allies to follow. The mizzenmast and jiggermast, more lightly defended, had already suffered significant damage, but mayhap he could put a stop to that. As little by little he cleared the decks, archers below were given a chance to target enemies aloft, speeding their removal from the lines and spars.

The bloody business continued for the better part of a quarter-mark. By then, the outcome had ceased to be in doubt. The majority of attackers lay lifeless, strewn about the decks or tangled amid the ratlines. Leaving nothing to chance, Ledron's order had the wounded swiftly put down. The few who remained scurried about like stubborn fleas, still seeking to damage the vessel rather than retreat, their offensive-minded focus only hastening their demise.

Kylac fought to the end, refusing to sheathe his blades until the last of the parasitic attackers had been felled—as cleanly as possible. He found the final assailant trapped by a clutch of Stonewatch against the bow rail. The arrow that had dropped him from the foremast had snapped upon his fall, leaving only a broken shaft protruding from his side. He held one arm close, favoring a shattered wrist. The other arm had dislocated at the shoulder, hanging as limp and useless as his legs, which stretched out before him in splintered angles. Though bruised and lacerated inside and out, he hissed at them like any cornered animal would, drawing laughter and jeers from a handful of bitter Redfists.

Fearing some might seek to make sport of the lone survivor, Kylac stepped forward to ensure a merciful end. Before he'd raised a blade, a pair of arrows whizzed past, striking the proud elf in the chest, leaving him to stare sightlessly, accusingly, through the bloodshot whites of his pain-wracked eyes.

Only then did Kylac lower his weapons, turning to trace the dead gaze aft, to see what remained of the *Vengeance* and her crew.

20

THE CREW'S EXHILARATION was short-lived, the thrill of victory sapped by a prevailing exhaustion and an all-too-swift realization of what their triumph had cost them. The smattering of soldiers who saw fit to cheer or congratulate one another fell quickly silent as they surveyed the aftermath. To a man, the enemy had been vanquished. But here or there, soldiers and sailors lay among them, dead or dying, and the ship herself appeared to be in tatters. Torn sails flapped loosely in the wind. Halyards, shrouds, and even stays draped limply from the spars or lay coiled haphazardly upon the decks. Blood and bowels pooled amid the bodies or pieces thereof, and streamed along the seams of the ship's planks. Scavenger birds circled overhead, shrieking hungrily, drawn by the pungent scent.

As the flush of battle seeped from his veins, Kylac felt not the slightest satisfaction, only grim acknowledgment and a nagging regret. He saw no reason for these Mookla'ayan natives to have become his adversaries. None had had any involvement in Dethaniel's abduction. None bore any particular stake or concern that Kylac could fathom in the bitter feud between Addaran and Grenarr. While long since inured to the ravages of combat and even murder, it troubled him to participate in such senseless slaughter. He and his crew were the invaders, outlanders who'd come uninvited, stolen from this native

people, and thus earned the elves' aggression. That the Sea Scribe
had been held against his will seemed in that moment a self-serving
rationalization—a petulant denial put forth against the encroaching
specter of guilt.

"Festering fiends," spat Sethric. The typically congenial Redfist
stood nearby, kicking the corpse of an elf sprawled at his feet upon
the foredeck. His sword still dangled in hand, blood running down
his arm and soaking his rent sleeve. "Ain't fit to serve as chum."

Elsewhere, a similar anger and resentment burned, as crewmen
took stock of injuries to themselves and their comrades. It caused
Kylac to wonder what effect such bodily damage might have had on
his own, more compassionate, outlook. Impossible to know for sure,
as he'd sustained none. But he found it difficult to imagine lament-
ing such an obvious risk. If willing to inflict injury, one should be
prepared to receive it.

"Stonewatch, see to the wounded," Ledron commanded. His tone
was grave, but the words impassive. "Seawatch, see to the ship."

Lieutenants and others within earshot echoed his orders, putting
an end to whatever respite the winded, weary fighters might have
elsewise hoped for. Kylac hesitated, uncertain as to where the captain
might wish him to serve. Would it be in tending to those crewmen
who required treatment, or in working to restore proper function to
their vessel before it ran them all aground?

He chose the former, believing his knowledge of bodily trauma to
be of use in examining injury and assigning priority to those whose
suffering was most severe. Whatever its condition, their ship's rigging
would be of no use if none remained to man it. If necessary, they could
anchor her out in the center of the river until repairs could be made.

Not that Ledron seemed inclined to suggest as much. "Maintain
course!" he shouted, as he ventured aft, summoning a Whitefist to help
him assess the most critical damage as he went. Pevrick approached
from the wheelhouse, making observations and giving commands
of his own. Kylac didn't doubt that there would be plenty of heated
discussion when the two met, and harbored no great desire to be a
part of it.

Had he been summoned, he might have reconsidered. But Ledron neither looked nor called for him while descending the forecastle, leaving Kylac to his own devices.

Finding the most grievously wounded wasn't difficult. For the greater part, their moans and screams were sufficient to draw attention. Those who bit down and better bridled their shock and agony still tended to attract thicker clusters of crewmen the more gruesome their injuries. Kylac simply targeted the packs of comrades-in-arms gathering round to lend aid, offer reassurances, or observe with morbid curiosity, then worked quickly to shove these bystanders aside—directing them elsewhere while worming into the heart of each huddle. His actions drew a few murmurs, but he spoke forcefully enough that none dared question him outright.

Not after bearing witness to the latest struggle.

To the others, those beside each of the wounded who genuinely wished to supply aid, he gave instruction where needed, or encouragement where he deemed matters already in hand. Directives on where and how to apply pressure, tie off a bleeding limb, or make an incision to relieve dangerous swelling were common. In mortal cases, he either urged the man to relax and bleed out, else smiled bravely and urged him to resist the encroaching darkness—as determined by what he believed the particular individual most needed to hear. In only one instance, that of a stomach wound that promised a slow, painful death, did the sailor—Erresh—see the truth in his eyes and ask him to end his ordeal more swiftly. With a firm nod and an abrupt draw of his blade, he granted the lad's request.

When those who could be helped had been, or were receiving suitable treatment, Kylac joined those engaged in addressing the graver injuries to their ship. Amid much bickering and dispute, he focused on actions—securing sails, running lines, reattaching shrouds and stays—that, little by little, restored function and stability. He labored relentlessly, tirelessly, pleased to engage in a productive effort and to establish an example that others followed. For the first time since the inception of their voyage, he sensed from a growing number of shipmates a brush of the camaraderie they exhibited toward one another, a feeling of acceptance—eager in some instances, grudging in others—that suggested he might finally belong.

Though widespread, the opinion was far from unanimous. An hour into the effort of securing, repairing, and cleaning the vessel, he found himself at odds with a pack of Redfists who'd taken to having a mite too much fun with the disposal of the enemy bodies. Unfortunate enough, in Kylac's mind, that there was naught but to heave the corpses overboard, ridding the ship of both the dead and the flocks of birds come to scavenge among them. Knowing not what rites these particular Mookla'ayans might practice, and understanding that expediency allowed for little else, he could overlook that much. But he saw no need to tolerate mockery, looting, or outright desecration, and didn't hesitate in telling the perpetrators so.

"Why concern yourself, eh?" asked Hamal, a leather-skinned brute with a natural squint made worse by the sun. "More than half these corpses is yours."

"Then those trophies aren't his to take," Kylac replied, gesturing to the pouch gripped in Kahrem's fist—full of bloody teeth the pack of Stonewatch had been harvesting from the Mookla'ayan dead.

The snakelike Kahrem recoiled, clutching his pouch protectively. "These vermin won't be missing them."

"Turn 'em loose."

"I know an apothecary back home who'd pay a silver finger for each, maybe more."

"Over the rail. Theirs or yours."

"You don't command us," grumbled Olekk in that sonorous voice of his. Better known to his compatriots as Thatch, he stepped forward to glare down at Kylac, folding his arms—hairy as they were thick—over his imposing chest.

"A request. Shall I ask again?"

"You going to compensate us, then?" asked the sour-smelling lad they called Crawfoot. He nudged one of the elven bodies with a boot. "Felled this one myself."

The four and another pair—Yoden and "Quill"—grunted in chorus. United against him, and growing bolder by the moment. Kylac sensed others approaching, made curious by the apparent stand-off, looking to observe if not participate. Better to end this quickly, before it spawned a full-fledged confrontation.

"I'm told your Grenarr prefer to carve their trophies from the living," he said, crossing his own arms loosely before him. "I's seen these natives do so firsthand. Should chance bring ya beneath their blades, would ya has me stand aside then as now?"

He shifted gaze from soldier to soldier, driving his point home, probing for the seam in their armored wall.

"I'll take my chances," Thatch blustered.

"And the rest o' ya?" Sensing Yoden's hesitation, Kylac pinned the lad with his stare. But it was actually Quill beside him who blinked first.

"Shards but you're a grieving damper," the notch-eared Redfist complained. He put his hand over the rail, revealing a palm full of trinkets—ivory and precious metal—pilfered from elven piercings. With a peevish scowl, he flung them into the river. "Satisfied?"

Kylac turned to Kahrem, who squirmed as if impaled on a hook. "We were promised plunder."

"Which ya can sells to me now, as a favor I'll remember. Worth more than a handful o' uncollected silvers, I assure ya."

Hamal scoffed. "And what, you'll betray the rest of us?"

"Ya seeks to reclaim what was taken from ya. As do they," Kylac said, gesturing to the corpses at his feet while casting a nod toward Ithrimir in the wheelhouse.

"What *you* took from them," Thatch snapped reflexively.

Kylac ignored him, focusing on the others. "If'n it's marauders ya's become, what difference between yourselves and the Grenarr?"

It seemed the right string to pluck, drawing shame and indignation in equal measure. Even as additional shipmates drew near, potentially bolstering the protest against him, Kylac watched the wind drain from Olekk's comrades, sapped by whatever mix of fear and pride he'd managed to stir within them.

"Ain't no tar-skin," Crawfoot groused, flinging aside a leather brace stripped from one of the elven dead.

Kylac wouldn't have begrudged the soldier such a practical artifact. It was the bodies he sought to preserve, not their belongings. But seeking to clarify as much might only spawn further irritation and confusion. So he held his tongue, eyeing again Kahrem's pouch.

"Cup of slag, this is," the Redfist muttered, seeking to ward off those who looked to him now with expectant expressions. "Is he to tell us next when we spit and when we swallow? Or are we to—"

"Enemy afore!"

The lookout's cry ratcheted through the bodies of the crewmen as it reverberated throughout the ship. Spines straightened and necks craned as duties and debates were set aside, heads turning as one toward the bow. Hamal, Crawfoot, and Olekk glanced first at Kylac as if he must be the source of the new alarm, then peered ahead like all the rest.

Kylac looked with them.

Positioned amidships, nothing came to view beyond the rise of foredecks. But the frantic reactions of those shipmates who *could* see what lay before them was sufficient to cast a pall over those who couldn't. As abruptly as that, petty dissension gave way to common urgency.

"Tend to them as you will, then," Thatch huffed, signaling to his comrades as he abandoned the remaining corpses and strode forward. Hamal, Crawfoot, and Yoden were quick to join him. Quill hesitated only briefly before finding their heels.

Alone, face to face with Kylac, Kahrem emptied his collection of teeth into the river. His sullen visage bore traces of both bitterness and pleading. "So be it. For your favor, yes?"

"See to these bodies," Kylac replied, "while I see what threatens yours."

Trusting the matter settled, he slipped forward amid a stream of others. Stonewatch, mostly. The majority of Seawatch remained focused on tasks essential to the ship's health or limping progress. Those Whitefists who could break away took to the rigging, bettering their line of sight through elevation—joining those comrades already aloft. After just a few strides, Kylac followed their lead, taking hold of a loose stay and shimmying skyward along its corded length.

To learn what fell challenge awaited them now.

While obscured by distance, the new peril seemed plain enough. Ahead, the river narrowed, squeezed again by encroaching shelves of lowland jungle. Another choke point awaited them, no more than a league hence. This time, however, a gnarled mass had taken root where banks east and west converged—a clog of timber and deadfall that, from this vantage, appeared to block further passage.

A dam.

But it wasn't the hazard itself that caused Kylac's stomach to knot in warning. It was the forms that scurried upon it like ants on a hill, their faint chirps and stark shrieks echoing across the watery flats with fiendish anticipation.

The Ladrakari, it seemed, hadn't finished with them just yet.

A cloud of uncertainty rippled throughout the crew. Murmurs gave way to objections tinged with dismay. To tamp down the rising panic, officers barked or bayed orders, advising courage and focus. Most hands, regardless of disposition, looked to their commanders, urgently seeking solution.

Kylac dropped from his line and hastened toward the wheel deck, to learn how Ledron and his lieutenants intended to respond.

" . . . appears but a crude barrier," Pevrick was growling as Kylac arrived. "At full sail, might be we can brush it aside."

"We're hardly capable of full sail," Taeg reminded him.

"They needn't stop us," Ithrimir snarled, his half-gaze fixed upon the forward horizon. "Merely slow us long enough to overrun us again."

The uninvited observation met with momentary silence, as the ship's commanders decided what to make of it.

"She'll not likely withstand another raking like the last," Brenham agreed in that complacent tone of his.

"And our prow?" Ledron asked. "Will it withstand collision with their damned nest?"

The patch in their hull. Rushed to completion and given little time to set. By all accounts reported over the last hour, the flooding below had been arrested, or near enough. But would the repairs hold if they were to ram headlong into the natives' barrier?

"Can we not reverse course?" Kylac asked, shouldering the stern looks that rounded on him.

"Apparently not," Ledron answered sourly, glancing at Ithrimir. "Seems the river at our backs has ebbed at some point. The route we've followed cannot be retraced."

"Those were not my words, Captain," the Sea Scribe objected. "Only that we'd be grounded for a fortnight before able to proceed."

Alas for the Shrouded Skein and its ever-shifting waterways. Judging by the expression on Ledron's face—and the interpretation already given—the Head wasn't about to delay them that long. And if retreat wasn't an option . . .

"The matter is decided then," Kylac said. To their narrowed gazes and furrowed brows, he added, "The slower we advance, the thicker their dam grows. Better to test it now than later, eh?"

He allowed them the span of a few heartbeats to disagree. When none did, he took his leave, striding forward again. Sure enough, the echoing shouts rang out behind him before he'd reached the maindeck.

"Battle posts!"

Whatever weariness might have weighed upon the crew gave way to the flush of raw energy preceding any mortal conflict. Ill-prepared as they were for another encounter—still in the process of securing, cleaning, and elsewise recovering from the last—their enemy had them in sight. The men would make themselves ready, or they would die.

Morale was another matter. However improbable, the Ladrakari host awaiting them looked to be even larger than the last. The natives must have marked the *Vengeance*'s course upon her departure from the peninsula, Kylac realized, and straightaway set upon blockading the southern waters. Shards, it may have been that the prior offensive had been a secondary endeavor all along.

One more reason to decry his shipmates' unseemly celebration.

It mattered little, save that the Redfists clustering into battle formations upon the forecastle recognized easily enough that their victory had been anything but. Seeing that their tormentors were in better position to wreak havoc than before—and recalling that they'd only narrowly escaped that previous assault—brought with it a prevailing sense of dread.

"Straighten those spines, lads," Kylac urged as he pushed and slithered his way toward the center of the bow rail. "These are no more fearsome than the last."

A few Redfists regarded him incredulously. Others nodded without any real conviction, or ignored him altogether. One or two, however, seized upon the scrap of confidence, using it to bolster their own.

"Repelled them once," remarked Talon, "we'll do it again."

"This is why we came to serve," Simalen reminded his nearest comrades.

"Rasp un buggered bones!" Creyl echoed with a gleeful sneer.

Kylac found Sanow, last of their Shadowguard save for Ledron himself, affixed at the point. For once, the lanky Blackfist seemed more welcoming than wary, receiving him with a grim nod. Wooten stood nearby, and at his elbow, Ysander, pole-axe in hand. A stout wedge, Kylac determined, having fought alongside each of the latter at his own cordon that very dawn. Their presence summoned a twinge of reassurance.

The *Vengeance* gained speed, girding up despite her wounds as if to show these troublesome elves her true, battle-tested mettle. Kylac felt a stab of unexpected pride. As the gap between her prow and the natives' dam shrank, she seemed to swell in size. The crude mound of knotted trunks and twisted brush, only loosely entwined, was indeed smaller than it had first appeared. Hastily constructed and thinly laid, it had little chance of halting their progress. Better yet, the narrowing banks were too low for the Ladrakari to swarm the ship's decks as they had from the overhanging promontory.

Suddenly, the obstacle before them didn't seem so perilous after all.

The awaiting elves seemed to recognize this, scattering from the crown of the dam as the *Vengeance* made her final approach, bearing down like a horse with the bit in its teeth. They'd done what they could, but seemed anxious now to clear the path. A rain of scattered arrows gave chase, ushering the retreat, launched by Seawatch bowmen positioned at the rail and within the rigging above. Together, Redfists upon the forecastle and Whitefists aloft raised a hearty cheer.

Kylac himself smiled, invigorated by the rush of wind and the surprising withdrawal of the awaiting horde. Then he spied the pair of elves stationed upon the western bank, standing straight and proud in a position of command. He knew them at once, less by sight than by the fell warning that pierced his blossoming euphoria like a poisoned sliver. The Butcher, Chitral, hooked and barbed and painted in the blood of his victims. At his shoulder, Ox. Forannenuk, Et'tanis had named him. He who'd first grudgingly welcomed them to Mistwall's shores and served escort throughout Kylac's initial visit. With Et'tanis slain, the leaders of this clan.

For what reason their presence disturbed him, he couldn't have said. Nor did he have time to contemplate it. With collision imminent, the *Vengeance* seemed suddenly to be sailing too quickly, heedlessly, recklessly. Cheers ebbed and smiles slipped as soldiers and sailors grasped abruptly for solid footing, bracing for impact . . .

A rending crash and jarring thud heralded the violent cracking of driftwood boles, the scraping of dead branches, the hiss and rustle of leaves. The *Vengeance* shuddered as the mesh of wooden debris stabbed at her, clawed at her, straining to reel her in. The fragments she tore past raked her sides with skeletal fingers, reluctant to let go, shrieking outrage amid the fervent cries of the elven host that had set them in place.

But outrage alone couldn't arrest their momentum, and the barricade itself could only slow it. With a scathing groan of her own, the *Vengeance* powered on, smashing aside trunks and limbs and roots alike, plowing through the makeshift snare and into the unobstructed channel beyond.

21

A SURGE OF WATERS went with them, unleashed from the splintering dam to rush south unimpeded. Atop the forecastle, toppled soldiers grasped and clutched at their nearest comrades, struggling to regain their feet. Kylac offered a hand where he could, even as he stepped to starboard along the bow rail. Peering aft, he watched Ox raise a fist to the air, punching furiously, while natives below him barked and yelped in a chorus of savage outrage. Amid the agitated throng, Chitral stood unmoving, the Butcher's hatred giving chase like a flaming arrow upon the wind.

Down at the waterline, the edges of the dam clung to the muddy shore, logs and branches reaching out like the tips of fractured bones. Farther back, the river churned, choked with scattered debris that bobbed and spun in the ship's wake. By all immediate appearances, the *Vengeance* was free.

A resurgent cheer went up as this realization took root among the crew, uncertainty giving way to cautious relief and then outright enthusiasm. With broad smiles, arm clasps, and slaps on the back, Redfist and Whitefist alike congratulated one another on their good fortune.

Kylac wouldn't begrudge them their revelry this time. None had been slain, be they ally or enemy. No blood needlessly spilled. Ahead lay only smooth waters, agleam with the light of the morning sun. While a kernel of misgiving lingered like a thorn in his gut, it appeared unfounded. Merely the residue of a false alarm.

So he nodded and smiled at those who looked to share with him some acknowledgment of their reprieve. He even managed a reassuring shoulder clap for half-mad Creyl, who alone seemed disappointed that the confrontation hadn't come to blows.

"Not the last of our perils, I'll wager."

Sanow gave the order for the assembled Stonewatch to stand down. As the already slack formations broke apart, Kylac started aft, seeking the most pressing duty with which to occupy himself.

He'd scarcely descended the forecastle when Aythef popped up from a hatch amidships. Though his shouts were trammeled by the usual flurry of deck activity, his flailing, stumbling emergence left little doubt as to his sense of urgency.

Those nearer the cook's position froze, giving ear to his frantic message. When two more hands surfaced behind him, similarly distressed, the thorn in Kylac's stomach twisted deeper, penetrating with fresh warning.

"We're breached!" the relay came to reveal. "Flooding! Flooding below!"

A lightning strike couldn't have set the crew to skittering more quickly. Though the recurrence of an earlier hazard, and a risk weighed even before punching through the natives' dam, the stark reality of that most fundamental threat to a waterborne vessel had men shaking their heads and hissing a common frustration.

A furious bailing effort manifested almost before the command was given. While sailors and soldiers alike fell into positions as before, Kylac descended a string of ladders to glimpse the damage firsthand. Witnessing the torrents of water gushing in through the buckled seams of their forward hold, he was unsurprised moments later by the official assessment delivered to Ledron in the wheelhouse.

"Nearly two hundred barrels an hour," Aramis reported.

"A rate we cannot hope to repel," Pevrick snapped.

As if those present couldn't determine the truth for themselves. Even Kylac recognized the figure as more than triple the scale of the previous flooding. If the latter had grounded them, what hope did they have this time?

Ledron grimaced. "We'll have to put down again."

"With those savages on our heels?" Pevrick asked.

"We'll drag along as far as we can."

"Even if her hull were intact, she's not oceanworthy," Brenham added. With his flat tone, it was difficult to determine which argument he embraced. "Before putting out to sea, her rigging must be repaired."

Seeming desperate for support, Leeches turned to Ithrimir.

"Chitral will have anticipated this outcome," the Sea Scribe agreed. "Anchor again on these shores, we will be overrun."

"So we find an atoll," Taeg proposed. "Far enough out that they cannot reach us."

"South of the isle?" Brenham shook his head, lips pursed with doubt. "A stretch to believe we could make it that far before the waters lay claim."

"Or the Grenarr," Pevrick spat. "Lest you've forgotten, they're out there trolling for us."

Taeg shrugged. "Then an island within the river. Using the shore boats to fetch supplies." Off their grudging silence, he added, "Or are we merely voicing objections?"

The most viable option—if not the only reasonable one before them. The sooner they embraced it, the faster action might ensue.

"What other choice but to abandon ship?" Kylac asked.

"And row ourselves where?" Pevrick snarled.

"Wherever we'd be most likely to commandeers another." He directed his gaze at Ithrimir. "Back at the cove, mayhap?"

The Elementer stiffened. "The Ladrakari—"

"Death by drowning or death by spear is all I'm hearing," Kylac explained. "The latter gives fighting chance. Might be we can remain hidden long enough to avoid a direct battle."

"I like his idea better," Brenham admitted, with a nod toward Taeg.

"As do I," Kylac admitted. He'd only intended to steer the commanding body more quickly in that direction—to shed a favorable light upon Taeg's plan by proposing a darker alternative. A vote of support might have been swifter, but, stemming from him, might also have only spurred a greater resistance. "But that's for our navigators to decide," he added, "if'n a suitable spot exists."

Ledron must have agreed, though his sour expression made clear that, as usual, he cared little for the taste of his own decision. "To it, then. There must be some rock or bar we can settle beyond the savages' reach. If not, we can . . ."

He trailed off as his gaze slipped to the forward window, reddened features crimping with curiosity. Kylac traced the captain's line of sight to a growing disturbance upon the maindeck—marked by a lengthening stream of crewmembers stunned into stillness. Strides slowed or halted, bent backs straightened, and busy hands went suddenly slack. An unnatural hush, given the demanding effort to keep themselves afloat. What could possibly . . . ?

And then he saw her, staggering among them on shivering, unsteady legs. A foal among wolves, save it was the wolves falling back in mute horror. An apparition, she must be. A trick of the light.

"Mother's mercy," Ledron whispered.

The Princess Denariel.

Kylac bolted from the wheelhouse, bounding down the first deck stair in his haste to intercept her. Though it might not be his place, the girl could scarcely keep her feet, and none other had yet moved to aid her. Astonishment filled his veins, but wouldn't arrest him as it had his shipmates. While questions fluttered through his mind like a flock of starlings flushed from their nest, none were more important than attending to her obviously impaired condition.

From atop the ladder to the maindeck, he noted the devious smile at play upon her lips, in tune with her defiant air. She was enjoying this, Kylac realized, whatever that might mean. Frail as she appeared, hers was a march of grim triumph.

He brushed past a slack-jawed Rehm and gaping Tareth to catch her eye. All at once, he slowed, the enmity of her gaze striking him like a crossbow bolt in his chest. As quickly as that, any doubt that it could truly be Denariel, standing before him on the deck of that foundering vessel, hundreds of leagues from where he'd left her, was consumed.

"As you are, mercenary."

She halted, so Kylac did the same. She seemed stable enough, swaying only lightly where she stood. As much as his arms itched to lend support, he knew well enough that she wouldn't welcome it.

Up close, she looked even weaker than she had from afar. Her dark skin—that telltale sign of her mixed heritage—hung looser than he'd remembered on her diminutive frame, and paler. Her eyes and cheeks had grown hollow, her limbs lean. The odor of her body and rank stench of the woolens that clung to it told him she'd gone too long without suitable cleansing. But then, that was as it would have to be, given their days at sea. Days that had worn on her like weeks.

Interminable, the moment in which they faced each other, before Ledron came thumping down the stair, shoving through the loose wall of paralyzed bodies with Leeches at his back.

"To work, barnacles!" Pevrick hollered. "We sink and you gawk? To work!"

In packs and individuals, the crewmen remembered themselves, snapping into action with a perceptible degree of effort, casting backward glances with every departing stride.

Ledron stepped past Kylac to loom over Denariel, his visage clenched in a rictus of disbelief. The princess held her ground, bold smile in place.

"Were you not informed, Captain, that the water is generally kept *outside* a ship's hold?"

"No!" Ledron barked. He raised his hand, looking for half a heartbeat as though he meant to strike her. "What game is this to you now? Have you no honor?"

Denariel hefted her chin, crossing her arms before her. Her left thumb still bore a thick splint, intended to immobilize the broken bone as it healed. "You do enjoy prating of honor. You and Father both. Hollow without results."

"You've doomed this mission."

"By my eye, you've done a suitable job of that yourself." She looked around at the frenetic activities of the crew, and up at the bloodied tatters of their rigging. "Perhaps if I had emerged earlier—"

"Who helped you?"

"Pardon?"

"Would you stand there and tell me you stole upon this vessel on your own? That you've remained hidden all this time without aid?"

"If it matters, I'll tell you precisely that."

Kylac chuckled. He couldn't help himself. Absurdity amused him.

Ledron whirled on him. "Have you word to add to this?"

"I'm as surprised as you are, Captain."

"So you say. You who claim to have swept this ship clean before we commandeered it, and again countless times after. You who even suggested to me the possibility of a stowaway. Match my gaze, Kronus, and tell me you had no hand in this . . . this . . . treason."

"You waste your time," Denariel snapped, while Kylac weathered the Head's glare. "He'll claim no merit for my presence, for he has earned none. And while I might delight to watch you rake his bones beneath our keel, I'll wager he's proven to be the only capable sword among you." With another sweeping glance at the surrounding damage, she added, "Inasmuch as *capable* might pertain here."

"Yet he finds this as humorous as you do," Ledron snarled, continuing to stare Kylac down.

"Thinks on it, Captain. How else could fortune possibly betray us?"

Precisely why he preferred a life of action and reaction, in which one need only be keen and swift to survive. A man committed to plans and expectations tended not only to be more predictable, but also less adaptable to the unforeseen.

The Head seethed, teeth grinding, eyes bulging beneath his livid brow. All around, shipmates marked the confrontation as best they could, gaping and murmuring while carrying out their more pressing duties.

"I'm here of my own volition," Denariel declared again. "If it soothes you to know how, I stole from my bedchamber following your refusal to let me join the expedition. Beneath the stars, I crept down to a deserted section of the wharf and swam up beneath your rudder. I scaled its housing with a grappling line, and from there climbed into the hold, where I've remained since. Her belly is large, and full of voids—even when half submerged at the head. That you, he, or any other failed to find me may speak more to your negligence than my cunning, but there you have it."

Kylac sensed at once that her account, if not riddled with lies, was at least laced with deceit. How relevant that might prove to their undertaking remained to be seen. More striking, in that moment, was his growing admiration for her strength of will. However she'd managed it, and for whatever reasons, she'd succeeded in a task few others would ever contemplate, much less attempt to carry out.

"In truth, the greater challenge was to resist exposing myself sooner, while suffering the blind echoes of . . . well, Eriyah's guess at what you've been doing to this ship."

Solitude. Deprivation. The prior flooding. The Ladrakari attack. She'd weathered it all, dredging herself up from below only now, when the incoming waters were too much to ignore. Aware, no doubt, that Ledron would turn back if she were to be discovered. Yet Kylac had to wonder if there might be more to it than that.

"Ya truly believes ya can help us find your brother."

"I truly trust none of you to see it through."

Ledron shook his head. "The mission is over. If not to the depths, we make from here directly for Addaranth. You hear, Lieutenant?"

"Aye, Captain," Pevrick agreed, eager as a man could be.

"Has ya some secret knowledge?" Kylac pressed, his focus still on Denariel. "Some vital truth ya's yet to share?"

"We tread this ground back in Avenell," Ledron snapped, "when waging argument with Her Highness then." He gripped the princess with his glare. "I said no. You said no. *His Majesty* said no."

"Yet here she stands," Kylac pointed out.

"To sabotage, once more, our best effort at securing His Highness's return." Again the captain shook his head, radiating fury, sorrow, disappointment. "I care not what she knows. I care not that she believes her will to be stronger than ours. I am my king's servant."

Denariel sneered. "Lickspittle, you mean."

"And you, Your Highness, are now my prisoner."

"Her disloyalty would account for our misfortunes, at least . . ."

"Majesty should have fed the black whelp to the wolves . . ."

"Always been an insolent runt . . ."

The murmurs trailed Kylac throughout the ship—abovedecks, belowdecks, and aloft. From the deepest hold to the highest spar, amid Stonewatch or Seawatch, location and company marked scant distinction. No matter the task, be it bailing, stitching, raising, lowering, sanding, knotting, or any other effort deemed critical to keeping the *Vengeance* drifting southward *atop* the waves rather than below, the sentiment rang the same.

"Were she mine, I'd have strung her up by her toes until that fevered blood boiled her brain . . ."

"Would sooner let her own brother die . . ."

"Can't help she's got tar for blood . . ."

To a man, it seemed, Denariel had become the scapegoat for every ill they'd suffered. It was her presence from the outset that had doomed them. Else her earlier disappearance and subsequent hindrance of His Majesty's accord with the Grenarr, which had necessitated this voyage to begin with. Interpretations varied, as did the suggestions of those who urged action against her now, before she made matters worse. But the consensus was swift and fervent and irrefutable. Denariel was to blame.

"Captain should try her as an anchor and sever the line . . ."

"Stuff her back into the bilge to rot . . ."

"Please me to hand her over to the tar-skins myself . . ."

Some muttered, some growled. Others only shook or bobbed their heads as their companions railed and cursed. Kylac felt almost guilty. Not so long ago, it was he who'd been the target of the crew's prevailing fear and resentment, much of it unfair. No matter how well founded some of the arguments against the princess might be, he couldn't bring himself to give them credence.

"I's heard folk back in Avenell suggest she wields a courage your king lacks," Kylac offered casually, while passing a fresh length of cordage up to Jahvid near the top of the mainmast.

"Boldness marked by ignorance," Jahvid huffed, "breeds only foolishness." Line in hand, the sailor set about securing a severed brace of their main-topgallant yard.

"Should've abandoned her to the Harrows when you had the chance," Nadrum mumbled, perched with Rehm in a set of foot-ropes nearby.

If any felt differently, they'd yet to raise voice within Kylac's hearing. Kylac himself, while privately resisting this common view, had seen no cause to openly challenge it. The revelation of Denariel's presence had done nothing to alter their current predicament. Let his shipmates be united in their anger, as long as it fueled them in their endeavors. Even a steady rotation between tasks couldn't keep the men fresh forever. And what harm to the princess while she lay locked away in a cabin belowdecks? With Ledron and Sanow personally overseeing those tending to her immediate recovery, she seemed suitably sheltered from the various acts of violence proposed by the crew. Giving open ear to their complaints provided Kylac a better idea of those he might actually need to ward against in the future.

Besides, while most of their assertions sounded to him prejudiced and ill-conceived, he couldn't say with certainty that they lacked any merit whatsoever.

So he'd gone about his assignments alongside his disgruntled shipmates, toiling in one manner or another, trusting in raw effort and blind fate to see them through. It had been four hours since their collision and Denariel's unannounced emergence. In that time, Ithrimir had charted for Brenham a remote cape, near the southern shore of the isle, upon which they might hope to put aground for repairs. A place where the land's features could potentially shield them from the Ladrakari pursuing them . . . *if* they could reach it. With that desperate aim in her crew's hearts and minds, the *Vengeance* had since lurched from one tributary of the Moravial to another, snaking southward through the enveloping jungle, ushered by the fierce cries and an occasional glimpse of the determined natives shadowing them by land.

An unnecessary reminder of what fell fate awaited those whose strength flagged.

With each hour, the effort had intensified. Further assessments had revealed damages that even Brenham admitted might prove fatal. At best, they would require days of repair, rather than hours. More likely, Brenham had confessed privately, they were dead already, merely in the throes of denial.

There was nothing for it but to press on, hoping for a taste of fortune's fickle favor. Even as the *Vengeance* sank deeper. Weighed down and listing ever more heavily to larboard. Hobbled, yet tenaciously refusing defeat.

A reflection of her crew, Kylac thought, regarding the faces of those Whitefists with whom he labored now. Haggard and harried, wounded and weary, yet stubborn and steadfast. Though rank with bitterness, those Kylac had striven beside, brushed in passing, or observed from afar sustained one another with a collective resolve, doggedly resisting the despair that threatened to overwhelm them. Unsurprising, he supposed. Were it elsewise, they'd not have been chosen for this hopeless errand in the first place.

"Marauder afore!"

Kylac turned, wincing as yet another grim announcement from the crow's nest sent shockwaves throughout their vessel. Those bracing the yard Jahvid sought to secure fumbled their hold, but remembered themselves and dug heel into their footropes, recovering swiftly.

"Steady, lads," Kylac urged.

From his lofty vantage, he found the enemy ship quickly—nearer than he would have expected. Stolen in from a veil of mist clouding the southern horizon. Bearing down on them in apparent ambush from no more than a thousand strokes out.

"Sangho's Tempest," Rehm cursed.

Kylac couldn't make out the ship's colors, but she was a full mast larger than the Reaver that had chanced upon them earlier. Marauder class, given the lookout's cry. The same as their own. Meaning that their enemies were multiplying, with Temerius Seahammer and his attending Prowlers still to be dealt with.

To that concern, he spied no attending vessels. Nonetheless, an urgency bordering on panic took hold of his fellow crewmen as orders went out and those who were able scurried to their battle posts.

Nadrum balked. "We're to fight? In our condition?"

"Would you sooner we try to outrun them?" Rehm asked with a scoff.

"Mother's mercy," Jahvid pleaded.

Kylac smiled. Just as chance could steal from under a man's nose, so could it offer blessing when least expected. "Look closer, lads, and sees it for what it is."

"The Fair Mother's final embrace?" Nadrum asked glumly.

"A boon," Kylac replied.

Jahvid frowned, his irritation only deepening. "Mad as Creyl, you must be."

Kylac winked as he took his leave, shimmying across the ratlines toward the nearest shroud.

"How is this a boon?" Rehm called after him.

Kylac paused upon reaching the shroud. "Here we're set to kiss the depths," he said, "and our enemy sees fit to deliver a fresh ship."

22

WITH A NOD MEANT TO COMFORT the ashen-faced Garryn, at post
in his most common relay position, Kylac entered the wheelhouse.

"A quarter-mark to intercept," Brenham was announcing to those
present, scratching notations upon the larboard chart table. "Maybe
twice that if we come about now."

"Can we lose them in the Skein?" Pevrick asked, scowling at Kylac's
arrival.

Ithrimir snorted. "Crippled as we are? We've no place to run
where they cannot overtake us."

"Shall I just keep heading toward them, then?" Taeg asked. He'd
reflexively nudged the wheel to larboard, edging them away from
their enemy, toward the mouth of another waterway.

"Put her aground," Kylac said.

Elementer and first mate regarded him as they might a roach at a
feast. Helmsman and second mate appeared only slightly less repulsed.

"Abandon ship?" Brenham surmised.

"To surrender to the savages?" Pevrick asked.

"The Grenarr would be fewer in number," Taeg pointed out. "Even
a Marauder's crew."

"We risk greater casualties in a shipboard fight," Kylac replied. "To
us, and to our ship."

"Our ship is finished," Pevrick groused. "With our diminished mobility, they'll sink us from a hundred strokes out."

"Not if'n they hope to retrieve Grendavan's lieutenant. Regardless, I meant our *new* ship—theirs."

"This song again?" Taeg asked, making no attempt to hide his amusement.

Heads turned as Ledron entered.

"Status."

"Runt here would have us flee afoot," Pevrick answered. "Each man to himself, no doubt."

"Flee?" Kylac echoed. "Put her aground, I said."

"He thinks to commandeer their ship," Brenham corrected.

Ledron's frown bespoke interest. "Surely more sprightly than ours." His gaze turned to Kylac. "How?"

"Captain," Pevrick interjected. "If we set ashore, the savages—"

"I'll hear your protests, I'm sure," Ledron said, raising a palm at his first mate. "*After* he answers my question."

"Afloat, they have us caged," Kylac explained. "Carrying a hundred, I presume?"

Taeg nodded. "Four seascore. Warriors all."

"Ashore, we can lure them out, bid them chase. I'll sweep their ship o' those who remain."

"What lure?" Ledron asked. "How to be sure they'll take the bait?"

Kylac shrugged. "Ourselves. Our guest the Shorecleaver. Her Highness, if'n it puts spur to their flanks."

Ledron scowled, his gaze narrowing.

"You hear?" said Pevrick. "Her Highness as bait. While he roams of his own accord?"

"Has ya seen me shirk a fight?"

"Which route here?" Taeg demanded, as they neared the approaching fork. "Or do we come about?"

"Wherever we can buy some time from our native hosts," Kylac urged. "There are small islands ahead, yes? A spit or mound that'll take 'em longer to reach?"

"At our pace and heading?" Ithrimir, frowning intensely, seemed to contemplate quickly. "I know a place. An hour it might give us, no more. Veer east."

"Veering east," Taeg echoed.

"And if the Grenarr choose not to set aground?" Brenham asked, his tone laden with caution.

Pevrick agreed. "Why would they, when they see the horde of savages set to do their killing for them?"

"Because they're tar-skins," Ledron determined, "and they'll not be deprived." Thinking it through, he added, "So we ground ourselves. Deploy a contingent with Tormitius to draw pursuit. Conceal another company within the *Vengeance*. A fair fortification on elsewise open ground. From savage and marauder alike."

The princess. Ledron meant to shield her as long as possible.

Kylac nodded. "Fair enough. As the enemy ranges, I'll sees to the ship. Shed its defenders. The hunters will turn back. Some, if not all. When they reach me, those ensconced in our wounded lady here emerge at *their* backs. Food for the crabs well within the hour o' the natives' arrival."

"Them or us?" Taeg quipped.

Ledron's visage suggested he was unconvinced, even as he muttered, "It could work."

"Or the runt could be feathered by a Grenarr sentry before setting foot to enemy ladder," said Pevrick. "Our runners chased down or intercepted. Those sheltering in this black bitch's carcass burned alive."

"Noted. Alternatives, Lieutenant?"

The *Vengeance* shuddered, her hull dragging against some submerged shelf or mound. Her larboard list had grown more pronounced. Swarming Redfists still scurried abovedecks and below, fighting their losing battle against floodwaters, while Whitefists grappled with the compromised rigging. Wind-chopped waves only added to the lurching, staggering sensation of her unsteady advance.

"We used the landscape to shed them before," Pevrick put forth dourly. "Barring that, we might do battle above the waves, or sink as they watch from afar."

Only the obvious. Gazes shifted, marking the Marauder's position on the southwest horizon. Nearer than before. Rotating to match the *Vengeance*'s heading. In the ensuing silence, not one of the three choices recounted by Leeches sounded more tenable than Kylac's proposal—not even to the first mate himself.

"Find us a landing," Ledron commanded his navigators. "Lieutenant, summon Jaleth, Sim, Sethric, and Olekk. Assembled here upon my return."

"Aye, Captain."

Kylac took to Ledron's heels as the captain departed. While the Head hadn't invited him to do so, neither did he demand elsewise as Kylac followed him to a deck hatch leading below. A pair of subdecks they descended, before venturing aft to a bank of cabins, one of which was warded by Redfists Ysander and Moh. Kylac returned a nod from each before slipping between them after Ledron.

Inside the cabin, Denariel sat upon a padded berth, cocooned in a coarse blanket and sipping stew spooned to her by Aythef with a tremulous hand. Sanow stood sentry against a wall. An undue precaution, it would seem, given the lack of exits, the bare furnishings, and the guardsmen posted just outside. Then again, this *was* Denariel. Doubtless, Ledron had instructed his fellow Blackfist not to let her out of his sight.

Their bodies quickly consumed what space remained in the cramped quarters. Aythef shrank to one side, seeming unnerved by their arrival—or by whatever grim news they bore.

"What fell word now, Captain?" Denariel asked.

Already, the dusky color had returned to her cheeks. Her short hair was a tangle, and her eyes set deep in recessed hollows, but her strength, Kylac suspected, wouldn't be long in returning.

"Find her some warm woolens and leathers," Ledron commanded Aythef. "Seems we'll be putting forth sooner than anticipated."

The cook acknowledged them with a curt bow, then cast about for someplace to set the bowl of stew.

"Take it," Ledron said. "She's had her fill for now."

Aythef bowed again, then scurried from the cabin, gaze averted, only too eager to be rid of them.

Denariel clasped her blanket to her throat. "And where . . ." A fit of coughing threatened to steal her words, but she fought through it. "Where do we sally to, Captain?"

"To one of your voids, if any remain above water. Wherever you can burrow and not be discovered." He turned to Sanow. "We founder, and the Grenarr are upon us. When we beach, I want her in the most secret—yet defensible—nook you can find. If we are to be caught, she will be the last. Understood?"

"Sir."

Denariel leaned forward. "Captain—"

"Report to the helm when she is ready to move."

The Head wheeled around, turning for the exit. Kylac slid from his path.

"Captain!" Denariel barked.

"Oh, and see to it that she is gagged."

The Head half turned to Kylac as if anticipating protest. Kylac had none to give. Seeming almost disappointed by this, Ledron marched on, reversing their path of descent, with scarcely a grunt for those they passed in the narrow corridors. Moments later, Kylac shadowed him back into the wheelhouse, where Pevrick, Brenham, Taeg, and Ithrimir were joined now by Jaleth, Simalen, Olekk, and Sethric.

"How fares the arm?" Ledron asked Sethric, gesturing at the Red-fist's bloody sleeve.

"A scratch, sir."

"Good." The captain gritted his teeth as he eyed his chosen crew-men. "I have need of you."

He proceeded to outline for the newcomers the plan as he envi-sioned it—much the same as Kylac had described it from the first. Once beached, he wanted three Whitefists—Brenham, Taeg, and Jaleth—along with three Redfists—Sim, Sethric, and Olekk—to each lead a squad ashore. Six companies, twelve men each, to fan out while taking flight from the Grenarr they assumed would give chase. Nearly the whole of their force, to give every appearance that they were abandoning the *Vengeance* entirely. Taeg's pack would be charged with escorting their prisoner and primary lure, Tormitius.

"Making me the stag in this hunt," Taeg noted dryly. "I'm hon-ored, sir."

Ledron himself, along with Pevrick, would stay behind with the remaining dozen—chiefly stewards and bowmen—who would prove sufficient, he hoped, to defend the ship from any tar-skins who sought to reclaim it. They would not truly be warding the crippled vessel, however, but His Majesty's daughter, hidden within. Whatever personal feelings they might harbor toward Her Highness, they would be expected to defend her with their lives.

Using the ship as a holdfast would strengthen their defense, while the ground forces, after stringing the attackers out, would be charged with circling back to help break any concentrated siege.

He went on to explain Kylac's assignment during this initial feint: to board the enemy vessel—by land or by water, depending on where the enemy dropped anchor—and clear the way for their own siege against it. Ledron's company would reinforce his efforts from behind, and help to secure the vessel as their own. The more distant companies would reverse course, crushing the enemy—caught between them—as they went.

Questions were raised and answered as to contingencies. If Kylac were to fail? An alarm would be trumpeted by those upon the *Vengeance* for their ground forces to battle back sooner. It might be that Ledron's company would have to sally forth to ensure the Marauder didn't slink away before they could reach it. The primary objectives were to ensure that the Grenarr forces engaged, were kept trapped between two fronts, and to pray that the enemy's numbers weren't too much greater than their own.

"Give me rein, and they won't be," Kylac promised.

Ledron glared down the boast. "However it plays out, it must do so quickly," he emphasized, "before the island's denizens arrive to have hand in matters."

By then, the ground chosen for their landing had been sighted—a mile-long, hook-shaped spit arcing south and west from the eastern bank of the waterway through which they slogged. Sandy at its point and grassy along its torso, yet marked by shelves and spires of jagged rock where it sloped up to abut the jungle shore. A suitable barrier against the Ladrakari, Kylac thought, but also a veritable palisade against any landward escape.

Fortunate enough, given that flight wasn't truly intended as an option.

Now firmly astern, the Grenarr ship chomped at their wake. Even though their adjusted course had led them to race *from* it rather than toward it, it was chewing up the intervening distance at an alarming rate. According to Brenham's calculations, it had closed to within twelve minutes.

"You have ten to assemble your teams and relay orders," the captain said. "Lieutenant, the wheel."

Brenham and Taeg exited alongside the other chosen commanders, leaving the helm to Pevrick.

"What of our Scribe?" Kylac asked, nodding at Ithrimir.

Ledron eyed the Elementer with distaste. "He'll avail us nothing if put to running back and forth upon the sands. Let him hunker with those aboard. I don't suppose you've any practice with a bow, have you?"

Ithrimir shook his head, cobalt eye narrowing in a piercing squint. "If it please you, Captain, I can hurl stores or sever a scaling hook easily enough."

"So be it," the Head replied with a dismissive wave, then turned to depart.

Again Kylac chose to trail him, this time to the command deck, where they entered the captain's quarters to peer down at the shackled Tormitius.

The Shorecleaver's gaze gleamed amid lantern-lit shadows, his bed and body tilted now—along with the floor itself—at a perceptible angle. "Do my senses deceive, or is this vessel rolling to larboard?"

Ledron looked to his posted jailors. "Bring him."

Cuffed at the ankle and wrist, Grendavan's erstwhile lieutenant was half carried, half dragged between burly Havrig and brawny Jorrand out to the starboard rail. Following Ledron, and with Kylac at his back, the Redfists delivered him from there down to the maindeck, where Taeg awaited with his company.

"Can he not stand?" the helmsman asked.

"Cannot or will not," Ledron replied. "I'd bleed him for it, were it not what he desired."

Taeg frowned, adjusting the tie that held back his gray mane. "That's not going to aid our attempt to cast a distant lure."

"Less distance to reel back," the Head offered in cold appeasement.

"Fine care you've taken of my lord's vessel," Tormitius observed. His mocking tone was laced with anger as he surveyed the condition of the rigging with a squinted gaze. "Too much ship for a knot of landsnakes."

The taunt went ignored as Denariel emerged from a nearby hatch, attended by Sanow. Dressed in oversized garb and gagged as commanded. Kylac wondered whether they would also bind her hands to prevent her from removing it. It surprised him that she would tolerate it willingly. But then, she'd already demonstrated a knack for keeping him guessing as few did.

Ledron gestured them toward the wheelhouse. Sanow nodded and nudged her accordingly. Denariel moved as prompted, without complaint.

Though half blinded by the sting of unfiltered daylight, and surrounded by crewmen mustering in one direction or another, Tormitius didn't miss the duo's passing. A broad smirk split his black face. "Fie, Captain. You told me not that the princess sailed with us."

"Find him a gag," Ledron instructed the Grenarrian's handlers.

"A lure you named me. For what?" Wincing from the glare, Tormitius peered astern, tracing gazes to find the closing Marauder.

"Your black ilk think to rescue you," the Head allowed. "Though I'd not give rein to hope."

Kylac took note of the startled recognition that rippled across their captive's features a moment before he chortled with coarse laughter. "No, Captain. It is you who should surrender hope."

"Choke on it, filth," said Havrig, as he presented the Shorecleaver's mouth with a strip of cloth.

"Hold," Kylac said. "He knows something."

Ledron frowned, but raised a restraining hand. "Speak to it, then."

Havrig withdrew, but hovered near.

"That is no Marauder that gives chase."

"Relieved I am to hear it. Shall we furl sail and welcome them aboard then with cups of mead?"

"Give eye to her colors, Captain, and to her figurehead. Do you not know them?"

Kylac looked. The ebony standard upon their pursuer's mast whipped in the wind, so that he couldn't make out its crimson device. The figurehead looked to be some form of creature enwrapped in billowing tatters, but revealed nothing, judging by the expressions of his shipmates.

"Vorathus, you have found. The Shrikeskinner. Master of the *Banshee's Wail*. Rebel. Cannibal. Kinslayer. Vorathus the Brutal, Vorathus the Barbarian, Vorathus the—"

"What of it?" Ledron snapped.

"By any name, a rabid renegade who slaughters without prejudice. Who has no allies, no allegiances, and seeks none. My foe, as surely as he is yours. He'll attempt no rescue."

Ledron shared an uncertain look with Taeg. "Bounty, then. If traitor he is, he'll seek to make you his hostage, to ransom you for—"

"Ransom? He has come for the bloodletting and nothing more. He and his brood of Banshees. To collect bones and skins with which to further decorate his cursed vessel."

As if in response, the wail of a shell horn shrilled from the pursuing Marauder, ushering a concentrated roar from its crew. Available hands clustered to the fore, cheering madly, brandishing their blades and bows. The trailing sun hid much in backlit shadow, but from the rails and rigging hung adornments that could in fact be human trophies as Tormitius described.

"Our death knell, Captain. He gives no quarter."

Amid the approaching furor, Ledron seemed suddenly concerned. "The value of royal blood would not escape him. Surely he would—"

"Your princess? He'll as soon ravish her battered, headless corpse," Tormitius promised, "as seek to sell her to her father. Prey, we are now. Carrion for the Vulture of the Seas. Nothing more."

A genuine fear underscored the cruel relish of the Shorecleaver's pronouncement. Suggesting he spoke truly. Truth or lie, the account had found purchase among those within hearing. The soldiers and sailors giving ear looked to their captain with fresh uncertainty.

"Why seek to convince us o' this?" Kylac asked.

"Only to say that, whatever you've plotted here, better would it be to scatter inland, to make his hunt more difficult."

"Brace for landing!"

Those who'd all but forgotten the impending landfall turned now with the rest of the crew to secure holds, grasp lines, or elsewise buttress themselves against impact. Drowning at the nose and half tilted to larboard, the crippled *Vengeance* scraped and groaned as Pevrick at the wheel and sailors manning the sheets heaved her shoreward alongside the westernmost edge of the spit. Timbers creaked and planks split as she grated through a nest of submerged rocks before jarring to an abrupt, shivering stop upon the sands, her bow wedged into a half-moon cove. There she hung, sharply canted, rolling slightly as if recoiling in denial.

As she settled into her unsteady berth, her crewmen looked to one another breathlessly, awaiting some unknown command.

"Ladders!" Ledron shouted.

Sailors and soldiers on the larboard side stumbled into action, tossing corded rungs and knotted lines overboard, spurred by the surging cries of the oncoming barbarian vessel. Those nearer the captain, Kylac observed, were slower to react, as if seeking some additional confirmation.

"We cling to our plan," the captain urged. He gestured at Havrig, who responded by cinching the ready gag into Tormitius's mouth. "And let no tar-skin—Grenarrian or outcast—seek to divide us."

23

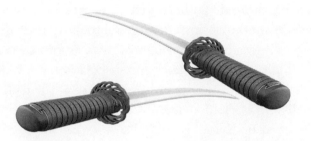

CROUCHED AMIDSHIPS AT THE larboard rail, wedged between a pair of storage lockers for cover against enemy lookouts, Kylac watched his shipmates spill from the *Vengeance* like fleeing rats. The companies comprised of Seawatch had gone first, scrabbling down ladders and lines behind commanders Brenham, Taeg, and Jaleth. After them now streamed the companies of Stonewatch, led by Simalen, Olekk, and Sethric. Strategy dictated that, when the sailors and soldiers turned back to reengage their barbarian pursuers, Redfist blades would form the front lines, protecting the Whitefist bows at their backs.

Sensible enough, save that the frantic haste with which Kylac's fellow crewmen were tearing along the sands of the spit made it difficult to imagine any did so with the intention of turning back at all. Formations, loose to begin with, quickly dissolved into ragged lines splintering out in all directions. Sailor or soldier, some men were fleeter afoot than others, with those of leaner limbs and longer strides outpacing their shorter, stockier compatriots. Within moments, the organized withdrawal had devolved into a mad dash toward high ground, each man running only for himself.

But then, that was by design. The first step in drawing the barbarians was to sell the feint of a desperate retreat. Thus far, Kylac was convinced.

He couldn't speak for the approaching Banshees, save that they appeared eager enough in whatever purpose had brought them. The larboard side of their ship's hull was even now scraping against the spit's embankment, coming in for a broadside landing as the *Vengeance* had before it. Kylac had anticipated a slower, more cautious approach—if not anchoring farther out—in order to minimize any damage caused by a direct beaching. He'd been given no cause to suspect the renegade Grenarr might sacrifice their vessel the way Ledron meant to abandon the *Vengeance*. Countering that, what information he'd been given was riddled with ignorance and speculation, not to be trusted.

Better to be patient and let observation reveal the truth.

The shell horn of their pursuers blew again, sending a chill of anticipation slithering up Kylac's spine. Whatever plunder these barbarians had come to take—the ship, its stores, its occupants—their ringing cries reeked of bloodlust. Mayhap, as Tormitius had claimed, they'd come not for loot, but for the challenge of the hunt itself.

If so, Kylac would be pleased to oblige them.

He checked the progress of the fleeing companies, slowed now by fatigue, yet staggering on through the swaths of seaweed and stalks of swordgrass covering the hook-shaped bend of earth. Tormitius, he noticed, jogged willingly alongside Taeg and those charged with his handling. Though hobbled by the injury to his foot, fettered still by the cords binding his wrists behind his back, and visibly hampered by the days of minimal rations and bedridden captivity, he clearly wanted no part of this Vorathus's crew. For all his talk of seeking death before permitting himself to be used to betray his people, surrendering to the so-called Shrikeskinner wasn't something he was prepared to accept.

The chill gripping Kylac's neck and shoulders burrowed a mite deeper.

Upon the enemy ship, orders echoed. An anchor dropped, plunging into the windswept waters. Booms shifted, and lines whistled through pulleys. Sails twisted or raised, working to arrest the vessel's momentum as she crunched along the stony foundation of the embankment. Kylac got a better look of the ship's figurehead than he needed as the sleek bald brow of the howling, skull-faced maiden upon its prow bit right up against the *Vengeance*'s stern, slow-charging bowsprit piercing some lower deck amid a shattering of glass and cracking of wood.

A shudder rippled through the already battered vessel at the intrusion, attended by a chorus of lusty cheers. Kylac looked reflexively at the hatch through which Ledron had departed on the heels of his shipboard regiment. None had broached the possibility of the *Banshee's Wail* skewering them from behind, essentially pinning the *Vengeance* upon her chosen landing ground. A broadside boarding had been deemed plausible, but dismissed as unlikely, given that the *Vengeance* was of equal size and thus even-matched, potentially, in terms of crew. Why would the barbarians tether themselves to so formidable an enemy without some idea of her strength?

Mayhap they knew she sailed at reduced force, or had observed her trammeled condition. Mayhap they'd witnessed the crew's exodus in time to alter their attack strategy. Mayhap they simply didn't care. A vortex of possibilities churned through Kylac's mind before dissipating in a scattered chorus. Their reasons mattered not. Only the result. Already, Ledron's strategy had been disrupted. There would be no defense of the *Vengeance* from an elevated position. There would be no time for Kylac to hide while the Banshees raced ashore before he began his takeover of their vessel. As fate would have it, he looked to face a stampede of enemies pouring over—and possibly through—the very ship upon which he stood.

The ship-to-ship battle they'd hoped to avoid.

Only, now it appeared he would wage it alone.

Options crowded his thoughts, demanding consideration. Hide, in hopes that the bulk of the assailing host would yet spill after the retreating crew as anticipated. Race to confront them, taking the fight to their decks so as to better prevent any from tearing through the *Vengeance* in search of the hidden Denariel. Stand his ground, so that whatever damage might be done to their surroundings would be inflicted against the dying *Vengeance*, rather than the barbarian ship they hoped to claim.

Flee? Slip into the jungles of Mistwall and abandon this folly, as Pevrick had accused him of plotting.

He dismissed the last, but gave further thought to the others as the assailing Banshees tossed hooked ropes and set down boarding planks, further securing their forecastle against the *Vengeance*'s stern. Their clustering ranks thickened, though none had moved yet to cross over. Kylac couldn't have guessed why, until the burgeoning wall of marauders split down the center, giving way to one who stepped forward among them.

Barefoot, clad only in breech clout, a quiver of arrows, and a brace of knives, the massive brute carried a bulbous waist and barrel chest striped scarlet and white with war paint. Similar markings carved crescent lines across his meaty limbs and the humps of fatty muscle that flanked his neck. A great black beard, salted in narrow strips, sprouted like a spearhead from his face and chin, matching the crown of hair that tufted up from the back of his head, styled into a pointed plume behind his bald brow.

Vorathus himself, Kylac suspected, given the deference shown him. In his left fist, he carried a large bow. With the other, he dragged what might have been a black-feathered cloak . . . until he trotted up the central plank laid between the ships to put foot on the *Vengeance*'s taffrail. There he paused to heft his right hand into the air.

Revealing the carcass of a shrike, gripped by the throat, pierced by a pair of arrows.

The barbarian captain howled, and those around him bayed in frenzied chorus. Kylac recalled the shrike his own shipmates had failed to bring down a day earlier—shards, had it truly been only a day?—upon escaping Grenarr pursuit through the Trellong. A bird presumed to have been sent by one Temerius Seahammer to obtain reinforcements or elsewise betray their position. Much like the one loosed earlier from their own shipboard rookery, Kylac had posited, by an enemy mole secreted aboard.

Whatever its origin, whatever its precise purpose, Kylac felt certain—trusting to his instincts—that he gazed upon the same bird now. Intercepted by this Vulture of the Seas. Bringing the Shrikeskinner down upon them.

Amid his crew's cheers, Vorathus flung the slain raptor upon the sterncastle and spat on its bloodied feathers.

Unleashing the barbarian charge.

In a mad rush, they boarded the *Vengeance*, racing across planks or swinging down from ropes amid their forward rigging. Borne upon a swell of raucous cries. Fueled by an unmistakable thirst.

Kylac drew his blades.

Reflex propelled him forward. He wasn't going to wait for them to surround him and pin him against the rail. Nor would he risk permitting them to flood the ship, whereby he might have to give chase to ensure Denariel's safety. He also had to make sure they didn't turn about and withdraw with their ship. All of which suggested he push to engage now. So they outnumbered him a hundred to one. His father had an adage for facing overwhelming odds. *How to scale a mountain? One stretch at a time.*

He dashed aft along the larboard rail. Swift, silent, twirling his blades in hand. Intimate he was with their heft and balance, their planes and edges, their blunt hilts and piercing tips. Yet there remained the weaving winds to consider, the subtle rocking of the ship at his feet, the ceaseless flow of invisible energies around him. All would affect his work in this particular setting. Natural forces he could define, and those he couldn't, he drew them near, basking in their touch, empowering himself in ways that physical training and muscle memory alone could never quite match.

They coursed through his veins, and he felt himself flaring like a hooded asp.

The first wave of Banshees met him upon the stair leading from the command deck to the wheel deck. He sensed their surprise, and fanned its flames by spinning his body while tossing his blades into the air ahead of him. He caught them amid circling flashes, which became arcing slashes. The Banshee to larboard fell against the rail, right arm severed near the shoulder. The Banshee to his left doubled over at the waist, then slipped and fell on his own entrails.

Before either could know what had happened to them, two, three, four more had joined them. Kylac stood his ground at the base of the stair, like a wedged boulder dividing a stream, while his enemies' momentum carried them past. His blades whirled, carving rather than stabbing, to remain unfettered by the weight of his adversaries. Blood bloomed and fountained, in sudden gouts and beaded strings.

Pain and death followed.

Neither did much to dissuade the Banshee charge. The knot of howling, ebon-skinned bodies pressed his position. As the tenor of their cries was altered by the startled keening of the wounded, the trailing waves shifted instinctively, pouring to the sides of those slowed by injury in the center. One man's haste carried him over the rail, but the bulwark served to corral those who followed him. To starboard, the surge simply spilled over the lip of the command deck, forgoing the clogged stair. These marauders soon rounded, recovering quickly from lost footing and entanglement with their comrades, to have at Kylac from behind.

With them were many of the wounded, retaliating with instinctive rage and refusal. Whether missing limbs or bearing mortal injury, they resumed the fight as best as their maimed bodies would allow. Howling all the while. Wide-eyed. Stinking of tar and filth and disease.

Kylac had intended to press onward, blocking and then turning back the barbarian surge by virtue of the narrow space, driving the fight nearer to the *Vengeance*'s stern. But the swiftness with which their numbers eddied at his back, and the ferocity with which they countered, had him withdrawing to the wheel deck and then the maindeck. Better to keep the majority of his enemies in front of him, and to have more ground upon which to roam. A stationary target, so severely outnumbered, could be overrun. The more fluid his movements, the harder he would be to pin down.

Banshees flooded down along the starboard rail unimpeded. Recognizing the threat, they curled to larboard, tearing across the slanted deck to descend upon him. It mattered little to Kylac, for these reinforcements would first have to fight through the nearer ranks to even reach him.

Their zeal to do so, however, took him by surprise, as they set to hacking, shoving, and bludgeoning their own in order to reach the front. While this cannibalistic behavior served to deflect or inhibit some of those who might have elsewise raised weapon against him, it shifted the entire flow of the melee in an unusual manner, altering its anticipated rhythm.

Reminding Kylac of the potential peril wrought by expectation.

He adapted readily, perceiving and reacting to the change without conscious thought. A smile tugged at his lips. The greater the challenge, the more alive he felt.

Even as the number of dead mounted around him.

The marauders seemed not to notice, or not to care. As they had from the outset, they betrayed no substantial awareness of pain, and none whatsoever of camaraderie or self-preservation. Another challenge, for they couldn't now be relied upon to react and behave as rational men.

Kylac, however, had faced such before, having fought more than once against the insane, the enraged, and those under the influence of drink or nerve-dulling medicines that made them immune to fear and all but impervious to injury. Shards, in the battle at Kraagen Keep, he'd battled an entire horde of Killangrathor's dragonspawn—creatures who displayed a similar lack of regard for themselves and their kin, and whose capabilities far exceeded these.

The harder they pressed him, the quicker he could cut them down.

He edged toward the center of the deck, forgoing the relative defense of the larboard rail at his back. The Banshees swarmed round, encircling him in a roaring torrent, hewing and jabbing with all manner of blade and cudgel. Tips and edges thrust and swiped at him, but were more likely to draw blood from an overeager companion than from their intended target. For all their unrelenting savagery, their attacks were reckless and clumsy and crude. Kylac was too swift, too agile, too familiar with a man's strengths and limitations to fall victim to—

An arrow shaft whistled as it skimmed past his ear. Kylac half turned at the short-lived yelp of the barbarian behind him, who took its head in the thigh. Without pause, he lunged to slip the tip of his longsword between the ribs of an opponent while parrying a thrust at his back with his shortsword, then pivoted away from a flanking blow aimed at his knee while stabbing rearward with his right hand and chopping with the left. Amid the ceaseless flurry, he traced the arrow's path back to a prominent figure atop the wheelhouse.

Vorathus.

Already, the Shrikeskinner was nocking another arrow to his string.

Awhirl within the frenetic tumult, Kylac could give the barbarian captain only passing attention, but recognized the new threat. At precisely the right moment, he withdrew behind a charging Banshee, and watched a barbed arrowhead sprout from the peak in the man's throat.

He expected then for the marauders to back off, giving their leader room to play. Instead, those nearest continued to assail him, while those farther back drew slings and bows of their own.

As abruptly as that, Kylac found himself showered and pelted with missiles fired or flung from almost every direction. Worse, many sailed at him haphazardly, as if launched without aim. Fast and fluid as he might be, he couldn't draw their fire to one area and evade it by redirecting to another if they were willing to arc or hurl shots randomly amid their own shipmates.

Who maintained their ferocious crush, undeterred.

Kylac used this to his advantage, shrinking his sphere of movement and allowing his enemies to draw closer, using their bodies as shields against the barrage. Even so, a warning pricked his stomach. While their fearlessness alone wouldn't win the day, their range weapons just might. For the way in which they were being brought to bear made this less a contest of skill and more a game of chance. Especially as more and more Banshees beyond his reach grew impatient and sheathed their swords and clubs in favor of bow and sling.

The writhing, convulsing dead began to pile around him. Barriers, but also walls that would keep him pinned. Barring some new wrinkle, he would have to abandon his increasingly stationary position. By his estimate, he'd slaughtered nearly twoscore—approaching half their number. Many more had been wounded—by his hand or another's. Surely, even a mindless enemy such as this had its breaking point. Mayhap, if he held his ground just a little longer, they would recognize the futility of their effort, and withdraw.

Alas, all sound and movement suggested elsewise. Despite their heavy losses, they seemed determined to depart these decks with his severed head in hand, or not at all.

As his foot brushed the edge of a deck hatch, Kylac remembered Ledron and crew, ensconced somewhere below. Were they to emerge now, somewhere at the barbarians' backs, Kylac might have all the distraction he would need to finish these stubborn fools. If not the Head's contingent, then those Addarans who'd fled the ship. Even if just a handful. Had that not been the plan? To draw the enemy out and seek wherever possible to flank them?

Evidently, failing to unravel the barbarians' knot meant that Kylac truly withstood their rampage alone. For he sensed neither aid nor favor, only the hostile whirlwind shrieking around him.

A searing pain slashed across his forearm. An arrow. Aimed or errant, it made no difference. As with the hammering jolt in his shoulder from a spinning stone. Kylac sprang backward, somersaulting to larboard. Reason suggested he might abandon ship, to gather a force with which to rally . . .

Foolishness, Kylac realized, dropping low and skewering a pair of enemies that loomed over him. He'd never outpace the hail of missiles that chased after him. Even now, stones riddled the backs of those who twitched at the ends of his blades. An arrow punched through the stomach of one, and from the mouth of the other. Both dropped almost instantly, exposing Kylac to the barrage that followed.

He avoided injury by spinning to his left, hamstringing a swordsman and severing the foot from a bowman. The latter brought a fierce grimace to Kylac's face.

He put a blade in the back of the bowman's neck as he slithered on, spinning forward again in a crouch. There was nothing for it, he'd decided. Forsaken but for his swords and the occasional aid of the enemy's own fire, he had but one choice left to him. Keep moving. Keep slashing. Slay them all.

With feints now serving little purpose, he moved to maximize his cover from the aerial assault. Barrels and capstans and rigging became as shields as he ducked and whirled and vaulted from the open maindeck back toward the wheel deck. It occurred to him that he might seek shelter belowdecks, but the risks were too great. Even if Ledron hadn't barred the hatches, even if he could set down his weapons long enough to fling or pry one open, there was no guarantee his enemies would follow. He still had to seize their vessel, which he couldn't very well ensure from within the bowels of his own. Besides, if they did happen to chase him below, and he ended up with archers drawing bead on him amid those cramped confines . . .

A bolt grazed his calf. Kylac snarled, tamping down the flare of pain. Laughter boomed amid the tumult. Atop the wheelhouse, Vorathus's great belly shook, even as the mad huntsman reached into his quiver for another shaft.

Kylac decided then, as he carved through the body of another Banshee, that if no others died, the Shrikeskinner would. Mayhap, upon witnessing the fall of their bestial captain, the remaining Banshees would scatter, or at least reconsider the wisdom of persisting in a fight that had already seen their crew decimated.

It seemed unlikely. Were that his only justification, he'd have abandoned the notion.

Fortunately, all he truly wanted was to see the Vulture bleed.

The sprawled forms of his victims and the pools of blood surrounding them challenged his footing as he worked his way aft. Hand-to-hand opposition had thinned, as most had surrendered their blades in favor of range weapons. A poor defense as he swept toward them, diving and rolling and lunging with a swiftness they'd not likely encountered before. Not that their swords and cudgels would have saved them against blades such as his. But it might have slowed his work. As it stood, he scythed through them like stalks of wheat, ducking beneath their bodies whenever possible to help deflect or intercept the missiles raining after him.

Pricked and nicked and battered as seldom before, Kylac returned to the larboard stair that ascended to the wheel deck. He found it clogged with corpses and peppered with clattering projectiles. There stood no more enemies to shield him. The remainder lay at his back upon the maindeck, save for Vorathus, taking fresh aim almost directly above him.

Kylac sprang up the stair, feinting toward the wheelhouse. Had he followed through, the Shrikeskinner's black arrow would have feathered the top of his skull. But his actual leap took him to the larboard rail, from which he flipped overhead to reach a web of ratlines, sheathing his swords in order to catch hold of the strands.

He let go almost as quickly, to evade the hail of missiles chasing after, but held on by hooking his knees and feet around a pair of lower rungs as he pitched backward. Hanging for only a heartbeat, he weathered a stone strike against his chest in order to avoid an arrow that would have pierced it. He then bucked upward again, swung round to the other side, scrabbled higher, and leapt out toward a nearby boom.

He never reached it, but he hadn't intended to. With his right hand, he reached for a particular line of cordage amid a sheaf of them. With his left, he drew one of his daggers, with which he slashed through a neighboring line within the bundle.

The severed line released a heavy yard serving counterweight. Maintaining his hold on the other length of that cord, Kylac was jerked skyward. He drew his feet in toward his chest as he went, projectiles arcing low beneath them, gazes and gaping mouths snapping up in pursuit.

He could have ridden the line halfway up the mizzenmast. Instead, he dropped, tucking and rolling, coming to a halt atop the wheelhouse at the feet of the barbarian sea lord, Vorathus. The Shrikeskinner chopped down at him with his thick bow, bladed at its edge above the handle. But Kylac slid outside the swipe, his dagger-wielding hand whipping out to bury his own blade in the back of the marauder's knee.

A lusty howl erupted from Vorathus as he spun, drawing a dagger of his own. But Kylac by then had a shortsword in hand, which he thrust up through the Shrikeskinner's gut. Tearing free just as swiftly, he rounded again, slashing along the barbarian's spine, before closing face-to-face, freed longsword piercing up through the dead man's jaw.

Even so, the Shrikeskinner seemed for a moment as though he might retaliate, staring at Kylac with blood-flecked eyes and flared nostrils. His entire body flexed, as tall and stiff as a flagpole, perched high upon his naked toes. His mouth pinned shut, he hissed and slavered through blistered lips peeled back in a mad grimace, stinking of rancid meat and decayed teeth.

But his thick arms hung in place, unthreatening, as the gleam in his bloody gaze dimmed. And the grimace was but a reflex, a rictus sure to remain long after the flesh had rotted from his carcass. When Kylac ripped his blades free, the towering brute fell with a jarring thud, bow and dagger still clenched in his meaty fists.

Kylac crouched, ready to spring down from the wheelhouse, when he realized that the remaining Banshees—numbering no more than a score—were gazing up at him in openmouthed disbelief, bows and slings dropping from their hands. Surprise swept through him, accompanied by relief and disappointment both.

No more need die, he thought, wondering if it might actually be true.

Before he could give it voice, the Banshees began drawing blades—those who didn't clutch them already.

With which they promptly slashed their own throats.

Kylac's astonishment gave way to an intrinsic horror. No doubt, a handful of those who stood were already mortally wounded, and thus only hastening the inevitable. But of those who still had the means to fight . . .

Amid the carnage, he caught sight of a Banshee rising from among the wounded, who hadn't yet registered the death of his captain or the mass suicide unfolding around him. Kylac leapt toward him, rolling against the deck to absorb the shock of his descent. Before the disoriented marauder could ascertain what had happened, Kylac struck him a blow at the temple, dropping him like an unfastened sail.

Though he cast about for others he might preserve, Kylac saw only throats awash in blood, some cut deep enough to cause the victims to choke and sputter on the fluid draining into their lungs. None he saw raised shout or whisper. None betrayed any sign of anguish or lament. They simply stood until their legs gave out beneath them, at which point they crumpled.

To lie in twitching heaps among the ghosts of the slain.

24

W ITH A READY BLADE, Kylac sifted through the carnage, probing for additional survivors. After such a pitched effort, he wasn't going to allow an unconscious Banshee to rouse at his back—or the back of one of his shipmates, assuming they intended to eventually rejoin him—and thereby tarnish his victory. At the same time, only dire necessity would cause him to bloody his weapon further. Already, he fended off the gnawing fear that he'd indeed slain them all—those who hadn't slain themselves—thus depriving him of prisoners who might be put to some better use than baiting hungry gulls.

He marked the *Banshee's Wail*, pinned to their stern by her bow-sprit, while he worked—giving ear to her creaking and groaning amid the river's wavelets, attuned to the rhythmic manner in which the surf set her nose to grating and grinding against the *Vengeance's* tail. He hadn't yet had a chance to inspect the barbarian ship for any rearguard or stowaways, and remained mindful of the possibility that such a force might yet seek to steal off with the vessel, else ambush him or his fellow crewmen from within.

Alas, one task at a time.

He found himself lightly winded. Only now, with the battle ended, did the vague threat of fatigue present itself, the thrill of combat bleeding out like the ebbing oscillation of a plucked string. His flesh

ached and stung in a dozen places, riddled with bruises and minor
lacerations. He would feel the wounds more keenly later, he knew.

An odd sensation, and vaguely annoying. For all his many skirmishes, he'd long since grown unaccustomed to receiving injury. To
recall a time in which he'd suffered this sort of battery, he had to
withdraw into his memories more than a decade, back to his early
youth at Talonar, while under the tutelage of his father and the school's
other battle masters. Even then, he remembered only one beating
akin to the one he endured now—orchestrated by his father simply
to ensure that Kylac wouldn't be entirely unaware of what effect pain
might have on a fighter's faculties.

Churlish he would have to be, however, to bemoan his condition
while treading amid the fresh corpses of some fivescore adversaries
who moments earlier had fought so fervently to take his life. That
they'd bombarded one another almost as heavily as they'd assailed
him would seem to have had an immeasurable effect on the outcome.
That roughly a quarter of them had taken their own lives in the
end . . . vital to any fair recounting. But one man against a hundred?
No matter how one might frame it, any bard or rumormonger foolish
enough to spread word of these events could expect to win only a
purse full of jeers.

He'd all but finished inspecting those fallen upon the maindeck—
turning up two more who might be saved, and putting down half a
dozen who couldn't—when a hatch opened atop the forecastle, and
the chief cook, Aythef, cautiously poked his head free.

"She's clear," Kylac called out.

At that distance, he couldn't quite see the other's gaze as it swept
the ship in cursory examination. But he sensed the emotional shift
as wariness gave way to astonishment. Kylac, still focused on his task,
chose to ignore it as he ventured aft, sifting through the tangle of
victims thickly piled about the larboard deck stair where much of the
fighting had been concentrated. At his back, the winds of amazement
grew, bolstered by the gradual emergence of those who'd sheltered
below.

"Bloody shards . . ."

"Dawning winds . . ."

"By Eriyah's grace . . ."

"I daresay your Fair Mother had no hand in it," Kylac said, turning at last to greet those wading loosely amid the carnage.

Ledron slipped past those sent ahead of him, to take the point among his scattered detachment. The sight of him triggered in Kylac a stab of irritation.

"Captain. I feared ya might has drowned in our flooded hold."

"Is this all of them?" Ledron asked bluntly.

"The ones I's come across. Perchance there's more hunkering in their vessel, the way some of us hid in ours."

Denariel was just now descending the forecastle, tugging at her gag a step ahead of her assigned shadow, Sanow. Between her and the captain, the others arrayed themselves loosely, regarding the sea of slaughtered flesh with varying degrees of awe and revulsion. Pevrick wore his typically surly expression, casting about as if seeking some flaw in Kylac's work. Trailing nearby, Ithrimir scowled grimly.

"Do none find mercy at the tip of your claws?" the Elementer asked.

"Three thus far. I fear I was in poor position to grant quarter."

"Bind the survivors," Ledron commanded Pevrick. "I would have them as captives."

"For all the use a captive tar-skin has proven to be," Leeches muttered.

"Lieutenant!"

"Aye, Captain." Half turning, he shouted, "To it, men! Lash and gag any who draw breath!"

"Shall we send signal for the crew to return?" Kylac asked, peering down the length of the spit to where the remainder of their shipmates had clustered upon the rocky high ground at the edge of the inland jungle. "If'n they choose their own timing as you did, we may not see 'em for days."

"Did you not request room to work?" Ledron asked him.

"Foolish o' me to thinks ya might look at least to serve some form o' diversion." He reached down to pluck one of the Shrikeskinner's arrows from the body of a sightlessly staring Banshee. "Mayhap loose a quarrel or two in my defense?"

He tossed the bolt toward the captain's feet.

Ledron eyed it archly. "By my view, the conflict was never out of hand."

"That would be your view from belowdecks."

The captain shifted as Denariel trudged near, the princess seeming untroubled by the massacre. An affectation, in some measure, given the way she held her breath as she stole among the corpses, trying a mite too hard to avoid looking at them.

"I wasn't going to risk Her Highness's life by exposing our position," said Ledron. "You knew this. As to our archers . . ." The Head made a show of turning his gaze inland, with a hand at his brow to shield against the sun. "Under separate commands, as I recall. We can request explanation, if you desire, upon their return. Though I'm not certain what aid you feel they may have been, at or beyond extreme bowshot range."

Kylac loosed a wry chuckle. "I care nothing o' your strategies, Captain, save that they scarcely resemble those we discussed."

Ledron shrugged. "Rare is the battle that ravels according to plan. I reacted as I felt—"

"Ya needn't justify your cowardice to me." Ignoring the lancing glare that Ledron fired back at him, he added, "My concern is only for your word. Be it kind or cruel, I expect ya to honor it."

The others were giving ear or elsewise taking note of the growing tension. Dead barbarians twitched at their feet. Mayhap it was only the tang of blood in the air, the cries of gathering seabirds, or the warm wind carrying the heat of the sun's rays, but Kylac felt the telltale twinge of anticipation stirring, spoiling for a fresh fight.

"The battle is won," Denariel interjected. "So why this mewling?"

Because, despite his father's adage that an ally was but another potential enemy, he wanted to believe that Ledron and crew understood their expedition was doomed without him. He wanted to believe that, after the trials he and the Head had endured together, their camaraderie—while forced—was not a complete charade. Because, in an inconstant world, the only dependability to be found was in carrying oneself—friend or foe—without deception.

As matters stood, he had to wonder now if Ledron had known or at least suspected the barbarians' true strategy all along. Might he have plotted this precise scenario from the outset?

"I'll wager this skirmish won't be our last," Kylac said. "And I would know now if'n I'm being led around by a noose."

Ledron flushed with indignation, jaw clenched, hackles raised. "Never have I made pretense as to my loyalties. You may trust me to serve my king's interests in all matters—not yours. If you cannot agree to that, you can remain here with this carcass of a ship and those set to breed maggots upon it."

"A tired threat, Captain. And laughable, given the carnage around us."

The Head was truly fraying, for he went so far as to lay hand on his sword hilt. "Would you seek to double your latest tally? Leaving you stranded if not dead?"

"Mother's mercy!" Denariel snapped. "Would that I could bridle you both. Do not claim to serve my father, Captain, and then bray about destroying our strongest asset." Turning to Kylac, she added, "And you. You posture and prate and flaunt your superiority, and then moan for want of trust? Absurd threats and pointless challenges, with breaths better spent determining how to proceed in the course of Thane's rescue."

Ledron's anger was unappeased. It simply shifted target. "I told you, Highness, this voyage is ended. You saw to that the moment you stole aboard."

"And if I hurl myself over this rail, or take knife to my own veins? What excuse would you then use to turn and flee home?"

Ledron gritted his teeth, taking pause to consider Pevrick, Ithrimir, and Sanow, who from separate directions had all drawn near. They hovered now at the fringe of the debate, while the remainder of their detachment mimicked Kylac's effort in sifting through the Shrikeskinner's slaughtered crew. With a deep breath clearly intended to tamp down his fury, the captain finally responded.

"Call me craven, if you wish. My devotion—"

"We all know where your devotion lies," Denariel intruded, with that incisive petulance of hers. "So tell me, what would my good father desire if he were here? Whether or not he laments my absence, he is—as he has been from the beginning—far more interested in

Thane's return than mine. Would you disagree?"

Ledron's mouth, hinged open with a ready rebuttal, clamped shut.

"Then the course you propose can yield only failure. So let us consider mine."

Pevrick bristled. "Is she, too, now an officer aboard this ship?"

"The waters work against us," Ithrimir snapped. "To wend north again through the Moravial, even in the more willing beast at our rudder, would at this point require weeks, not days. Circumnavigating the isle entire could take longer."

"Suggesting we sail deeper into the Abyss as a matter of convenience?" Pevrick balked.

"Be buggered, the lot of you," Ledron snarled. "We've a crew to signal, a new vessel to sweep, and an old one to scuttle. When that is accomplished, then will I decide where the winds may take us."

Aft he stormed, shedding them like a moldy cloak, climbing toward the wheel deck and on toward the command deck. Kylac stood among the others, unmoving, watching him go until he disappeared into the captain's quarters, as if to seek better advice amid the council of his private thoughts.

"It's to us then, eh?" Kylac surmised.

Leeches cast him a glare before turning away. "Signal the crew!" he shouted.

"I suppose I'll sees to the *Wail*," Kylac decided.

"Let my shadow do it," Denariel determined instead, with a nod toward Sanow.

The Blackfist stiffened. "My orders are not to leave your side."

"The boy is spattered in blood, and I would know how much of it might be his."

"Your Highness—"

"You think yourself a more suitable protector than him? Prove it. Go clear the rats from this new vessel of ours, should any remain."

Kylac was surprised by the hint of protectiveness in Denariel's stance. "My injuries are meager enough," he assured her.

"Did I ask your assessment? You've earned your day's keep, mercenary. And I would limit your blood loss or the risk of rot, that you might do so again on the morrow."

"Humbled I am by your concern. But I—"

"Concern? As I would have for oiling my dagger or cinching my saddle. A tool you are, make no mistake. The surest means by which to deliver my brother. These others"—she said, casting a disparaging glance at Sanow for emphasis—"are but mummers in comparison." Turning back, she added, "Were it not for that, I'd gladly watch you fester."

Kylac glanced at Sanow, who lacked sufficient boldness to argue further, and at Ithrimir, whose mask of disdain made it clear he cared not a whit, one way or the other.

"As ya will, Your Highness."

Leaving behind the gruesome sights and cloying stench, Kylac followed the princess down and aft to the cabin in which Aythef and whoever else had been tending to her earlier.

"Sit," she commanded him, when they'd reached her makeshift quarters, empty now of attendants and sentry-jailors, leaving just the two of them. It made the space seem larger than before. Or mayhap it was the gulf between them, its air thick and discomfiting. If she hadn't made her feelings plain abovedecks, she did so now with her petulant scowl, her stony silence, her refusal to meet his gaze—as if doing so would be beneath her. A matter of station, one might have guessed, if unaware of the history between them.

Kylac could claim no such ignorance.

"Tunic and breeches," she said sharply, having completed her cursory examination. She turned toward a small basin, into which she poured water from a half empty skin hanging on a nearby hook.

For a brief moment, Kylac considered defying her demand, to argue again that he could see to his injuries himself. To remind her that they weren't on Addaranth, and he neither servant nor subject. But he tamped down that reflexive urge, choosing to acquiesce. A paltry concession, all in all. A small means by which he might hope to allay some minuscule measure of the enmity she bore him.

He set aside his blades and boots as well, feeling more exposed for lack of his weapons than his garb. Clear it was that she would as soon plunge one of his daggers into his back as wash the cuts that striped his skin. Should the attempt soothe her, she was welcome to try. Had he been bound and blindfolded, he could yet subdue her before she put hand to hilt.

He suspected she understood as much, but that it wasn't fear that held her in check. Rather, it was her aim, as professed, to see her brother freed from the clutches of his abductors. Barring that, he didn't expect she would undertake such elaborate measures to strike at him. She'd have simply lashed out the moment he fell within her reach, consequences to herself be damned.

He'd seen it before.

"Turn," she said, as she faced him with a soaked cloth in her unsplinted hand. Trying not to look at the other—at her broken left thumb—Kylac again obeyed, giving her his back and bracing himself against a low-hanging beam.

With the way she attacked the lacerations found there, he wondered if he hadn't underestimated her. The sting of seawater turned shallow trenches into canyons of fire. And she scrubbed with a vigor that seemed less intent on cleaning than it was on peeling his skin away in broad strips. Why seek simply to stab him if he was fool enough to stand there and let her flay him to death?

But the blazing intensity was quick to subside, and nothing he couldn't endure, even at its worst. Even so, he winced from time to time, giving vent to the pain rather than absorbing it, hoping it might bestow upon her some pleasure or relief—then quickly questioning himself as to why he should do so. Had he truly wronged her to such a terrible degree? Had she not played a significant role in the events for which she viewed him with such violent loathing? Were his ongoing efforts to make amends truly so inadequate?

"I daresay your decision to join us has dismayed our fair captain," he offered, when tired of respecting her silence.

Her nails raked at his ribs through her wet cloth, exposing another trailer of flame.

"I care not for his feelings, so long as he serves as I desire."

"The rest o' the crew may be even less enamored than he."

"And you think I've any more concern for their opinions than his? Or yours?"

I suppose not, he thought, marveling at how foolish she made him feel for merely sharing the observation. As if it were some lame attempt at currying favor, the threads of a rope that might one day help to bridge the chasm between them. *I am your friend,* he may as well have pleaded. *Mayhap your only friend aboard.* Even if true, to what end?

The cloak of silence returned, heavier than before. Not an absence of sound. Aboard a ship, there was no such thing. The creak of boards straining always against their seams, the thud of boots on the planks above, the muffled shouts from Pevrick and his detachment, the slosh of floodwaters within their hold and the break of wavelets without . . . these and a myriad other noises from vessel and surroundings alike scratched at Kylac's ears as they had for weeks. To that end, true silence might have been a welcome relief. Yet, in this instance, the collective sounds seemed woefully insufficient, unable to fill the deafening void between him and this young woman who held him accountable for her life's greatest heartache.

He sensed it better not to tread there. But when she forced him around to have at the array of slashes across his chest and shoulders, he couldn't help but brush at the heat of her seething hatred. The way a child might at the flame of a candle. Entranced by the savage intensity belied by its mesmerizing appearance.

"Ya's a rare certainty in your own convictions." In response, she jabbed at him with her rag as if he'd insulted her. He denied her this time the satisfaction of a reaction. "A point o' survival, it must seem, when your own father would sacrifice ya to his greatest enemy."

Denariel's short laugh was biting. "As ever, you presume too much."

"Do my words offend Your Highness?"

"Your very breath offends me, mercenary. Your words do but season the insult."

"Then it's not that I'm wrong."

"But you are, if you believe my actions to be rooted in self-pres-ervation. It is the fate of my people I care about. The future of . . ." She trailed off, her spilling proclamation stoppered by a sudden surge of emotion that she choked down. As if she might conceal it from him. As if it hadn't already slapped him like a wave.

Her lover. She laments the future denied them. However that might have looked. Whatever she imagined it could have been.

Her harsh scrubbing resumed. "Fortunately, I wouldn't trade a bucket of bilgewater for your beliefs."

"I believed it wrong to sees ya leashed by their overlord," he reminded her. That earned him a quick glance, accompanied as it was by a prideful stiffening of her shoulders and another clawing scratch. "Where mights ya be now, were I wrong about that?"

Her lips, small and tight, formed a snide grimace. "Until death intervenes, was my vow. It made no mention of the means. Do you sincerely believe I would have let that devil live a day beyond Thane's release?" At last, she fixed her gaze upon him. "You did me no great favor by slaying him before I could."

Kylac stared back. The bottom half of her face protruded slightly, lending her a pugnacious appearance. Well fitted to the cant of her brow, and the dark expression etched into the flat planes and sharp angles that formed her cheeks and jaw. A face made for extending challenges—and accustomed to winning them.

"Ya may have found that harder than ya suppose."

"Because you think me incapable." She dropped to her knees to dig and swipe at a slash across his left thigh.

"Because I thought ya'd suffered enough." Even allowing that he might have freed her later—or that she might have freed herself— there'd been no guarantee as to what horrors or indignities she might have endured in the interim. It was for this reason, despite all the arguments demanding he stay his hand and let Grendavan carry off with her as Kendarrion had agreed, that he'd taken action to ensure no further harm would come to her.

He wasn't going to let her cause him to regret it now.

"And so my brother now suffers—likely far worse—in my stead. How much easier would all of this have been, do you suppose, had we simply waited for the tar-skins to return Thane to *us*?"

Assuming they'd ever actually meant to do so. She herself must have doubted their intent to comply, given her own renegade actions in fleeing to Kuuria in search of aid.

He stopped short of saying as much, which she must have taken as a capitulation.

"Clearly, you didn't think this through," she huffed.

Mayhap. But that aligned with his belief that a plan could carry only so far before other, unforeseen factors intervened. "Address the enemy facing ya, I was taught, before turning to the one at your back."

"Already, the tar-skins may have erected a mast from my brother's bones, flying a flag of his skin." Seeming determined to complete her task, she turned to a pair of nicks just below his right knee. "So do not hiss at me with platitudes, or of deeds for which you feel I should thank you. Like Ledron, you will do my bidding, else I'll pluck and cast you away like the thorn you are."

Amid his own self-certainty, Kylac felt a twinge of doubt, a seed of potential remorse for the mistakes he may have made. Could she be right? Would it have been better to trust in her to defend her own interests? Had he but come to meddle in matters that had naught to do with him?

A consideration he'd faced before, and a possibility he couldn't deny. But that was the risk he'd assumed—a risk he'd come to live by. Once before had he stood aside, permitting a friend to tend to matters of a personal nature while ignoring the inner urge to help her in doing so. He'd sworn never to make that mistake again.

He considered explaining this to her, but tamped down the impulse. It'd likely make no difference in how Denariel viewed him, and he'd not use Brie in such an attempt.

Some ghosts were not to be unleashed.

Instead, he let the silence return, listening to the thud and clatter above, waiting on the princess to steer any further conversation. Upon completing her initial scrubbing, she tossed her rag and reached instantly for a pungent salve from a netted sack, which she began applying to his deeper wounds. By then, Kylac could hear the muffled shouts and measured knocking of the rest of their crew returning, come to board the *Vengeance* once more—likely for the last time.

He half hoped that one of his shipmates—with no preference as to which—might think to check on him, or the princess, and thus disturb their awkward solitude. Alas, if any sought to do so, it would seem their commanding officers redirected them, having other duties in mind.

It left him with nothing to do but stand there and contemplate his actions, past and future, while stewing in the hatred and bitterness she felt for him. Even as she worked to mitigate the damage he'd suffered in her defense. To ensure that he survived long enough to do so again.

And he would, he resolved, as she finished with him and strode wordlessly from the cabin.

Whether she valued it or not.

25

As the hour allotted them by the Sea Scribe waned, the urgency of the crew intensified. Though none had yet sighted or heard sign of the Ladrakari, Kylac could sense the elves like a gathering storm, a tang of menace on the winds that swept down out of the jungle growth. His shipmates, while lacking his skills of perception, nonetheless exhibited a common fear—an apprehension that put spur to weary muscles and gave speed to their labors. Some sought to deny it, welcoming the natives to attack, boasting of the number of savages they would gladly slay if besieged. Yet even these, Kylac observed, cast their fair share of anxious glances out across the spit, searching the low ridgeline from which all expected their tenacious pursuers to spill.

And whether blustering or genuine, their comrades and commanders were quick to shout them down and keep them on task.

Their work had taken longer than anticipated. A search of the *Banshee's Wail* had revealed a hold heavy with plunder, yet lean on provisions. The price of being a renegade, mayhap, unwelcome in any port. Regardless, with no clear knowledge of how long their voyage might persist, it was quickly determined that they should transfer whatever stores they could from the *Vengeance*. This entailed salvaging barrels and crates from half-flooded holds and compartments, culling usable contents from spoiled ones, hoisting them up from below, rolling them across the narrow planking bridging the vessels, and depositing them in the belly of the *Wail*. Others had been tasked with sorting and removing less critical wares from their new ship to make room. Lacking sufficient time to wait and complete one task before the other, it seemed men everywhere were butting heads and setting heel upon another's toes, all coming and going at the same time.

Amid this general disorder, a team of Whitefists led by Brenham set about familiarizing themselves with the *Wail*'s rigging. While similar to that of the *Vengeance*, she'd undergone various modifications under her mad captain's rule, given what Kylac heard of the second mate's assessment. Another team, led by Taeg, had been charged with a final scuttling of the *Vengeance*, stripping the once-proud Marauder of what sheets, lines, and supplies might most readily be used to piece her back together. Though Ithrimir claimed that the Ladrakari lacked the skill with which to restore the wracked vessel, Ledron was taking no chances.

They'd found the *Wail* empty of resistance, at least, her strength expended to a man in the Banshees' attempt to take the *Vengeance*. It caused Kylac to wonder at their obsessive effort in doing so. Had they recognized her as Grendavan's former flagship? Or would they have assaulted any other vessel with the same savage intensity? With Vorathus felled, had Kylac rid the Grenarr of their only barbarian outcast? Or were there others of the Shrikeskinner's ilk? Sailing the *Wail*, would they be hunted any more fiercely than before? Any less? What advantages and shortcomings might they expect to inherit with this change of vessels?

Questions that could wait, in Ledron's estimation. A quartet of surviving Banshees—the three Kylac had discovered, plus one more Pevrick's men had retrieved—had been sequestered belowdecks under armed guard, not to be disturbed without permission. Kylac might have probed Tormitius, but Ledron had swiftly stashed the Gre-narrian away—as before—in the captain's quarters of the new ship. Whatever the truth, Kylac suspected the Head was right. It wasn't as if he could learn anything that would alter their immediate course. Better to focus on helping where he could to ensure they embarked as quickly as possible.

"What o' the shrikes, Captain?" he overheard Pevrick ask of Ledron at one juncture.

The Head's jaw clenched. "Butcher them in their cages."

"Aye, sir."

"Ya no longer wish to keeps them as barter?" Kylac asked.

Leeches glared at the intrusion.

"I'll not waste our limited efforts on hauling cages and birdfeed," Ledron explained. With a meaningful stare, he added, "Nor will I risk one stealing free. Lieutenant."

"Sir."

Weathering another scowl from the departing officer, Kylac added more quietly, "A raptor or two could prove lure to whoever freed the last."

"All the more reason to deprive him. *If* that's what occurred. I've not the time or means to ferret out this supposed traitor of yours."

Hence the bait, Kylac thought to say. But the Head had turned away to address other matters, and Kylac saw no firm reason to press the issue. While the identity of their shipboard mole might prove critical, even he didn't feel it to be of immediate concern. Not compared to the many others arrayed against them. Not when they remained uncertain there even was a mole. Given their losses in the earlier skirmishes against the Ladrakari, it was possible the guilty party, if he existed, was already dead.

Too many scenarios to consider, and thus another bevy of questions that could wait. Had Kylac been tasked with slaughtering the birds himself, he might well have resisted, regarding them more as victims than accomplices. But the captain hadn't asked him to. Nor could he deny the danger the birds presented if left alive. If Leeches had it in him for that kind of butchery, let him have it. Mayhap it would help cool his ever-boiling blood.

As he marked Ledron's departure, a secondary reason for dropping the debate wormed through Kylac's chest. Truth unfettered, he remained raw with the captain for his inaction in the fight against Vorathus and his Banshees. Still vexed by the degree to which the Head had clung to his single-minded pragmatism—or mayhap annoyed more with himself for failing to foresee it—Kylac had reflexively decided to withdraw somewhat from his self-appointed advisory role in this venture, and to let Ledron take whatever action he deemed most prudent.

Better than to trust again that the Head would comply with what Kylac might mistakenly believe to be a joint decision.

Leaving him to react, as it should be, without expectation.

He found it easier to detach himself, in part, due to his *new* self-appointed role: that of Denariel's personal warder. No, she wanted nothing whatsoever to do with him, forcing him to maintain an appearance of distance. Yes, she still had Sanow clinging to her, alert to any potential harm. Even had she been left alone, she was likely in no real peril, despite the crew's ongoing expressions of distaste. But as Kylac marked the stolen glares and surreptitious murmurs against her, he continued to feel the stirrings of indignation. As she herself was untroubled by their opinions, he supposed he had no cause to be offended on her behalf. Yet, he couldn't deny the protective instinct it spawned in him.

Mayhap because, notwithstanding her abiding rancor, he took solace in her integrity. However resentful her views might be, they remained steadfast, reliable. With regard to him, and with regard to her aims on this mission. He couldn't say the same—not with equal certainty—of any other aboard this ship. Not Ledron or Pevrick, not Brenham or Taeg, not even Ithrimir, whose life he'd saved. To some extent, the motives of each lay veiled in mystery.

All but hers.

Or mayhap he was simply reacting to the lingering specter of guilt. Well-intentioned as he may have been, he was at least partially responsible for events that had brought them together in this time and place. He'd not have embarked on this particular mission elsewise.

For the moment, at least, Denariel moved freely among them, lending aid despite her weakened condition. Ledron appeared to ignore the fact that she did so. As if he'd tired of debating with her as Kylac had tired of debating with him. Relinquishing responsibility for her fate.

Better for all, thought Kylac.

With none to direct her, she worked where and how she chose. For the better part of the past hour, that had been aboard the *Wail*, removing an assortment of grisly ornaments such as the string of human skulls that dropped now from a forward spar to clatter against the foredeck.

Forced to sidestep the falling obstacle while hauling one side of a trunk from the *Vengeance*, a startled Crawfoot looked up with a ready shout, only to bite his tongue and hiss instead to Hamal, at the other end of his load, "Too vain to sail with the dead, is she?"

"Your pardon, Highness," Hamal muttered mockingly. "Would that we had time to raise sheets of satin and strings of pearls."

Kylac noted their derision as he dumped a load of unfinished ivory over the rail, dredged up from the *Wail*'s hold and passed to him by Graves. Valuable, yes, but not when weighed against essential provisions such as water, food, and weaponry. Even a quarter-mark ago, he might have questioned it. Graves surely would have. But it had been given to the more senior Jaleth, positioned below, to determine what should be tossed in order to make room. They and others in line had learned not to question those decisions, but to carry them out.

"Can she not find a more meaningful task?" Yoden asked, rolling a filthy cask toward Quill.

"With fortune's favor, she'll slip from her perch," Quill observed, "and it'll be her own skin tossed overboard."

"Might be more'n vanity she strives for," Kylac interjected as the cask came to him. His nose wrinkled at the stench of whatever had spoiled within. "Some o' these trophies are fresh enough to draw flies."

"Flies? The least of our worries."

"And the disease they bear?" Kylac heaved the cask out after the ivory.

An obvious benefit that he and his shipmates should have acknowledged on their own, if giving the princess fair due. A petulant grimace tugged at Quill's cheeks. Resentment steeped in chagrin. "I'll call us blessed if we live long enough to tally illness among our woes."

A man too long separated from malady, Kylac thought. His own recent brush, suffered in the Addaranth wilderness, remained far too fresh to regard so brazenly. The mere recollection conjured a wave of lightheadedness and an uncomfortable tightening in his gut.

He didn't speak of it, though, nodding instead a companionable acknowledgment. As before, he saw little to be gained by aligning with Denariel outright. A pebble's toss here or there, just to test the waters of the crew's opinion and mayhap form a ripple of uncertainty, was as much as his own tenuous standing would seem to allow.

A sack of mealy flour was passed to him next, followed by a crate of buckles and a sack of leather shoes. Kylac tried not to think of where the latter might have come from, especially given some of the small sizes. Children falling under the thumb of Vorathus wasn't something he cared to contemplate—though it gave him a surge of satisfaction to know that it couldn't happen again.

Sanow, meanwhile, worked to discard the ornaments that Denariel continued to cut from the rigging. He did so dutifully, even while plying her with the occasional plea to descend and seek rest. That his tone rang hollow, lacking any real earnestness or deference, was something else Kylac tried not to consider too closely. Likely, the Blackfist was simply loath to show full and proper respect while surrounded by his shipmates, who eyed him almost as grudgingly as they eyed his royal charge. Or could it be that he, sworn member of the Shadowguard, was no more enamored of the troublesome princess than the rest of the crew?

These and a score of nagging thoughts akin to them tugged at him like the day's restless breezes, each worthy of attention, but none so strong as to merit alarm. While all seemed to carry the potential of breeding future threat, Kylac refused to fret over what *might* happen.

Particularly when so many open threats loomed already before him.

The first of those finally manifested when a distant flock of birds lifted free of the jungle in a squawking, stuttering cloud, surging free of the patchwork foliage with raucous complaint. The strident tones formed a telling chill at the nape of Kylac's neck before eddying down his spine.

Ladrakari.

He glanced skyward to make sure their oft and present lookout, Jahvid, had marked the disturbance. The Whitefist had, though slower he was to draw conclusion. Restrained by denial, mayhap, or circumspection. High in the *Wail's* crow's nest, the sailor fumbled at his spyglass. Kylac, meanwhile, accepted a bolt of moldy roughspun from the leather-faced Hamal and cast it out amid the rest of the flotsam gathering in the shallow surf against the spit's embankment.

By the time he looked up again, the jungle had begun to shiver, and the first faint flutter of a small horde whipping through the brush began to whisper amid the dissonant chorus of river and shipboard sounds.

"What's that, eh?" Hamal asked, squinting as he drew nearer Kylac's elbow.

"Our departure bell."

Not until the first elven scouts advanced beyond the scraggly treeline, however, did Jahvid call it out.

"Enemy to larboard!"

By then, the Ladrakari war cry had been raised, there at the rugged juncture where the spit abutted the mainland. Initiated by just the handful of scouts filtered out from the fringe, but swelling quickly with the strength of the throng hidden upon their heels, until the very jungle seemed to thrash and scream.

The scouts descended, lithe forms springing down the rocky climb. Ledron, having emerged upon the command deck from wherever he'd been occupied, didn't wait for even the vanguard to join them. Turning to a crier, he immediately issued the orders that all were anticipating. *Drop your load. All aboard. Prepare to shove off.*

The resonating shouts tore quickly through both ships, and the crew's members raced to comply. Redfists abandoned whatever loading task they'd been engaged in, casting aside crate, barrel, sack, or net, and scrambling into defensive position along the larboard rail of the *Banshee's Wail*. Whitefists took to the ratlines of the new ship like ants streaming up a rotting bole, one after the other, before fanning out along various spars and cords. Soldiers and sailors fleeing the scuttled *Vengeance* moved with greater haste, Kylac noted, rising from her holds and sprinting across her bloodstained decks as if worried their captain meant not to wait for them. Put to it, Kylac wouldn't have wagered elsewhere.

He searched for Denariel, and found her repelling along a loose

line dangling from the outer reaches of the foremast. Sanow awaited
her below, bracing as if to arrest her potential fall, while also seeking
to shelter against the loose stampede of men surging past his position.
Kylac shifted in that direction, seemingly without purpose, but neither
allowing himself to be diverted. Only after Denariel had touched
down safely, and he'd watched Sanow trail her into the wheelhouse
to hover at Ledron's shoulder, did he slink back to the larboard rail
to join those eyeing the elves' lusty charge.

As they had at dawn of that same day, they came like a closing
surf, gushing down the spit's length at full force, voices howling, feet
kicking up a spray of sand beneath the thick swaths of swordgrass.
Their numbers were the greatest Kylac had seen yet, as if their continued trek across Mistwall's shores had drawn others in their wake,
to multiply beneath the jungle screen. Three hundred, four hundred,
more. The soldiers around him muttered silent oaths, bluster given
over to tense disbelief.

They needn't have worried. Ledron and those under his command
were risking no encounter. Amid the shrieking of the natives and the
shouts of their own crewmen, the *Wail* creaked and shuddered as she
pulled astern, drawing clear of the wrack of the *Vengeance*. Shards of
glass and broken strips of wood from the impaled vessel rained from
the wound as their bowsprit scraped free, growling its reluctance. Like
the gnashing teeth of a rabid dog straining against its master's leash.

The sails filled, and the master's tug won out. Abruptly, the *Wail*
calmed, no longer struggling, but set to seething amid the slap and
splash of the deepening river waves.

The Ladrakari were incensed. But the face of their front lay yet a
hundred paces distant. Their dreadful caterwaul was the only weapon
that could reach the departing prey. And though it raked and skirled
sharply on the prevailing wind, the *Wail* no more than huffed, indif-
ferent to their cry.

Their furor met this time without cheers, without jeers, without a
single wasted arrow. Save for the seamen who called to one another,
diligent in their tasks, Kylac's shipmates clung to a sober silence, having
lost their taste, it would seem, for celebration. Casualty to a common
exhaustion. Or to the sight of the trammeled *Vengeance*, forsaken

upon the spit with her slashed sails, broken spars, and the slaughtered barbarians heaped upon her decks. Or to the grisly filth of the stolen vessel in which they now sailed, laden with the trappings of murder.

Else mayhap they understood that their departure here merely marked the continuation of a voyage that had thus far reaped only narrow escapes and outright failures.

Giving no reason to revel in the latest, or to hail the arrival of the next.

26

THEY SAILED UNTIL DUSK beneath a radiant sun, then on into night
under a canopy of unfiltered starlight. The waterways of the Moravial
broadened, branching less frequently, its shores retreating to either
side. Taeg and Jaleth, in turn, nonetheless kept steady hand on the
ship's wheel, with Ithrimir at either man's shoulder to warn against
various hazards that continued to creep up from below.

The rest of the crew had been sorted into shifts and given to
either rest or resume clearing, sorting, and scouring their new vessel.
Denariel's Wail, many had come to call her. And despite their harsh
snickers, Kylac had heard none correct them.

For the most part, Kylac had busied himself aloft, helping to tear
down the ornaments of the *Wail*'s former occupants from reaches not
easily accessible. He did so more for the sake of assisting than out of
any personal desire to shed the barbaric symbols. There'd been some
debate as to whether they might be better off leaving the notorious
Marauder mostly intact, recognizable, in hopes of dissuading any
other ships who might sight her. But Ledron himself had supposedly
given the order to strip and scrub her so as to make her as indistinct
as possible, and her scent more palatable to those aboard. Her flag was
now a stark black square lacking device or symbol. For what purpose
or advantage, Kylac hadn't asked. To elicit hesitation from anyone

they might come upon seemed a suitable guess.

He'd kept mostly to himself, seeking what distance he could from the recent flurry of events, and from his shipmates' interpretations of them. The relative silence helped him to avoid puzzling over matters he couldn't control, or to assess actions he might or might not take. To remove himself from the emotional chaos—churning in and around him—and to realign himself with the deeper, calmer currents of the natural world. To find that distant place where he was most at peace, most ready to respond.

Most lethal.

His fellow crewmen left him to it, mayhap sensing his withdrawal, mayhap merely busy with affairs of their own. It wasn't until the Raven's Hour that Creyl stole upon him, clomping up the stair to the poop deck where Kylac busied himself twining a fresh rope.

"Cap settin' eye for ya. Reel un me, tah?"

Kylac glanced up at the splay of crooked teeth that marked the Redfist's feral grin. For half a heartbeat, he considered ignoring the summons. Let the Head seek him out himself, if he had need. Kylac would decide then whether or not to grant the man audience.

But that came from a place of petulance that Kylac misliked in himself at once. It meant that his frustration with the captain continued to fester. While resolving to keep a measure of distance, he hadn't allowed Ledron to draw him into playing petty games of control, had he?

"Where is he?"

"Nav hole."

Kylac offered Creyl the frayed end of rope. "Care to do some braiding?"

The Redfist scowled. He cared no such thing. Yet he took the line and accepted an encouraging pat on the shoulder as Kylac brushed past.

Ysander stood sentry, but promptly stepped aside as Kylac approached the navigation cabin from its lone, larboard door. A reverse configuration from that of the *Vengeance*, which had opened to starboard. But any meaning this might have among the Grenarr held none for Kylac, save to remind him that he sailed uncharted waters in more ways than one.

Returning the Redfist's wooden nod, Kylac entered.

As it had aboard the *Vengeance*, the cabin served antechamber to the captain's quarters, the inner door to which stood closed. Within, the walls were ringed with tables and cubbies papered or stuffed with maps and charts, logs and ledgers, of a nautical nature. Less orderly, it all seemed, compared to that arrayed upon the prior ship. But that might have been due to whatever effort had taken place here since their coming. Like a shorefront after a gale, littered in this instance with scrolls and parchments—several of which Kylac recognized as having come from either the *Vengeance* or the Sea Scribe's vaults—strewn, splayed, or elsewise spread about in what appeared a haphazard fashion.

All was lit in flickering lamplight, with shadows dancing amid the flames held captive in swaying lanterns. The writhing interplay lent a false sense of motion to the sketches and drawings, bringing them to life. It had the opposite effect on the faces of those gathered, causing features to appear drawn and haggard. The murmur of voices ebbed, and eyes turned to him.

"Ya summoned?"

Ledron gestured vaguely at Denariel, shadowed even now by Sanow. "Her Highness insisted you be present."

Kylac glanced at the princess. Though she declined to meet his gaze, he offered her the slightest tip of his brow. He knew better than to find flattery in her invitation, or to take it as a sign of trust. Pevrick spat, proclaiming his own distaste. Whether that was more to Kylac's involvement, or the strength of voice being afforded Denariel, he couldn't say.

Brenham stood centrally over a splay of maps, his normally unflappable expression riven by a mild grimace. Ithrimir hovered at his shoulder. The crew's three most senior officers, plus the pair of strays picked up along the way. The cabin air hung thick between them, seasoned by lantern smoke and the scent of melted tallow.

"Has we some matter at hand?" Kylac prompted.

"Only that of destination and course," Ledron replied, a weary edge to his voice.

"Our destination is known," Denariel corrected, "if this one can be believed." Her left hand, with its splinted thumb, gestured vaguely at Ithrimir.

"If the Blackmoon Shards you seek," the Sea Scribe muttered defensively.

"A folly if it is," huffed Pevrick.

Kylac glanced reflexively at the door leading to the captain's cabin, in which he presumed Tormitius to still be shackled. A place of luxury compared to that inhabited by their captive Banshees—or almost any other man aboard. He wondered to what degree the Shorecleaver marked their words, or those that had gone before.

"Do we raise again that argument?" Denariel asked, her harsh tone suggesting they didn't.

Pevrick's bitter silence—together with the angry flush upon which his leech-like throat tattoos gorged—seemed to mark a furious capitulation.

"We go to rescue His Highness Dethaniel," Ledron clarified with a heavy sigh. "And while we've found no chart upon this black bitch to light our course, our devoted Sea Scribe has given us a pair of options."

"Swift or safe," said Ithrimir.

"As you've been troubled to join us," the captain continued, with a fleeting glare at Denariel, "we may as well hear your vote."

The princess straightened. "To nudge the pendulum."

"Vote or no," Pevrick growled. "It is the captain's decision."

Nudge the pendulum. Meaning they were at a stalemate. Impossible with five present prior to his arrival, unless one or more had abstained. Noting again Pevrick's distant position and cross-armed stance, as well as his stubborn insistence that they seek some other heading altogether, Kylac had his best guess as to who'd heretofore refused to cast lot.

"Swift or safe, ya say," Kylac echoed, then arched a brow in question.

"Speed is of the essence," Denariel blurted, exposing her own preference. "As it has been from the outset."

Kylac checked for any clues from the others, but found only stark visages and inscrutable masks. "As I recall, we chose that route before," he reminded them, thinking back to when they'd first brought the Sea Scribe aboard and debated whether to sail north or south from

Mistwall. "It very nearly spelled the end of us."

"And cost us much time regardless," Brenham added. "Even swift is not always *swift*."

Ah, thought Kylac. By his reckoning, that outburst put their second mate in the scale opposite the princess.

He shifted his remaining focus between Ithrimir and Ledron. Yet it was Denariel who pressed the argument. "Once he's made the decision to kill Thane, the new Grendavan will almost certainly mount a retaliatory invasion. War will ravage our shores as never before."

"All the more reason to accept our sorrows," advised Pevrick, "and return home."

The prince is lost, he could have said. A fair point, as it had been from the first. From the moment Kylac had decided to put a stop to the so-called accord that would have had the Great Grendavan hauling Denariel away from Avenell as his wife, to lay claim to the region of land promised his people in exchange for her brother the crown prince's return. Kylac had to wonder, as all of them did, whether the retaliatory strike Denariel spoke of wasn't underway already.

But they had to assume it wasn't. That there was no full-scale invasion, and that His Highness Dethaniel still lived. That, despite the Addarans' apparent treachery, whatever party or parties had filled the power void left in the wake of Grendavan's demise would continue to cling to their greatest asset and give Kendarrion one last chance to surrender to Grenarr demands, for the sake of his son's life.

"If'n we permit that His Highness is dead, the Grenarr already exacting retribution, we fight a lost battle here either way—be it swift or safe."

Denariel leaned forward, lamplit eyes gleaming with anticipation.

Kylac shook his head. "As I'll not presume failure, I say we move swiftly, before they may change their mind."

The princess cast a victorious sneer at Ithrimir, suggesting that the Scribe had been the other to hold out against her. That put Ledron on her side of the scales. Yet if the Head was pleased by Kylac's alignment, he did a poor job of expressing it.

"Tell us, then," the captain growled at Ithrimir, "of this more perilous course we've chosen."

The Scribe fixed his gaze on the chart spread before Brenham. Somehow, Kylac still felt the chilling stare of his dead eye.

"A shorter, more direct route to the archipelago of Haverstromme," he said, a yellowed nail clawing eastward on the map. "But it will carry us directly through Eominn Ghornach, the Thousand Tempests, a storm-tossed region whipped by gale, further wracked by underwater quakes and the whirlpools they spawn. At the heart of this fury lies Durnifwyr, Eddaron's Rift, Dread Maw of the Deep. A vast maelstrom that has been churning for more than six centuries—and which we must skirt, for its precise boundaries are ever ranging."

"Have you seen these great terrors?" Ledron asked. "Or do you merely recite legend and rumor?"

Ithrimir looked up, his depthless black eye seeming to bore into the captain. "I have seen."

"Waters lightly traveled, if'n dreadful as ya claim."

The Elementer rounded on Kylac, bright eye squinting, but ceded him a slight nod. "Particularly now, with winter's ebb still upon us."

"Perhaps not so perilous, then," Denariel suggested. "For we'll be less likely to encounter prowling tar-skins."

A grim silence seemed to settle the matter—for the moment, at least. Brenham, having listened pensively throughout, capitulated with a shrug. "Might be the stink of this ship will be enough to keep them at bay."

THE FOLLOWING DAWN brought them to a broad bay framed to the west by a curving peninsula. Beyond the land's narrowing tip lay only boundless ocean, its gray-tinged expanse veiled by a thin curtain of mist. Before they could sail free, however, the mists thickened, gathering in gossamer folds, obscuring the world beyond. Spearing ahead, the *Wail* herself was consumed, the fog shrouding bow from stern, and decks from rigging. Abreast the maindeck, Kylac watched crewmen huddle nearer one another, as if unconsciously seeking some manner of tether amid the void.

Then the sun burned through, and the haze fell astern, to brood sullenly on the aft horizon. A cheer went up as men's hopes were confirmed. Mistwall and its Shattered Skein lay behind them. Its natural snares, treacherous waterways, and bloodthirsty denizens could haunt them no more. A final tally of gains and losses resulting from their prolonged visit could now be taken, the stakes and bids of this voyage reset.

Kylac shared his shipmates' relief, the weight of the isle dropping like a yoke from his shoulders. The open seas to the south took on a sapphire cast, agleam with the sun's rays. Ceaseless waves carried with them the tingling promise of limitless possibility. With a rearward glance at its lingering stain, Kylac determined that he wouldn't soon miss Mistwall's shores.

"There's a rock I'm glad to be rid of," Kahrem muttered, coming to stand at Kylac's elbow. "Even letting go the few treasures she fleeced from me."

Kylac ignored the thinly veiled accusation at the heart of the feigned jest. It wasn't the faceless isle that Kahrem felt cheated by, but Kylac himself. The embittered Redfist would still be seeking some form of compensation, then, for his handful of looted Mookla'ayan teeth. Kylac considered suggesting that the soldier consider the fingers and palms still attached to his wrists payment enough. But he saw nothing to be gained in stoking further conflict.

"Might have taken more'n she did," he offered instead, tugging at a frayed strip of cloth fluttering from a bandage at his wrist. "Be glad we's fortunes to reap ahead of us."

A common sentiment among the crew, he discovered, as he went his way about the ship over the next several hours, taking his turn at various mundane tasks before stealing away for a moment's solitude. While some continued to fret and grouse over perils believed to lie ahead, most seemed suitably grateful for those challenges put to their rudder.

For a time.

Such tempered enthusiasm, as Kylac might have predicted, was poorly equipped to survive the week of drudgery that followed. By and large, the Redfists were the first to grumble, unnerved by the vast reaches of empty ocean, and by the seemingly infinite repetition of rising and falling amid its swells. Though mocked by their Whitefist counterparts, they complained of the madness of any who would willfully take to the seas, to beg of forces as volatile as wind and wave to be delivered safely again to the rock and soil upon which men were born to stand.

Truth unfettered, neither were the men of the Seawatch immune. Sailors, yes, but never this far from their homeland shores. The seas were their practice yard, yet ruled by their enemies and whatever mysterious creatures lurked within. Those aboard had already ventured longer and farther than any Addaran had in generations. Though some carried this knowledge more comfortably than others, Kylac could read the attending uncertainty in their anxious gazes and the lines of their weathered faces.

As he'd shared their relief, so did Kylac feel their discomfort. Though he chose not to admit it, he, too, soon longed again for land. A form of the fear that overtook him in enclosed spaces found similar purchase here. For with the same, endless view awaiting him at each point and corner of the compass, it was easy to imagine they might be the only inhabitants in all of Eddaron. A humbling sensation, underscored by interminable loneliness, as they surged along, day after day, in their grim vessel. No matter how deep they cleaned, the blood and rot in which this ship had bathed had seeped into her pores, to become as ingrained in her planks as the pitch between her seams. Trapped in such grisly confines, steeped in her carcass stench, more than one man came to question whether they weren't dead already, and merely scurrying about a bier set drifting through oblivion.

The only true respite lay in activity, with tasks that served to distract the senses and ward the mind from darker thoughts. Most of these labors, however, had become so routine as to be carried out by muscle memory alone. Basic repairs and endless scrubbing, the netting of fish and preparation of meals, the sharpening of blades and fletching of arrows, the inspection of stores, the study of weather, the examination of maps, the futile search for markers amid the undulating *sameness* of their drowned world . . . At times, the monotony of such toils seemed only to serve reminder of the limbo in which they'd willfully placed themselves, and from which there remained no obvious escape.

Even when they pretended elsewise, Kylac heard it in his shipmates' voices, and spied it in the slouch of their shoulders. The gradual onset of depression, weighing heavier each day. Moreover, Kylac himself felt its stealthy yet certain encroachment. Like a burgeoning storm cloud, hovering invisibly overhead. Masked by the lie of the incessant sun.

So he set hand to whatever chore he happened upon, and, in the interim, resumed his various routines of exercise and swordplay. The latter served better to stoke his fire and fuel his spirits—particularly now that he was able to draw willing shipmates here and there into his training sessions. But no shipboard scenario offered challenge greater than those already faced, and so even these drills left him increasingly dissatisfied. As if being stuck out here were hampering his development as an athlete and bladesman, limiting his life's progress.

Leaving him to wonder vaguely where else he might be, had he chosen a different path.

He knew the folly of such thinking. Not only was it too late to remove himself from the situation, but there was no true reason to believe he should do so. The expectation was that he might have happened upon more fulfilling circumstances. But the likelihood was just as great that he would have become ensnared in worse. So why waste time in lament?

Countering that, there seemed plenty of time to waste.

No matter how he engaged himself, or where, he continued to take silent stock of those around him. Having earned some measure of his shipmates' respect, he found himself less actively shunned than he'd been prior to their detour through Mistwall. Though loath to admit it, the closest to one he might call a friend would have to be the half-mad Creyl. But most others treated him companionably enough—even Kahrem and the rest of the pack he'd confronted over their lack of respect for the Ladrakari dead. He wouldn't claim to have earned their trust, and had reaped no cause to offer them his. But at least, for the greater part, they no longer carried themselves as adversaries, granting him greater access to their motives and opinions.

Enabling him to better gauge any who might have cause to betray them.

There remained a number of notable exceptions. Leeches, who glared on those rare occasions in which he failed to avoid Kylac's gaze altogether. Ithrimir, who by order or desire clung to the wheelhouse or navigation cabin, and stiffened irritably whenever Kylac happened to enter, snorting as if to repel an unpleasant odor. Denariel, who once checked on his rapidly healing wounds, but said nothing and thereafter left him to his own devices, keeping belowdecks where he seldom found sufficient cause to tread.

And Ledron, grim and taciturn, who had staunchly denied Kylac access to their Banshee prisoners as he had to Tormitius. Who persisted in gritting his teeth and offering only curt, grudging responses, seeming intent on making Kylac beg for every scrap of information. As Kylac sensed quickly that there was little new knowledge to be gained under these conditions, he soon tired of the captain's stern rejections and let the stubborn Head keep to his shell.

So it was, at the close of that interminable week, that Ledron surprised him by tracking him down atop the forecastle, where Kylac had been set to mending nets alongside the Whitefist Warmund and Redfist Talon.

"Walk with me?" the captain asked, a weathered scroll in hand.

Kylac obliged him, withholding inquiry, trusting that Ledron would give voice to his need in whatever space and manner suited him. It didn't come until they'd retreated deep belowdecks, venturing aft through a cramped string of lower holds.

"We may be lost again, if ever we weren't," the Head muttered without preamble.

"Oh?" Kylac asked, to ensure the other he was listening.

Ledron huffed, wending onward by the light of a lantern he'd taken up in his free hand. "Brenham has come to question our Scribe's directions, based on his own study of the charts available to us."

"Charts we's no great reason to trust."

"As I reminded him. But the codger has also contradicted himself, as Brenham tells it. More than once. Reinforcing our original fears. Does he truly know where the Shards lie, or is he mistaken? Does he mean to take us there, or does he have some agenda hidden from us? Is he but foaming mad? Who among us can say?"

And which would be worse? Kylac wondered. For if his father's wisdom could be trusted, *that* was the scenario they could expect.

"Would ya has me go and speak with him?"

"The Scribe? To what end? His tongue has been loose enough. We simply don't trust it."

Kylac resisted the urge to suggest that he might have better luck—to remind the captain that there were many means of gleaning truth from lie.

"Fortunately, his is not the only tongue available to us," Ledron mumbled.

Kylac glanced at the scroll the captain carried, and knew then where they headed.

"We've let our barbarian friends stew long enough. Time to see how well they've softened."

At last. While he'd have preferred a go at Tormitius, Vorathus's surviving Banshees would surely have knowledge of the seas around them, and quite possibly of their target destination. An initial interrogation should have taken place days ago—at least to determine where the prisoners' loyalties might lie. As members of a renegade crew that had shunned allegiance to the Great Grendavan, they might actually be quick to sell word of the Shards' location.

Or so he could hope. For these wouldn't easily be swayed by threat of death or torture.

"Any particular seed ya'd like me to root out?"

Ledron half turned to peer over his shoulder, eyes narrowing with his deepening frown. "I'll tend the questions. Your presence is merely to remind them of your talent with a blade."

A potential detriment, in this particular parley. Given the self-massacre of their comrades upon the Shrikeskinner's death, what reason was there to presume *these*—rendered senseless in battle—might respond favorably to the sight of their last known foe?

But Kylac wasn't going to heap further doubt on a matter already buried in it. Anxious he'd been for another chance to affect matters, rather than merely suffer them. He'd not decline this one.

They neared the end of a narrow corridor formed by stacks of crates and barrels stowed to either side of this rearward hold. Yoden warded a small portal in the aft wall ahead, his only companion a lantern of his own. Leaning heavily against a barrel, the Redfist straightened quickly upon sighting Ledron.

"Captain?" he greeted questioningly, as if to verify everything was in order.

The Head nodded. Yoden unlatched the door behind him.

"Would you have me join you?"

"Thank you, no. Wait here."

The soldier saluted and turned aside, giving them room to pass.

Ledron went first, pushing the door wide and stepping over the raised threshold. The darkness beyond withdrew reluctantly, like a scavenger interrupted in the midst of its meal. Kylac couldn't have said what spawned that mental image . . . until he caught the trapped scent of the cabin's stale breath—the choking tang of spilled bowels overpowering the mold and dank.

The captain drew up a forearm to cover his nostrils, reflexively tightening grip on the chart in that hand. He hefted the lantern in his other, its globe falling over the quartet of Banshees salvaged from the now week-old slaughter. All sat together, securely bound amid sacks of gravel and sand used for ballast, heads lowered against their chests.

Ledron kicked at the leg of the one nearest him. "Rouse, filth."

"Ya needn't bother, Captain." Kylac shook his head, a sense of vindication overcoming his momentary confusion. "They're dead."

27

LEDRON CAST KYLAC A TART GLANCE, then bent to see for himself. The four Banshees slumped rigidly against one another, eyes lidded, lips flecked with foam. One had retched before his death, leaving flakes of dried vomit upon his chest and adding a rancid tinge to the already pungent air. Given the smell, all four had soiled themselves upon breathing their last.

"Yoden!" Ledron barked, recoiling in anger.

The Redfist sentry thrust through the portal. "Sir."

"Who was the last to enter this hold?"

Yoden blinked, a slight panic gripping his features as he came to realize the condition of his charges. "Sir, I . . . One of the servers. The pocked one. Aramis."

"None other entered?"

"On *my* watch, no. Sir."

Kylac crouched nearer the dead Banshees. Victims, he supposed. Another act of sabotage from the mole he believed to be ferreted among them. For even if they'd taken their own lives, they hadn't done so without assistance in some form.

Regardless, his feeling of vindication gave way to bemused irritation. Another foolish decision by their captain, to have waited this long. An opportunity squandered.

"I see no surface wounds," he said. No blood, no bruises. He looked up at Ledron. "At a glance, I'd wager poison."

"Assemble the servers," the Head demanded of Yoden, "all who set foot in here. I'll see each of your fellow sentries, as well."

"And all others who may have touched their meals?" Kylac prompted. "Or the stores used to make them?"

He felt the weight of Ledron's frown, heavier for the shadows in his visage, gathered against the lantern light. "Suggesting what?"

"That it may be easier to question those who *didn't* have access." A ship this large remained a ship. If one man aboard had found opportunity to have hand in this matter, *all* could have.

"If this is a saboteur's work, I'll have him flushed here and now."

"And share our suspicions with the entire crew? To sow rampant mistrust?"

Ledron gritted his teeth, but glanced at the lingering Yoden with sudden hesitation.

"Whoever did this is unlikely to reveal himself," Kylac said, pressing his point. "And reluctant I'd be, for the sake o' morale, to set about wringing forth the truth."

"This was *your* suspicion from the outset. Would you let the matter go unchecked?"

Kylac considered the timing of the deed. Assuming murder, what had prompted it? If aimed to silence the prisoners, why not earlier? Mayhap the risk had been too great, and thus undertaken only when the captain's intent to question the prisoners had been announced. "Who knew ya meant to seek this audience?" he asked, thinking again that it might be easier to ask who hadn't.

"I told only Pevrick and Brenham, immediately before coming to you."

Then there hadn't been time for that particular whisper to take flight. Kylac turned his gaze to Yoden, who stood frozen, as wide-eyed as a startled buck. Given the genuine cloud of shock and fear emanating from him, he seemed an unlikely suspect—opportunity notwithstanding.

"An inquiry is warranted," Kylac agreed finally. "I merely suggest a more subtle means, so as not to go tearing at our own throats."

Ledron coughed, choking on the stench. When Kylac looked to him, his sleepless eyes had narrowed. "What means?"

Jorrand bowed expressionlessly when relieved of his post, and exited the captain's quarters with brisk strides. Making Ledron Kylac's only ally as he stepped into the hazy streams of daylight penetrating the cabin's misted portholes.

Tormitius met their arrival with a baleful grin. "The captain and his asp."

Another week's captivity had taken visible toll of the proud Grenarrian. He lay limply in what had been Vorathus's bed, no longer straining against his shackles. His muscles had softened with disuse, once-chiseled edges rounding like the crags of an eroding bluff. His cheeks had lost their former fullness, and his eyes gleamed dimly now within deepening hollows. Even the bitterness in his gaze appeared to have cooled, making way for an eerie calm.

Kylac mistrusted it at once.

"Of what service am I to avail you now?" the Shorecleaver asked.

"Come to warns ya of a contagion aboard," Kylac replied, "laying claim to your ilk."

"The Vulture's Banshees?" Tormitius chuffed, his throat hoarse from thirst and lack of use. "No kin of mine."

"Dead, nonetheless."

"Pity."

Kylac marked the tug of a smirk at Tormitius's lip. *He already knows.* "A contagion carried by *rats*, mayhap?"

"You'll find worse, surely, festering in the bowels of this wretched beast."

"Will we?" Kylac asked, advancing slowly, casually. He felt Ledron tense behind him, but the captain held his ground, trusting to the terms they'd agreed would govern this interrogation—ceding Kylac full rein of the conversation, provided he caused the valued prisoner no harm. "And yet, only those who made home aboard this vessel before us—those most familiar with its environs—have thus far been stricken. Four, perishing together. While ours who warded them remain hearty."

Tormitius cocked his head, smirking his black amusement. "No mysterious taint, then. Merely a brood of traitorous vermin seeking relief from the foulness of their own skin."

"As their shipmates did before them," Kylac allowed. "But these perished from within. Begging the question, where might this poison have hailed from?"

"Perhaps they carried it in their veins." With Kylac's frown, the Shorecleaver's smug grin broadened. "A venom suppressed by the sun's rays. Bound below, untouched by natural light for half a fortnight? Sufficient time, one might guess, for it to seep forth and lay claim."

No stranger to poisons, Kylac was unfamiliar with the breed Tormitius described. Which didn't mean it couldn't exist. His foray through the Harrows had introduced him to more than one lethal toxin he'd not been exposed to in his studies at Talonar, reminding him that he tread now in a different world. A glance back at Ledron, however, earned him only a scowl. The Head knew naught of this, either.

It *would* explain the curious timing of the incident. Nonetheless, it struck Kylac as just a shade too clever, and a mite too convenient.

Particularly when he considered Tormitius's surprising knowledge of the Banshees' shipboard location.

"And if'n I told ya they'd been dangling all this time from yardarms?"

The black grin slipped, but only momentarily. Instead of summoning excuse or denial, he changed course entirely. "Then perhaps they swallowed their tongues upon realizing our heading."

"Oh?"

"Plagued by superstitions, Vorathus. Among them, that falling prey to lightning or maelstrom amid the Thousand Tempests would see a soul forever lost. His Banshees may have deemed it better to die aforehand."

Kylac advanced another step, to hover directly over the prisoner's bedside. Personal superstition, he'd not attempt to argue against. But Tormitius continued to demonstrate a remarkable amount of knowledge for one sequestered as he'd been.

"And what makes ya believe these Tempests are our course?"

"A Grenarrian can feel his way in the swells, and hear it in the winds."

An unlikely boast, but Kylac let it go. "Impressive. And not one in four might have resisted? We's yet to glimpse a storm cloud or vortex that might threaten. Would none have waited for the peril to manifest?"

Tormitius laughed. When he shifted his thinning bulk, Kylac observed a smattering of small sores that bruised the underside of his naked arms. "Perhaps I'm mistaken. They may have sought only to spare themselves the indignity of slavery. Or to safeguard the location of their families, secreted away on some distant atoll."

"He toys with us," Ledron groused.

Kylac didn't flinch. *O' course he toys with us.* The only thing more unsettling than the Grenarrian's apparent knowledge was his slack handling of it. It was too much to hope that this willing communication reflected weariness or eroding resolve. His focus remained sharp, his tone calculating. If fearing betrayal from his own tongue, one such as Tormitius could be trusted to say nothing at all, jailing his thoughts entirely.

At least until claimed by delirium.

Such was weeks away—if not months—under these conditions. Kylac hadn't entered with the futile belief that the Shorecleaver might be clumsy enough to reveal any specific information he wished to withhold. Only to gauge any change in the prisoner's temperament, confirm certain suspicions, and allow Tormitius another opportunity to make himself the object of Ledron's ire.

That Kylac might soon be permitted to hasten matters along.

"Release me from these irons, Captain," the Shorecleaver taunted, "and there are other games we might play."

"I have pledged already to do so, if you will but help to deliver my lord prince."

"A pledge reforged from the shards of a lie."

Kylac shook his head at the tired refrains. "Is their conviction so much greater than yours?" He waited for Tormitius's glare to turn back on him before continuing. "A pack o' renegades. *Vermin*, ya calls them. Yet dead they are, in defense o' their beliefs. So I wonder, why aren't you?"

He felt the Shorecleaver's seething hatred like the simmering heat of a sun-baked earth. For a moment, he half expected the prisoner to lunge at him. Kylac leaned in, daring him to do so.

Instead, Tormitius forced another laugh. "*My* life is of no consequence, since I know what little you will gain of me."

Suggesting again that he understood keenly the potential threat the Banshees had posed. That whether or not he'd somehow orchestrated it, he was pleased by the elimination of an element beyond his control.

"Our destination is charted," Kylac reminded him. "The chance for ya to prove valuable to us is drawing to a close."

"Then spare me your foul breath and the stink of this odious vessel. Cast me to my death, that the winds may carry you that much swifter to yours."

"I KNOW NOT whose tongue I'd sooner sever and boil," Ledron grumbled, "his or yours."

They'd departed the prisoner's quarters only moments earlier, turning Tormitius back over to Jorrand and climbing aft to the poop deck. The captain's expression had been enough to dissuade any from joining them. So they found themselves alone now at the taffrail, peering back at the swath of foam cresting in their wake.

"You yap and yammer," the Head continued, "yet say nothing. Did he have hand in this, or did he not?"

"He knows he has an ally aboard," Kylac asserted, "be it a lone wolf or a pack."

"Why? Because he assumed we stashed his so-called Banshees in a lightless hold?"

"Because he wasn't surprised to learn they'd perished."

"Was that also not to be expected? Their entire crew slew themselves."

"Ya said yourself he was toying with us."

"As he has from the start. To sow confusion and dissent."

"Fearless he was, when last we spoke. But now he's become confident."

"Confident?" Ledron's incredulous look turned scornful. "More than a fortnight we've been at this, only to lose a ship and very nearly *our* entire crew. Confident he is that we'll never find the Shards. Confident that this voyage is doomed to fail, one way or another. Posture as you will, he told us nothing in there we didn't know already."

Kylac regarded the tirade with a shrug. "We's given him no reason to do elsewise."

"You still believe you can carve it out of him?"

Did the captain still believe they had a choice? While they might peck and nibble at clues and insinuations, whatever Tormitius knew of the real truth—about their mole, their location, their destination—he'd not share it unless compelled to do so.

"It needn't be bloody, if'n it's the mess that concerns ya."

Ledron cast a withering glare, then pressed a sigh through his gritted teeth. "We've stumbled into the rushes here. I came to you with concern as to the *Scribe's* reliability. And it seems to me, he's as suspect as anyone in the barbarians' murder."

What hope Kylac might have had that Ledron should relent on the matter swiftly dimmed.

"If it's a neck you must wring, let it be his."

Seeing nothing to be won with further delay, Kylac tipped his brow to the captain and headed forward, descending to the command deck. While no longer tethered as he'd been aboard the *Vengeance*, Ithrimir had nonetheless maintained over the past week a near permanent residence in the *Wail's* wheelhouse, scowling upon the horizon or scribbling away at his chart table under the wary eye of helmsmen, navigators, and any others given cause and permission to venture inside. The far greater majority of crewmen, including Kylac, had suffered no inclination to intrude upon that inner circle.

Would that he could say the same now.

Odd, the knot of uncertainty that twisted in his stomach whenever giving thought to the Scribe—present since his slaughter of those

Ladrakari who'd assailed the decks of the *Vengeance* on what his ship-mates had come to call the Day of Bloodletting. Kylac wasn't given to baseless fears or inexplicable misgivings, and had been unable to rationalize this one. He knew only that it had failed to dissipate. In that regard, better to deal with it now, he supposed, than allow it to fester any longer.

A single glance from the Elementer's clouded black eye left him doubting again.

"Captain would have me speak with ya," Kylac said as he entered the wheelhouse, defying the unsettling look and his own inner hesitation.

Ithrimir snorted. "To ply me with questions he fears to ask himself." He bent back to the chart in front of him—if chart it was. From Kylac's vantage, it appeared nothing more than a profusion of hooks and whorls weaving senselessly across the wax-covered tablet.

Taeg eyed him sidelong from his position at the wheel, a slight shrug and headshake suggesting that he knew not what the Scribe was so intently about, either. And that it might not be wise to press him on it.

But Kylac felt they'd tiptoed around the matter long enough. Having come full circle to where this line of questioning had started, he was determined to come away with something resembling an answer.

"Mayhap," he allowed, bypassing the helmsman to hover nearer Ithrimir's gnarled shoulder. "The only specific fear he voiced was the soundness of our course."

Another glance from Taeg, this one sharper with caution. Kylac ignored it. If determined to reap honesty, he intended to sow it.

"Threatened every time one of you draws me from my work," the Elementer groused. The wattles at his throat shook as he turned the blunt end of his stylus upon his tablet and rubbed furiously to erase a pattern of swirls. "The waves are ever unbridled, and the Dragon's stirrings have spawned a turmoil unwitnessed in centuries."

Quickly he poured fresh wax, scarcely waiting for it to cool before spinning back to the pointed end of his stylus and redirecting a series of arced lines along a curving new path.

"His ravings are consistent, at least," Taeg offered.

Indeed they were, to Kylac's recollection, echoing the same threats and admonitions the Scribe had uttered while imprisoned in his temple keep.

"Is there nothing to ease this creature's restlessness?"

"Am I to know? I read the devastation wrought by his movements, not the source of them."

"What devastation?"

"Sudden surges and compounding swells, violent flows and wrenching ebbs, all twining and growing toward inescapable cataclysm."

Kylac refused to meet Taeg's patronizing look. Mad as it all sounded, he didn't want to dismiss the matter solely for his own lack of understanding. And yet, he wasn't sure how to pursue this particular thread. Was this Dragon a physical monstrosity, or some symbolic representation of natural forces? Did it matter? He felt vaguely foolish even contemplating it.

He decided to aim for the heart of it. "Does nothing we might do matter?"

Ithrimir's bark might have been a laugh. "Should the ant ponder the range and sway of its skittering? It crawls as it can, seeking shelter from the rains, high ground amid the floods. Eluding death, but never escaping it."

A fair assessment, if not particularly helpful.

"At least you're out here skittering," Taeg observed. "And not spread from the branches of some tree upon your isle. Were it not for our visit—"

"Were it not for your visit, Chitral would have been unable to rouse his clansmen against Et'tanis. He may not have been sufficiently emboldened to try."

Kylac's stomach clenched, knotting anew at this confirmation of an earlier fear. It was *his* calling that the Butcher had used to spur a previously bridled revolt, convincing the Ladrakari that Kylac's coming and their Sa'ahla's unapologetic intractability meant the time had come for fresh leadership. Et'tanis's blood was on *his* hands, along with those whose needless killing had followed. For *he'd* been the pebble to trigger the resulting landslide.

Waves.

The Scribe's veined hand continued in its scratching, even when his dead eye again found Kylac. "Ever unbridled."

An eerie chill scraped along Kylac's spine. He shrugged it aside. While serving to explain a measure of his unease, the revelation—along with what seemed a piercing insight—did little to answer Ledron's concern as to whether the Elementer could be trusted.

"Ya did beg passage aboard our vessel."

"And for lack of options, here I am. Was it not the same that led you to seek my guidance from the first?"

The Scribe turned his unnerving gaze upon Taeg. Had he learned it was the helmsman's proposal that had brought them to him? If so, the searching frown Taeg flashed at Kylac suggested he hadn't been the one to mention it.

Mayhap the perceptive Elementer had known all along. His observations certainly seemed to reflect some level of preternatural intuition. Should that surprise them? Had they not brought him aboard precisely for the unique knowledge and powers he was rumored to possess? Powers said to be of mystical origin?

Magic or madness, the Scribe seemed to have the right of it. He was relying upon them as much as they were relying upon him. Unless he had some further agenda he'd managed thus far to conceal, they had little reason to mistrust him.

No more than he did them.

"Then spare me your captain's suspicions," Ithrimir growled. Along the side of his tablet, he drew a descending series of unreadable characters like marking numbers in a ledger. "Unless you happen upon one better capable of charting the course *he* has set for us."

A reasonable request, Kylac decided, knowing even as he bowed and took his leave that it meant departing yet another interrogation in which he'd gained nothing by way of justifiable assurance. All he had was his sense, present almost from the beginning, that Ithrimir spoke truly—insofar as he saw it. A dangerous proposition, when belief alone couldn't suppress physical reality.

He was forced to admit as much just moments later, when Ledron cornered him with senior officers Pevrick and Brenham in tow.

"Well?"

"Strikes me as lucid enough," Kylac answered. "No more mad than the rest of us."

It was difficult to say which of them frowned deepest.

"And his inconstant directions?" Brenham asked.

Kylac put forth a bemused expression. "Seems an inconstant task, tracking wind and wave. I won't pretend to comprehends it, but neither would I think to tells ya *your* business."

"Sailing and navigation must be as sword and sheath," said Pevrick. "If he cannot justify the maneuvers he asks of us, we shouldn't be performing them."

Brenham nodded. "We needn't reroute for every cap and breeze to make our destination. Twice now he's damn near had us crawling in circles."

"He peers at shades invisible to me, I grant ya. But does so to keep us from danger."

"Real or phantom?" Brenham asked, an edge to his typically un-flappable voice. "We've glassy seas and nearly cloudless skies. Just what is he steering us away from?"

Kylac couldn't say. He preferred to simply accept and abide by the Scribe's purported expertise. But therein lay Brenham's frustration. A master he was, of the same craft, and thus finding it difficult to disregard his own, more conventional judgment. Kylac might have felt the same, were Ithrimir advising him to parry with a blade when he knew he should thrust.

"Believe in him or don't," Kylac said, shrugging for emphasis. "Only saying that, from what I's heard and seen, this is *his* element. And I wouldn't necessarily wait to finds myself at the edge o' this Eddaron's Rift 'fore I asked him to guide us clear."

Their frowns persisted. Ledron appeared to be mulling it over, in that bitter, dissatisfied manner of his. Pevrick and Brenham held surprisingly silent. Doubtless, they'd made their opinions on the matter plain already.

"If we deny him chance to bring us to the storm's edge," the captain said finally, "we'll not know whether we can rely on him within its grasp."

Leeches crossed his arms, his scowl deepening, while Brenham's energy seemed to flag.

Ledron himself cursed beneath his breath before adding, "If some evidence should prove me a fool, do bring it to me at once."

28

THAT VERY NIGHT, they found their storm front.

It greeted them in the moonlit dark with a blanket of cold and a smattering of rain. Kylac, sleeping abovedecks in one of the canvas-covered shore boats, was awakened by the abrupt chill and slow, scattered tapping. As he peered to the east, a distant flash of lightning illuminated the mountain of black clouds that hunkered on the forward horizon. It was several heartbeats before he heard the dim crackle of accompanying thunder.

Within moments, however, the rains began to descend in earnest, while a mournful sigh arose from the winds gaining pluck amid the rigging. Kylac tucked further beneath his canvas shield, but soon surrendered to the heavy drumming and slipped out in search of better shelter. En route, he spied Ithrimir hunched at his table beside Jaleth in the wheelhouse, scowling through the rain-streaked window. Other dark forms, cloaked and hooded, huddled in various positions throughout the decks, manning their lines, watch stations, or relay posts. The few who eyed him did so with a grudging air, amid halos formed around the lanterns holding back the night.

By the time he reached the desired hatch leading belowdecks, he had to wrestle with the wind to close it again, drawing a shrill whistle of protest when he pulled it shut. The lantern below, guttering at the intrusion, flared with relief. Kylac followed it into the surrounding darkness, listening to the *Wail* creak as she listed to larboard and back again, riding the rogue swell that heaved beneath her.

In the deck's corridor, he found himself face-to-face with Pevrick.

The first mate still bore the weight of his interrupted slumber, heaviest about the shoulders and eyelids. But the unexpected sight of Kylac in those tight quarters proved jolting, judging by his quick gasp and stiffening lurch.

The Whitefist's cheeks flushed with anger. "What brings you slithering down here?"

Kylac resisted the urged to fling the same question back at him. He was, after all, the ship's second-in-command, which probably gave him right to know. "Something unpleasant brewing topside. Just came down to escape the gale."

Leeches scoffed and shook his head. "Burrow deep, little tick. Stay snug while the rest of us steer you to safety." With a contemptuous grunt, he pushed past, muttering unintelligibly as he found and climbed the nearby deck ladder.

Kylac lingered momentarily, measuring his actions against the other's animosity, calculating whether he'd done enough to provoke it. It didn't seem so. But then, every man's tolerance was different. Mayhap, to Pevrick's nose, he simply smelled foul.

The winds howled sharply as Leeches opened the hatch, then quieted as he slammed it shut again. Kylac directed his gaze down the now-empty corridor. Farther aft lay Denariel's quarters, beside those taken by Ledron and the other senior officers. As another swell rolled under their keel, he thought of the princess's own poor tolerance for seafaring. For half a heartbeat, he considered looking in on her . . . before abruptly recalling Pevrick's reaction to his unannounced presence. A warm embrace, he suspected, compared to the response he might receive from Denariel or her assigned warders.

So he turned and traveled forward instead, descending to a dry hold filled with grains and powders stacked about in canvas sacks. Uncomfortably cramped, like all else belowdecks, yet blissfully empty of crewmen, which made it seem more spacious. The drumming of rain and shriek of the wind persisted as but a soft echo and dull whisper. Save for the rock and sway of their vessel, he could almost forget the elements railing outside.

As he arranged a small pile of sacks to better accommodate his reclined frame, Kylac thought back to the sea storms that had assailed him on his earlier voyage from Pentania—a long, bitter fight that had ended in shipwreck upon the northern coast of Addaranth. Given Ithrimir's admonitions about the region into which they now sailed, these promised to be even worse. He could only hope that, whatever their severity, they wouldn't reap similar calamity.

"DEATH?" OLEKK MANAGED through cold-clenched teeth. "A relief, were it to end this misery."

Several of the surrounding Redfists, as soaked and pallid as their sonorous comrade, muttered agreement. Kylac, who stood centrally among them as they swayed in their hammocks, wondered where his tale had gone awry. He'd just finished recounting for them the destruction of *Denariel's Return* and the decimation of her crew . . . of the survivors who'd struggled ashore that dark night, only to be hunted by the monstrous, juvenile tarrocks inhabiting the reef they'd struck upon. He'd done so to bolster the spirits of those he sailed with now, by reminding them that their situation wasn't yet as dire as some.

Alas, he seemed to be mining little in the vein of appreciation or perspective.

"Better a sharp, swift bite than trapped in this boundless swirl," said Crawfoot.

Kylac had been overhearing similar laments for days now. So had Ledron—presumably why the captain had asked him to see what he might do to sow encouragement among those most dour. A dubious charge, given that Kylac would be lying were he to deny having to fend off his own dark sentiments over the past ten days. Ten days that had seen them hammered and tossed incessantly by furious winds and savage seas. Pummeled by rains and deafened by thunder. Torn and battered, they'd weathered on, climbing mountainous swells only to be shrugged back and forced again to scale the next. Twisted and spun. Wrenched and dragged and thrust aside by violent gusts and surging waves wrought not by nature, it seemed, but by some darker, primordial power bent on destroying them.

"What difference, reef tarrock or ocean shark?" asked Wooton, implying that the latter fate awaited at least some of them.

Difficult it was to find fault in their despair. Like the soldiers around him, Kylac had no training for this. They were helpless, chained to a bit of wood and pitch adrift amid the unyielding tempest. Shivering in dank darkness. Thrown from one foot to the next. Retching into the same buckets and barrels from which they spent hours bailing endless surge waters. Blind to the world that raged outside. Tormented by its ceaseless caterwaul.

And that when safely belowdecks.

"Suppose I'd sooner drown," Quill determined thoughtfully.

"Lightning, for me," huffed Hamal.

"So why lay here shivering?" Talon asked irritably, his eyes closed in a futile attempt at sleep. "Plenty chance at both topside."

Indeed, they seemed to have forgotten that the Whitefists had it worse. Charged with keeping rein of their vessel, those abovedecks had to contend with the shriek and scrape of strafing winds. With sheeting rains that struck like iron shards. With rogue wave crests that swept continuously over the ship's decks, each seeming larger and more threatening than the last. It was said that Garryn had been washed away by just such a wave when the knot of his safety line had come undone. Neglecting his tether altogether, Tareth had toppled over the starboard rail, caught by an abrupt roll of the ship to that side. And Jahvid, their chief lookout, had been lost to a fork of lightning while hunkered in the crow's nest.

"Only a matter of time for the rest of us," hissed Kahrem. "At some point, she'll tire of gnawing on us and gulp us down."

Rest assignments brought little relief. The *Wail*'s motions were too violent, and the men typically soaked through from their shift's labors. The best they could do was strip from their sodden garments, wring the ocean from them, and cocoon themselves in their blankets while cloaks and tunics and breeches hung abandoned—never long enough to completely dry before the time came to don them again.

"Brought it on ourselves," said Graves, clutching his pouch of knucklebones as if a charm that might bring them better fortune. Kylac hadn't seen the Redfist toss them in sport since the deaths of Rags and Lisp. "Never should have brought that madman aboard."

Another well-worn refrain, though Kylac had yet to hear it so brazenly uttered by anyone who knew him to be within earshot. Ithrimir was to blame. Doubted by the ship's officers when it had seemed he might be misreading or intentionally delaying their progress toward this stormy region, he'd come to be viewed now by the bulk of the crew as the reason they couldn't escape it.

"A barnacle-eyed turtle could have steered us better," said Mutton.

Hamal scoffed. "You think we flail about by accident? Probably means to sacrifice us to his watery gods."

"Could he be brewing this himself?" asked Yoden.

"Of course he is. No storm so savage lasts this long."

"Or might be his gods mean to punish him—and us in the bargain."

Kylac kept quiet as the theories were tossed about, waiting for the meat of the matter to emerge.

"His own followers claimed he'd lost his powers, did they not?" asked Quill.

Kahrem spat. "This or that, sooner we scrape that barnacle free, sooner we might find our way."

And there it was.

Kylac waited for their gazes to gather upon him. Some eyed him warily. Others intently. All did so with some measure of expectation.

"Anyone take this to the captain?" he asked.

The question drew only murmurs, while gazes turned aside. No matter. He knew already that more than one of them had. There'd been objections to the strange Elementer joining them from the first. The desperate stages of their flight from Mistwall had overshadowed those complaints for a time, but by the close of that first storm-shrouded day, they'd begun to resurface. By the fifth day, the rumblings had gained sufficient intensity that Kylac himself had gone to Ledron, informing the captain that if he didn't wrangle the matter, *he* would.

The Head had simply grumbled that if any intended to toss the Scribe overboard, it might be wiser not to stop them.

Kylac had from that moment been more watchful of Ithrimir's occasional movements about the ship. While respecting the Elementer's obvious desire for seclusion, he wouldn't allow the eccentric codger to come to harm. True enchanter or charlatan, Ithrimir had saved his life at least once already. While it might be said Kylac had paid that debt in advance by sparing the old man from ritual torture, he hadn't done so merely to bloody his own hands later.

Regardless, he believed none of this superstitious prattle, and privately derided the collective fear that had spawned it. He, too, worried that the sea might devour them at any moment—simply crack their vessel like an eggshell and suck them down into its fathomless gullet. But only greater harm could come from lashing out in irrational response. And eliminating from their crew the one man who claimed to be able to navigate these waters struck him as absurd.

"It was you who brought him on," Hamal remarked pointedly, punctuating the accusation with that squinted stare of his. "Should be you who persuades the captain."

Heads bobbed amid a chorus of enthusiastic grunts.

Kylac chuckled. "And if'n the captain should ignore my pleas?"

"Then it might be someone more prudent should be in command."

It was Olekk who'd given voice to the idea. But the ensuing silence told Kylac that others had already been thinking it. Mayhap even discussed it among themselves. He waited another moment, giving chance for someone—anyone—to raise protest.

The storm outside sang unchallenged.

He considered his response. If it had come to this, it would be foolish of him to speak openly in the captain's defense—to align himself against them and lose what shred of confidence they were offering him. Countering that, he doubted they'd trust him if he appeared too eager, and didn't want to risk being accused as a potential conspirator, should any present be secretly opposed to mutiny.

"Has we another better suited to the task?"

"The captain himself is no sailor," Hamal reminded them.

"And has too little to lose," Olekk pressed. "Easy to lay wager in desperation. Yet it is *our* lives he gambles with."

"And how much o' the crew might we lose in opposition?"

"There is but one other Blackfist aboard," Crawfoot observed. "The Whitefists would surely prefer to follow their own."

And if this many Redfists would risk the topic in open conversation, odds were the rest would be willing to follow.

Especially if they perceived Kylac and his blades to not be elsewise set against them.

Kylac put a hand to his chin, rocking on his feet with the sway of the ship. His deliberation was only partly feigned. While he, too, had wondered whether Ledron was ideally suited to lead them, he shuddered at the prospect of turning control over to Pevrick. Would it not be better, though, to follow popular sentiment willingly, in hopes of redirecting matters at a later juncture? Easier to influence the outcome and oversee the treatment of any to be deposed—Ledron, Ithrimir, Denariel—if he were to support the common aim, rather than resist it.

Or should he simply start cutting the throats of these dissenters, and hope it left him with enough able-bodied men to keep the *Wail* afloat?

It was his *father's* taste for intrigues he needed here.

He looked around, weighing their individual stances, expressions, gazes. As a whole, he smelled trepidation, which gave him time. Just how much would be harder to determine.

"I'll not fall prey to any man's madness," he said, and drove the claim home with a steely glare. "Give me leave to remind our captain and navigators o' this. I'll let ya know whether their answers suit me."

He considered going straight to Ledron with word of the crew's wavering loyalties. But there seemed little to discuss. Doubtless, the captain was aware of his tenuous standing, and needed no specific reminders. And without any definite stratagem of which Kylac was aware, he'd be delivering little more than vague warning. For that, he ran risk of appearing a rat to the bulk of the crew, and might trigger a preemptive response from Ledron that could make matters even worse.

For now, the Head would have to maintain his own guard as he had from the first.

His greater concern was still for Ithrimir. Not only because the Scribe remained the underlying target of the crew's anger in this situation, but because it was the Elementer upon whom their lives truly depended.

And the Elementer who had answers yet to give.

With inquiries made to a handful of green-faced sentries, Kylac learned that the Scribe could be found at that moment not in the wheelhouse, but deep below among the bilgewater bowels of the ship. He'd been spending more and more time in those depths of late, examining whatever it was he found so fascinating within those waters. Having men hoist buckets from below, full for him to sample, had proven both difficult and dangerous, and often angered those called upon to carry out the work. Though it meant leaving his post beside the helmsman, he must have come to prefer this course.

When Kylac found him in the foremost hold, the Scribe was submerged to his waist—or his knees, depending on the ship's lean—muttering to himself while raking with his fingers at the agitated waters sloshing heavily to and fro. A mix of waves and rainwater that had spilled down through portholes and hatches, or seeped up from below. So as not to disturb, Kylac waded to within a half dozen strides before settling against a beam, giving feel to the alternating push and drag, but learning nothing from it beyond its brackish chill. Warmer than the seas cradling his homeland to the north, at least. For that, he supposed he should be grateful.

"That stench muddies my work," Ithrimir grumbled.

His scent must indeed have betrayed his presence, since the Elementer had yet to turn eye to him. "Your pardon. Ya wouldn't has a phial o' rosewater to share, perchance."

"The oils of your skin trouble less than the blood of your veins. But neither is more potent than those damnable spines you carry."

"Spines. My blades?"

"*His*. Pungent were they an ocean away."

Kylac drew a dagger to have fresh look at it. The only light at this depth of the hold glowed from a lantern some seven paces behind him. But he didn't need light to examine what he'd studied a thousand times—he and every bladewright or smith he'd come upon over the years who might be able to tell him something more about the strange material. Exotic. Exquisite. Resembling steel, but lighter and stronger, with a pearlescent sheen. Unbreakable, insofar as he'd experienced, against implements of metal and stone many times thicker and heavier.

Could it be?

Forged with sorcery, some had claimed, with mystical grains woven into its folds. But Kylac remembered well where and how he'd found them—in a remote cove on the eastern coast of the Skullmar Mountains, lying abandoned amid hundreds if not thousands like them. Who could have forged such a trove? Who would have done so and then left it to bake upon the stony, surfswept sands? They certainly resembled the spines of a fish—something he himself had suggested before. Only, what breed of fish wore such an array of knives and swords and spears?

But then, Ithrimir had already told him.

"The Dragon," Kylac recalled. "Your *Dread Eye of the Deep*."

Ithrimir grimaced, but issued no denial. Implausible, it still seemed. Yet, Killangrathor had been riddled with spines. Who was to say the magnificent beast wasn't cousin to some great monster that lurked yet amid the primordial depths?

A strange warmth bloomed in the pit of Kylac's stomach. To whatever extent he chose to believe, a question carried with him for the past three years had been given answer.

"The leviathan that shed these . . . The one ya fear . . . Has it a purpose?"

"Ask as soon why day chases night, or the wind strafes the shore. He *is*, and we but the grains stirred by His passing."

A foolish question, mayhap. Kylac chose to redirect, nearer his original intent. "Odorous as they may be, these spines may be all that now separate ya from the crabs."

Ithrimir's cough carried with it a mocking derision. "Kill me, and they'll take their own place amid the bones of the deep."

"I's staked my own belief as such. But I fear my opinion counts for little with this brood." Kylac sheathed his dagger and waded forward. "Is there nothing ya might do to justify their faith?"

"Am I a jester now, to seek the applause of skeptics and simpletons?"

"Twice now I's seen ya bend water to your will," Kylac replied earnestly. "When wresting me from that subterranean flow, and again when that Reaver was bearing down on us in the Trellong."

The Scribe turned to him at last, peering at him with his more natural eye. Scowling as if wary of deception.

"Would ya denies us the benefit o' your power simply because we cannot fathom it?"

The scowl softened. If Kylac wasn't mistaken, the old man's gnarled shoulders sagged upon his crooked frame. "My ancient forebears, the Aggethrehn of yore—theirs was the true power to mold and manipulate. A mere echo am I, amid the roar of their great legacy. The chill of a passing shadow."

The Elementer scooped a palm full of the waters frothing past him as the ship pitched and rolled, spilling them from one bony hand to the other. Kylac felt the weight of his bitter lament.

"Yet, my sight is strong. Though my command be weak, the waters hide little from me. As a guide, my value is real."

Kylac felt his own lingering doubts drain in response to the confession. In their place, he found the dregs of a minor guilt. Truth unfettered, he'd come not quite knowing whether he should confront the Scribe for help or for blame. Mayhap it was the gossip of his shipmates digging under his skin like ticks . . . or the Scribe's rancorous mien . . . or simply the wearing effects of the enduring storm. But having so often been underestimated or misjudged himself, he should have been more diligent against such suspicions.

Ithrimir slapped at the waters in which he stood and turned back to resume his study. Irritated, no doubt, that he should be so challenged by those he was endeavoring to preserve.

"Has ya any estimate, at least, as to how much longer we may be trapped in this gale?"

"We shall find Durnifwyr on the morrow, beating at the Tempests' heart. Only then will we have traversed this savage wasteland by half."

Kylac's own heart plummeted. Whatever encouragement he'd found in his rejuvenated faith, it couldn't withstand the disappointment of learning that each stormy day they'd endured thus far must be matched again on the other side of this Eddaron's Rift.

Assuming they ever reached it.

"So if you've any other festering concerns, you may as well ask them now, while my concentration is shattered," Ithrimir grumbled. "For our path grows more perilous as we approach."

Dozens of questions Kylac could have asked—about his blades, this *Dragon*, Ithrimir's ancestors, and the present voyage. But all seemed unduly selfish, if serving distraction that might further endanger all aboard. Whatever Ithrimir's immediate task, the Scribe clearly held it crucial. Would any of Kylac's questions truly matter if the old man failed in it?

"I'll buy ya what time ya need," he promised. "Though it may mean blood in these waters."

Ithrimir snorted. "With you, it always does."

29

FOR THE ELEVENTH STRAIGHT DAY, the dawn failed to arrive.

If the sun had risen, it hid behind impenetrable layers of roiling black clouds that served backdrop to a heaving seascape—churning gray waters blanketed with foam. Sheeting raindrops blew sideways, hurled by relentless winds that sought to pull Kylac from his feet. Beneath him, *Denariel's Wail* bucked and rolled amid the darkness.

Still he climbed higher.

Below, Whitefists wrestled in packs with loosening lines and unruly sheets, slipping and stumbling upon the tilting decks. Waves struck the *Wail's* hull with the force of hammer blows, reverberating throughout her battered shell. Even near the top of the foremast, inching skyward past the fore royal sail that flapped loosely in the wind, he felt her shuddering response. A marvel, that she should withstand such constant punishment. Of constant concern, the moment in which she might succumb.

She already had, in bits and pieces. The hour had yet to pass, it seemed, in which she hadn't loosed a knot, torn a sheet, or thrown a spar. The web of lines by which her rigging was strung together simply couldn't withstand the wrenching shifts caused by the raging storm. A wiser, less desperate crew would have long ago furled sail and simply battened down against the sea's wrath, letting it blow and toss them where it willed before collecting themselves later.

No, Kylac amended, a wiser, less desperate crew would never have entered this savage stretch of ocean at all.

But that choice had already been made. With it, they had no true course save the one they were on. This deep into the Thousand Tempests, escape wouldn't be found without forcefully attempting to navigate in one direction or another. They were as well off seeking to maintain their eastward heading as slinking off to some other point of the compass. Difficult and costly as that continued to prove in lost or broken materials—and lost or broken men—there was no help for it now but to see the voyage through.

Soldiering on in fits and starts and all-too-frequent repair efforts such as this.

As he reached for the next handhold, an abrupt lurch threw the *Wail* to starboard. His palm stretched wide. His feet slipped against the rain-slicked wood. For a moment, his entire body flung free, tethered only by the rung gripped in his left fist.

Though he couldn't hear them over the storm's roaring din, Kylac sensed the anticipation—fretful in some cases, eager in others—of those below who marked his climb, waiting for him to fall.

Maintaining his calm, Kylac held fast until the ship rolled back beneath him. Mayhap he'd been overzealous in volunteering to reattach the fluttering corner of sail aloft, rather than lowering its yard. This would be swifter, he'd claimed, and require fewer hands, buying them precious moments in a venture that could ultimately be decided by mere heartbeats. True enough, though truer still would have been to confess that he'd come to seek any such challenge, if only to avoid one more moment moldering belowdecks.

He wondered if, peering down, he might take better stock of those wagering either for or against him—and of how many were hoping he'd fail regardless. Not likely, from this height, and in these elements, with most scattered about, engaged in duties of their own. So he settled for the telltale itch of their gazes—the prodding of those urging him safely skyward, amid the plucking of those praying for his fall—and continued to focus on the more urgent task at hand.

When properly positioned, he crept out along the larboard arm of the royal yard, riding it up and down with the ship's wildly erratic pitch and roll. Beneath him, the loose corner of sail snapped and stammered its protest amid the howling wind, flapping uncontrollably. As instructed prior to his ascent, Kylac began reining it in, stretch by stretch, from the center, re-securing it with the robands supplied him—one eyelet at a time—to the jackstays. He'd been warned to respect the wind's strength, and found it easy to do so, given the ferocious tug of just a short span of cloth against his grasp. Overzealous? Wrestling with such merciless forces so high above the tempest, the ship rearing beneath him, struck him now as downright foolhardy.

A worthy contest.

He'd reached the corner eyelet, the sheet's railing reduced to a whimper, when the ship yawed viciously to starboard while tilting heavily to larboard. For a dizzying moment, the world turned sideways, leaving him to stare down the tip of the yardarm into the churning frenzy of the sea below.

Amid the prevailing darkness, a shadow loomed. Kylac heard the dim echo of cries from his shipmates, and looked up as the towering wave rolled in.

It crested over the *Wail* as if to consume her, a great deluge that slapped and pummeled and tore. Near helpless out at the end of his spar, Kylac could but hunker and cling as if death itself were dragging at him. Surrender to this, and he'd be surrendering to everything.

On the seventeenth anniversary of his birth, no less.

Interminable, it seemed, the wave's cold, clutching grasp. Until abruptly, its weight fell away, its bulk thrown past, leaving only the briny waters dripping from his already sodden garments, and the shrieking of the winds riding its wake.

The spar threw him back again, as the *Wail* somehow righted herself. Kylac held fast. *Keep clawing, girl,* he thought, even as he looked below, to see what damage the rogue wave had wrought.

He spied nothing but its remnants, at first. A foaming surge sheeting over the starboard rail. As the ship rocked to the other side, an ankle-deep wash flooded back across the deck, sloshing about in whorls and eddies. Sailors clinging to lines and shrouds, rails and capstans, emerged like mussels from their shells, probing warily. Others had been saved only by their tethers. All arose gradually, taking stock, as he did, of themselves and their surroundings. Hard-pressed to believe that all remained intact.

Then came the echoing shouts, faint amid the tumult, of terror and pleading. They drew Kylac's attention out amid the swells. One . . . two . . . three men he counted, dark specs adrift among the churning whitecaps. Whitefists whose safety lines had torn free, slipped loose, or elsewise failed them. Dead men, for all their thrashing and denial. For in this gale, there was no coming about, no pole or hook that could reach them, no net or line with which to reel them in.

Not for lack of effort. As the doomed sailors were spotted, their comrades searched for those lifesaving implements nearest at hand. But even in calm seas, the distance from deck to waterline of this great Marauder was such that only a man who'd swum right up against the hull might hope to take hold of strand or loop or ladder rung. The crewmen who'd been swept away in this fell hour were exhausted already from their labors, from the constant trial of keeping the *Wail* on course. And they kicked not against smoothly rolling swells, but heaving mountains that served to erase a dozen desperate strokes with a single, implacable shrug.

Already, their cries were diminishing, devoured by the swiftly growing distance.

A new furor kindled below, nearer at hand. Another wayward Whitefist, netted amid the ratlines of the mainmast. Slipped down from above, or hurled up from below. Entangled now, and, given his thrashing, in no small degree of discomfort. Yet it wasn't his voice that drew attention, for if voice he had, it failed to reach Kylac's position. Rather, it was the frantic shouts and fevered scampering of those who rushed to his aid that bespoke concern.

Suggesting a man of importance.

Biting down against the knot in his stomach, Kylac bent to finish the knot in hand. Negligent he'd be called, were he to curtail a task volunteered and accepted in order to take up another. Only when confident he could do no more to secure the fore royal did he slither back across the yardarm, seeking the nearest halyard from which to begin his descent.

By the time his feet struck decking again, the larboard shrouds of the mainmast were awash with a half dozen Whitefists, all clinging and tugging like spiders around their ensnared shipmate. Others shouted or cursed from where they'd clustered below, eyes wide with apprehension. Pevrick stood among the latter, barking like a foaming hound, his unbridled fury underscored by a genuine fear.

Spurred by their distress, Kylac slipped through the clutch of onlookers and clambered up among those fighting so feverishly to free their comrade. The victim was but a faceless tangle, from Kylac's view, enwrapped in cloak and hood. Yet it quickly became evident that he was being strangled by the cords caught round his neck—with the weight of those straining to reach him only hastening that end.

"Clear!" Kylac shouted as he scrambled past the slower, clumsier hands barring his path. He brought a dagger to bear, slashing at various strands to cut men loose and relieve the pressure on the one choking on their weight. He listened to their grunts of surprise and complaint, and paid them no heed.

Within heartbeats, he'd scurried beyond the lower-hanging re- sponders, angled in among the highest, and severed the rope encircling the trapped man's throat. Yet it was a purpled face that fell free to gape sightlessly back at him, his neck a chafed and bloody ruin around his crushed windpipe.

A plummeting sensation cored through Kylac, even as the *Wail* bucked upon another swell.

Brenham.

Luckless timing, a waxen-faced Taeg observed, that Brenham had chosen in that moment to venture from the navigation chamber to his quarters belowdecks. Would that he'd spent a few minutes more in the wheelhouse in passing. Or a few minutes less. Quite likely, fatigue had played some role. The second mate had slept but a blink or two amid the past half dozen arcs—two hours, mayhap, amid the last thirty-six.

"He knew better," the haunted helmsman had muttered amid his shock.

None other had anything to add as to how it had happened. Traversing the decks one moment, dead the next. Alongside him, the other three Whitefists—Tornow, Jurich, and Adaeus. Men whom Kylac had known but little, but who'd been well liked and well respected by their shipmates. More so in retrospect, Kylac sensed, their lives afforded greater value for the circumstances in which they'd been lost. Leaving the rest of them that much more shorthanded. Increasing the burden on those who remained.

There'd been no formal eulogy or ceremonial parting. After being cut free and shown to Ledron, Brenham's body had been fed to the sea. Only the Fair Mother knew when they might elsewise have returned his corpse to Addaranth, or in what condition. His token of rank was given to Pevrick to deliver to his widow, should the opportunity ever manifest, but sentimentality was elsewise trammeled by expediency. Before half the crew had even heard what had happened, Brenham was gone.

Few seemed willing to accept it. Or knew not how. Shipwright, navigator, second mate. Three crucial roles, lost in a single mishap. Few aboard, if any, could claim to serve greater purpose on this voyage. To Kylac's eyes and ears, the episode had served devastating blow to the crew's already battered morale. Be they Redfists or Whitefists, the men he happened across in the hours that followed were no longer soldiers and sailors, but drowning rats seeking any hope of escape.

And the key to those hopes consorted now with the crabs.

Kylac found himself wondering how much more they could tolerate.

By midday, he had his answer.

He'd taken to trailing Pevrick, who'd been tasked by their captain with selecting Brenham's replacement. *Replacements,* Leeches had growled at once, emphasizing the severity of their loss by pointing out that no *one* man among them could assume all of Brenham's duties. Ledron hadn't bothered to argue, only insisted that he see it done quickly.

From that moment, Kylac had misliked the first mate's mien. His expression was no darker than before, his neck no stiffer, his unblinking eyes no narrower. But the sight of him triggered a slithering sensation in Kylac's stomach, like that of an adder bearing down on its prey. So it came as little surprise when Kylac took root in a hold compartment adjoining the one in which Olekk had begged Pevrick for a meeting, and discovered their whispers to be bent on mutiny.

"What oath can you give that the Stonewatch follow you?" Leeches demanded.

"What oath but one?" Olekk huffed, his sonorous voice resonating amid the stores and through the slats of the compartment wall. "I stake my life on it."

"And mine in the bargain. So you'll forgive my caution. We'll have but one chance at this. If you've any doubt, best to wait."

"What doubt can there be?"

The question met with momentary silence. Even through the partition, Kylac felt the weight of Pevrick's glare.

"He's pledged no part, for or against," Olekk admitted.

"He'll seek to thwart us," Leeches spat, and Kylac knew from the venom in his voice that they spoke of *him*. "Killed or subdued, I say. Until then, we're pissing against a gale."

"And a very real gale outside, that even now tears us asunder."

"So see it done. Tonight. Bring me Kronus's skin, and I'll give you Ledron's. And a homeward heading by daybreak."

"You speak of it as if some simple matter."

"Is it not? Creyl has his confidence. Use it against him."

"I'd not counted the half-wild among our ranks."

"He's a bloody Redfist, is he not?" Pevrick huffed his disapproval. "So use him unwittingly. Or must the baitworm know its purpose in order to serve it?"

Another heavy silence marked Olekk's lingering hesitation. "I'd hoped—"

"Hope and holler and the seas might turn to dust. The vagabond was never going to side with us. If elsewise, only until he spied some other purpose more to his liking. Wiser you'd be to tear steak alongside a brood of shrikes. Can you do it?"

"Of course I can do it."

"So set deed to word."

The *Wail* creaked and the storm thundered. Pevrick's tromping feet announced his departure, followed moments later by Olekk's. Kylac sat back, considering his options. Nice it would have been to hear how the Redfists intended his demise. Not because he needed to know their strategy in order to thwart whatever clumsy attempt they might muster. Merely to discern if there might be a way to forestall it without having to kill half their number.

And what might that number be? To know with certainty which of his shipmates were desperate enough to take hand in his slaying, he'd have to wait until the very moment in which they came at him. Taeg? Warmund? Talon? Shards, mayhap even Creyl. Were they to entrust him with the opportunity, what great cause had Kylac to believe the half-wild might shy from it?

The image carried with it a tincture of sadness. Had he met none along this voyage who might value his companionship beyond what suited their own benefit?

It scarcely mattered. Friends or pawns, he in their game, or they in his, the only commitment he'd made was to reunite Dethaniel with royal sister and father. Whatever his next move, it would be that which bettered his chances of attaining that objective.

The rest served only so much distraction.

Mayhap the time had come to expose the conspirators to their captain. Any other action Kylac might undertake without leave would surely invoke Ledron's ire. So might any *inaction*, were the Head to later suspect that Kylac had withheld prior knowledge of any mutinous dealings.

Be cursed or be damned, his father might have said, *but bury your thrust.*

Still deliberating on the direction in which he might aim, he headed topside. He was weighing the notion of another "accident" involving a senior officer of the ship when he sprang the forward deck hatch and ventured back out into the squalling darkness.

And dismissed the matter as his gaze caught upon the horizon.

Out beyond the bow rail, past the chop and heave of tempest seas, churned a monstrous maelstrom breathtaking to behold. An immense crater swirling amid the storm-riven expanse. Black clouds roiled overhead, but flashes of lightning in near constant chains spread an eerie, flickering radiance over broad swaths of its vast reach, providing dire hint of its fathomless depths.

Eddaron's Rift.

Unmistakable, given Ithrimir's description. Yet a tame account, now that Kylac witnessed it for himself. A crushing vortex of immeasurable strength, immutable power, that looked for all the absent stars like a rent in their world, a portal to the Abyss.

And, as madness would have it, they were still sailing toward it.

He hastened aft to learn why. Chaos ruled the decks. The scramble of reserve sailors filtering up from below suggested a shipwide alarm only just now sounded. As did the paralyzed reactions of those Kylac passed—crewmen awestruck by the Rift's size and fury. Kylac cast more than a single backward glance himself, half hoping he'd been mistaken, half certain he *had* to be. Yet the Dread Maw remained, sucking and whirling as if to drain the whole of the ocean into its cavernous gullet.

"How did we permit this?" Pevrick was demanding of Taeg as Kylac scampered into the wheelhouse.

"I daresay our rudder holds meager sway in this brew."

Leeches surveyed the scene through the streaks of rain pelting the forward window. "Larboard tack," he determined. "Broad as she'll reach."

"Starboard," Ithrimir corrected, as the first mate turned to leave.

Pevrick whirled, turning his glare upon the Scribe. "The bulk of the Maw lies to starboard."

"So drives the prevailing current. Challenge it, and we shall be engulfed."

"Says he of mystical insight," Leeches snarled, reddening with fury. "Who has brought us to the very edge of its boundaries."

"I admonished all as to the capricious nature of—"

"You have put us upon the precipice!"

"Lieutenant!" Ledron barked upon entry.

But Pevrick was beyond verbal restraint, driving past the wheel to lunge at Ithrimir. "By choice or folly, we teeter here at *your* command!"

A dagger came to the first mate's hand. Before any could know the precise fashion in which he intended to use it, Kylac slipped forward, a quick slash of his longsword swatting the blade from Pevrick's grasp—and drawing just enough blood to caution the enraged lieutenant against retrieving it.

Leeches whirled, gripping his wounded wrist, eyes gleaming with murderous intent.

"No!" Ledron shouted. A plea, more than a command. When he saw that Kylac had Leeches cornered, sword tip pricking the apple of Pevrick's throat, he added hastily, "After. We sort it out after. If *after* there is. Until then, weapons sheathed, and let's get to work."

Without relinquishing Leeches from his gaze, Kylac returned his blade to its scabbard. "A sensible request, Captain."

"Which heading, then?" Taeg asked. "Or shall I split the difference and aim for the chasm's heart?"

"Starboard," Ithrimir insisted. "Else our next council shall convene in the depths."

Gazes shifted toward Pevrick, whose bloodlust heaved against the inner wall of his chest.

"Lieutenant?" Ledron asked.

"What voice have I, but to abide the captain's wishes?"

Ledron's jaw clenched, teeth gritted against the first mate's insolent obedience. "Starboard it is, then." Peering eastward at the watery gulf ahead of them, he muttered, "And may the Mother grant us sure footing along her southern rim."

The Head stepped aside, freeing a path to the wheelhouse door. Kylac mimicked the movement. Anxious to be rid of them, Pevrick thundered past and out through the opening, to loose his wrath against the storm.

Kylac followed, far enough aback so as not to draw ire, but near enough to intervene as circumstances might demand. It struck him that Leeches might sooner they all perish than permit Kylac to assist, but he was determined to keep abreast of the crew's effort to circumnavigate the Dread Maw all the same, on the chance that his talents be required.

And to ensure that the embittered first mate intended to execute as instructed.

On that count, Leeches didn't disappoint. Though many of the nuances of sailing continued to be lost on him, Kylac had learned enough to see and hear that the sailors responding to Pevrick's directives were making every effort to angle booms and trim sail so as to veer sharply southward. The prevailing wind blew astern, running them forward along an easterly course. Kylac couldn't help but wonder whether it wouldn't be wiser to furl sail and seek to slow the pace of their advance. He had to trust that, were that the case, someone more experienced than he would have given the command.

More critical it must have been that they maintain what speed they could muster amid the storm-tossed waves. The slower they sailed, the less effective their rudder, as Taeg had suggested. Better to race headlong with some semblance of control, it seemed, than to dig in their heels and be tossed about like flotsam.

He could only hope the theory proved correct.

The savage intensity with which Pevrick tromped about and hollered orders amid the howling din suggested a conviction that Kylac found suspect, given the first mate's deep-seated hatred of those whose wishes he conveyed. Mayhap he only intended to demonstrate to them their folly by performing precisely as commanded, whereafter he might gloat in those final moments before their bodies were chewed to pulp amid the bones of their vessel.

The maelstrom itself only grew larger and more ominous as they drew nearer its western rim. Almost as if reaching out to them with ravenous anticipation. Not just waves, but winds shrieked toward its center. Kylac spotted now the dark specs of scavenging galefishers a'flock around its edges, darting now and then to retrieve some morsel—living or dead—swirling about the perilous borders. As he watched, more than one ventured too close, to be caught in the vacuum—of wave or wind—and prove too weak to flap free.

It caused him to wonder if the *Wail*, too, had already crossed some invisible barrier, hazarding beyond a point of no return.

Lightning forked and splintered across the sky, its rumble underscoring the roar of the maelstrom and the bellowing of the tempest. Rain sheeted across the tilting decks, salted by windblown spray. Mere seasoning for the surge waters that continued to slosh about the ship in a foam-filled wash, stealing footing from those who dared out of necessity to scramble about. As if to deny them fair chance to complete their already daunting task.

Kylac marked those scampering movements, darting in more than once to help a sailor to his feet or give extra pull on a line where needed. For the greater part, the crew seemed to be holding its own despite the savage elements. Though fickle winds and combative waves compelled them to make ceaseless adjustments to keep the *Wail* on course, she seemed willing enough to submit to their urges and commands, as if sensing her peril and relying on them to guide her free.

Whether that faith would prove well founded remained difficult to gauge. Though the winds still ushered her more east than south, with the Dread Maw yawning westward as if to receive her, the *Wail* staggered and clawed along a trajectory that appeared might carry her clear of its gaping mouth. Kylac wouldn't have cared to lay wager on their success. By his estimation, the margin was yet too close to determine.

Then fell fate intervened.

Kylac was peering aft when he heard the high-pitched crack, but turned in time to watch the staysails at the fore of their vessel collapse to starboard. Weighed down by their bowsprit, he realized, which had snapped near its base to twist and fold broadside against the bow. Not only robbing them of their jibs, but dragging the compromised rigging back against the foremast, to effectively disable those sails, as well.

Even to the untrained eye, a devastating blow.

Drawn by the echoing shouts of dismay, Pevrick tromped forward from the mainmast to survey damage to the rigging. Kylac ventured further forward still, to have look at the wounded bowsprit. Tethered more by the forestays, now, than by the splintered fibers of wood still clinging to the bow. Like an arm kept dangling by a few strands of skin and muscle, when bone and ligaments had been severed.

"Stretch those lines!" Pevrick cried, staring skyward along the foremast—where pinned foresails chafed against the tangle of loose rigging, effectively reducing the *Wail*'s sailing capacity by a quarter strength or more.

To that concern, Kylac wondered that they didn't simply cut the offending jib lines altogether. As he understood it, the staysails served chiefly in stabilizing the vessel and contributed only slightly to its propulsion. With no obvious way to anchor them at the fore, would it not be better to focus on restoring proper function to the foresails and dealing with the jibs as a secondary endeavor?

Yet again, he was given to trust in those whose seafaring knowledge and skills exceeded any he might soon develop himself. It was quite possible, he reckoned, that without those forestays, the integrity of the entire foremast would be threatened—particularly in a gale such as this. For if even their mighty bowsprit had succumbed to the strain . . .

Kylac recalled the moment in which that same stout spar had skewered the *Vengeance* from behind. On how many other occasions had the infamous Shrikeskinner, Vorathus the Brutal, issued order to ram a ship in such a fashion? Had it been a battle-weakened horn that had betrayed them? Or had the *Wail* herself, demonstrating loyalty to her erstwhile captain, simply waited until this moment to reveal her treachery?

The latter view may have owed to the superstition of the White-fists drawing near.

"Traitorous bitch!" Rehm cursed upon approach.

"Her very marrow festers!" Nadrum agreed.

The forecastle dipped low, inviting the crest of a wave to spill over them. Nadrum held on, while Rehm slipped aft, taking Warmund with him. As the *Wail* righted, the pair struggled forward again, this time with Pevrick on their heels.

"Splints and braces!" Leeches roared, lips flecked with either spittle or sea foam. "Pin her fast!"

"A tar-skin's beak!" Nadrum groused. "She bleeds rot!"

Pevrick seized the despairing Whitefist by a fistful of hair. "Buttress this spar, seaman! Or dangle from it!"

With a glare thrown at Kylac for good measure, the first mate released his charge and spun about to ensure his orders were followed.

He needn't have doubted. All hands had been summoned, and

every available sailor, it seemed, had within moments come to cluster
upon the forecastle. Together they formed relay lines, larboard and
starboard, along which fresh supplies were passed. Damaged parts
were shuttled aft or discarded, as determined by those in supervisory
positions. Kylac soon found himself dropping back to permit his shipmates the room they needed to effect their repairs. He watched men
wrangle cordage with hooks and pulleys, while others handled planks
and timbers of wood amid plates and bands of iron. He observed those
who climbed aloft, fanned wide, or even scrabbled over the rail into
harnesses along the outer hull, to better reach whatever vantage was
required. He listened to the mingling echoes of their calls and cries,
until he wondered how a man was able to distinguish those directed
at him from those that weren't.

All while marking the slow, unsteady tack of the wounded *Wail*
as she drifted ever closer to the looming chasm of Eddaron's Rift.

Amid the unrelenting chaos, the crew appeared to be managing
what Kylac hadn't thought possible. With the forestays shifted to deck
cleats serving as temporary anchor points, tension on the bowsprit was
released so that its broken base could be splinted with poles and braces.
More critically, foresails and even the lower jibs were enabled along
newly strung lines, attached to a pair of provisional spars that extended
beyond the bow like a pair of tusks. With teams of men making sure
those poles remained pinned against the foredeck, Whitefists worked
the clew lines to trim the various staysails as commanded. For all the
fuss and furor, mayhap a non-mortal injury after all.

Or so the men prayed. For the Dread Maw had all but laid claim.
Peering over the larboard rail, Kylac set eye upon the outermost
threshold of its swirling border. They were edging south of it now,
but only by the slimmest of stretches, skirting precariously along its
collapsing rim. The *Wail* continued to heave to starboard, leaning
as best she could to avoid the incessant tug nipping at her keel. An
opposing gust, a single errant wave, might be enough to tip her
toward oblivion.

Or a diving galefisher, come spearing down from the sky to strike
at the polished cranse iron at the nose of their farthest-reaching spar,
set to anchor the jib of jibs. Amid the flapping and screeching of the

startled raptor, the sheet's line tore free of its shackle. Unsecured, their topmost staysail fluttered free, snatched by the wind.

Kylac couldn't have guessed what difference that single sheet might make. But Pevrick must have deemed its loss unacceptable. For as Irryn retrieved the rogue line upon the forecastle and Warmund looked with Stannon as to whether they should draw the entire spar and its remaining jibs back in, the first mate grabbed the free end himself.

"No time!" he shouted, and ventured over the bow rail.

Kylac rushed forward to offer aid, but Leeches was already on his way, crawling out along the rain-slicked spar, his only potential safety line the one gripped in his teeth. Even without the stunned gazes of the crewmen around him, Kylac recognized the folly inherent in the lieutenant's undertaking. He also knew there was little he might do to forestall it, and that it wasn't his place to do so.

So he watched breathlessly alongside his shipmates as Pevrick navigated that spindly perch, hauling body and line from handhold to handhold, while the tempest shrieked and the maelstrom roared.

The *Wail* bucked and twisted, but couldn't deter Leeches in his aim. Clinging stubbornly, he gained the spar's tip, where he shackled the line anew with a practiced hand. He then signaled back to Irryn, who adjusted the line's tension, measuring the flap and luff of the attached sail against the violent, volatile winds.

And the jib of jibs flew again.

Daring mission accomplished, Pevrick held fast to his precarious position. Solitary and exposed, he yet continued to fight, staring at the canyon-sized vortex gaping beneath him, shouting inaudible curses into its grinding gullet. As if it had become a personal contest pitting his will and strength against that of the Rift. Crewmen throughout the ship fought their own battles, all far more critical to their cause. But it was difficult not to take particular pride and interest in the struggle waged by their first mate at the very nose of their beleaguered vessel, who looked as if he alone were straining to draw them clear of the enemy chomping at their flanks.

"Hold fast!" Warmund shouted, while working to attach a safety tether to a spear-length gaff.

Even as Worm and his fellow crewmen endeavored to extend the life-saving line to their senior officer, Kylac felt a stirring anticipation of the greater conflict drawing to a close. Still veering as sharply southward as she could manage, the *Wail* had begun to increase the distance between herself and the Rift. Though its outer waves continued to clutch and claw at her—currents and riptides reaching out like hooked lines sent to reel her in—the strength of its overall pull was subsiding. As its draw weakened, the crew's resolve strengthened, until cheers went up, hailing the expected triumph . . .

The Dread Maw fell astern, marking the final outcome with a slow, gradual yielding. The timbre of its own growling song echoed unchanged. Kylac heard neither rage, nor lament, for the quarry that had eluded it. A tiny morsel, *Denariel's Wail*, gained or lost. The Rift would simply keep on churning, hungering boundlessly for the next.

The only cries of dismay were those that echoed abruptly atop the forecastle. Kylac spun back toward the bow, searching along the tusks serving as temporary bowsprits.

To find no sign of Leeches, save for the empty tether dangling from a gaping Worm's outstretched hook.

30

For another ten days, *Denariel's Wail* clawed eastward, chewing an unsteady course through the Thousand Tempests. In escaping the grasp of Eddaron's Rift, she'd but traversed the storm-wracked region by half—as Ithrimir had forewarned, and continued to remind the more despairing members of her crew. Though murmurs held that this was merely an ongoing attempt by the Sea Scribe to deflect doubts about his ability to guide them, he had, in ushering them past the Rift, won sufficient goodwill from enough crewmen to merit patience. If ten days he begged, ten days they would give him.

So urged Kylac, Ledron, and Taeg, raised from chief helmsman to first mate following the loss of Pevrick. The latter had struck Kylac as bittersweet. He'd not soon miss Pevrick's hateful disposition, that which had fueled—or been fueled by—his bitter resentment of their captain's authority. And it was only through his drowning that the mutiny planned by Olekk and others had been forestalled. Yet, however loathsome his prior conduct, the first mate had given his life in an effort to save theirs. To what degree his endeavors had affected the outcome had sparked some measure of debate. But none could argue against the nobility of his intent.

His sacrifice may have further contributed to the renewal of cama-raderie taken root among his surviving shipmates since. No stranger to the bond formed among men who'd endured a common crisis, Kylac understood that their death-defying brush with the Dread Maw may have served in and of itself to restore their faith in one another. But given the reverent whispers with which many spoke of their former officer—along with his own newfound respect—Kylac chose to attribute much of the crew's ensuing solidarity to the example Leeches had set with his final act.

Wondering only how long it might last.

Unsurprisingly, tempers had begun to flare and fellowships to fray no more than midway through day seven. Though no more had perished, and the *Wail* herself continued to withstand the elements better than any of them had rightful cause to expect, whatever support Ledron and his newly appointed officers may have enjoyed wouldn't long subsist, it appeared, were the Tempests to maintain their grip. Ithrimir in particular, unofficially assigned as chief navigator in Brenham's absence, would be held scapegoat the moment his estimates proved unfounded. And the shipboard dissent and resulting machinations would sprout anew.

So it was that here on day ten, with noon scarcely an hour hence, mistrust reigned. When the winds began to weaken, the crew took notice with scornful pessimism. When the rains slackened, reactions softened only slightly, making way for glum skepticism. Only as the skies brightened did the reactions of a few stout souls veer toward wary optimism.

Fortunately, the sun demanded no welcome before knifing through the thinning cloud cover, sending clear signal that the dreaded Tempests might at last be falling astern. The piercing rays were met with a resounding cheer by believer and cynic alike. After so prolonged an absence, many had come to fear that they'd been blown into a darkness from which they would never sail free. To partake again of the sun's blessed rays, however fleeting they might prove, brought more than one man among them to tears.

Others laughed or sang or looked to their mates as the skies continued to clear, setting aside fights and grudges in exchange for clasps and embraces. Redfists Mutton and Graves hooked elbows and stomped a circling dance upon the forecastle. Olekk and Kahrem joined Creyl

at the larboard rail, to hurl jeers at a shiver of sharks awaiting their
arrival—gathered amid the calming waters as if to feast upon the
storm's leavings. Aloft, sailors whistled and hooted to one another
amid the rigging, making gestures of gratitude to their Fair Mother
or the sea's benevolent graces.

Rehm, promoted to second mate in order to assume some of
Brenham's non-navigational duties, suggested a barrel be raised for a
toast to fortune before it could flee. Taeg agreed, and within moments,
cups and skins were being passed around and a measure of ale freely
distributed to the crewmen on hand. This and the rest of the growing clamor drew Ledron and Denariel from belowdecks, the former
attended by the porter sent to fetch him, the latter by her assigned
warder, Sanow. Though the new arrivals carried with them a cloud
of suspicion, it couldn't long abide the delight of the others who
streamed forth to join the burgeoning celebration. All around, a
sullen weariness had given way to fresh hope. Even Denariel, Kylac
observed, permitted herself a small smile of relief.

Which, regrettably, he couldn't bring himself to share.

He thought to give warning, to seek to quiet the revelry, but the
pinch in his chest told him he was already too late. He settled instead
for venturing forward, gaze brushing the horizon, probing amid the
fragmented banks of storm clouds for sign of the darkness brewing
in his stomach.

Their lookout spotted it first.

"Ship afore!"

In the distance, amid the lingering mounds of ashen haze, a beetle-
like form emerged. Dead ahead, or near enough not to matter. Too
far off yet to identify clearly. But the pall that fell over the *Wail*'s
decks echoed Kylac's dread misgivings.

"Ship to starboard!" came the follow-up cry from the crow's nest.

Almost before anyone could turn in that direction, Creyl yelped
from his position on the opposite side of the ship. "Ay! Larboard, tah!"

With a sweeping search, Kylac quickly confirmed the second and
third sightings. A veritable cordon, by seafaring standards, and them
sailing headlong into it.

"Festering fiends," Nadrum muttered, drawing near Kylac's shoulder.

Others cursed and mumbled in his wake, a thickening clutch of merrymakers suddenly crestfallen.

"Stations!" Taeg bellowed.

The gathering disbanded. Amid their scampering departure, Kylac followed those taking aim at the wheelhouse.

"Of all the cursed reaches," Rehm was griping, with a sidelong glare at Ithrimir, "this is where we emerge."

"Stow that tongue, Lieutenant," Ledron snapped. "I need reports, not laments."

"We don't yet know them to be Grenarr," Taeg added encouragingly. "Could be a merchant convoy."

Denariel snorted. "Scattered about? Sniffing the boundaries of a storm such as this?"

"Whoever they are, I want no part of them," Ledron huffed. "If merchants, they'll not take kindly to this Marauder."

"They're Grenarr," Kylac assured them.

Their prickly gazes turned on him as if to ask how he knew this, but none voiced the question. In their hearts, they knew it, too.

"Nearest to larboard!" Aramis called in from his relay post.

"Veer south?" Rehm urged.

"We might duck back the way we came," Taeg suggested. "Seek to lose them in the Tempests."

"How did they find us?" Jaleth wondered from his place at the wheel.

An echo of Rehm's observation, in but a gentler tone. Fairly asked. Even Kylac found himself looking to their navigator for a response.

Ithrimir bristled at the attention. "The swiftest course to Haverstromme, you demanded. Did you not believe our pursuers might divine this?"

A pointed glance from Ledron told Kylac that the captain was thinking of their mole. But Kylac shook his head. While in the teeth of the Tempests, and without any shrikes aboard, their suspected traitor would have been hard-pressed to direct word of any kind. More likely, it was as Ithrimir suggested. Given that their enemies had been awaiting their initial departure from Mistwall, their ultimate destination had surely been betrayed as well. The Grenarr needn't have gathered any additional information to lay wager as to what course they might set. A guess, mayhap, but an informed one.

"We's long known they'd be trolling for us," Kylac reminded them. "Might be they's vessels setting ambush along other routes, too, and it only *seems* lucky o' them to find us here."

"Should we raise the Shrikeskinner's standard?" Taeg asked. "Unless they know we switched vessels, it might give them pause."

Ledron grunted dismissively. "A prize we'd be, in either vessel. Cling to the storm front, I'd say. Edging south to maximize distance?"

The question in his tone was directed at Ithrimir. The Scribe responded with his piercing stare and a shrug of his good shoulder. "Our destination lies to the northeast. Our hunters know this."

"Another vote for the south, then," the Head determined. "Make it happen."

The calls went out. Halyards shifted, and sails reached. Relay shouts were kept to a minimum, the sailors opting for hand signals wherever possible. Though no order had been given for silence, the men had taken it upon themselves to limit sign of their presence. As the *Wail* reversed tack, slinking back toward the cover of the storm from which she'd only scarcely emerged, Whitefist and Redfist alike took to holding their collective breath.

"Mother embrace us," Denariel murmured, peering through the forward window of the wheelhouse.

To Kylac's ear, her arch tone evinced little faith.

The prevailing wind blew from the northwest, ushering the *Wail* southward while challenging her westward tack. As the cover of the storm seemed more critical to their endeavor, the crew would have gladly traded those compass points, given the choice. Increasingly so, as the clouds around them continued to dissipate, the fringe of the Thousand Tempests dissolving before their eyes. Succumbing to the strengthening midday sun, else speeding away on an altogether different set of currents. Whatever the driving factors, the conceal-ment they so desperately required appeared to be slipping quickly from reach.

Within a quarter-mark of the sun, it became evident that their pace couldn't match that of the storm's withdrawal. Despite their concerted effort, its sheltering borders continued to elude them, remaining just out of reach.

Amid the retreating clouds, four more ships were sighted—one to the west, another to the north, and two to the south. No longer a cordon, but a snare.

"It appears again," Kylac observed, "that your Fair Mother wants no part of our squabbles."

Denariel flashed him a reproachful look. Before she could voice a more specific objection, Aramis interjected, relaying the latest observations from the crow's nest.

"Vessels closing! Fore, aft, and larboard."

The snare was tightening.

"We're spotted," Taeg admitted, long after all had silently realized it.

"What heading?" Jaleth asked, a bridled panic giving edge to his voice.

"Dawning winds," Ledron growled. "Whichever may help to evade capture."

The captain stormed from the wheelhouse, leaving the matter in his officers' hands. Denariel trailed after, an agitated Sanow on her heels. Their departure left Kylac with Taeg, Rehm, Jaleth, and Ithrimir. He regarded each with a searching look while determining what aid—if any—he might be to them.

"Begging pardon, I think I'll sees now to the ship's defenses."

Ledron had initiated the muster already, summoning Redfists Simalen and Sethric as squad commanders, and assigning them fore and aft. Olekk and Moh he divided to larboard and starboard amidships. Ten soldiers per regiment, with all available Whitefists set to man the ballistae ringing the decks, else climbing aloft with their bows. A thin ring, when spread as such around the whole of the ship. But, whatever the final maneuvering, the Head fully expected to be surrounded, compelled to wage battle on all four fronts.

"And where would the captain have me posted?"

"As it suits you, Kronus. I'd as soon seek to halter a rampaging grackal."

Praise, it might have been, were it not for the Head's disgusted tone. "What of the princess?"

"Below," Ledron answered curtly, trampling whatever protest Denariel might have summoned. "Sanow will see to it."

The Blackfist gave no acknowledgment, his focus on one of the distant beetles swelling in size off the larboard rail.

"Lieutenant?"

"Below," Sanow echoed finally.

"Yourself?" Kylac asked.

Ledron glared, as if sniffing accusation. Spawned by guilt, mayhap, from his inaction in their last battle. "A position of central command. Should I fall, you've my permission to die as you please."

With that, the Head wheeled to starboard, trudging away to rain curses upon a pair of porters who'd spilled a bundle of ballista spears.

"Seven ships," Denariel observed quietly, marking the movements of their enemies. Though barely perceptible at this range, they'd led to a near uniform circle around the *Wail*. "If we fail to slip their noose, we'll have no chance to survive them."

"Echoes a proclamation I's defied before," Kylac replied calmly. "More than once."

"Spare me your bluster. Feigning fearlessness will not turn them away."

The tang of her own fear was sharp and ill-fitting, like a king in soiled rags. Unsettling, emanating from her. "What cause for fear?" he parried. "No man among them can match me."

Her laugh was short and acrid. "An empty boast. Trumpeted by many a proud fool put to rot by the hand of another."

"None as lethal as I." He knew not the source of his certainty. Only that it had always been there. Arrogant, yes, but founded upon a litany of deeds. True or not, he didn't stake the claim to be boastful. He did so believing that, contentions aside, she and others around her—such as Sanow—needed reminder.

"Cling to it, then," she scoffed. "I only pray I live long enough to kiss the feet of the wretch who proves you wrong."

"Must we perish on this voyage, I'll indeed go first," he agreed. "To serve vanguard for Your Highness against whatever comes next."

With a tilt of his brow to Sanow, he shunned her sour expression and took his leave, setting upon a circuit around the decks to ascertain the mood and readiness of the remainder of the crew. In doing so, he happened across a fair mix of trepidation and aggression in various measures. By and large, he discovered the Seawatch to be more fretful, the Stonewatch more likely to tamp their fears beneath a fire of hostility. He might have presumed as much, given a Whitefist's comparative lack of combat experience—into which they felt certain they were heading. Else mayhap the average Redfist, being less knowledgeable about sailing, was miscalculating their odds of escape.

He found outliers, of course, amid the various companies—men from either faction who might have been better suited to the other, or those like Creyl, Warmund, and Aythef, whose muddled or tightly hoarded emotions defied ready perception. But Kylac's overriding sense was that the soldiers aboard, if somewhat deluded, felt equal to the task, and that the sailors, while mistrustful of their chances, would be fueled by their desperation.

As prepared for the onslaught as he might hope to expect.

Kylac himself was almost itching for it—the opportunity to trade endurance against the elements for a battle whose outcome he might more directly affect. His cuts and bruises from the massacre against Vorathus's Banshees had all but healed, exposed for nearly a month now to the salty winds and saltier spray. Time to learn whether any would have lingering effect.

His willing presence seemed to instill confidence, in varying degrees, so he remained on the move, flashing a smile, a jape, or the deft twirl of a blade as he deemed necessary to bolster flagging spirits. Reminding all that they'd faced down many a savage enemy already, and would do so again.

Meanwhile, their navigators were making every effort to eliminate the need. Taking aim at the larger gap between enemy ships to the southeast, those piloting the *Wail* seemed intent on dashing clear of the trap laid for her. To Kylac's eyes, it seemed unlikely, with how quickly the Grenarr ships lying along that course were closing in front of them. Ithrimir must have agreed, or Jaleth, for the *Wail* veered westward again, as if to cut behind the southernmost ship before it could come about. But the smaller vessel proved impressively nimble, adjusting quickly to remain in her path, while at the same time retreating southward itself.

Far enough to avoid a direct engagement, Kylac realized, as its brethren closed round.

So it went, as the *Wail* tried one tack or another, probing for escape. Even more impressive than the handling of the individual ships was the expert manner in which they reacted in concert with one another. Five Prowlers, they numbered, amid two Reavers. Outmatched, any one of them, if separated from the others. But like a pack of predators encircling a larger prey, they took turns harrying or withdrawing in response to the *Wail*'s movements, seeming to anticipate her maneuvers, expertly discerning feint from run—ultimately shifting and tightening rank without foolishly exposing one of their own.

Refusing to engage until their full strength could be brought to bear.

As he watched these Grenarr coordinate their approach without any visible communications between them, Kylac came to better appreciate some of the dread respect he'd heard heaped upon their kind.

"Do they fight as well as they drive?" he asked of Taeg in a moment that found them together just outside the wheelhouse.

"Better," the first mate mumbled, peering through his spyglass.

Mayhap he was wrong not to be a touch afraid himself. After all, he was still quietly assuming they meant to board the *Wail* in an effort to take at least some aboard alive. Should they prove content to feed all to the sharks and crabs, their combined bombardment might reduce the Shrikeskinner's treacherous vessel to tatters and cinders before any came within reach of Kylac's blades.

"Ah," Taeg added, "looks to be our erstwhile friend, the Seahammer."

"Ya say?"

"Same standard. Can't make out those of his friends, yet."

"How did he overtake us?"

Taeg's brow furrowed. "Must have sailed north from Mistwall, rather than grinding through as we did. Heading due east, skirting the Tempests' northern edge, could have put him well ahead of us."

"Better tallied among this brood, I suppose, than lying in wait with another."

An obvious reckoning. And yet, it didn't provide the small surge of hope that Kylac might have expected. *The most headstrong,* Tormitius had told them. Most beloved of his father, and loving in turn. If driven by vengeance, there seemed a greater chance that this Seahammer, Temerius, would seek to capture his father's murderer alive, delivering himself—or at least those under his command—into Kylac's hands. But if the vessel's identification spawned anything, it was a raw disquiet that knotted uncomfortably in the pit of Kylac's stomach. Surprise, that the same ship to ambush them in their departure from Mistwall had come to ambush them again. A grudging admiration, even, for the resolve and insight that had played part in bringing it here. The understanding that, when motivated by revenge, there was often little a man wouldn't do to see it through.

Or mayhap his was merely a byproduct of the crew's unease as the observation was echoed by other lookouts and spread around the deck. An ill harbinger, some muttered. Others hailed it fiendish fortune, or cursed magecraft. To a man, it seemed, they viewed it an inauspicious sign.

"We left him stranded once already," Kylac reminded those now marking the Reaver's approach from the larboard rail. "Grasping at air." *Howling like a madman,* he recalled privately, but chose not to remind them of it. "If'n called upon, we'll offer stronger dissuasion this time."

Creyl granted him an eager sneer. The rest within earshot only grunted or ignored him, scarcely taking their eyes off the advancing Reaver.

"She's near to range of our deck catapults," Rehm observed as Ledron approached.

The captain snorted. "Given perfect aim. Let's not discard our limited ammunition in a panic."

Kylac judged the nearest vessels to lie about four hundred strokes distant, with the others no more than a hundred strokes beyond that. Even if they struck true, their missiles weren't liable to do as much damage as they would at closer proximity. If their enemies—whose weaponry this was—hadn't fired yet, mayhap it was because they knew something the landsnake Addarans didn't.

The *Wail* herself had ceased to dance and adopted a direct heading to the southeast at full sail—harvesting the whole of the wind's strength, and intending to swiftly disable the pair of Prowlers in that area, if possible, before those coming astern could join the fight. Kylac didn't believe they'd succeed in the latter, given the Grenarr's demonstrated ability to read and react. A better hope might be that the sheer size and volume of the *Wail's* sails would enable her to overtake her target vessels and keep ahead of those at her back.

Yet the *Wail* was a wounded bird, battered and torn from her three-week flight through the Thousand Tempests. The Grenarr vessels, whether come through the Tempests themselves or skirted round along another course, appeared unharmed, their movements crisp and fluid and swift. Even were the *Wail* at full strength, Kylac questioned whether her crew could match the expert handling of her enemies, given their own self-doubts. Alas, it would have been nice to put them to the test.

He might as easily wish the oceans dry or the sun to trade watch with the moon, for all the difference it made. Such hollow prayers merited no more than a fleeting fancy.

He turned aft, taking but a pair of strides before the drums began. A slow, steady beat throbbing from the Seahammer's ship before being echoed by the others. Pipes followed, shrill and piercing. Within moments, a skirling, discordant song played upon the winds, driven by a pulse-pounding rhythm, circulating around all points of the compass. Tuneless, but each layer resonating a promise of death.

"Let them prate, eh?" Olekk suggested. "Their melodies cannot harm us."

Part bluster on the Redfist's part, Kylac sensed, intended to mask a rising swell of fear. But he let the sentiment stand, lest it fool the others.

"May they blister their palms on their drumsticks," Kahrem agreed, "sapping grip on their swords."

"Grend un peel dor charred hides," added Creyl.

Then came the rasp of a dagger, and the startled yelp of a woman's voice. "What are you—"

"Back! Back!" barked an aggressor's. Sanow's. Kylac found it at the heart of a nearby stir, where soldiers were retreating with grunts of surprise and murmurs of confusion.

He slipped through the seams into the clearing deck space, and there found Sanow backing toward the rail, an arm around Denariel's chest and his dagger at her throat.

"Lieutenant!" Ledron shouted, overlooking the developing scene from atop the ladder to the wheel deck. "What in Sangho's Tempest—"

"Enough!" Sanow cried, arching his head back and clenching his eyelids as if to drown out the drumming din.

Kylac crouched, measuring the distance between them. Yet he hesitated, and with just cause. For in the next heartbeat, Sanow targeted him at the inner edge of the encircling crowd.

"Try me, Kronus. Let us learn how fast you *really* are."

The air hummed and crackled in a profusion of raw emotion— chiefly shock. Denariel's was turning already toward indignation, the crew's toward grim delight. From Sanow, Kylac sensed only desperate resolve. Whatever else this turned out to be, it was no bluff. And none but mayhap Ledron could be counted to have his back should he act in favor of the princess. The sum of these realizations served to stay his hand.

"Lieutenant!" Ledron bellowed again, as he crowded through at the opposite end of the circle. "Put down that blade."

"Unhand me!" Denariel agreed, wrestling in his grasp.

"Begging forgiveness, Highness, I'll take no more orders from you."

"Is there an order ya'd give, then?" Kylac asked. Had Sanow merely snapped? Been their mole all along? Whichever, Kylac couldn't quite fathom the Blackfist's intent. Slit her throat. And achieve what?

"We are Shadowguard," Ledron growled.

Sanow laughed. "That we should live and die for the whims of a festering waif such as this?"

"As we have sworn."

"Oathbreaker," Denariel hissed.

"Why must we perish for her, eh? Or her brother, for that matter? Or her father? How can one life weigh greater than so many?"

Irrational as he might be, his sentiments struck a chord among those clustered near, and those who now ventured from their own stations to glimpse the scene for themselves. Even as the drums throbbed, and the pipes shrilled, across the constricting expanses between them and their enemies.

The Head gritted his teeth. "And what do you intend?"

"Intend?" Sanow echoed, voice tinged with a madness befitting his conduct. "To let *her* serve shield for once. To save the rest of us."

"You've lost your wits," said Taeg, his own tone dry with mockery. A conscious effort at distraction, if Kylac's senses sang true. "The Grenarr will kill or enslave us all. Murdering her but spares her the indignity of capture."

Sanow's anxious eyes flitted back and forth, gleaming with indecision. When next his gaze met Kylac's, they narrowed with sudden certainty. "Murder? A shield, I say."

Without further warning, the Blackfist squatted low, dropped his knife, and seized Denariel about the knees. Kylac lunged, even as the princess herself swatted at Sanow's neck and shoulders. She'd have done better to jerk free. For as she rained her futile blows, and Kylac strained to close ground, her assigned warder hefted her high . . .

And heaved her over the rail.

31

Dₑₙₐᵣᵢₑₗ's ᴘʟᴜɴɢɪɴɢ ꜱᴄʀᴇᴀᴍ ushered her descent, raking Kylac's spine as he reached for the rail. Grimacing at the slap of her body against the ocean's surface, he searched for her telltale splash amid the waves . . . finding it, and then her, as she resurfaced, bobbing amid the foam-crested waters sliding swiftly aft along the larboard hull of their speeding vessel.

Instinct gripped him, and he surrendered to it, given so little time for rational thought. A knuckle punch to the center of Sanow's torso left the traitorous Blackfist breathless, slumping to his knees. As stunned now as the rest of them. Incapacitated for whatever punishment their captain deemed appropriate.

"Shore boat!" Ledron cried.

No time, thought Kylac. He leapt up, feet perched atop the rail.

"Full stop!" the captain shouted. "Prepare to come about!"

Kylac hesitated, troubled by the order. Not for any cause he might explain, save that it was the simplest response, and thus to be expected. "No!" he shouted back. He peered ahead at the gap between closing Prowlers. "Run the blockade!"

Ledron's glare radiated a stubborn refusal. "My oath demands—"

"Damn your oath," Kylac insisted. His hand found the hilt of his longsword, sparking confidence in his unformed decision. He sought out Taeg and captured the first mate's gaze. "Maintain course. I'll send our Scribe signal."

He glanced toward the wheelhouse, glimpsing Ithrimir through the forward window. Feeling the Elementer's piercing gaze, and taking further strength from it.

Then he jumped.

The wind whipped at his loose-fitting garb, whistling mockery in his ears. A wave swelled to receive him . . . and swallowed him whole, eclipsing the light with a crystalline filter. The shock of its embrace engulfed him, chill and crushing. He held his breath, sensing the vast weight of the passing *Wail*, continuing on without him, and the unfathomable reaches of the ocean into which he'd cast himself. Tetherless in that void, he recalled his last ill-fated plunge, and worried all at once that he'd made a dreadful mistake.

His head breached almost before he realized he'd been kicking skyward, and fresh breath filled his lungs. He had to cut it short as another swell buoyed and then crested over him. He surfaced again, more quickly this time, and took his bearings. Salt stung his eyes as he wiped the water from his face, to peer northward. There, to his left, he spotted Denariel, bobbing amid the waves, some three hundred strokes back. As adrift as he was, and even more alone.

The *Wail*'s stern rushed past, the near tail of its foaming wake sweeping over him. The feeling of solitude that enveloped him in that moment caused him to long for Ledron's shore boat, for the *Wail* herself to circle back as initially commanded. Hopes bred of fear, he realized, and turned his thoughts back toward Denariel.

Swim!

Swim he did, stroking overhead with as much haste as he could muster. Not his proudest skill, but neither was his body unfamiliar with the motions. He quickly found his proper pace amid the rhythm of the swells, and settled into it. Kick and reach, kick and reach, breathe. Kick and reach, kick and reach, breathe . . .

With time now to contemplate his actions, he endeavored to reconcile instinct with rationale. Had he erred in urging his shipmates to carry on without him? If the *Wail* did come about, she was certain to be cornered. A fight it would be, she and her crew against the seven

Grenarr ships and theirs. Though part of him relished the challenge, at what cost? When the damage was complete, and the last blood spilled, would there be enough left of vessel and men to carry on?

Whatever else had spurred Sanow's treachery, it had been done with the hope of diverting their closing enemies, increasing the *Wail*'s chances of escape. Given that they'd failed to forestall the attempt, it seemed sensible to let it carry through.

That at least the bulk of them might be spared.

Delving deeper, Kylac understood that this voyage was slipping away from them. Defeat this pack of Grenarr, and they'd likely face another on the next horizon. Attrition in this contest wouldn't serve. And, as his father had taught him, only the foolish or the incapable sought to overcome a losing battle with the same strategy that had placed them at a disadvantage.

Kylac was neither.

What had truly inspired him atop that rail—aside from the urgent desire to aid Denariel as quickly as possible—was his simmering belief that this overall effort to reach and rescue Prince Dethaniel required a new point of attack. A shift in tactics to help alter the flow of battle. Though he had scant idea yet as to how it might all play out, here he was, shaking the table, letting the die be recast. Disrupting a largely failed pattern of strikes and parries in hope of setting foot upon more favorable ground.

Or any ground at all, given his present situation. Mayhap he was only giving over to delusion, seeking to justify a mostly senseless gamble. In striving to prove more clever than his enemy, succeeding only in outwitting himself.

Should that prove so, he could always hope Ledron and the others would ignore his hastily offered advice, overruling any wisdom they might find in it. Indeed, recalling the stubborn captain's history, was it not far more likely that Kylac had given his recommendation in vain?

If so, a pity he'd not kept his opinion to himself and leapt sooner, that he might have found himself that much closer to the princess now.

The waves rose and fell between them, alternately revealing or stealing her from his line of sight. By whatever measure it might avail them, she appeared to be swimming toward him, helping to close the gap. The observation caused him to wonder what she might think of his latest deed. Would his apparent courage in diving after her serve to thaw her bitterness toward him?

He found it difficult to imagine. Were she to throw her weary arms around him there upon the swells, it would more likely be to drown him than thank him.

The dispiriting thought settled over him like a yoke. What was it that had prompted him to undertake such a taxing and unappreciated endeavor? He was a champion of close-quarters combat, unfit for paddling about the boundless seas. What if he and Denariel were simply abandoned, by allies and enemies alike? How long would they be able to tread water before succumbing to the ocean's insatiable pull?

As his pace faltered, he recalled not only his underwater flight through the limestone foundations of Mistwall, but a prior swim months earlier, near the headwaters of the Emerald River in the northern reaches of the Kalmira Forest—when fighting to escape the ravening demon sent to thwart his journey to Mount Krakken. On both occasions, he'd only narrowly avoided failure. Truth unfettered, he *had* failed, and been spared each time only by fortune.

The memories chided him, countering his lethargy and causing him to redouble his effort. If he was indeed to perish out here, it wouldn't be as a victim to despair.

He'd closed to within a hundred strokes when he began to feel an ominous itch upon his belly, as if exposed to some invisible danger. Belatedly, he remembered these to be shark-inhabited waters. Though it stung his eyes to do so, he opened them beneath the waterline, searching for shape or shadow that might threaten. Thick schools of brightly colored fish abounded, but none near enough to cause alarm. Mayhap it was only their sudden flashes of motion he'd sensed, the residue of their constant, frantic movements designed to elude predators amid the deep.

His anxiousness, however, wouldn't be dispelled, leading him to focus as much upon his underwater environs as his target. Despite deep visibility through remarkably clear waters, he couldn't shake the feeling of imminent peril.

When Denariel pulled up abruptly, thrashing and spinning in place, a cold dread pierced him with understanding.

It wasn't *his* peril he sensed, but hers.

A pair of dark fins slid past her, staggered to either side, before diving slowly from view. Her shrill yelp echoed across the expanse, peaking above the murmuring waves and hammering of enemy drums. A terror-stricken panic radiated outward. Whatever fears she'd conquered in life, however intrepid her spirit, she hadn't inured herself to this—being hunted by nightmare creatures rumored to relish the rare taste of human flesh.

Put to it, neither had Kylac. He'd faced in his time savage beasts of shocking variety, natural and elsewise. He'd fought and defeated demons. He'd even survived encounter with a dragon. But all had been with his feet beneath him, most often with weapon in hand. Where he was capable of affecting the outcome, and not merely falling victim to it.

These monsters, in this watery element, presented another challenge altogether. A challenge that rendered a great measure of his skills meaningless.

An all-too-common occurrence, since striking foot from his homeland shores.

Encumbered by a growing sense of helplessness, Kylac nonetheless surged toward Denariel, determined to reach her before the sharks' wary curiosity surrendered to craving. A pair, he'd seen, but assumed others to be present, given the number he'd witnessed earlier from the decking of the *Wail*. Foolish, he'd been, not to wait for the relative shelter a longboat would have provided. Nor did it appear now that any would be lowered. *Denariel's Wail* remained visible only by her shrinking stern, becoming less distinct as she drew farther adrift. Of scant consolation, her potential escape, should he and the royal charge she'd been renamed for serve in the end as chum.

Whatever his own counsel at the time, it felt now as if they'd been forsaken.

The ship nearest their position was the Grenarr Reaver flying the standard of Temerius Seahammer. Suggesting that, if they *were* to be rescued, it would be by the most deeply aggrieved, most irate of their enemies. Kylac had anticipated as much—or of being delivered promptly thereto. He just hadn't envisioned their bodies being reeled skyward by way of a shark's belly.

He did so now, actually smirking at the imagined disappointment on the Seahammer's face. A gallows contentment, to be sure. But if his ultimate fate was to serve himself meal to a shark, he meant to take what satisfaction he could.

Denariel tried again to swim toward him, then halted anew to resume her thrashing as the fins reappeared before her. A third circled her now. Kylac was near enough to mark the shadows of their dark bodies—some six or seven paces in length, with sufficient girth to swallow the princess whole.

Should fortune prove kind enough to spare her the gnashing of those razored teeth.

"Away!" Denariel shrieked, spinning and splashing at the encroaching creatures. "Away!"

Kylac knew better than to interpret her plea as a warning for his own safety. Had it been so, he'd have ignored it all the same. As he closed to within twenty strokes, his drifting focus tightened, morbid fancies and fretful emotions consumed by the ushering tingle of mortal conflict. It filled his veins like liquid fire, burning away his fears, bringing him to that euphoric, enigmatic state of pure calm and ultimate passion.

At ten strokes, he drew a dagger for each hand. Sacrificing reach for increased mobility, given the thick, heavy medium. Prod, he might, with longsword or short, but if called upon to slash . . .

Four sharks now clustered round, their gray skins marbled with rust-colored streaks and overlaid with scars. Kylac's reckless approach had him cutting through their circle on the tail of one, with the head of another drawing near. The latter redirected as he passed, tossing its snout as if at a foul stench. He twisted his body to keep eye on the beast, to witness its upper lip curling high to reveal a wall of tissue staked with teeth. A black orb stared him down, cold and unblinking. An implacable opponent, fueled not by anger or fury, but sheer, primal hunger.

Then Denariel was upon him, clutching, whimpering. For a moment, he worried that she indeed intended to drown him—if not consciously, in response to her shock.

"Blade!" she cried. "Give me a blade!"

Kylac righted himself there in the water, putting his back to her in order to face their predators. "At my waist," he invited her. "Your back to mine."

He felt her groping, coming away with the shortsword on his right hip. Suitable enough for her, he supposed, hoping at the same time that she didn't drop it. For if fumbled to the depths, its potential replacement lay a world away.

A distant and selfish concern. He resumed focus. Denariel's terror, while still palpable, seemed to subside with weapon in hand. As if she, too, had been alarmed more by her defenselessness than the sharks themselves. She positioned herself now as requested, her back to his, their feet kicking at each other's as they fought to hold their ground by swimming in place. He sensed her exhaustion, but felt also the prevailing fright that lent her strength. He didn't worry for its measure. If it was weariness that took them at this juncture, they might consider themselves blessed.

His arrival seemed to have agitated the sharks. Their circling motions felt less smooth, more twitchy and restive than before. But they hadn't backed off, either. Like irritated horses tamping and tugging against their riders' restraints. Kylac knew little of what their behavior might indicate. Sharks were a rarity off Pentanian shores, the tales to which he'd been exposed fraught with embellishment and ignorance. All he had was his warrior's sense that, while presently checked, their appetite hadn't diminished.

A fifth came to join the shiver, and then a sixth. The thickening cluster circled closer, its individual members taking turns making exploratory advances before darting away again. As with any pack of assailants, Kylac did his best to attune himself to their *actual* intentions—ignoring these feints—so as to avoid fixating on a false threat that might expose them to a real attack on its flanks. Inhuman, these animals. Yet Kylac's experience assured him that all living creatures shared similar characteristics at a primordial level, with comparable fears and desires comprising telltale directives of energy. In that regard, the aims of a shark felt not unlike those of any other man or beast he'd faced. A unique dialect, but a familiar tongue.

Of course, the first day he met an animal that disproved this theory might also be the last. Making him careful not to rely too heavily on such convictions.

The hard-charging prow of the Seahammer's Reaver continued to cleave the northern waves over his left shoulder, drums and pipes beating their rhythm, bearing down on their position. Leaving little doubt as to the *Grenarr's* intentions. Whether they meant to fish him from the swells, or simply plow him under the ship's keel, he couldn't say. But he knew that he and the princess had been spotted, and faced the prospect of a painful afternoon, should this Temerius have say in it.

An attending Prowler approached from the south, as if to cut them off should they seek escape in that direction—as if they might somehow outswim pursuit. The other ships appeared to still be taking aim at the *Wail*, her own prospects difficult to discern from this vantage, but unfurling in a grim light. The Grenarr had styled themselves like sharks, after all, from the sleek design of their vessels to the ubiquitous fin tattoo on the side of their throats. A deserving correlation now, as they drew up against the *Wail* to nip at her shanks as surely as the actual creatures that nipped at his.

It remained only to learn whose fate—his or his fleeing shipmates'—would be determined first.

"Do something!" Denariel urged.

An odd request, considering their predicament. She knew his skills well enough. Or did she think he might have some additional capability hidden from her?

Her strength was flagging, he realized, heightening her desperation. A disregarded concern rearing its head.

In that moment, one of the circling sharks—the smallest among them—overcame its caution to strike at the princess. Kylac twisted to his left to intercept its lunge, dagger slashing at its gills. It peeled away at once, thrashing horridly, a cloud of blood leaking from its wound.

Kylac whirled back, resuming his watch against the others. Most had increased their distance, granting him wider berth, their chilling gazes reflecting accusation. The murky black orbs reminded him of the Sea Scribe's dead eye. The one that saw nothing . . . or mayhap everything.

Though he hadn't injured it too severely, the wounded shark continued to convulse, blood blooming around it, attracting more sharks
still. Kylac waited for its brethren to tear into it, as he'd heard the
creatures were wont to do. Instead, the gathering animals were keeping their distance, twisting and darting with increased agitation, yet
holding up just beyond the borders of the trailing blood cloud. As if
the fluid were somehow tainted . . .

It made him wonder that he and Denariel had yet to fall victim
to a feeding frenzy. Might his own blood bear some taint he couldn't
comprehend? Ithrimir had suggested as much, more than once. *Not on
you. In you,* the Scribe had muttered upon their first meeting, when
raving of dragon's blood. And again more recently, in the bowels of
the *Wail. The oils of your skin trouble less than the blood of your veins . . .*
Cryptic statements, or so they'd seemed. Was it possible the Elementer
spoke more bluntly than Kylac had heretofore believed?

More likely, the sharks' behavior owed to the presence of his blades.
Neither is more potent than those damnable spines you carry. Another of
Ithrimir's refrains, unforgotten, which had served significant role
in the hasty thinking that had brought him here. For it was by his
blades that he'd hoped the Scribe might be able to trace him and
Denariel to whatever destination lay in store. *Pungent, were they an
ocean away.* True or not, if a dragon had shied from the weapons, why
not a shiver of sharks? Especially if the blades hailed, as proclaimed,
from *the* Dragon, Ithrimir's Dread Eye of the Deep?

By this or some other spark of fortune, Kylac and Denariel remained
unscathed, untouched, as the Grenarr Reaver's hulking shadow fell
over them. Kylac watched the kraken figurehead surge past, spearing
tentacles outstretched. It did so slowly, sheets of foam sweeping over
the nearest waves, as the vessel eased its pace.

Eased, but didn't stop. A net dropped from the side, to dangle
from an outrigger boom.

"Deep breath," he warned, resisting the instinctive urge to dive
or swim wide. Uncertain he could have if he'd wanted to. Instead,
he curled tight, folding limbs and daggers in close, and told himself
again that this was the correct course. Even if they could manage

to keep the sharks at bay, they weren't going to be able to swim to wherever Dethaniel was being held. At the very least, mayhap they could learn something while in the clutches of their enemy that they hadn't been able to discern from without.

Sadistic jeers rained from above, amid the barking of commands and the unrelenting drums. A raucous din as the net swept over them, gathering them up in its mesh and dragging them along in a twisted, choking tangle. Kylac swallowed a reflexive panic, keeping tightly coiled against the wrench and tug of the net, seeking calm against his fear of confinement. Nonetheless, for several pulse-pounding heart-beats, he wondered if they'd staked the correct wager in assuming the Grenarr meant to retrieve them, and not merely drown them . . .

Then the crushing, invasive flow of water softened, and he felt himself hefted skyward. Denariel's squirming body pressed against his within the netting, cords cutting at his skin. He heard her grunt and sputter, coughing water from her lungs and throat as they lifted free of the waves, to drip and sway as shouts rang and the winds of their continued passage whistled in his ears.

"From one shark . . . to another," the princess growled, a grim res-ignation replacing the desperation in her voice. Huffing and writhing, she added, "Appears your recklessness . . . has finally caught up to you."

He couldn't determine whether this pleased or disappointed her, only that she was regaining already a measure of her typically stout demeanor. At least *these* sharks, she must have supposed, could be reasoned with.

Considering his options, Kylac hoped she was right.

32

THE WORLD TURNED AND SWAYED in confusing glimpses, obscured
by strands of netting and a limited line of sight over which Kylac had
almost no control. Though he could determine little through the
inconstant patches of visibility, he heard clearly the muster of men
tromping near, howling like huntsmen who'd brought their quarry
to bay. Their savage glee scalded him like steam from a cauldron,
fueled by the flames of a vengeful menace.

"Spear ring!" a gruff voice shouted, followed by the slap and rasp
of bladed shafts coming to hand, and the flexing of bows as arrows
were nocked and drawn. Sensing the tightening presence of those
sharpened heads, Kylac told himself that the Seahammer wouldn't
likely have fished him and Denariel from the swells only to skewer
them while still in the net.

Acknowledging at the same time how little he actually knew as
to his enemy's thinking.

That none of the hovering weapons immediately pierced his back
seemed as much reassurance as he was likely to find. He did wince
as the end of a pole struck him in the ribs, but quickly perceived it
to be no more than a deckhand bringing the catch under control.
Other hands reached in, to stop the net's spinning. The world stead-
ied, Kylac's skyward view settling upon a tower of billowed mainsails

trimmed to starboard.

"Release!"

The net's drawstrings were loosed, and the walls of their prison fell away, dropping him and the princess to the deck. Kylac bucked forward to land on the balls of his feet. Denariel proved less fortunate, grunting as she tumbled roughly upon her side, still caught up in the mesh. Encircling hands leaned in expectantly, spear tips leading.

Kylac spun, daggers slashing. For all their preparation, the ready movement caught them by surprise. Most fell back a step, giving him more room to work. "Hold!" a voice shouted, arresting those who might have reacted more aggressively. In that space, Kylac sheathed his daggers and crouched over Denariel, yanking her torso upright while snatching his shortsword from her startled grasp.

The spearmen leaned in again, and arrows were trained, but not before he set his blade's edge against her throat.

"Begging pardon," he said, and smiled as his enemies froze. "Not until ya pay for her."

The demand drew silence from his audience, its members stunned or disgruntled in varying measure. Grenarr, one and all, of towering height and muscled limbs. Most bore an array of scars and tattoos upon their ebony skin, to accompany the shark's fin inked on the left side of their throat. Their flesh was largely shorn, where not naturally smooth. Features that, along with the spiked and serrated trinkets sewn into their spare woolens and leathers, gave them an almost Mookla'ayan look.

If painted in soot and swelled in strength to rival that of a bear.

For all their formidable attributes, however, they'd lost their tongues to the young upstart before them. Were it not for the enduring song of drumming pursuit, amid the ceaseless railing of wind and wave, a toss of the knucklebones would have struck in that moment a terrible clatter.

A short moment. For in less time than it would have taken the dancing bones to fall still, the crewmen pressing him erupted in laughter.

With exception. Some scowled. Some snarled. One even hissed at him. But the dominant reaction, given time to unfurl, was unquestionably one of cold, cruel mirth.

That, too, proved short-lived. Even as the amusement bloomed, one muscled in among them, fist raised in a signal of restraint, spawning a respectful hush as he glared down at the day's catch as if to judge whether it had been worth reeling in. He did so with eyes like livid coals—not in color, but in the searing heat emanating from them. Reminding Kylac that, if free of the cauldron, he'd by no means escaped its fire.

As the newcomer beheld the captives' stance, however, sighting Kylac's blade at Denariel's throat, he, too, smiled.

An unsettling gesture, given the visceral hatred radiating from him. But he betrayed a genuine exhilaration now, as well. A sense of triumph he could scarcely contain. He recognized them, or thought he did. And while surely he or his lookouts had done so already, judging by the effort taken to retrieve them, the further act of identifying them so near at hand, securely in his clutches, carried with it an entirely new level of satisfaction.

"Welcome," he sneered, "to the *Kraken's Reach.*"

He lowered his fist. As if given rein, the bridled laughter around him resumed.

Kylac smiled alongside, seeming untroubled, refusing to be cowed. *Temerius Seahammer, I presume.* Yet he refrained from doing so openly. His enemy needn't know what the Shorecleaver had revealed to them. Supposing the information was true, better that he appear ignorant of the grievance this son of Grendavan had against him. His best play at this juncture, he'd determined, was to pretend that he'd intentionally brought the princess over in order to sell her to them. Harder to believe, were he to admit knowing himself to be marked.

"Princess Denariel," Temerius added, with a wolfish smirk to match his growling voice. "A most pleasant surprise."

"Spare me your filthy—"

"In the flesh," Kylac interjected, choking off Denariel's tart response. "Or what passes as such, for the bastard royal she is."

The laughs and snickers gave way to a smattering of confusion. Temerius turned his gaze upon Kylac, eyelids narrowing. "And you call yourself what?"

"Flotsam, for what purpose it might serve. It's my bounty here that should concern ya, Captain . . . ?"

"You think to fence with me, boy?"

Kylac dared a glance off the starboard fore, seeking to place the *Wail*. Though the *Kraken's Reach* and its attending Prowler had fallen off the pace, they'd positioned themselves already along pursuit trajectories. As had the other Grenarr ships—all but the pair that lay in the *Wail*'s path. However bleak the prospect of escape, it was clear now that Ledron and crew had at least decided to make the attempt. Whether upon Kylac's urging, or some determination of their own, he couldn't know. But mayhap his parley here might buy them some time, if he could assure their captor that Denariel—and himself, if need be—were prize enough.

"Barter," he replied. "Rewarding those who's so doggedly pursued us."

The scales shifted back toward amusement, a chorus of rasping chuckles largely lost to the thrumming song of pipe and drum.

Temerius, for his part, continued to stare heatedly at Kylac, grinning darkly, hand caressing the bone-handled hilt of a knife at his waist. "You supposed Her Highness to be my target? *Surprised*, I said, that she should join us."

"Acknowledging my part in bringing her to ya."

"Confessing my astonishment that she is not tucked away in some chamber of her false father's borrowed castle."

Kylac let his own smile slip, using the touch of a frown to feign confusion. "Would ya's paid more for the Shorecleaver, then?"

Denariel squirmed abruptly in his hold. "Snake!" she hissed, as he clutched her fast. "My father should have gutted you and sold your organs to Horghanni spicers!"

The outburst led Kylac to believe that she understood what was required here. Or mayhap she truly believed he intended to sacrifice her to save himself—seeking profit along the way.

"Or was it your lord's ship ya meant to retrieve?" he asked. "If'n so, I can tells ya where ya might find her remains."

Temerius's smirk crept higher, though his eyes retained their dangerous glint. "Clever, you must think yourself. Or me not at all."

Kylac arched a brow, maintaining his mock ignorance. "Speak plain, Captain. By all appearances, ya's further matters to attend."

"You pray I've not been fed your description. Is that it? For it would seem unmistakable, *Kronus*."

Kylac tipped his head in due deference. "A rare repute, I's acquired. And earned, I suppose, for what portion bears truth. Ya must knows, then, that I can serve priceless ally, or costly adversary. As our princess here can attest."

"What I know," Temerius growled, "is that it wasn't the princess who slew my sire under a flag of truce."

Kylac took a moment to appear unsettled, though the admission but confirmed what the imprisoned Tormitius had already claimed. Hunted by one of Grendavan's sons, apprehended for the sake of retribution. Would that remain Temerius's primary purpose, now that he had Denariel within his grasp? By all indications, yes. For the Grenarrian captain seemed entirely unconcerned with the lingering threat on the princess's life, and hadn't so much as turned his back to mark the status of the ongoing pursuit of the *Wail*.

He already had before him that which he desired most. Whatever might come after were but dressings upon the feast.

"A regrettable business, that with your father," Kylac replied finally. "Ask, and I'll gladly repay ya in the skins of Addarans—Kendarrion's own, if'n ya seek it."

The Seahammer forced a snarling chuckle. "As if the Pretender's feeble life, or those of a thousand landsnakes like him, could equal that of my sire."

"So take *his* life," Denariel urged, bucking again in Kylac's grip. Kylac let her thrash, using the struggle to further extricate himself from the loose strands of netting draped upon his feet and hooked over a pair of hilts at his waist. "Consider it a gift from *my* father. Take me as your bride, as yours meant to do, and return my brother as agreed upon."

"He'll have your tongue," Kylac hissed, "if'n ya continue to let it slither." Having twisted and shrugged free of the ensnaring cords, he shook her and tightened his hold, making a show of reestablishing his tentative grasp on the situation.

"An offer most kind, Your Highness," Temerius agreed, his mocking tone thick with derision. "Though it bears scant gratitude toward one who has so valiantly defended you."

The Seahammer wasn't biting. He believed the offers of betrayal between princess and warder to be a ploy. More convinced of it than Kylac himself was.

"I's ventured here on her behalf, yes," Kylac confessed. "For the reward to be gained in her brother's return. I'm granting ya the chance to make a better offer. Else, given the circumstances, whatever coin ya can spare."

He cast about at those whose weapons were trained on him, seeming less certain of his standing. A continued affectation, as he absorbed the signs—visible and elsewise—of Temerius's most likely intentions. What would the vengeful lad do if Kylac permitted himself to remain captive? How might he react if Kylac chose to bolt? His own life, he was confident he could defend. But which was liable to cause Denariel the least amount of harm?

Temerius pretended to consider, all the while reflexively stroking that bone-handled dagger in a manner that revealed his savage desires. "Inconstant proposals, from each of you," he observed. "You, Princess, have been opposed from the outset to any such arrangement between our peoples, have you not? Given chance to barter yourself for the welfare of your brother, you chose not to. My wife, you say? Long enough to drive a stake through my sleeping heart, I'll wager."

The Seahammer's shipmates grunted and murmured threateningly, awaiting a rebuttal that Denariel didn't bother to give.

"And you," Temerius pressed, fixing Kylac with his hateful gaze, "could have let her be wed and waited to learn whether we would honor the accord between her kind and mine, yet chose to intercede on her behalf and seek to steal back the landsnake prince. You have shown your colors, yet seek to sell me a different loyalty?"

Kylac shrugged. "I am but a seeker o' fortune, scratching for profit where I may. Had the prince been delivered by your people, what chance would I's had to fetch him and earn the bounty for his return?"

"You are an impetuous vagabond," Temerius corrected. "And the only bounty you shall reap is that of your betrayal."

The threat twisted openly in the wind. Yet the standoff persisted. Whatever the Seahammer intended, he'd determined to take Kylac alive. Elsewise, he'd have signaled to his spearman by now—or the bowmen backing them—and ordered Kylac impaled or feathered on the spot. Though an observer might have thought it was damage to the princess that the Grenarrian hoped to avoid, Kylac, at the center of the storm, continued to sense elsewise.

The only reason Temerius hadn't attacked already was his rabid hunger—increasing by the moment—to prolong and savor Kylac's demise.

A greedy aim. And Kylac intended that it should prove, as greed often did, too far-reaching.

"Mark engaged!" a lookout cried.

Kylac's gaze shifted out to sea, where the *Wail* appeared on the verge of collision now with the pair of Prowlers clamping down on her. Enemy missiles rained upon her decks from either side, triggering an even heavier bombardment in return. A strange pride, Kylac took, in watching the great Marauder weather the combined storm, like a mother wolf snapping back at a pair of pups come to nip at her flanks.

Temerius, he noted, declined to turn, continuing to peer aft, keeping his true quarry fixedly in sight. His ring of spearmen likewise maintained discipline, refusing to be distracted. Confident, most likely, that matters with the *Wail* were in hand.

A terrible grinding echoed over the intervening expanse of ocean, the screech of the *Wail's* hull scraping past those of the pinching Prowlers. Denariel cringed in Kylac's grasp. A few more Grenarr heads turned to observe, but only those of sailors—none of those who'd been tasked with restraining the prisoners.

"Mark free!"

Grenarr stationed aloft, along with warriors positioned elsewhere upon the decks, hissed and shouted their displeasure. Temerius was unmoved.

"Maintain pursuit," the captain ordered calmly.

The tempo of the shipboard drums, along with the pitch of the pipes, altered slightly. As did the echoing refrains from the pack's neighboring vessels. But no commands were given to modify course.

The Seahammer had anticipated this, Kylac realized. He'd known that the Marauder was still the stronger vessel, and, while less maneuverable, faster given full sail.

He seemed equally confident that those advantages would eventually wear thin. Now that they had her, they would stalk her until they ran her ragged, or had completely hemmed her in.

"Like all rogues," he sneered, as if privy to Kylac's thoughts, "inevitably brought to heel."

A pleasure it would have been to dispute him, to sap even a small measure of the captain's smug certainty. Alas, Kylac had nothing upon which to found such foolish optimism.

"I leave it to you, then," Temerius gloated, "to determine how long you stand there posturing before yielding. Knowing that for every moment you deny me, your pain shall endure."

Kylac was still mulling it over, weighing his instinctive fear of confinement against the harm Denariel might suffer should he liberate himself, when the lookout overhead hailed an unexpected cry.

"Rogue afore!"

A different breed of rogue, Kylac saw. Directly astern of the *Wail*, the ocean had risen . . . and risen . . . to form a rapidly steepening slope against the Prowlers at her rudder. Though they sought to climb it, the towering wave flung them backward before cresting over their bows. Even at a distance, amid the song of pursuit, Kylac heard the dismayed shouts of crewmen who slipped and careened about their ship's decks as the pair of vessels were shrugged aside by the sea's sudden, heaving wash.

Buying the *Wail* a few more precious moments.

Kylac smiled. He'd all but forgotten about the Sea Scribe's powers—how useful they'd proven already, and might again. Ithrimir's self-effacing assessment days earlier, while in the throes of the Thousand Tempests, had caused Kylac to believe that the manipulation of ocean waters was a far cry from a river surge, and thus beyond the Elementer's skill set. It appeared now that the limitations to which Ithrimir had confessed pertained less to the size of the body of water, and mayhap more to the duration of his influence.

Merely a guess, erected upon his assumption that the Scribe was

involved at all. But the timing was too perfect, the result too beneficial, for Kylac to believe anything else.

"Matters may not be so well in hand, Captain."

Temerius frowned, but remained fixed in his stance. A Grenarrian
at his shoulder gave assessment. "A hummock, liege lord. Ill-formed,
yet set to pass."

The deck beneath them reared and fell again as the rogue's remnants
gushed by, rolling beneath their hull. But the prow of the *Kraken's
Reach* knifed through cleanly, slicing along her keel. A moment's
disruption, the wave served, before expending itself.

Nor had it caused the other pursuing vessels much distress. For all
the attention it had drawn, a fleeting disturbance.

"Smooth ahead!" the lookout announced.

Temerius's furrowed brow smoothed in turn, reflecting his black
amusement. "The sea is *our* ground—swells, surges, and all."

"Maelstrom!"

This warning drew greater unease than the last. Making no attempt
to mask a genuine surprise, Kylac eyed the slow-forming outline of
the new hazard. On the heels of the rogue, a deepening depression
in the *Wail*'s wake that spanned the stretch of ocean across which the
Grenarr gave chase, gradually beginning to churn.

No Dread Maw of the Deep, but cause enough for alarm.

The pipes shrilled a new tone, as the drums thundered a new
cadence, seeming to echo his assessment.

"Then ya knows well," Kylac said, "she never tires o' surprises."

"Permission to veer," the mate at Temerius's ear requested.

At that, the Seahammer turned his head, disbelief vying with fury.
It was all the opening Kylac needed.

He acted instinctively, as he so often did—as was most comfortable.
Setting aside his questions and doubts about possible scenarios, he
seized upon his impulse in that moment to release Denariel and fling
himself toward Temerius. The Seahammer was already turning back
to him, but had ventured too close. Ducking one spear and swatting
past another, drawing a second shortsword to complement the first,
Kylac spun in to rise with blades in upthrust scissor formation at the
captain's throat.

Temerius froze, sucking in a startled breath. His hand gripped his bone-handled dagger, but failed to draw it. Wisely so, if a conscious decision.

"Back!" Kylac shouted, loudly enough to ensure a widespread audience. He pressed his blades tight, forcing Temerius's jaw higher. "Else I takes his head."

For half a heartbeat, he considered doing so anyway, on the chance that the Seahammer's crew might eliminate themselves the way Vorathus's Banshees had. But the latter seemed a unique loyalty among the Grenarr. Grendavan's retinue hadn't slain themselves upon *his* death, and he their overlord.

More than that, Kylac yet had need of this particular crew.

The nearest spearmen, whose lunging counters had brought them to within a step of his exposed left flank, held their ground. He'd positioned his back against the starboard rail. On his right flank gawked the Grenarrian mate, who, like Temerius, had found his blade, but not the time to draw it. The bows overhead seemed the greatest danger, yet Kylac continued to trust that none would fire without their captain's permission.

Else they'd have done so already.

The Seahammer's incensed gaze flashed with explosive rage— weighing his chances of escaping this snare, if Kylac wasn't mistaken, against the fierce pride that would deny any such fear.

"Fool," he finally hissed. "You but thrash in your noose. Do you think I'll not sacrifice my life to destroy yours?"

"Has I asked for your life, Captain? Bounty, I seek. If'n not from your coffers, the one I set forth to claim."

"Should I fall," Temerius proclaimed, his rasping volume rising to a roar, "vessel and command to he who slays this wretch!"

"I mean to proves it," Kylac pressed. "Ya want revenge? Ya'll has your chance, if'n ya takes me to Dethaniel."

The ship shifted to starboard. Though permission had yet to be given, the helmsman had evidently taken the liberty to steer her in that direction. The rest aboard, whether scattered about the decks or perched amid the rigging, fixated upon the modified standoff.

"The prince, hear?" Kylac asked. "Blackmoon Shards, Red Sun

Wastes . . . your own chamber pot, if'n that's where he's stashed. Deliver me to him, and we'll meet again."

Temerius scoffed. "I'll carry you nowhere."

"I'll makes my own way," Kylac agreed. "Just remember, the only way ya lay eyes on me again is using Dethaniel as lure." He glanced at Denariel. Hunched upon folded knees, ignoring the hedge of enemy spears around her, radiating surprise and confusion amid her unrelenting disapproval. "Treat his sister as ya will."

Her stunned reaction struck him like a jab in the ribs. *What was he thinking?*

"You've nowhere to flee," the Seahammer reminded him, confidence returning. "You've but a choice between my mercy and that of the sharks."

"So it seems." Kylac checked again the lay of his surroundings—the neighboring ships, the yawning of the developing maelstrom, the positioning of individual enemies clustered around him. He reassured himself of the Seahammer's boiling need for retribution, while disregarding the withering heat of Denariel's wounded expression. Did he truly believe this desperate gambit could harvest anything but failure?

"Ya has my terms," he said with finality. "And, given your present demeanor, I'd sooner not wait around to be flayed, keelhauled, drawn and quartered, or worse." He straightened his arms, to keep his blades at the captain's throat as he leaned back. "So I believe I'll return now to finish that discourse with the sharks."

Before he could reconsider, he sprang backward, onto the gunwale. From there, he flipped high and wide—beyond the reach of thrusting spearheads—while sheathing his shortswords and drawing daggers in their stead. Smaller blades in hand, he stretched into a dive.

And back into the sea.

33

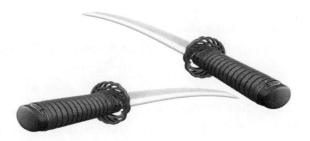

He entered the waters headfirst, daggers clutched before him in a reverse grip, as a razored welcome against whatever awaited his return. A massive shark approached at once, the largest he'd yet seen, its battle-worn skin nicked and scarred from untold conflicts. Kylac rolled head over heels to right himself, blades poised to receive it. Misliking the look of him—or mayhap his scent—the creature swatted its tail and turned wide, edging past with that dread, merciless expression of primordial craving.

More than a dozen others lurked nearby, racing along beneath or astride the *Kraken's Reach*, as if serving escort to her impressive hull. Kylac kicked toward the passing Reaver, until its ominous bulk came within reach. He stretched out with his nearest blade . . .

And caught the ship as she was about to slip by, dagger tip gouging her skin before gaining purchase just an arm's length from her transom. He clung fast, still holding his breath, as the pressure of driving waters sought to dislodge him. When confident he could withstand their tug, he reached forth with the other dagger, driving higher in his aim. Stout as the planks were, his blades pierced the wood with relative ease. Hand over hand, he scaled toward the waterline, begging patience of his lungs amid their stinging cries.

He breached amid a foaming rush of waters that continued to

drag against him with the weight of the vessel's momentum. Already, however, that momentum had begun to slow. Kylac couldn't make out the voices that echoed somewhere above—not over the growling surge in his ears. But the urgent tone seemed to support what he already sensed.

The *Kraken's Reach* was coming to a halt.

Fitting, he supposed, with the Seahammer's aims. Temerius wasn't going to simply trust the sharks to do his killing for him. A body would be required to appease his hatred, even if—as Kylac had imagined earlier—it must be carved from the bellies of its devourers.

Keeping low to evade enemy sight, Kylac gave audience to his racing mind and thundering heart. Conscious of the sharks eyeing him from below. Of the men above who searched the surrounding waters, waiting to see where he might surface. Of the attending Prowler drawing near—flying a familiar spear-and-trident, and with lookouts of her own. He sensed the other ships farther out, the nearby maelstrom as it gained in strength, and the frantic efforts of the former to escape the latter. Somewhere beyond, the *Wail* waged her own desperate struggle, crewmembers wrestling with all that had transpired. Flush with resolve in their immediate purpose, scarcely ready to consider the despair and confusion of whatever must come next.

Next? Kylac could have laughed at the absurdity. Here he was, clinging desperately to the tail of a vessel that seemed intent on shrugging him free, half expecting to fall prey to sharks, and with no reasonable idea of what his move should be. Amid all the howling turmoil, within and without, his most pressing concern was for Denariel. Had he just condemned her to torture and death? Her betrayed expression haunted him, knotting in his chest. While careful not to lie outright, he'd deliberately led Temerius to assume that he sought Prince Dethaniel for the sake of coin. An accusation Denariel might make, hardly reflective of his actual intent. Would he ever be able to profess as much to her? Could he ever convince her to trust him again?

She never trusted you to begin with, an inner voice mocked. He found some solace in the reminder. He'd lost nothing in terms of her esteem, and shouldn't have cared were it elsewise.

Might his gnawing discomfort owe solely to his ridiculous, half-formed strategy? Tempt the vengeance-minded Temerius to seek out Dethaniel. Find a way to stow himself aboard, stealing a ride to that same location under the captain's nose. Leave Denariel to the relative safety of a shipboard cabin—even if manacled—trusting in her inherent worth to these pirates to preserve her from undue harm.

A vague plan, however noble his intent. Fraught with any number of fragile assumptions. And he need peer no farther into the future than his current, precarious position to admit it.

Yet, even the prospect of failure—likely as it seemed—wasn't what weighed on him. More troubling was the sense that he'd somehow shirked an open challenge posed by Temerius and his crew. Was it necessary that he'd done so?

Less selfish would have been to surrender his weapons and remain with Denariel as a prisoner, trusting in a later opportunity to spring them both. But the fury in Temerius's eyes had told him that he'd not have been kept prisoner for long. Be it late or soon, he'd have been forced to fight his way free in a weakened state, to kill or maim most of the crew, leaving him with a crippled vessel and no idea of where to steer her even if there remained hands enough bent to his will to do so.

He might have battled then and there, else manipulated the crew by keeping their captain as his hostage. But that, too, had felt wrong. At some juncture, they would have defied him and revolted, with or without Temerius's command. Denariel might have easily been killed in the resulting conflict, or executed in a demonstration of will.

Neither course of action had seemed likely to keep the princess from harm—nor put him in a position to successfully coerce his enemy to steer the vessel toward Dethaniel's place of imprisonment. Had he not been sparring on that count with the captive Tormitius for weeks now? Hamstrung as he'd been in those particular negotiations, he'd come to respect the rare resolve to which these Grenarr lay claim, and understood that the only certain means of reaching Dethaniel would be through their genuine desire that he do so. For even if Ithrimir could make good on his promise to deliver them to Haverstromme, what guarantee could he provide that the abducted prince was to be found upon the archipelago's shores? Or where, precisely?

Deliberating now over what he'd scarcely more than *perceived* above, he did spy a framework of reason that might support his actions. He could only hope Temerius would seize upon the bait, and that he'd successfully convinced the captain he cared nothing for the princess beyond her limited mercenary value—thereby eliminating any reason to kill her out of hand.

But if his justifications were warranted, why did they still trouble him?

As the *Kraken's Reach* continued to slow, and the tug of passing waves to lessen, Kylac growled away the doubts and the guilt. His greatest skills were those of intuition and adaptation. So he'd landed himself in a terrible predicament. He would just have to find a way to work himself free.

As well as those he'd jeopardized alongside.

His most immediate concern was avoiding detection. Not only were those aboard the nearing Prowler likely to spy him eventually, but he could make out now over the calming surge the shouts of Grenarr above clambering out over the rail, descending the hull's exterior on ladders and scaling ropes, seeking sign of his whereabouts. Peering up along the contours of the starboard side, he spied a shore boat creaking in its davits, teeming with Grenarr warriors, preparing to lower. The longer he remained in one place, the more certain became his discovery.

But where to go? Unless he were to sprout a pair of gills, he couldn't hope to remain submerged long enough to elude them. Nor was he entirely convinced the sharks wouldn't come to recognize him for the morsel he might serve. For whatever length of time they might remain at sea, he needed to board a vessel. Preferably this one, to better keep watch over Denariel. The others might turn away, risking what could prove a permanent separation. The *Reach* was his best hope for gaining the Shards, whether at its captain's behest, or redirected by Kylac himself at some later juncture. Whenever or however, he needed to slither back aboard the very vessel he'd just departed, and it appeared he would have to attempt it much sooner than anticipated.

There was no scaling the hull in this light, nor even at nightfall as long as there remained so many eyes—and scouring hands—upon its skin. Where else might he find purchase? He looked aft over his left shoulder, toward the rudder housing. The means by which Denariel claimed to have accessed the *Vengeance* in secret. If he could enter that cramped void without being seen, he might ride his adversaries out for some time, shielded from their eyes and their bows, killing any who sought to climb in after him and casting suspicion for those deaths on the sharks.

With the added benefit of reducing the number he might have to kill later.

Of course, Temerius might put in for reinforcements at some enemy port other than the one holding Dethaniel—or burn the ship entirely—in an effort to remove any chance of infestation. But that . . . that would expose a whole new skein of possibilities that Kylac needn't contemplate at this time.

His platter of concerns was overflowing already.

A chore it was, putting the welfare of others above simple self-preservation. The resulting complications made his head ache. But he couldn't turn away now. He'd assumed certain responsibilities that he intended to see through—for the sake of his own integrity, if nothing else. And if the fun was in the challenge, well, these circumstances promised to prove downright exhilarating.

With the *Reach* heaving to a crawl, he pulled his head above the waterline for a fresh breath.

And promptly felt an arrow speeding toward his back.

He leaned to his right. The barbed head thudded sharply against the ironwood hull just over his left shoulder before careening into the water. Alas, his indecision had cost him. Turning to peer at the advancing Prowler, he found that an archer upon its forecastle already had him squarely in sight.

He finished drawing his breath, then yanked his daggers free and pushed off, delving beneath the surface as another arrow chased after the first. So much for departing without a trace, leaving his adversaries to guess as to what might have happened to him. Preferable, that they believed him to be alive. But harder it would be to avoid detection if they *knew* rather than merely *suspected* him to be aboard.

So it was that he swam beneath the keel of the hovering vessel, from starboard to larboard, venturing forward as he did so. Having been spotted so near the *Reach*'s rudder, taking aim at the housing now would be too obvious. If he was to throw them off the scent, even momentarily, he would have to lead them down another path and seek to backtrack later.

An ominous proposition, as he eyed the sharks—now some two dozen in number—with which he shared these waters. He had to believe that something drew them, for so many to flock to one area. And, as best as he could tell, he remained the only potential meal within range. What were they waiting for? Could they truly be so fascinated by him and wary of him at the same time?

He marked their rust-streaked bodies, their bone-chilling gazes, and continued to wonder how long their hunger could possibly be held in check.

His expiring breath forced him to surface amidships along the larboard side. Shouts greeted him, as spotters aboard the *Reach* pinpointed him almost at once. *Good,* he thought, before taking another breath and diving again. Let them think he was swimming about in circles. He'd only gone to the far side to make it appear as though he wished to escape the attending Prowler. To draw eyes without making it obvious that he was intentionally doing so.

Because a clever cat knew when it was being baited by the mouse.

The mounting danger, of course, was that he would become so exposed that he'd be unable to conceal himself on the way back to his original destination. On land, in a chosen setting, he could vanish so completely and abruptly that some might accuse him of magecraft. But underwater, with his trade skills limited by slower movement and his body's need for breath, passing unseen could prove harder than usual.

He would need a distraction. Fortunately, he already had one in mind.

But one matter at a time.

He swam deeper to avoid a lancing harpoon, Temerius's crewmen taking to hunting him like a fish or whale. Sensible enough. The

Seahammer desired him alive, but not necessarily undamaged. Better, in fact, that he were disabled—speared through the arm or leg—so as to make a second escape less likely, once they reeled him in.

His plunging course brought him face-to-face with another shark, this one surging up from the shadowed deep. Kylac got a good look into its opening gullet, encircled with jagged rows of razored teeth, before a sweeping dagger drove the animal aside with an angry swish of its tail. The creatures appeared to be growing bolder. Or less patient. How much longer did he dare press his luck?

He took aim at the *Reach*'s stationary prow. He didn't surface again until gaining shelter beneath the angle of her cutwater. Gripping the ship's face with his daggers, to rise and fall with the passing swells just above the waterline, he took fresh assessment.

Less than a hundred strokes to the larboard fore, the maelstrom was losing strength, its churn slowing, its broad basin smoothing. A brief fury apparently expended. But the whirlpool had served its purpose. Like the *Kraken's Reach* and her attending Prowler, the other five Grenarr ships had stalled or veered wide. By all appearances, the *Wail* had gained sufficient distance to evade capture.

For the moment. Kylac couldn't know how long she might continue to do so, or what would become of Ledron and crew should they manage to avoid future ambush. Would they attempt to track him as he'd intended? Round about and make for home? Turn renegade and become pirates themselves?

A future concern. He'd done what he could to help cover their escape, and would have to satisfy himself with that. The greater jeopardy now was to his own freedom. Already, lookouts aboard the spear-and-trident Prowler were whistling and shouting at their brethren aboard the *Reach*, betraying his current position. A pair of shore boats—one to each side—were rowing forward along the Reaver's flanks, while her outer hull was swarming with other Grenarr set to spy or hunt him from ladder or harness. The number of sharks continued to grow, seeming to spawn from every quarter.

If he was to make his own escape, he saw little reason to delay any longer.

Down he went again, aft along the keel before edging back to larboard, away from the Prowler. Eyeing the boots of a Grenarr warrior perched at the bottom of a scaling ladder with harpoon drawn, he lunged from the water to slash at the man's ankle tendon. The harpooner, facing down and out to sea, failed to see him emerging from underneath the curve of the lower hull. And while the injury inflicted was by no means mortal, it proved sufficient to shed the Grenarrian from his perch with a grimace of shock and burning pain.

The muted cry and resulting splash drew the attention of others, so Kylac dove again at once. Even underwater now, he heard the shouts from above—among them, Temerius's own enraged cries spurring his crewmen to action. Whatever else there remained to accomplish, the hornet's nest had been stirred.

He kicked away, increasing his distance from the wounded man, whose leg trailed a bloody cloud. He looked to the sharks, marking their reaction, hoping now that their reluctance didn't bespeak an utter lack of hunger or aggression.

He needn't have worried. One moment, the harpooner was splashing amid the waves, righting himself and reaching back for his ladder. In the next, half a dozen of the nearest sharks surged toward him. They set into him like a pack of starving wolves, mouths tearing, bodies thrashing. In a matter of heartbeats, his screams had ceased, and nothing remained but a billowing soup of shredded meat and floating scraps of organs.

Kylac observed the carnage with a measure of awe. Not all tales of sharks, then, bore embellishment. He watched others flock toward the detritus, long after any meaningful morsel had been snatched up. Only to wrestle and snap at one another in apparent agitation at having been denied.

Looking already for the next feeding opportunity.

Kylac half feared he might be it. Though confident by now that they were repulsed by him, they hadn't been in any kind of obvious frenzy before. Man or beast, bloodlust had a way of suppressing inhibitions.

So he observed for another moment, kicking backward underwater to increase his distance from those still being drawn toward the surface.

Then set out to provide them another target.

He returned to starboard, pausing for a breath before taking aim this time at the shore boat on that side. Overfilled with harpooners perched around the gunwale, the craft made for an easy mark. He simply waited for a sizable cross-swell, then kicked up from beneath to give the boat an extra heave amidships. One Grenarrian failed to compensate for the sudden lurch, and that momentary imbalance was all it took to carry him and two of his comrades into the water.

The sharks no longer required the invitation of an open wound. Doubtless, they could smell the bloodstreams circulating within. A pack honed in on the men's splashing bodies.

And promptly devoured them in bloody chunks.

Grenarr aboard the shore boat retaliated with their spears and harpoons—even their oars. But this only incited the sharks further. As Kylac stroked away from the massacre with all haste, the larger sharks turned on the boat itself, nudging it with their powerful noses, swatting it with their tails, surging from the water with mouths agape. Hammered and spun from all directions, the craft quickly shed most of its remaining passengers—all but a handful hunkered fearfully at its center.

And the bloodbath grew.

Sharks multiplied out of the darkness. Again Kylac looked to see whether any drew bead on him. But those that swam past continued to skirt round, shying from him with cold-blooded disinterest. Focused on the feast in progress.

Continuing to give him a fighting chance.

His human adversaries, however, showed little sign of being deterred. Arrows and harpoons rained down, striking back. Sharks now bled among the Grenarr, and, unlike the pup Kylac had wounded earlier, some of these fell victim to their own kind in a gruesome display of cannibalism.

A melee quickly spiraling out of control.

All the while, those under the Seahammer's command sought to trace his movements as best they could, and to attack where opportunity presented itself. Sharks took advantage of this, lunging from the water at the ship's edges to drag lower-hanging Grenarr from their ladders and harnesses. Fins and teeth cut through the now roiling sea, whose foaming surface had been dyed red and littered with bloody fragments of bone and flesh. This only hid the greater nightmare beneath, where sharks savaged their prey and one another in a chomping, sawing, rending orgy of butchery.

Kylac had seen enough.

Amid the blooming blood clouds, he returned to the *Reach*'s underbelly, peering back and forth in search of shark or human pursuit. None of the Grenarr he found below were in any position to give his away. Most were but twitching pieces of their former selves, torn and tattered about the edges. Those who could defend themselves sought to do so, only to be attacked from behind. The rest clawed frantically skyward, screaming vainly for aid or for mercy, receiving neither.

As he swam aft through the inky waters, lungs pressured by his jailed breath, the question returned as to what Temerius might do if he believed Kylac slain. Might he still proceed to the Blackmoon Shards or wherever else Dethaniel was held? It seemed reasonable to expect that the captain might seek to convene with whatever council or individuals had come to lead their people, now that he had the princess in his clutches. To re-determine, mayhap, the next course for their people, with both of Kendarrion's royal children under their control.

But why guess and wonder? He would seek to learn the captain's intent from Temerius himself, once he'd climbed aboard. Should he fail at that, the rest would matter little.

So he focused on making his way through the haze of eviscerated bodies beneath the cover of the *Reach*'s keel, while dead black eyes, thrashing fins, and tooth-filled jaws flashed by in glimpses. Even now, his tiring muscles tensed in anticipation of that single rogue attack that might take from him a limb or worse. Though evidence suggested he should be safe, his overwhelmed senses couldn't be sure.

Ahead, the lean silhouette of the ship's rudder materialized amid the murk. To one side, trapped beneath the stern, floated the remains of a severed torso. Without examining it too closely, Kylac prodded the mutilated mass before him until he reached the edge of the transom, then pushed it out beside the rudder on the starboard side, where the Prowler still hovered.

As the freed torso floated to the surface, Kylac stabbed one of his daggers into the transom's base, deep beneath the waterline, and there left it. A beacon, as it were, for Ithrimir to mark the *Reach*'s movements. Assuming the Elementer could do so. That he would wish to. That Ledron would resist any further overtures from his crew to rid themselves of the Scribe's presence. That the Head himself retained command, without falling victim to mutiny . . .

The potential setbacks seemed without end. But Kylac's lungs were near to bursting, and the bloody torso had already drawn a pair of sharks. With their snapping, gnawing assault chewing the water around the torso to foam, Kylac surfaced to larboard and the opposite side of the rudder. Assuring himself that none were watching, he clawed his way up into the protective housing. A stab of grim pleasure went with him, as the screams and desperate shouts of Grenarr reverberated through the air. Delighted not by the terrible nature of their demise, but by the Seahammer's plan for recapturing him having failed expectations.

Order o' the day, he thought, recalling the moment in which the Grenarr had been sighted and his own crew's plans had begun to unravel. And this the result. The *Wail* set fleeing upon the fastest wind, Denariel a prisoner of the enemy, and himself settling into the cramped void of the *Reach*'s tail end for a moment's rest. Daggers in hand should any manage to search for him from below. Realizing only now that he dare not penetrate further quite yet, lest his dripping entry into the ship's bowels leave obvious sign of his infiltration.

Leaving him naught but to catch his breath amid those stifling confines. Reflecting upon the ill turns this day had wrought, and what fell fortunes might yet follow before the sun could set.

34

THE SONG OF SCREAMS PERSISTED throughout the day, as Kylac hunkered there within the curved shielding of the rudder housing, waiting for the furor of his escape to subside. Temerius hadn't surrendered easily. Hours after Kylac had used the feeding frenzy to slip from view, the Seahammer's men had carried on the hunt, slaughtering sharks in droves—and perishing themselves—in their captain's desperate desire to produce Kylac's body or some evidence of its ruin. Telltale sounds suggested that the crews of the other Grenarr ships had been brought in to reinforce the search, to scour the waters around the *Reach* in longboats, sifting with nets and hooked poles through the detritus of the savage feast. Even when the wailing screams of dying or half-eaten men had diminished—indicating the Grenarr to have gained the upper hand—their lingering echoes rang in Kylac's skull.

The shouting continued thereafter, the ongoing din of those set to prowl the surrounding seas in a seemingly ceaseless circuit. More than one boat stroked about the stern of the *Reach*, to examine rudder and stock. But Kylac was able to press himself up against the inner wall of the protective housing, beyond their angle of view. Others came at him from above, twice emerging from the access hatch within the ship. These would have found him, had he not heard the thud and scratching of their movements as the hinged service portal was unlatched and drawn open. On each occasion, he'd had ample warning to shimmy back down the rudder, to hide again beneath the swells and the ship itself while waiting out their cursory inspection.

Fortune had it that the search teams neglected to probe his place of hiding from both directions at once, enabling him to remain undiscovered from one or the other without shedding further blood—and mayhap triggering a whole new round of alarms. Still, the back-and-forth nature of concealing himself in that limited area had the helpless feel of an animal pacing in its cage. And every time he was forced to submerge, he had to begin the slow process of drying out all over again, preventing him from entering the vessel proper, keeping him pinned.

Not until after nightfall was the hunt concluded, the various teams of searchers recalled to their ships, and the *Reach*'s sheets unfurled to the wind. Even then, Kylac chose to remain in his secret berth. Concerns as to Denariel's unknown treatment almost forced his hand, but he resisted the impulse, trusting to instincts that urged patience.

Shortly before midnight, the search from within came again, forcing him back down beneath the waves. This time, he had to cling to the rudder stock with his daggers, dragged along at the head of a frothing wake. He held his breath for as long as he could before resurfacing, to emerge as the inner hatch was being shuttered back into place.

A tiresome game.

He waited only a few moments longer before deciding to make his incursion. It was quite possible that they would continue checking the rudder routinely every few hours, and that, unless he wished to spend another day or two seeking to calculate their precise—or imprecise—inspection schedule, his best wager was to simply enter on the heels of the last and trust that it would afford him a sufficient window of opportunity to mask his tracks after entering.

Of course, it was equally possible that they'd posted a sentry inside, who would now be waiting to ambush him. But after measuring his options, with significant consideration given again to his own intuition, Kylac made his choice.

After wringing excess water from his tunic and breeches, he

climbed higher upon the rudder's stock to reach the service hatch—finding it increasingly difficult to believe Denariel's claim to have done the same. How would she have managed it, lacking his agility, his special blades . . . nursing a broken thumb, no less? To trip the inner latches, she'd have had to be at least somewhat familiar with the nature of the hatch's seating—knowledge he'd gained aboard the *Wail* only after he'd heard the princess's tale and decided in a quiet moment to investigate its plausibility. Skeptical of her account before, he found it even less conceivable now.

But if her method of stealing aboard had been a lie, what was the truth?

Questions for another time. After listening for sign of enemy presence—largely futile, given the echoing roar of passing waters in that cramped void space—he slipped a pair of his slim blades along the edges of the hatch to negotiate the latches beyond. Upon working the bolts from their cradles, he wasted no time before opening the hatch and—sensing no imminent danger—hauling himself up through the portal.

Empty darkness awaited him. The absence of the suspected sentry caused him to wonder if his adversaries had surrendered the possibility of him being there. Surely, at least some aboard assumed he'd been devoured. Others might doubt his ability to navigate the tricky penetration point, as he questioned Denariel's. Or was their lack of vigilance merely a ruse to tempt him?

Looking to find out, he battened down the hatch and crept quickly forward, trusting the patches of wetness giving indication of his presence to dry swiftly—or at least before anyone returned. Given the late hour, and the violent struggles of those that had preceded it, he might hope that most of the crew had been permitted to rest, limiting the number he would have to avoid while skulking through the ship's bowels.

Assuming at the same time a full watch.

Either way, he'd returned to a more comfortable element, and gained fresh confidence as a result. He'd have preferred open environs and fresher air. But at least he was no longer paddling awkwardly about, surrounded by flesh-eating monsters, unable to breathe. Stealth was all that was required of him now—a trade since birth. And while the ship remained an enclosed setting, it offered him plenty of spaces in which to hide, no matter how heavily patrolled.

Shards, if Denariel had been able to mask her presence as long as she had, so could he.

He proceeded in darkness, feeling his way through the dank, inky confines of the utility hold. He carried no flame, and no simple means of igniting one. Nor would he have chosen elsewise. Aside from increasing his risk of exposure, light afforded him nothing he couldn't determine by way of his other senses. Already, he felt his hearing, his scent, his touch, sharpening with heightened awareness, tingling in anticipation of being called upon. Anxious to serve greater role in the absence of his sight.

He paused upon reaching the forward wall of the tiny compart- ment—scarcely more than a crawlspace, really—and there waited in a crouch beside the seams of the inner hatch. Attuning himself to his new surroundings. Seeking the heartbeat of the vessel and its dealings. He'd not yet been aboard a Grenarr Reaver. Both the *Vengeance* and the *Wail* had been of the larger Marauder class. Giving him less room to play, and a smaller margin of error.

His primary objectives were threefold. Locate Denariel, and reas- sure himself of her safe condition. Eavesdrop on the captain or his lieutenants, and thereby apprise himself of the Seahammer's intent. Finally, food and drink for himself, as it had been too long since he'd tasted either.

As all three aims were critical to his ongoing mission, the order in which he accomplished them mattered little. Enabling him to venture forth largely as permitted, and see where circumstances took him.

When convinced that no immediate danger awaited him on the other side, he opened and slipped through the hatchway.

And his own hunt began.

It lasted throughout the night. Though the bulk of the crew slept, Temerius had in fact ordered a thick watch contingent and tight patrol schedule, owing chiefly to the chance—the hope—that Kylac had been foolish enough to steal aboard. Or so grumbled those displeased with the decision, who muttered among themselves when confident no one of rank was listening. Whatever their protests, the assigned crewmen carried out their captain's command with due diligence. As a result, Kylac found many of the deck ladders warded by sentries, some of whom stood fast until relieved. While he could have slain one or all without raising a whisper, the eventual discovery of the bodies—or even the absence thereof, should he trouble to dispose of them—would have removed any doubt as to his enduring presence, undermining his intent that his hosts be permitted to proceed of their own volition.

And yet, leaving them untouched necessitated as often as not that he backtrack and seek alternate routes about the vessel, slowing his progress.

His circuitous course did serve to increase his knowledge of the ship's layout, giving him cause to probe its more isolated reaches—often forcing him to find creative methods of doing so. But he'd determined quickly enough that such intimate explorations were largely unnecessary. Though slighter in scale, the design of this particular ship proved to be strikingly similar to those with which he was already familiar—a puzzle comprised of the same basic pieces. Cabins and holds were smaller, or fewer in number. Corridors were tighter, or replaced by adjoining walls cut through by doorways. But the essential arrangement of quarters and workspaces and armories and storage bays proved consistent. Dictated by efficiency, mayhap, in function or construction. Or suggesting a rigid order imposed by a domineering overlord. Whatever the rationale, it hadn't taken Kylac long to become acquainted with his new home.

However long it might serve as such.

Having started in the ship's bowels, he'd come across his food and drink first. A ration of dried plums, hard bread, and pickled pork had satisfied the former need, skimmed from a number of containers rather than whole ones—which could more easily be tallied and found to be missing. He did the same with his ale, tapping it from multiple barrels. He'd been schooled since birth in deprivation, learning to subsist for longer periods on far less. But without knowing where matters might take him, better to nourish his body while he had the chance.

He'd encountered Denariel next, relieved to find her housed in an aft ward room and not shackled in some half-flooded bilge compartment. She'd been tethered to her assigned bed, but appeared elsewise unharmed. His view was obscured, somewhat, in that he was unable to gain direct access inside, but rather forced to carve a sliver of a peephole beside an upright storage locker hammered into a sidewall. Nonetheless, her scent was of soap and oils, telling him she'd been cleansed, and he spied no marks on her exposed flesh in the light of her bedside lantern. Some scuffs on her wrists, mayhap, likely due to her own stubborn struggles. In the near half-mark that he remained with her, she slumbered peacefully enough, undisturbed by her captors.

Alleviating concerns that she might have been made to suffer for his insolence.

It had taken him much longer to reach a similar window into the captain's quarters. Though the suite was situated but two decks above the cabin given to Denariel, its layout and guard positioning was such to deny any easy access. Kylac ultimately found his by worming into a secret bolt-hole beneath the flooring that he only knew to look for based on Tormitius having made use of a similar void when Kylac had tracked him down aboard the *Vengeance*. Even then, he'd had to stand upon a borrowed crate to reach a ceiling underneath, and trigger a latch meant to be opened only from within, in order to release the rope ladder by which he gained entry. A tedious process, given his need for quiet, and the sentry who came pacing through that particular stretch of corridor at irregular—and often untimely—intervals.

Tedious, but for one as calm and skilled as he, merely a matter of patience.

Once settled into that compartment, he'd given ear to Temerius's restless pacing, which carried the captain from one corner of his cabin to the next. For what purpose, Kylac couldn't discern. The floorboards above permitted no light, and by every indication, the Seahammer was alone. Unable—or unwilling—to sleep. But beyond that? A decanter clinked when the captain poured himself a drink. Wind and sea huffed and roared when a portal was opened onto the aft balcony. Kylac heard a trunk open at one point, and a rustling of what might have been scrolls. Sometime thereafter, the Seahammer took to throwing a knife, by the sound of it, at his forward wall. Over and again, a hissing grunt, the whistle of a spinning blade, the thud of sharp steel biting into wood. Followed by the slow, steady scrape of sandaled footsteps as the weapon was retrieved, and the game begun again.

For reasons he couldn't have explained, Kylac found himself recalling the bone-handled dagger Temerius had been fingering during their brief interrogation, and wondered if this wasn't the blade's song.

On it went until, after a time, Kylac had retreated into a vague form of half sleep, in which he rested eyes and limbs without ever relinquishing his vigilance. He gave thought to the waning hour, and wondered whether this particular void space would be safe to inhabit should the daylight find him still hunkering within. As suitable as any place aboard, he determined, and likely better than most. He wondered how many of them he would come to know before their journey was done.

He thought of Denariel stowed away aboard the *Vengeance*, steeped in bilgewater and her own seasickness. He imagined her feasting on rats and roaches. He wondered again to what extent he was accountable for her suffering, and what sort of penance he might be asked to serve as a result.

With the predawn hour somewhere between the Sparrow's and the Thrush's, there arrived a knock at the captain's door.

"Come." The hollowed, grating voice belonged to Temerius.

The door creaked open. "A message, liegelord. Retrieved by Jairus while in port at Orenthrok."

"Barkavius." The dagger flew, biting into the wall.

"Would you have me respond this time?"

"You may tell the lapdog we're on our way."

"Which way, sir?"

"His."

A moment's silence preceded a pair of booted feet stepping into the cabin. The door closed behind them. "A claim that will displease him."

"Is it *his* pleasure you serve, or mine?"

The visitor's tone offered grudging apology. "We'll not be welcome. To forewarn him of our arrival would seem unwise."

"Welcome," the Seahammer echoed dully. Then, as if sneering through gritted teeth, "I need beg no steward's welcome. Grenathrok belongs to all of us."

Amid the other's silence, Temerius strode forward to wrench his dagger from the wall.

"Nine you've rallied to your command," the dissenter said finally. "Less than half of those petitioned." His voice matched that of the mate who'd stood at Temerius's shoulder when Kylac and Denariel had been apprehended. The Seahammer's chief lieutenant, it seemed. "The remainder—"

"The remainder are cravens, and will be dealt with as such." Again the blade flew, and struck home. What sounded like a chip of damaged wood skittered free.

"If Barkavius believes we mean to challenge—"

"So tell him of our cargo. Let the puppet know we carry the bastard princess, to reunite her with her brother. Share with him the impudent goad of my sire's murderer, if further cause must be given. But do not ask me to forgo my chance at revenge."

"And if it proves a sliverstray's fantasy?"

Kylac didn't know what a sliverstray was, but understood the question well enough. He all but held his breath while awaiting the Seahammer's delayed response.

After the ominous silence, "You've come then, to these quarters, to question my resolve?"

The seeds of aggression that had mustered in the lieutenant's tone scattered like roaches in a sudden light. "No, my sarki."

"Should the urge befall you, I beg you speak first with Oracus, and read what you will from his rotting rictus."

Boards creaked as the visitor leaned forward in what might have been a bow. "I leave you to your rest, liegelord." His steps retreated toward the door. "You *should* rest."

"When this is done," said Temerius, and sent his blade spinning into the cabin wall.

35

THE SLAP OF SANDALED FEET against the dock's planks overtook the lapping of waves against the pilings below. Kylac, submerged in the dark waters beneath the dock's underbelly, heard both as he swam silently shoreward on the heels of the company advancing overhead. The Seahammer's shore party had disembarked at king's tide, so the water level here at land's edge was high, leaving but a short span between the lagoon's surface and the boarded walkway above. Just enough room to breathe, really, as Kylac made his approach. Though confining, the tight, lightless quarters helped hide his presence from any who might have elsewise spied him from either side of the broad pier along which the *Kraken's Reach* had moored. The only witnesses to his arrival were the mussels and barnacles that grew from the wood in glistening clumps, along with whatever fish, shrimp, and clams swam, scurried, or nested underfoot.

His toes had encountered but the first grains of that sandy ground, still a dozen strides from where the dock abutted the shore, when the footsteps above him stopped, the Seahammer and his attendants coming abruptly to attention. Kylac paused along with them, easing forward another stride so that he needn't tread water while giving ear to the looming confrontation.

"You take great liberty in coming here," a stern voice nearer the shore bid in chill greeting.

"As do you," Temerius growled, "in addressing a liege captain as such."

The words were muted, muffled by the intervening planks and the grotto-like setting in which Kylac sheltered. The huffing of the lagoon's seawaters formed a competing echo as they rose and fell around him. Yet nothing could mask the rancor between the pair of disembodied voices squaring off above.

"*Sarki* Temerius," the challenger hissed grudgingly.

"You received my shrike, did you not?"

"Announcing your arrival, but failing to justify it."

"Justify?" Temerius echoed, his tone like a blade being drawn from its sheath.

"Your orders—"

"Do not prate to me of orders, *steward*. I've suffered already the insolence of your missives. A fell mistake to believe I'll stand here and endure also the lash of your tongue."

Bold words, given that Temerius had disembarked with only a dozen men against the hundred or so spear-wielding Grenarr mustered to receive him. The Seahammer outranked this land-based steward, Barkavius. Or clearly *believed* that he did. But the latter's posturing, from what Kylac had witnessed while drawing into port, was anything but subservient. It caused him to wonder anew at the ripples of Grendavan's death, and the unknown vagaries of Grenarr succession. With their overlord slain, how safe was it of Temerius to assume that traditional standings would be honored?

"Let us speak then of *my* duty," Barkavius rumbled at last. "To defend this atoll and its inhabitants, according to the commands given *me*. Your presence, in defiance of an acknowledged directive, constitutes a violation of—"

"I pay for the privilege," Temerius snarled. A scraping sound, accompanied by a muffled grunt, gave indication of Denariel, bound and gagged, being thrust forward among her captors. "A gift for your master. Would you refuse it?"

Whatever forewarning the steward had received regarding the princess, he seemed unsettled to set eyes upon her, given his sudden hesitation. "My lord's instructions—"

"Mean little," Temerius snapped, "with this unraveling of events."

"Events not unforeseen," Barkavius replied flatly. "Aggrieved we are," he added, regaining confidence, "all of us, by this treachery in the Pretender's court. We have mourned the loss of a great—"

"He was not *your* sire."

"A great and revered leader to us all. One who knew the risks, and accepted them. Who availed himself honorably to the end." The steward's tone remained firm, even as it edged toward conciliation. "I'm not insensitive to your desires. But this new aim of yours, it is not part of the contingency to which all agreed."

The Seahammer was unmoved. "It is a *new* contingency. Vengeance owed me, in exchange for the Pretender's daughter. Else I slit her throat and cast her to the crabs, with you as my witness."

"If that is your choice, knowing you will be held accountable."

Temerius spat. "Cursed spawn. Is it treason you fear? Rebellion?"

"Would you not? Were it a member of *your* crew acting as *you* do here?"

A small, blue-spotted fish approached Kylac's elbow before darting away again. He wondered if it, too, could sense the font of rage simmering above.

"Then permit me ashore, and me alone," Temerius said. "My crew shall remain aboard the *Kraken's Reach*. Only, entertain the favor I seek to purchase of you—at a fair price."

Another indignant grunt drawn from Denariel served to accentuate his proposal. Kylac's hands ached for his hilts. *He* was the favor Temerius sought, after all. But patience thus far had served him well. And action now would prove . . . messy.

"Liegelord," a familiar voice interjected. The Seahammer's first mate—Nemarus, if properly named in the snatches of conversation Kylac had happened upon over the past six days at sea. "I cannot advise—"

"If your advice is needed, I shall summon it," Temerius assured him. Nemarus fell silent.

"Well, steward?"

Seabirds called to each other on the evening wind. Waves licked the shore. Though none other sought to sway the outcome, Kylac felt the knuckling tension of those gathered to either side of the debate above, awaiting resolution.

"As you will," Barkavius agreed finally. "Sarki Temerius, in honor of your fallen sire, your petition is accepted, under terms that you submit to my guardianship, and that your prisoner be relinquished to the same. Your crew shall enjoy safe harbor upon your vessel, provided no effort is made to incur upon these shores, and you do nothing to violate the trust I extend to you."

"Done," Temerius snarled. "Preening wretch."

His footfalls had him stepping forward from his attendants, dragging Denariel alongside. The princess offered only the barest display of resistance, judging by her shuffling steps and the muffled grunts that escaped her gag. Enough to protest being bartered here and again like livestock, but not so much as to admit fear. If she was to proceed now into Barkavius's hands, it would be on unspoken terms of her own.

A contingent from the steward's ranks advanced to encircle both prisoner and liege captain, forming an escort ring that proceeded to tunnel inland through the other assembled defenders. Kylac remained where he crouched, giving ear to their route of departure while suppressing the urge to follow. He wouldn't be able to learn much more until he crawled out from underneath the pier, and he needn't attempt that—risking discovery in the light of day—with dusk only an hour out. He suffered a mild ache of regret at letting Denariel be hauled off again to unspecific circumstances, but having restrained himself this long, he intended to hold out just a little longer. This close to learning the whereabouts and condition of her royal brother, she wouldn't appreciate any intervention that didn't prove absolutely necessary.

If she had it within her to appreciate anything at all.

Barkavius's assembly had whittled itself down to just a score of dockside watchmen before Nemarus and the other spurned attendants from the *Kraken's Reach* turned heel and retreated to the comfort of their ship, moored at the head of the pier. Only then did Kylac wade farther in amid the deep shadows, to climb the crude slope of slick, algae-covered rocks beneath the dock at shore's edge.

Where, amid bounding sand fleas and scuttling rock crabs, he settled in to await the onset of twilight.

A BITING WIND swept across the craggy hillocks, chewing at the rugged landscape in a series of gusts and lulls like the ebb and flow of the surf below. The threat of a chill nibbled at Kylac's skin, clammy beneath his still-wet tunic and breeches. Despite the pleasant warmth of water and skies during the day, the temperature had waned with the sun. In the cloud-filtered moonlight, his damp, lightweight garb did little to repel the wind's cooling embrace.

It didn't help that he'd spent so many days now steeped in dank shadow, unable to draw on the daylight's rays. Nearly a week had he been constrained aboard the *Reach*, venturing about to eavesdrop as he was able, yet spending most of his time resigned to the bilge level. His loathing of such spaces notwithstanding, the crew's ongoing vigilance had dictated that he take no foolish chances at being discovered, which meant avoiding any of the more open or heavily trafficked areas of the ship. Only twice had he crept topside, and then at night, before delving again belowdecks. To offset his anxiety, he'd kept telling himself that if Denariel had managed it, so could he.

In that regard, a relief it was—in any conditions—to be out roaming again on dry land. Having withdrawn within himself to escape the discomfort of his confines, it hadn't been until land was sighted that he'd realized just how truly worn and stifled he'd become. Their approach to the atoll, witnessed through a thin portal in the forward hull, had seemed to span days, rather than hours. A rugged mass of earth, with stony crags scattered about her shore and shouldering skyward through thickly forested slopes, her appearance had been less than inviting. Like a thorny crone ashamed of her appearance, bristling beneath unwelcome gazes. Kylac could have greeted her with a kiss all the same.

She'd appeared uninhabited, until they'd sailed north around a western crease and down an inlet that had opened into the vast, crescent lagoon. That's when Kylac had spied the shipyards at the southern point, where he'd counted no fewer than twenty vessels resting in their berths. Colossal, leviathan-sized ships that dwarfed even Marauders like the *Vengeance* and *Denariel's Wail*. Transports, by their bearing. Light on armaments, but each boasting five, fully-rigged masts that towered over multi-level decks and a bulbous hull that might carry five hundred men or more—along with the provisions needed to sustain them over a prolonged period.

The ships and the clover-shaped docks in which they were clustered had swarmed with activity—hundreds of Grenarr at work amid the huffing of saws, pounding of hammers, scraping of sanders, and more, at a distance to merely echo labors that had been accomplished heartbeats earlier. Like ants, the workers crawled over and around their creations, streaming down from the heights of a forest that had been heavily logged, bearing fresh timber and other raw materials. The smell of smoke and pitch and sealing tar weighed heavily upon the air, refusing to be brushed aside by the persistent wind. The odor of ceaseless industry.

Curious as he may have been for a closer look, Kylac had been borne not south toward the shipyards, but north toward a network of piers on the opposite side of the sprawling lagoon. That's when he'd seen the large contingent taking up arms in order to welcome the *Reach* into port. Having recalled the conversation between Temerius and Nemarus in the Seahammer's quarters on his first night aboard, along with similar discussions whispered throughout the ship since, Kylac had recognized straightaway that he needed to place himself near the heart of whatever debate was to ensue between shipboard captain and land-bound steward. That they'd been permitted to venture this far inland without opposition might signify a lesser degree of hostility than Kylac had feared. It might also indicate any other number of tactics, including that Barkavius had used his ships instead to wall off any retreat.

To avoid being spotted, he'd slipped back out through the rudder housing before swimming up beneath the pier—after assuring himself, as he had throughout his journey aboard the *Reach*, that Denariel remained undamaged.

His first order of business now was the same.

His route appeared obvious—a broad, solitary roadway that snaked from the lagoon shore along a northerly route toward a mountainous pinnacle of rock. The only other road of significant breadth hugged the lagoon en route to the shipyards, and that wasn't the direction in which Barkavius's company had departed. Kylac had avoided, and continued to avoid, the road itself, for it was heavily trafficked even now, well after sunset, brightly illuminated with flaming stanchions and the lanterns of passersby. But there dwelled to either side thick pools of shadow amid the sparse fields, barren ridges, and wildgrass slopes of the flanking landscape, cut through by ravines and animal trails, dotted with spiny growth. Under cloak of nightfall, aided by a partial screen of clouds, more cover than he required.

He carried with him a nervous roiling, not unlike that which had accompanied him in his quest to liberate the Sea Scribe. An elsewise rare and discomfiting sensation that he knew better than to ignore. Yet, as before, he couldn't let it stop him. Merely a byproduct, likely as not, of the mounting stakes here within the heart of the enemy, amid the Blackmoon Shards. If in truth that was where he'd been delivered. The only name he'd overheard for their destination while aboard the *Reach* was that of Grenathrok. A promising sign, given its obvious resonance. Grenah. Grendavan. Grenarr. However widespread their settlements, if this turned out to be anything but their central atoll . . . well, he'd staked and won more on less likely wagers.

As he drew nearer the mountainous peak at the end of the twisting roadway, he came to realize an increasing number of pinprick lights as lamps and torches burning within the bluff's pitted face. Caves. The mountain was riddled with them. A stronghold, then, fashioned among the tunnels and caverns that likely honeycombed its interior. A shelter against invasion, yes, but more commonly against the savage sea storms inhabiting this region of the world, said to spawn with little warning and lay waste to low-lying landmasses such as this.

Cresting a rise between slabs of crumbled limestone, he came to see the glow of a village at the peak's base, comprised of hut-like structures erected of wood and reed. Impermanent buildings that had likely been rebuilt more than once over the nearly two centuries that the Grenarr had resided here. Sturdy enough, but poorly suited to any finer comforts. At this distance, the overall settlement resembled a patch of mushrooms sprouted amid the roots of a rotting tree stump. Plain it seemed as to why this people would want to return to Addaranth—or its more hospitable regions, anyway. Ancestral homeland or not, its fertile soil and other resources offered a bounty of sustenance difficult to achieve or maintain here, no matter how well supplemented by ill-gotten means.

He considered slipping down and through the village proper, to see what more he might learn from the people themselves, before deciding it could wait. Denariel and Dethaniel—Nara and Thane—remained his priority. After learning where and how Kendarrion's children were being held, *then* would he set about determining their most likely method of rescue. During which time he would likely find ample opportunity for further explorations.

So he scaled instead a sheer, fissured escarpment that brought him to a ridgeline stretching down from the peak like a root tendril, and followed that narrow, inaccessible track to reach the outer skin of the mountain proper. He spied no watchmen, though he sensed the gazes of men set as lookouts amid some of the peak's more elevated ledges. Had he been carrying a flame, they might have spotted him. Trusting as he did to dim starlight and his own sure footing, he stole upon their fortress without alerting them to his presence.

For his entrance into the mountain, he selected a dark cave mouth along the southern face, slightly elevated from his position of approach. Here, he was forced to proceed more cautiously. For all the strength of its limestone foundation, the peak's weather-worn hide was encrusted with loose rock, easily fractured were he lazy with his grip. A sprinkling of dust or pebbles wasn't likely to betray him. But he didn't wish to trigger a larger rockslide that would.

He paused upon reaching the targeted cave mouth, listening to the rasping echoes from within, reading from them what he could. Impossible to predict just where this particular tunnel would lead, or how fully interconnected the mountain's inner passages might be. Hearing nothing to suggest a dead end, he set forth to find out.

Stealing like a wraith amid the shadows, he spent the better part of the night exploring the warren inside the peak, committing to memory the various branches of its twisting, twining layout. Through corridors and caverns he delved, many of them inhabited, others filled only with stolen riches and supply hoards. He measured distances as he proceeded, gradually mapping within his head its halls and chambers, chutes and chimneys, open pockets and hidden caches. A sprawling complex, spanning levels that wormed over and around one another. Much of it felt random, formed by nature. Other areas had clearly been shaped and guided by human hand, molded to specific purposes.

The latter was what led him eventually to the skyward reaches, where he finally happened upon a cluster of prison cells nestled along the eastern face. He'd intended to reach them sooner, but had incorrectly guessed that such a dungeon wing would be found nearer the foot of the mountain than its peak. He came to understand why, if more accurate in his ensuing assumption, when he found a corridor among the cells that led to a precipice overlooking a plummeting gorge. Even from its towering heights, he could make out the faint reflection of wan starlight where it met with the broad pile of bleached bones below.

As effective as any gallows, it appeared.

A pair of sentries at dice within a forward antechamber alerted him to a closed door behind them at the deepest heart of the dungeon complex. After gauging the position of their unseen charges beyond, he returned to the execution platform, if that's what it was, and used it to venture out again along the peak's face. Navigating another bluff that few men would dare attempt to scale—particularly at these heights, buffeted by treacherous wind gusts—he investigated a series of barred vents serving as high-set windows, peering in on the rough-hewn chambers beyond.

The first chamber lay empty. As did the second. Though the cliff wall steepened as he rounded the next fold, he continued undaunted. The anticipation of his voyage coming to a long-awaited resolution served to counter his simmering, undefined anxiety. Attainment in some substantial form lay near at hand. He need only extend his reach, just a little farther.

His resolve rewarded him moments later with a view of Denariel curled up in a corner of her cramped cell. She rested upon a thin sleeping pallet no more than two paces beyond the wall of rock that separated them, shivering beneath a threadbare blanket. An iron collar around her neck shackled her to the inner wall. She'd been fitted with a branks, presumably to bridle her tongue. Amid his relief, Kylac felt a familiar pang. Had she not endured enough already, that she should be made to suffer petty torments such as this?

Tamping down a natural impulse to free her then and there, to let her know he hadn't abandoned her as she must suppose, Kylac proceeded past, skirting along a toe-deep crease in the rock face that ran toward the next window. Finding it empty, he continued to the next.

And there discovered Prince Dethaniel.

Or so he presumed. For who else could it be? His skin was much paler than his sister's, yet that was to be expected of a full-blooded Addaran. Seeking more suitable comparison, Kylac tried to see in him some aspect of Kendarrion's frame or facial structure. But the prisoner's conditions mirrored Denariel's—spare pallet, chained neck collar, and a rag of a blanket that left little to gauge. His exposed cheek was covered by an unruly beard, coarsely trimmed. So, how to make certain?

The corridor beyond the inner bars of the cell lay dark. The attending sentries were stationed at its far end, on the opposite side of at least one ironwood door. Kylac considered the risks in waking the presumed prince, and deemed them minimal. Should he panic or cry out, Kylac could scuttle from view and leave the guards to think their captive had been stricken by nightmare.

He tried a warbling whistle. The prisoner's slumber was restless already. Kylac didn't believe it would take much to wake him.

When that failed, Kylac pried a small stone from the cliff face and cast it through the bars of the window vent. The captive prince reacted at once, slapping his own ear and repositioning himself on his pallet, albeit without opening his eyes.

Kylac whistled again. This time, it brought Dethaniel's lids fluttering open. A moment later, his sleep-fogged gaze found Kylac staring in on him.

"Shards—"

Kylac hissed for silence. Dethaniel obliged him, though his chain clanked as he scrambled into a sitting position, pressing his back against the wall and drawing his knees to his chest.

"I's not come to harm ya," Kylac said, his voice a whisper just heavy enough to be heard. "Your Highness?"

The prince blinked and rubbed at his eyes. "What? Who are you?"

"Show me your hands."

"My hands?"

"Your fingers."

He waited another moment for Dethaniel's hazy awareness to crystallize. When it did, the prince obliged him by raising his hands, spreading his fingers to reveal the gap where his royal signet ring had once resided.

A ring and finger sent months ago to his noble father—and then his sister—to warn against further delay in complying with his captors' demands.

"I am Dethaniel," he confirmed, withdrawing his damaged hands from view. "Son of Kendarrion." An invisible darkness brewed about his furrowing brow. "You must be Kronus."

Kylac's surprise was mild and fleeting. "I fear again, my reputation precedes me."

"A rough account only, shared by my captors, of events at my sister's wedding." The prince's voice was raspy, harsh with more than thirst. His tone conveyed disappointment, accusation. Understandable, given that his suffering had been prolonged on account of the actions to which he referred.

Kylac's actions.

By contrast, Kylac could scarcely bridle his delight. Dethaniel was alive—of no guarantee since the moment of his abduction, and steeped in greater doubt since the now infamous wedding. Beyond that, he appeared in remarkably good health for one help captive in these conditions for so long. Filthy and sleep-deprived, but unbattered, unbruised. Save for his finger, unharmed in any way that Kylac could discern. And even that injury appeared to have healed over as best it would.

"What exactly did they tells ya?"

"That you slew Grendavan. Stabbed him in the back before slaughtering his entire retinue. All of whom were unarmed."

Not quite, but near enough. Kylac saw no need to set straight the details—even if he'd believed the captive prince might be receptive to them.

"My sister's doing, surely. Yet they hold my father to blame."

"Neither spurred my hand. The deed was my own."

"For what cause?"

"Yours, ultimately. Or did your jailors not tells ya to expect me?"

"They made mention of such intent." Dethaniel coughed. "They're going to kill you. And me, most likely. And Nara, now that you've dragged her out into this."

As if she hadn't been deeply involved and terribly endangered already. Prepped like a lamb for slaughter. Served to Grendavan in exchange for her brother's freedom. Judging by his present frustration, Dethaniel hadn't been particularly troubled by that arrangement.

"They's kept ya this long," Kylac reassured him. "Only to discard ya?"

"You murdered their kiros. Why should the next repeat the folly of his predecessor?"

"Because your father is now doubly beholden to them. They's gone to a great deal o' trouble to forgo their fiendish accord now, has they not?"

The scowling prince closed his eyes, kneading the root of his nose with a thumb and forefinger as if to ward off headache. "We can only hope."

"Then they hasn't professed some other aim?"

"For what value it may hold, no. If they don't kill us . . ." the prince's features tightened with his contemplations. "It would be as before. Return me as promised, now that Nara is in their possession. They'll want to land their colony ships first, of course, as assurance against further treachery. For that, they'll need to petition my father's consent."

"And how long might that take?"

"The delivery of their demands, and reception of a response—even if acknowledged and accepted forthwith—would require no less than a week. And that a'wing on their cursed shrikes."

"Anything else they might be waiting for?"

The angry furrows in Dethaniel's forehead deepened. "Such as?"

Kylac couldn't know. Hence the question. The nervousness in his belly had yet to be appeased. Finding the prince and confirming what he'd already been told had done little to satisfy it. Meaning there was more here, yet to be learned.

But as the prince had suggested, he could hardly expect a captive to know precisely what his jailors intended, and would be foolish in any case to accept such knowledge as truth.

His concerns just now were more practical in nature. "Just wondering how long we might has."

"For what?"

"Springing ya from this cage."

Dethaniel laughed. It burst free before he could prevent it. He stifled it at once, maimed hand covering his lips, but looked all the same to the inner bars of his cell, anticipating response.

None came. Kylac himself was unconcerned. The sound had been no louder than the winds skirling through the window or clawing at the peak's rugged hide.

After a moment, Dethaniel lowered his guard, though his voice reclaimed its whisper. "When? How? Unshackle me from this rock, and where would we go? Have you a ship and crew standing by? One that has any hope of bearing us away before the Grenarr catch up to us?"

"I'll sees to it before I makes my move."

The prince shook his head, causing the links in his neck chain to clink softly. His warring emotions were difficult to read. An odd measure of seeming contradictions—relief and anger, humor and sadness, triumph and defeat. Unsurprising, Kylac supposed. After so many weeks in captivity, this abrupt turn must have constituted a significant shock.

"Perhaps it'd be better for me," Dethaniel reckoned, "that you not interfere."

"Too late for that, most would say." Off the prince's frown, he added, "I see not how it'd harm your chances. Me, they want for revenge. You, for gain." Were they to be recaptured, what would change? If Dethaniel truly believed the Grenarr might kill him, attempting escape seemed a fair gamble.

The sullen prince had no response. After double-checking his precarious surroundings, Kylac proceeded then to question him about logistical matters. Did they tend to transport him between cells, or was this his sole location? What were their guard rotations? How often was he fed? He received mostly flat, tentative responses. He couldn't quite tell if Dethaniel's hesitation bespoke a willful deterrence, or genuine ignorance. Either way, he took note of the prince's reluctance and uncertainty, and weighed the information's potential worth accordingly.

"Tell me this," Kylac begged at last. "What makes ya believe the Grenarr may honor their accord, when your sister is adamant they won't?"

An honest regret seemed to settle about Dethaniel's shoulders, and resonate in his sigh. "Nara has ever been wild. Her hatred consumes her. Above all, she cannot forgive the Grenarr for our mother's . . . what they did to her."

Her ravishing. The one that had resulted in Denariel's birth. "And *you* can?"

"Whatever my grievances, I'm in a poor position to argue them."

Granted, easier indeed to protest when not shackled and made subject to the enemy's whims. The prince's abduction had denied him the same freedom with which Denariel had been given to act. Still, Kylac would be willing to wager that, even now, the princess would gladly submit to torture and death if it meant defeating the Grenarr's aims. Her brother clearly had a stronger sense of self-preservation.

"I'll sees to any arguments from here," Kylac assured him.

"And your stake in this is what, again?"

"Just cling to your wits, and summon your strength. The next time ya sees me, we makes for your royal home."

36

Leaving the shackled prince to hiss furtively after him, Kylac retreated back along the mountain bluff. Dethaniel might have further questions, but Kylac had answered all he cared to at this juncture, and asked already more of his own than necessary. The Woodcock's Hour had given way to the Shrike's. Half the night had passed, and he still had matters to accomplish before daybreak.

He hoped he hadn't made a mistake in revealing himself to the prince. Difficult it would have been to verify the prisoner's identity elsewise, and to confirm that the assumptions he'd been acting under remained valid insofar as Dethaniel knew. With the prevailing fear that his assassination of Grendavan might have caused the Grenarr to alter their plans, he took it as a great relief to learn that all likelihoods indicated they hadn't. Still, a risk to have exposed himself. Might the prince surrender word of his presence, willingly or *unwillingly*? If so, how might that complicate his plans for their escape?

Of course, *plans* would be a generous description. As Dethaniel had observed, freeing the prince and his sister could prove troublesome enough. Escorting them safely from the atoll constituted another challenge altogether. They couldn't hope to sail an ocean-worthy ship by themselves, even if they managed to steal off with one. And it seemed highly unlikely that he'd be able to persuade an entire crew of Grenarr to serve him in doing so. Which meant he was still relying on Ledron and Ithrimir to find their way here with the *Wail*. But how long might that take? How to know if they were even progressing along that course?

If for any number of reasons his former companions failed to arrive, Kylac trusted that, at some point, the Grenarr would pack up Kendarrion's stolen children and carry them elsewhere—hopefully back to Addaranth, as promised. Whatever, he would deal with that eventuality when it arose. The more immediate question was, where to lure the *Wail*, should she come, so as to escape the notice of Grenarr lookouts or patrolmen scattered around the atoll's perimeter?

For that, he continued scaling higher upon the weathered slopes of the mountain stronghold, seeking a better vantage of the surrounding terrain. Having drawn near its summit, he took pause upon a narrow shelf to see what the starlit heavens might reveal. As the highest ground upon the atoll, it actually provided a mostly unobstructed view of the crescent-shaped landscape below, from the lagoon south, to the forests east and curling farther south, and to the ocean waters that cradled it all.

In surveying those distant expanses, he spied numerous freestanding rock formations, posted around the atoll's shores like ageless sentinels set at watch. Most, however, appeared too squat, too lean, or poorly angled—in one or more ways insufficient to mask a tall-masted vessel such as the *Wail* from searching eyes. Others that might prove large enough sat at a distance difficult for him to reach. Ideally, he required a meeting location that could both conceal the ship's approach *and* enable him to remain ashore Grenathrok, so as to maintain vigil over the pair of royal captives he intended to free.

He permitted himself time in this endeavor, setting his gaze adrift, quieting his thoughts and allowing instinct to guide him. He settled at last upon a cluster of tusklike monoliths forming a sort of cage not more than a league offshore to the east. Farther than he would have liked, but offering suitable cover in the absence of dead angles. Though he searched awhile longer, he found no better option.

Feeling determined if not confident in his choice, he committed a number of landmarks to memory, then began his descent.

An hour, it took him, to wend and scurry his way down the peak and back across the outskirts of the now mostly sleeping settlement to return to the lagoon. Retracing the route of his arrival beneath the pier, he swam out to the stern of the moored *Reach* and plucked his dagger from her transom. No reason to leave it there, now that he had a better location in mind.

The remainder of the Vulture's Hour and the beak of the Sparrow's saw him cutting east across the rocky woodlands comprising the atoll's midriff, veering northward as he approached the far shoreline. The Sparrow's tail marked his league-long swim out to the cluster of towering rocks he'd dubbed the Tusks. Relieved he was to discern at that point—with a series of sweeping dives—that the waters were deep enough to accommodate a Marauder's draft, should one seek to anchor among them. Hoping he wasn't mistaken, he planted his beacon-serving dagger within a limestone fissure beneath the low-tide waterline, then crawled to a crevasse perch atop a barnacle-laden outcrop.

There, within a craggy, salt-stained nook, he discovered an abandoned gull's nest, and so helped himself to the eggs. By then, the Thrush's Hour was fast approaching. Given the sky's color, the final full hour before dawn. Thinking to conserve his remaining energies for a time in which they might be put to better use, Kylac folded his limbs in close, leaned back against the scabrous rock, and closed his eyes, settling in to wait.

Once again, to wait.

HE AWOKE just before midday, when a surge of sunlight chased the shadows from his nook and warmed him from his dreams. A momentary panic gripped him when he failed to recognize his surroundings or how he'd come to inhabit them. The mournful cry of a seabird, however, followed by the restless moan of waters heaving against the base of rock below him, triggered a string of memories that carried him from the bowels of the *Kraken's Reach* through the events of the previous night. Abruptly, he recalled where he'd secreted himself, and why.

He searched the ocean's horizons. Finding nothing but the glint and glare of sunlight sparkling against vast swaths of rock-strewn waters to the north, east, and south, he turned his focus west, through a window in his rocky shelf to the atoll of Grenathrok. Its forested ridges appeared quiet. From this vantage, the small land might well be deserted.

Knowing elsewise, Kylac set forth to see what other secrets it might harbor. A better use of his day than sunbathing amid the briny growth and tiny creatures clinging to the Tusks. The swim proved invigorating—due in part to his accompanying search for sharks or other sea-dwelling life that might enjoy stripping the flesh from his bones. By the time he crept ashore again, the unusual disorientation and lethargy that had plagued his waking had burned away like morning mist.

He caught and feasted on a pair of crabs found skittering through the shoreline undergrowth, and washed the raw meat down with milk from a shagnut harvested from a tree at the forest's fringe. He supplemented this with some wild roots and berries once he'd ventured deeper into the coastal woodland. Along the way, he kept watch for any sign of Grenarr patrol or native wildlife that might differ in the daylight hours from what he'd seen at night. As before, the land was mostly silent, inhabited by little more than insects, birds, and rodents.

He steered a southwesterly course, following the contours of the shoreline, thinking to explore the foot of the atoll as he had its head. The woods grew thicker to the south, the earth a mite less rocky. He observed a vast number of grompike groves, the rare tree no longer seeming rare at all. Doubtless, a key reason why the Grenarr had settled here, as it provided them ample quantities of the precious sap used in the construction of their ships. Or mayhap they'd settled the atoll for other reasons and discovered the grompike's special properties later. Regardless, it appeared to be *one* valuable commodity, at least, of which they had plenty.

Of life, he continued to find scant sign. No villages, no hamlets, no settlements whatsoever beyond the occasional outpost erected amid the trees or bald bluffs around the atoll's perimeter. And most of these were deserted. More and more, it appeared the Grenarr lived only within or at the base of their rocky stronghold to the north. While it remained possible he might find encampments deeper within the forest interior, he came across no trails that would suggest as much.

And why should he? Settlements required resources. Soils in which to sow and harvest crops. Fresh water in the form of river or spring. Packs of wild game for huntsmen to chase. Kylac found none of that here to the south. A Grenarr Prowler strayed past at one point, its nets squirming with captured fish. And he did happen across a mother and son collecting oysters from a sediment-laden promontory. But it seemed again that what little was to be reaped from this atoll was as easily gathered nearer the lagoon at its heart.

His circuit brought him at last to the southern rim of that body of water, where stood the shipyards witnessed upon his arrival. These bristled with activity. Upon closer examination, Kylac saw that the majority of the vessels remained unfinished—though nearing completion. The laborers and craftsmen passing over and through the ships were engaged chiefly in final touches—sanding, binding, carving, sealing, and the like. Bits of lumber lowered or carried belowdecks gave indication of internal construction still taking place, but nothing of a structural nature. He saw no frameworks, nor a single empty berth. This clutch of leviathans had been raised together as a single brood, and would reach maturity at roughly the same time.

A time fast approaching.

Colony ships, Dethaniel had mentioned. Surely, these were one and the same. For Kylac couldn't imagine a more suitable purpose for this impressive collection of colossal vessels. He wondered in the same breath as to the lack of warships—to make no mention of the warriors themselves. If the northern peak served indeed as Grenath-rok's only settlement, then the atoll held no more than seven, eight thousand souls in all. Could that truly constitute the heart of the Grenarr nation?

But then, the heart of their nation was said to be seafaring. *More than a hundred great vessels,* Tormitius Shorecleaver had boasted. Pirate crews, one and all. Kylac had to wonder how many of these were now harrying the Addaran coastline, taking what petty vengeance they could upon the Pretender and his landsnakes for the murder of their overlord. He considered how much time had passed, and wondered at the damage that might have already been inflicted. He wondered as to what the ultimate cost might be—to both sides—before this conflict subsided.

While observing the streams of shipbuilders passing to and from the surrounding woodland, he considered abducting one or more for interrogative purposes. But he hesitated to set off any unnecessary alarms that might result in increased vigilance on the part of his adversaries. The more time that passed without incident, the less guarded they were apt to be against his impending rescue attempt. He could of course dispose of the body in a manner that made the death appear accidental, but he didn't relish having to kill any who might be innocent of this power struggle initiated by their leaders. Assuming such innocence, he couldn't expect to learn much of import from them in any case.

In the end, he decided against it. He knew what he needed to. The remainder was little more than dressing. If important, it would come to light in due time, to be dealt with as required.

He spent the remainder of the afternoon and evening crisscrossing the southern forests themselves. Doing so confirmed what he'd already supposed. Here and there, he happened across Grenarr foraging for all manner of vegetation—berries, flowers, roots, leaves, mushrooms, oils, and more. Others collected worms, beetles, ants, and leeches, or ensnared snakes, lizards, mice, and rabbits. Birds were felled or netted, and eggs gathered. But he encountered no boar, no deer—nothing larger than an island fox. Nor did he brush paths with any but small, scattered groups of gatherers. He discovered no grain fields, no vegetable plots, outside those cultivated nearer the lagoon and village. He ran across no wells, and only brackish streams. The atoll's freshwater supplies appeared to be collected entirely from rainfall, funneled into cisterns. Else delivered in stolen barrels, along with all other materials used to supplement this people's meager subsistence.

Were it not for their pirating efforts, Kylac conceded, life here would be much worse. Sustainable, but only barely—and for far fewer than inhabited the atoll now. It fostered in him a newfound respect for the Grenarr's tenacity, their ability to persevere. It caused him to wish that people could work as diligently at resolving their differences, learning to share.

But those were larger issues, beyond his ability to affect. As of late, he'd found the balancing of smaller, personal injustices to pose challenge enough.

With twilight's descent, he turned east again and swam back out to the Tusks, there to spend another night's vigil in anticipation of the *Wail*'s arrival. But the dawn revealed the same vista of crystalline waters, empty save for the peppering of sentinel rocks lording over the swells. So he returned to Grenathrok, foraging and exploring as he had the previous day. This time, he concentrated on the northern half of the atoll. Finding little of interest, and less of concern, he chose again to penetrate the mountain stronghold and make further study of its worming halls. Therein, he looked in on Denariel and Dethaniel, but resisted the temptation to engage them. Aside from verifying their safe condition, his focus was on keeping an ear out for any stray gossip echoing through the halls, and on searching for potential escape routes. After all, he wouldn't be able to lead them from the mountain along even a tenth of the routes he himself used. He would need a more straightforward pathway—one that wouldn't result in any dead ends.

He repeated this process the next day, when Ledron didn't arrive. And again the next. And again the next. Roaming by day, returning to the Tusks at night in hope of sighting the *Wail*. Staying active, making use of his time, helped to quiet the foul whispers in the back of his mind. That his former shipmates weren't coming. That he might have to maintain this routine for weeks or even months before the Grenarr made a move. The uncertainty formed a thorn in his resolve, urging him to rethink his own motives and decisions.

Nothing he couldn't endure. His choices were limited enough at this point that it scarcely helped to reconsider his course. Even if he was inclined to abandon this venture, he was trapped until occasion should present him the opportunity to depart.

Nor would he seek it. He'd come too far to forsake the princess and her brother now. Doing so would only reinforce her opinions of him. If nothing else, he intended to deny her that particular satisfaction.

Whether through faith, patience, lack of options, or sheer willfulness, his persistence was rewarded when, in the darkness before dawn of the sixth day of his vigil, he stirred to an unusual sound amid the rhythm of the swells. Rousing from his rocky perch amid the Tusks, he looked toward the disruption, and smiled to find a skeletal-faced maiden gliding toward him over the black waters, the ghostly outline of a barbarian Marauder limned in starlight behind her.

37

"WEAK WINDS?" KYLAC ASKED, as he climbed from the rope ladder through a gap in the ship's rail to find Ledron awaiting him. Flanking the captain were burly Havrig and brawny Jorrand, their pikes at the ready. Taeg stood at their backs with a secondary clutch of Redfists, who marveled at the sight of Kylac's return.

The Head scowled. "Meaning?"

"We arrived six nights past. I'd expected ya sooner."

Ledron gritted his teeth. "Where's Her Highness?"

"Unharmed," Kylac assured him. "Well tended."

"*Where?*"

"A cave ashore. Atop a natural stronghold. Prince Dethaniel is with her."

Ledron stiffened, his countenance wrangling both skepticism and hope. "You've seen him? His Highness?"

"Spoken." Kylac eyed again the ready pikes of the Head's attendants. "If'n the captain will permit it, I'll gladly tell him what more I's learned."

Feeling foolish for it now, he'd anticipated a warmer welcome. Upon spotting the *Wail*'s final approach to the Tusks, Kylac had waved to her lookouts, then descended from his perch to retrieve his beacon blade and swim out toward the slowing vessel. A string of familiar faces had lined the rail before the ladder had been cast down, inviting him aboard. They'd greeted him wordlessly, mindful of any noise that might betray them. But their expressions and gestures, teeming with unspoken relief, had revealed a general excitement at having found him again.

That was before they'd been brushed aside or drawn back by Ledron and his gathered soldiers. Their quiet enthusiasm continued to spread throughout the ship, accompanied by a prevailing sense of awe. Those reactions, however, had been supplanted by the captain's cheerless, appraising reception.

Finally, the Head gestured. Havrig and Jorrand eased in their stances, leaving Kylac to wonder, what might their response have been had he delivered less promising word?

Irrelevant now. The captain turned on a heel, beckoning Kylac after. Havrig and Jorrand waited for him to follow. Taeg spared him a nod, then motioned to Irryn, who promptly bent to retrieve the rope ladder at Kylac's back.

Kylac took a pair of strides in pursuit of the captain before halting and calling ahead. "We'd do better to retreat east." The Tusks may well have screened the *Wail*'s nighttime approach as intended, but they would be less apt to do so throughout the long daylight hours. "Best to make our plans farther from sight."

Ledron frowned, but nodded at Taeg, who promptly signaled the nearest Whitefists. "Prepare to come about," said the first mate.

While the command and the crew's reactions rippled outward, Kylac proceeded aft on the captain's heels. Those whose gazes he captured continued to reflect amazement. For all his own doubts over the past few days, Kylac could scarcely imagine those of his erstwhile and newfound shipmates. They'd have had only Ithrimir's claim to go by, that he could sense and track Kylac's movements. This tacked on to the assumption that Kylac still lived and could lead them someplace worthwhile. Leaving them nothing more than their trust in a rogue outlander and wild Elementer—and their own desperation—to sustain them in the dubious endeavor.

And Ledron.

"A testament to your leadership, Captain, this reunion of ours."

The Head half turned to reveal an arched brow. "Is that gratitude?" He snorted. "Save it for that relic of a creature you call the Sea Scribe, and for Taeg's faith in him."

Unsurprising. But the ship's ultimate voice belonged to Ledron. The argument that both Denariel and Kylac—and even Dethaniel— were dead by now would have been vocal and widespread. That their mission was therefore hopeless would have been difficult to refute. That they might do better to steer for home? Impossible to deny. Whatever the counsel of his chosen advisors, it was Ledron who would have faced down that mounting pressure from the majority of the crew. A dutiful commander, ever loyal to his king's wishes.

"What o' Sanow?" Kylac asked.

The captain's roiling expression blended fury with sorrow. "An example."

Executed, then. Kylac felt the sting of Ledron's regret. Unfortunate, but necessary, if the captain had resorted to such. Though shorthanded already, what guarantee would they have had that the Blackfist wouldn't simply seek again to sabotage their efforts? Unstable as the crew had become, and with so much uncertainty still ahead, the Head must have determined he had no choice but to renew his convictions in a manner that all would witness and remember.

"Any sense he opposed us from the outset?"

A difficult question, scraping against a raw wound. But Kylac wanted to know how likely it was that they yet had a mole aboard.

Ledron glanced at his attending Redfists before answering, his angry expression still pained. "He gave no such indication. But who's to say?"

Kylac caught just a glimpse of Ithrimir eyeing him from the wheelhouse as the captain descended a hatch amidships. With a gesture of salute to the Elementer, Kylac followed belowdecks, Havrig and Jorrand on his heels.

They continued aft to a vacant, windowless cabin, stacked with pallets built into either sidewall. After motioning Kylac inside, Ledron commanded the pair of Redfists to stand sentry.

"None enter unannounced," he said, then closed the door.

Kylac had hoped for a general council including the ship's other officers, so as to be able to relay what he'd learned only once. But he could understand if Ledron wished to hear it all for himself first, and thereafter determine what might be shared. Already, Kylac felt the itch of confinement. He wondered if Ledron had selected this location with his discomfort in mind.

The captain turned to face him, his body blocking the exit, folding his arms against his chest. "So. Tell me."

"Is there a plan, then?" asked Taeg.

With his back to the ship's wheel, the first mate stood awash in the morning rays streaming in through the wheelhouse window. Kylac could scarcely eye him against the intense glare. After two hours of sail, the *Wail* had left Grenathrok beyond the western horizon, anchoring finally near a shoal beside yet another spear of rock upthrust from the submerged seabed. But they'd left her facing east, into the freshly risen sun.

"There is," said Ledron, "if his account is to be believed."

His account being that of Kylac's adventures since their separation, relayed first to the captain, and now *by* the captain to Taeg and Ithrimir here in the wheelhouse. The former conversation, held in private, had consumed nearly two hours, marked by a boundless stream of questions from Ledron, and followed by a thorough discussion regarding possible strategies for springing the royal captives. The latter recounting had passed much more swiftly, with the Head omitting events and observations deemed of lesser interest, to focus on what Kylac had learned about the nature of the atoll and its inhabitants.

"Has I given the captain cause for doubt?"

Ledron gritted his teeth, then gestured at the larboard chart table. "Show them."

Kylac advanced, accepting the stylus offered him by Ithrimir. As usual, he could read little from the Elementer's expression, save that he was less than pleased, and probably less interested in pleasing. Prior to Ledron's recitation, Kylac had thanked both navigator and first mate for their faith and perseverance in following him here. Taeg had confessed that he'd initially feared the Scribe might be misleading them in that pursuit, claiming to be able to track Kylac for no better cause than a perceived life debt. But Ithrimir had evidently dismissed that notion as absurd. Any such debt had already been paid. Moreover, if the Dragon continued unchecked, they were all likely to perish soon enough. He swore only as to what he *could* do. He made no assertion as to whether they *should*.

Hardly encouraging when Kylac had heard it, and no more so to think on it now. A sad reminder that he had no allies among this crew. Even when individual actions might suggest as much, he could assume other, more selfish interests to be at play.

Stylus in hand, he leaned over the blank wax tablet provided, with the cabin's occupants looming in turn over his shoulders.

"We'll launch from the Tusks," he began, making his first marks, "within a pair o' shore boats. As we did upon the Scribe's isle," he added, with a purposeful glance at Ithrimir—to no reaction. "Two teams this time. A small company under our captain's direct command, a pair o' decoys with me. We travel together here, to their stronghold, and enter along a series o' natural bolt-holes. After freeing the royals, we separate. The pair with me, disguised as Dethaniel and Denariel, will serve diversion, drawing pursuit, while the captain's crew leads our real highnesses back out along a mapped course."

"Like that?" Taeg asked. "Without resistance?"

"The number o' guards is limited. I do my part, Captain should be able to handle any strays."

Taeg grunted, but eyed Ledron with a wary look.

"Captain returns east, to his boat, and makes for the Tusks," Kylac continued. "Those with me divert south, toward the lagoon, as if'n to steal a ship. Here," he marked, after tracing a vague outline of the lagoon shore, "we scale a cliff by way o' pulley system laid by their work crews. Climb, cut the ropes to stall pursuit, and return to the remaining boat. Challenge will be to reach the *Wail* before she sets sail," he acknowledged, with an edge to his tone. "But if'n I can misdirect the enemy hunt as intended, it should take them some time to scramble their own ships—and on the wrong side o' the atoll. And once we reach the water, our Scribe here can mark my progress, so ya won't have to wonder when and where I'm en route."

Kylac hoped that these latter conditions would prove sufficient to buy Ledron's patience. The Head had threatened already to depart without him and his decoys if for any reason they were detained. Agreeable enough, in that any claim to the contrary would have been an obvious lie. Still, Kylac would sooner they wait, and genuinely believed that the agreed-upon strategy should allow for it.

"Short a few details, I'd say it sketches out reasonably enough," Taeg admitted. "Taken from a man once dead already, I suppose I'd be foolish to wager against it."

They dedicated the remainder of the morning to clarifying the particulars to which the first mate referred. While Taeg disseminated the proposed strategy and selected crewmembers for specific assignments, Kylac worked with Ledron and Ithrimir to map the precise course the captain was to take in his escape with the royal captives. Concerning the latter, Kylac had expected few arguments, as he'd been the only one to explore the warren in question. But Ithrimir did interject at one point to indicate a length of tunnel beneath the stronghold that Kylac hadn't considered.

"That stretch is submerged."

"Only during the king's tide," Ithrimir contended. "During the knave's, it is exposed, and would cut the length of retreat through these burrows by half."

Kylac thought to question the Scribe's assertion, but decided that it touched too closely upon the unfathomable nature of the Elementer's particular domain. "Then it would depend on the hour," he remarked instead.

"Cling to your timetables, and the tube will be clear," Ithrimir insisted.

Kylac looked to Ledron. "I won't be with ya at that juncture. Your call."

The Head looked as if he'd been asked to drink sour milk. "We've come too far for me to refuse either of you my faith now." With a heavy sigh, he determined, "We'll take the shorter route."

Which would grant the captain's company an even greater advance

Eldon Thompson

on the *Wail* than before. Kylac considered reducing the length of his own diversionary course in response, but ultimately resolved against it. Ledron was indeed placing an incredible amount of trust in him with regard to this venture. He would simply have to demonstrate in the captain a similar confidence.

An uneasy choice, given prior experience on this voyage.

When all had been settled as best it could be in advance, they went over it a second time in painstaking detail, this time with those individuals Taeg had selected to accompany them. Then they reviewed it again, for good measure. With the heat of the afternoon bearing down on them, a weary Ledron finally ordered their shore party and the bulk of the crew to rest, in anticipation of a long night.

Upon waking, they revisited the plan one last time. By then, those going ashore had committed their roles to memory. Ledron would be joined in his escape by Redfists Havrig, Jorrand, Sethric, Simalen, Jethmus, and Moh. Assigned to Kylac with the aim of impersonating Dethaniel and Denariel were Talon and Creyl. Though he'd been offered no voice in their selection, he could think of none he'd prefer in their stead.

Whitefists Nadrum and Warmund would row one boat, Irryn and Stannon the other, and would remain at watch over the vessels. Upon Ledron's return from the stronghold, Simalen, Moh, and Jethmus would stay behind with Irryn and Stannon to await Kylac's arrival, making room in Ledron's boat for the prince and princess. It would fall to Sim to determine how long they tarried, with the understanding that, should he wait *too* long, he risked abandonment of his entire party alongside that of their favorite rogue.

Threats and cautions notwithstanding, Kylac liked their chances. A nagging form of the anxiety that had deepened in him since his arrival upon Grenathrok seemed to suggest he must have missed something. He paid it scant heed. Triumph or tragedy, the night promised a measure of excitement that had recently gone missing.

As dusk settled across the sea, Taeg gave the command to weigh anchor. Moments later, the Marauder come to be known as *Denariel's Wail* filled her sails and eased westward, in slow pursuit of the setting sun.

38

KYLAC ALLOWED THE JAILORS at the table to look up before letting his daggers fly. Not to offer them a fighting chance, because they had none. He just felt it courteous, when stealing a life, to meet the man's gaze before doing so.

Whenever possible, anyway.

The jailor to his left fumbled for the bone whistle strung about his neck. The other reached hastily for his sword hilt, knocking a pair of alabaster figurines from the table and whatever game of strategy they'd been engaged in. Before those figurines had struck the floor, Kylac's spinning blades had pierced the jailors' throats.

Both men stiffened in shock, fighting reflexively to carry out their final motions, yet able to do little more than glare defiantly at their murderer's approach. The left-hand jailor did manage to bring his whistle to his lips. But in his attempt to draw breath, he inhaled only a choking gush of blood.

"Begging your pardon."

The thrust of a shortsword up through the base of their skulls—Whistler first, then his companion—soothed their distress, and ended any resistance. As quick and painless as circumstances permitted, for whatever comfort that might provide. Kylac eased their corpses onto the ground and retrieved his throwing knives as Ledron and company hastened forward from the outer corridor.

"Bring them," Kylac instructed, motioning at the bodies.

He'd intended to be more gracious in their incursion, binding and gagging Grenarr watchmen rather than slaying them. But Ledron had been adamant during their planning stages that they take no chances. While Kylac had argued that hobbling an ankle or knee would be sufficient, in this matter, to forestall pursuit, the Head had made it known that he would kill any tar-skin Kylac left alive—and not in any merciful fashion.

Kylac had taken Ledron at his word, and hadn't seen fit to test the captain's resolve. Fortunately, the path he'd chosen through the stronghold had already been mapped out so as to minimize the number of enemy encounters. The pair killed here, at the entrance to the dungeon wing housing the royals' cells, matched the total number of Grenarr slain previously in their night's endeavor.

A minimal toll.

His only other petty consolation had been in leaving Ledron to handle the dead after he'd felled them. Small solace, as the captain had been swift in both prior instances to delegate the task to his accompanying Redfists.

He did so again now, gesturing at Havrig and Jorrand to each collect a body and drag it after. Kylac had moved already toward the inner door. He hadn't yet passed through this way on any of his prior incursions, so he didn't know for certain what lay beyond the portal. But given the unlikelihood of an unwelcome visitor venturing even this far—or a prisoner escaping their cell—he anticipated no resistance.

He opened the door boldly, as might one of the jailors had they decided to pass beyond. Creeping through tentatively seemed more likely to suggest unusual circumstances to anyone posted on the other side.

He was met only by a lazy breeze and a faint wash of moonlight that softened the shadowed interior of the proceeding tunnel. A cave to the right served as a storeroom. Beyond that, a caged work area housed rusted bits of iron and lengths of chain, much of it serving host to cobwebs. Blades, spikes, and other implements of torture lay upon the tables and racks, or dangled from the ceiling. But all of it looked to have gone long unused.

Following a bend in the corridor brought him to a bank of cells he well recognized. As expected, the first two lay empty. The third brought him to Denariel, who stood as near to the cell door as her shackled collar would permit.

"So soon?" she remarked archly. "And here I've not quite fully festered."

Her bridle had been removed, Kylac was pleased to see, though he'd have preferred silence just now. Grime painted her brow and cheeks, and sleeplessness had bruised the wells of her eyes. Elsewise, she appeared hale enough, albeit in sore need of a bath. Clearly expecting him. Because her brother had let her know he was here, or because she, like Temerius, had believed he would come. Whichever, it relieved him to learn that, whatever her doubts, she hadn't been stewing all this time in hopelessness.

Kylac put a finger to his lips, gesturing in along the corridor.

"The guards stepped out," Denariel claimed. "I'd wager a quarter-mark before their return."

While Kylac dipped his head in acknowledgment, Ledron and his companions moved up beside him, into her view. At this, the princess evinced genuine surprise.

"Why, Captain, I'd more than half expected not to see you again."

"I live to serve, Highness," he grumbled, already moving past.

"It was the living portion that seemed uncertain."

The Head paused, scowling his irritation. Before an argument could bloom, Kylac pulled on the release lever embedded in the wall above Denariel's cell. A set of lock bars grated upward, and the weight of the cage door caused it to ease open.

"Keys," Ledron commanded his men, motioning toward the fallen jailors.

"No need, Captain."

While Simalen and Sethric bent toward the corpses held by Havrig and Jorrand, searching the pair for keys, Kylac entered Denariel's cell with ready picklocks. She flinched, initially, from his advance, but straightened quickly, defiantly. Kylac withheld a smirk as he probed the collar's lock. "Hold still."

A flick and a twist, and the collar fell free. Denariel rubbed at the chafed skin of her neck.

Ledron had moved down the tunnel, past the adjacent cell to the one beyond. The echo of his hissing voice grated against the scabrous walls. "Highness. Prince Dethaniel!"

Denariel's expression softened, taking on an urgent cast. Reading her intent, Kylac stepped aside, allowing her to exit.

On her heels, he gestured at Havrig, who nodded. As the Redfist hauled Whistler's dead companion into the vacated cell, Kylac joined the princess and Ledron at the entrance to Dethaniel's cage. The prince was just now stirring, as the Head wrenched on the lever to unlock the barred door.

Denariel knelt beside him. *Dethaniel. Denariel.* With the pair reunited, Kylac was going to have to start addressing them—privately, at least—with their more familiar names.

"Thane," Nara said, laying a gentle hand upon his shoulder. "Thane, wake up." Her hands moved to his, to caress the gap of his severed finger.

The prince's eyes drew focus, and quickly narrowed. "Sister," he greeted stiffly, withdrawing from her touch to sit up on his own.

A harsh reaction. Kylac pitied Nara the pinch of heartache that flared from her in response, though she shaded it quickly with that petulant frown of hers.

He reconsidered his earlier assumption, wondering now when last the royal siblings had actually seen or spoken to each other. In his stolen conversation with Thane, the prince had admitted to being confined to this one cell, but had made no inquiries as to his sister's presence or condition. Kylac had therefore assumed that the royals had at least conversed in some capacity since Nara's arrival. Given the strain of their interactions now, he was no longer certain. It felt more likely that he was witnessing their first true encounter since Thane's abduction.

"Forgive me, brother," Nara said flatly. "I never intended . . ."

Thane had already looked past her to Kylac. "I'd come to believe you had a change of heart. Else recognized the futility of your intent."

"We must go, Highness," said Ledron, waving Jorrand near. The

Redfist approached, dead Whistler in hand.

Kylac laid a hand on Nara's shoulder, much as she had her brother's. Predictably—and even more harshly—she swatted it away.

Kylac presented his picklocks.

Thane pushed to his feet. Nara thrust to hers and spun aside, brushing at the exposed skin beneath the tatters of her garb as if Kylac might have blighted her with his touch. He took no offense, and gave little thought to the bitterness between brother and sister. The prince seemed well within his right if harboring a measure of resentment toward Nara for leaving him in this position. Provided it did nothing to interfere with their escape, their dispute wasn't Kylac's concern.

"You mean to go through with this, then?" Thane asked, as Kylac worked at his collar.

"Our ship awaits," Ledron assured him. "Kronus will cover our escape."

"Un us, tah?" Creyl added, punching Talon in the arm.

"Stride swiftly, Your Highness," Talon pleaded in a dry tone. "I'd sooner not be burned or buried with this pair."

Freed of his collar, Thane shuffled into the corridor. Ledron met him with a supporting hand, beckoning Sethric and Sim for additional aid. As an afterthought, the Head nodded toward a brooding Nara, all but pressed into a natural alcove. "Moh. Jethmus. See to Her Highness."

Kylac helped Jorrand clap Whistler into Thane's neck collar, and to cover the dead jailor in the prince's blanket. They then closed the cell door and scurried back down the corridor in pursuit of the main party. Whistler's companion now occupied Nara's cell, locked away and covered in the princess's place. A minor ruse, but one that might help to buy them a few extra moments.

They gathered again in the antechamber in which the jailors had been slain. Kylac closed and latched the door behind him before assuming point. Creyl and Talon were on his heels, with Ledron and Havrig on theirs. Sethric and Sim remained in position to escort and defend Thane, while Moh and Jethmus tended in similar fashion to Nara's flanks. Jorrand had drawn rearguard.

"Halfway home," Kylac said with a smile.

Only Creyl smiled back, unashamed of the odor leaking from his crooked teeth.

Gods, don't resist my charm now.

Back through the stronghold they plunged, delving along a twisting array of coring passages. They traveled in silence—or what passed as such, with the members of this company. Had they been students at Talonar, they'd have been flogged severely for the slap and scrape of their footfalls, the rustle of their garb, the huff of their breath. Magnified by the close, bare environs, each slight sound rang as a screech or a shriek in Kylac's ears.

But the bulk of the stronghold's inhabitants slumbered at this late hour, amid reaches far removed from the caverns and tunnels comprising Kylac's carefully chosen path. And it seemed unlikely that many would share his keen sense of hearing, even had they been awake and alert. In the course of his life, he'd met few who did.

So he put the noises of their passing out of mind, in order to focus on the echoes of those that might signify danger—to themselves, or to anyone they might happen across. No simple feat, given the eerie chorus of clicking, clanking, warbling reverberations that hummed through these earthen halls. Yet he'd spent enough hours roaming within to distinguish sounds native to this stronghold from any that might not belong, and to discern relative distance even if unable to recognize the precise source.

Thus far, he'd detected no threat.

He might have preferred elsewise, in order to justify the itch that had come crawling upon his neck. The closer they came to freedom, the more insistent his reservations became. Something was amiss, though he couldn't seem to place it. Nor did this seem the ideal moment in which to try. Time and again, he cast rearward glances at the members of his company. All appeared safe and alert, though their faces gleamed with the sweat of their anxiety. Mayhap it was only *their* apprehensions that gripped him.

In descending a short flight of crudely hewn steps, they reached the level at which he was to part ways with Ledron. He just needed to steer them eastward, around and through a set of kitchens. No sooner had he taken aim in that direction, however, than a shrill whistling, yet distant, caught his attention. It soon spawned an echo, and another. Not the same sound, but a host of new ones mirroring it, like a spark giving birth to flames.

An alarm.

Too soon, he thought, and the first hint of a thrill quickened in his blood.

"Listen," Ledron said a moment later. "Is that—"

"They's found one o' their watchmen," Kylac confirmed. The first killed, most likely, down here near the base of the mountain. Fully mustered, it wouldn't take them long to find the others. "Tread lively, eh?"

He hastened his pace, trusting his companions to follow. They did so without comment, without complaint. Twice he looked back to check on their charges, Nara and Thane. Though staggered and off balance, both seemed willing and able to suffer the swifter strides— spurred, no doubt, by their fear of recapture. Kylac wanted to reassure them that he wasn't likely to let that happen, but imagined that it would sound, under the circumstances, like an empty boast.

With whistles and shouts seeming to surge from all directions, accompanied now by a clamor of footsteps and gathering of arms, Kylac led their company through a larder and down into a boarded-off access tunnel beyond. Through a narrow fissure they passed, into a small cavern that opened onto an empty corridor. A pocket of near-silence greeted them, temporarily muting the enemy uproar.

"Map in hand, Captain. This is where we leave ya."

Ledron fumbled at a scroll tube tied to his waist, drawing forth the scrap of lambskin on which his escape route had been inked.

"I can scarcely see," the Head complained.

"You're facing east," Kylac said. "Tunnel wends straight, more or less, for some thirty paces. There ya'll find the store o' candles I promised ya."

The Head grimaced uncertainly.

"I's my own duty in this," Kylac reminded him.

"Go then," Ledron growled. "Don't be late."

Leaving the Head to guide the others in the remainder of their retreat, Kylac reversed back up through fissure and tunnel to the larder. Creyl clung eagerly to his heels, close enough to share with him that personal odor of smoke and vinegar. A step farther back, the beak-nosed Talon followed dutifully enough, however less ardent in his enthusiasm.

"Wish I knew what I'd done to offend the captain so," the Redfist muttered.

"If'n he means to be rid of us, let's take pleasure in disappointing him."

"Brecken 'im coltris ire," said Creyl, followed by a short, hacking laugh. Whatever the statement's meaning, he seemed blissfully amused with himself for uttering it.

"Cowls," Kylac instructed them. With a smirk, he added, "You're royalty now, so give us your most regal bearing, yes?"

Creyl sneered. Talon grumbled. But both drew the hoods of their cloaks overhead.

"Keep close now."

They emerged from the larder and turned south. The stronghold buzzed like a hornet's nest under attack. Shouts and cries echoed through the tunnels and vents, in a manner that confused the ear and defied traceability. Voices raining at their backs might belong to men at a level above or below them, in no immediate danger of crossing their path. Others, sounding distant, might lie directly ahead, muffled by a craggy bend.

But Kylac was no longer greatly concerned with escaping notice and avoiding confrontation. Their purpose now, in fact, was quite the contrary.

To that end, he was actually surprised somewhat by the lack of resistance. While still amid the stronghold's more deserted regions, he hadn't expected to progress this far without meeting opposition in some form. A lookout, a snare, a gate—something. Particularly given that the alarm had been sounded earlier than he'd anticipated, effectively putting him behind schedule.

Suggesting only that the Grenarr were slow to mobilize, he hoped, rather than that he'd failed to properly estimate their response—or any other, more sinister, possibility.

Whichever, nothing to do about it now but carry out his task.

Rounding a bend, he followed a short ramp that spilled into a meeting hall through one of several side portals. Here at last, he found an
assembly of Grenarr warriors at the north end who, judging by their
anxious milling, appeared to be awaiting an absent figure of command. Resisting the instinctive urge to remain hidden, he stepped out
beside a crude pillar and waved his cloaked companions toward the
hall's southern opening. The challenge here was to be seen without
looking as if he wanted to be seen. A delicate dance.

It was Talon who ultimately gave them away. Turning his ankle
on a loose stone amid the shadowed perimeter near the exit, he
hissed with pain. Heads turned from the front of the chamber. Gazes
narrowed with suspicion. Kylac looked back at them while pushing
his companions through the exit with a feigned sense of desperation.

And the hunt was on.

"Curse it all," Talon snarled, wincing at every stride placed upon
his injured ankle.

Kylac disagreed. "Flawless timing."

"I'm hobbled."

"All the better for your disguise. If'n it can't bear weight, Princess
Creyl here will aid ya."

"I crutchen them shanks," Creyl agreed, grinning and sidling close.

With a snort, Talon pushed the half-wild Redfist away. "I'll manage."

Kylac wasn't sure which boded better for their chances—Talon's
despair or Creyl's reckless fervor. Better should a little of each round
the edges off the other.

Having been sighted, the net around them gradually began to
close. No matter how swift their stride, there was no outpacing the
shouts and signals that went echoing ahead of them. As intended.
The Grenarr couldn't know how well Kylac had committed their
tunnels to memory. They couldn't anticipate how quickly he might
deviate from a primary path, or redirect back onto one. Expected
or not, they couldn't prevent the ruthless efficiency with which he
would dispatch any who sought to bar his way.

Through what must have seemed a dizzying combination of sprints,
veers, feints, and retreats, Kylac cut a course for him and his decoys
through the stronghold's lower levels. He did so in a web-weaving

fashion, effectively drawing the scattered patrols of Grenarr in loops and spirals through their own home, buying the added time he believed Ledron would require. Twice, he allowed himself to be cornered by small packs, only to whirl right back around and hew through those who thought him trapped. These attacks served to incite the others who chased him about—once again, by design. His aim was to sow confusion, not death. He therefore chose to disarm and disable, rather than slaughter needlessly. Before long, the wailing of the wounded was but another disturbance amid the furor, further stifling the enemy's effort to organize against him.

But organize they did, little by little. As the routes available to him began to close, sealed off by various obstacles, Kylac looked to make his exit. After feigning a rush toward the mountain's central mouth, surely gated by now against him, he carved a serpentine route through what served as a sick ward. Therein, he'd discovered the opening to a smuggler's tunnel leading out and beneath the surrounding village. Even in a community as small and carefully cultivated as this, there existed those who would risk whatever punishment to profit where they could on the side. Else, what need for dungeons and execution platforms at the stronghold's peak?

However infamous the Grenarr were for their slaves and hostages, Kylac had found none of either—apart from Kendarrion's royal children—on this particular atoll. Regardless, he had yet to encounter a human settlement, big or small, unplagued by outlaws. Especially where resources were scarce.

Sickly Grenarr eyed him strangely as he passed through their cavern, redolent with human filth. Some smelled of leprosy and other diseases without cure. Kylac had never proven particularly vulnerable to illness. He hoped for his companions' sake that they didn't, either.

At last, they came upon the entrance to the tunnel he sought. He knew not the precise purpose for which it had been dug, nor when it had last been used. He'd found it grated at both ends. But the masonry in which the bars had been set was old, and his blades sharp. It had taken little effort to loosen, remove, and reseat the barrier, in preparation for this moment.

Now, as Kylac hovered protectively at their backs, Creyl hefted the grate free.

"It reeks," Talon complained, sniffing at the opening.

"Remain, then," Kylac offered, "to serve as rearguard."

Creyl pushed past his hesitant comrade to enter the odorous void. Giving ear to the cries of pursuit, Talon gripped the Redfist's shoulder. "Right, then, *sister*. Make way for the crown prince."

The half-wild sniggered as he cleared a path. "Spur, then. Or done shine that crown with your entrails a'grease."

Talon snorted, then disappeared into the dank darkness beyond.

39

THROUGH THE DARKNESS THEY DELVED, feeling their way over muck-filled ground riddled with worms, beetles, and other slithering, skittering creatures slimy or shelled. Talon continued to snort and cough, clearly troubled by the fetid stench. At one point, he stopped to retch. But Creyl and Kylac crowded him forward, giving him no chance to tarry.

"Only way out is ahead," Kylac reminded him.

The stricken Redfist needed no stronger prodding.

The echoes of pursuit gave chase. Kylac was less concerned with what followed than what might lie ahead. If any among the Grenarr knew of this tunnel and where it emerged, they'd likely have a patrol racing by now to head them off. Kylac didn't relish the thought of having to carve his way past them. Though, if the alternative meant being trapped for any length of time in this lightless tube, he'd certainly do so.

When an infiltration of moonlight began to expose the tunnel's features ahead, Kylac pushed past his comrades to take the lead. A quick survey brought relief. The exit lay clear.

Removing the grate himself, he pushed out into the open air, reaching back to help haul his companions after. Behind them, to the northeast, the village stirred with shouts and torches. Citizens residing outside the stronghold were being urged back into their homes, else arming themselves and mobilizing alongside watchmen and warriors now spilling from the stronghold. A pack of Grenarr had already broken from the mountain's mouth, taking aim at the ravine in which the intruders had emerged. Kylac straightened upon the ravine's ridge, allowing himself to be seen.

Quickly spotted, he urged his cloaked comrades down toward the lagoon, glancing back to take stock of those Grenarr gathering in his wake. Lighter in number than he'd expected. He hoped again that this didn't indicate a greater number having somehow marshaled in pursuit of Ledron. He wondered briefly how the Head and his company might be faring. Well free of the stronghold by now, if all had gone to plan. Halfway across the atoll to their waiting boats. He neither saw nor heard any activity that might indicate a secondary path of enemy pursuit, which suggested their party had indeed slipped away undiscovered.

So why did he not feel better about it?

Hissing at the evasiveness of his own senses, Kylac took flight, reclaiming the point among his more immediate companions. Grenarr mobilized ahead of them now, as well, those set at watch upon the docks. He also saw crewmen astir upon the *Kraken's Reach*, moored still at the end of her assigned pier. He wondered if Nemarus and those under his interim command would seek to muster against him. He wondered if they would be permitted to.

Veering east, he and his Redfists reached the main road skirting the lagoon. They traveled it for a stretch, putting themselves in a direct line of sight of both their pursuers from the stronghold and those preparing to receive them down by the docks. Doing so served to incite their enemies. Flushed into the open, they were now within grasp.

Or so he let them believe, luring them south as designed, farther from the true hunt to the northeast. He imagined the shock and disappointment to be reaped this night, when all had played out. Temerius's fury. Barkavius's outrage. He wondered which of the proud leaders, if either, would survive the confrontation likely to follow this debacle.

When bowmen upon the docks began loosing arrows at him, Kylac redirected east, shading away from the lagoon. The arrow rain was short lived. Presumably, someone in command had determined that the captives—Thane and Nara, at least—were not to be harmed. Which meant their deception had yet to be discovered, or word of it yet to spread.

They kept to their altered course, however, clearly abandoning the lagoon and any pretense of stealing a ship now in favor of a footrace to the south. A race they were already losing. The Grenarr were taller, faster, stronger, no longer hampered by stealth and misdirection. Alone, Kylac might have outdistanced them, but with Creyl and Talon beside him, there was little hope of doing so for long. Talon in particular was struggling, as his ankle swelled in protest against the rigors of their flight.

"Just a mite farther, lads," Kylac urged.

Some six hundred strides later, their faltering pace had surrendered enough ground to their enemies to jeopardize their escape. Talon limped along only haltingly. Creyl wheezed, lungs working like a saw. As they neared the southern shipyards, a dozen Grenarr watchmen gathered. Blades in hand, Kylac dashed forward to meet them. He took their weapons, their appendages, or severed the tendons and muscle sheaths for putting them to use. Two he left dead, and three more likely wishing they were. None would soon rise against him.

"Go!" he cried to his companions, waving them on toward the bluff that loomed ahead.

He lingered a moment longer, eyeing his victims to make certain they posed no further threat, then peering back at the advancing mob who most certainly did. Gauging the time left to them, he spun about and darted after his companions.

He found them at the foot of the bluff, doubled over, hands on their knees.

"We're to scale this?" Talon asked incredulously.

Kylac could scarcely fault the other's skepticism. The jumble of ropes, pulleys, and attachments spilling down from the ridge appeared a netted tangle, and the crest they must reach lorded high above their heads. At full strength, they might manage to haul their weight skyward. In their present, exhausted condition, the proposed task surely struck them as insurmountable.

Kylac hurried forward to show them elsewise. "Like raising a sail." He selected a bucket from amid the assorted bins, hooks, and loops used to ferry materials up and down the cliff's face, and set foot into it. Finding the appropriate counter rope, he began pulling, hoisting himself with relative ease by way of the pulleys through which the lines were threaded.

"Reel un up," Creyl rasped, breathless as he approached.

Kylac lowered himself, and gave his bucket over to the eager Redfist, putting its matching draw line in the other's hand. "Reel quickly."

He turned to Talon, who staggered forward willingly enough, and helped to find for him a bucket and line.

"A precarious perch," Talon observed, setting his good foot into the bucket.

"Pick a larger platform, then. But ya'll have a pair o' ropes to pull in concert. Lose one, and ya'll totter sideways."

Talon took the rope handed him, and began to heft himself in pursuit of Creyl.

Kylac permitted them another moment's lead, while peering back again at the closing pursuit. If any were to follow, he wanted to be the first they caught up to.

So that he could dissuade others from doing the same.

Finally, he stepped into a loop and joined his companions. Ropes squeaked and squealed through the pulleys as they climbed, hand over hand. The buckets swayed, bumping here and there against the bluff face. Talon was clearly having a harder time of it than Creyl, but the latter wasn't exactly soaring skyward. Kylac slowed in order to remain below them, while continuing to mark their wavering, unbalanced progress.

By then, the Grenarr had reached them, spitting threats and shouting curses, gathering below like a roiling brew. Kylac searched their rabid faces, but recognized none among them. Neither Temerius, nor Barkavius was present. Farther back yet, he supposed. Tending to the chaos closer to home.

Those who *had* come took to tugging or shaking the loose ends of rope being used by Kylac and his companions. Of small effect, given that the discarded lengths bore no tension. Other Grenarr, showing better understanding, mounted attachments of their own, while directing their comrades to hoist them in pursuit.

A race to the top, then. Kylac resumed focus on his own ascent. Though, when the enemy foolishly made use of a rope within his reach, he took pause, freeing one hand long enough to draw his longsword and sever the line.

He was still smirking at the frustrated cries of those tumbling earthward when an echoing command peaked amid the tumult.

"Imposters! Arrows! Bring them down!"

The cry came from a herald at the head of another pack running hard to join the congregation. On whose authority the order had originated, Kylac couldn't say. But it seemed to bear the necessary weight. All at once, a handful of archers reached for their bows.

"Pull, lads!" Kylac urged.

He did so himself, while eyeing now the iron-tipped shafts streaking toward him. The first batch were hastily fired, and errantly aimed. With each new draw, however, the bowmen came nearer to striking their marks. As the lowest and therefore closest member of their fleeing company, Kylac had to curl left or right more than once to avoid being struck.

Alas, it was their highest and farthest member, Creyl, who yelped when a bolt struck home. Kylac looked toward the piercing cry, to find the feathered shaft protruding from the Redfist's ribs. The half-wild laughed, then grimaced. When he coughed, blood spurted from his mouth.

He kept pulling, though. Somehow, he hefted himself higher, even as his elbow knocked against the buried arrow shaft. The ridge crest was almost within reach.

"Pull!" Kylac shouted again, dodging another arrow of his own.

Creyl did so, even after a second quarrel pierced his back. But as his hand reached for what might have been that final pull, it slipped, losing grip. The Redfist eyed it curiously, as if uncertain as to why it had betrayed him. He looked then to his remaining hand, still clutching the rope, holding him in place.

"Pull!" Kylac urged once more.

Creyl tried, wincing with the effort. Sagging, he grinned down at Kylac.

Then fell.

His cry of descent was more animal than human. But it bore neither terror, nor pain. Only savage euphoria escaped his lips as he plummeted. Reaching out, the Redfist managed to snag not only one, but two ascending Grenarr, yanking them from their ropes and dragging both in a spinning, pinwheel tangle to the ground.

Blood surged through Kylac's veins upon their final, crushing impact. The cheers that accompanied it set that blood aflame. An over-powering impulse urged him to release his own rope and slide down after, to scatter the wolves before they could beset his companion.

But Creyl was already dead. Past any solace but what vengeance might buy. Resisting that fruitless temptation, Kylac instead hastened his ascent, leaving the enemy's arrows behind, quickly passing Talon en route to the top. There, he scrambled over the crest and set about severing the lines that carried his pursuers.

Relishing the resulting screams, as their revelry soured into fury and frustration.

The remaining lines parted swiftly beneath his blade's edge. All save Talon's. Easier it might have been to cut the injured Redfist loose. With their ruse exposed, he would serve now only to slow Kylac's retreat. But Talon had done nothing to warrant such treachery, and Kylac was reluctant to add another thorn to his conscience.

Creyl's loss was irritation enough.

So he bent instead to assist his lone companion in cresting the ridge, ignoring the more practical voices that continued to whisper with sinister persuasion. A mere push now. Who would fault him? Who would know? *Suffer the weak,* he heard his father say, *and you will suffer their weakness.*

"You'd do better to leave me," even Talon observed, when standing sweaty and breathless beside him. Either the Redfist was being mag-nanimous, or he'd recognized the conflict in Kylac's eyes. Together, they peered back over the precipice, to where the maddened Grenarr were dispersing north and south with frantic haste, forced now to circumnavigate the bluff. "You'll be faster alone."

"We's all the lead we need," Kylac replied, "if'n we don't squander it."

He turned and set the pace, eased for the sake of his companion, but sufficient to reach their boat, he hoped, within acceptable range of the designated time. Though he huffed and grunted with pain, Talon loped alongside as if determined to justify Kylac's faith in him. Kylac didn't bother to admit that his choice had little to do with any value placed upon the Redfist's life, and more with opposing his father's teachings. No reason to sap the other's confidence.

The barking and howling of the Grenarr gradually diminished as they fell farther back in their pursuit. A temporary ebb. Once they'd gained the heights, they would recover ground quickly. The only question was whether he and his companion would still be ashore when next the enemy sighted them.

Whichever, a less harrowing retreat than his underwater flight with the Sea Scribe from Chitral's Ladrakari. Similar circumstances, but without the accompanying sense of helplessness. For all the uncertainty as to whether he and Talon could reach their boat in time, whether it would still be there, whether Ledron would wait for them to row back out to the *Wail*, at least he had all the breath he required, and might determine his own path. Better this than trusting blindly to the mercy of some immutable underground torrent. Even knowing the outcome of that prior venture, he wasn't certain he would agree to repeat it.

For more than an hour they ran, scrabbling over and through stepstone ridges, knotted groves, and bramble-filled ravines, along the route Kylac had chosen to carry them back to their landing site upon the atoll's northeast shore. Talon lurched and staggered over much of the terrain, wincing and grunting, each breath rasping as if it might be his last. But he clung dutifully to Kylac's heels, never once asking to rest, soldiering on despite his aches and discomforts.

Amid the gullet of the Shrike's Hour, they emerged at last from a scratching stretch of wild growth atop an eastern overlook that served view of the Tusks. Even knowing to search for her masts amid that cluster of monoliths, Kylac had a difficult time spotting them in the moonlit dark. More readily visible to one seeking it was the small craft rowing its way toward those rocks over the intervening swells between ship and shore. Ledron's? Or their own?

Kylac didn't stop to seek a definitive answer. The shouts of their pursuers were within a few hundred paces. So he continued to scrabble along the narrow, sandy track ahead of him, wending his way down to the pebble-strewn headland below. After a few turns upon the trail, the desired sight came into view—five furtive figures hunkered around a shore boat, reeking of anxiety.

When one among the figures perked abruptly and began motioning to the others, Kylac knew that he and Talon had been spotted. Still on course, then. Though the Grenarr—and Talon's injury—were going to make this final stretch of the race closer than he'd planned, it seemed they'd successfully avoided any significant snags in this night's enterprise.

With apologies to Creyl, of course.

"Just the two of you?" Simalen sought to confirm, as Kylac hustled up to him.

Kylac nodded. Sim grunted, but said nothing more. Together, they waited on Talon, hobbling now over the final distance, while listening to the thrashing advance of their enemy upon the heights.

Irryn and Stannon were already aboard the beached vessel, oars fitted and ready. Upon Irryn's command, Jethmus retrieved the small anchor rope, then joined them. Moh stepped forward to greet Talon's arrival with Kylac and Sim, half catching the stumbling Redfist and aiding him into the boat before urging his companions in after. Kylac obliged him, peering back at the heights as Moh shoved at the bow. With but a moment's resistance, the shore released her hold, and Moh leapt aboard.

Together, they watched Grenarr stream down the cliffside path in pursuit. Some bypassed the winding switchbacks to slide and skid down the sandy banks—only to go reeling and tumbling as the treacherous ground crumbled beneath them.

"Bah!" Jethmus snorted gleefully. "Masters of the swells they may be. But a tar-skin ain't fit to tread upon solid ground."

The others remained silent, more circumspect.

"Any trouble for the other crew?" Kylac asked.

Moh shook his head. "Captain set forth intact. Their royal highnesses with him."

Success. Kylac let the word echo in his thoughts, in defiance of his lingering unease. The Grenarr might rant and howl—might even swim out after them. But he spotted no ships, no boats. Without which, their enemy would be unable to catch up. Not unless it were later, upon the high seas.

On this night, at least, victory was theirs.

Irryn and Stannon stroked earnestly, steadily, over smoothly rolling waters. They covered the distance to the Tusks in a third of the time it had been taking Kylac to swim it. Amid the murmur of waves, the lingering shouts of the enemy echoed after them. In return, Kylac bid a silent farewell—and well riddance.

Upon rounding the Tusks, they found the *Wail* awaiting them. Only a handful of men at the rails peered down at them, silent and grim-faced. Kylac had thought to find them in a more celebratory mood. Too early, mayhap. Not that Ledron would have condoned it, regardless.

The falls for their shore boat hung suspended from the davits, just where they'd left them. Irryn and Stannon rowed into place, directing Moh and Jethmus to secure the lines. After signaling their readiness to sailors Hessel and Vosh overhead, the windlasses began to turn, and the boat to rise.

Amid the creaking ascent, Talon, who'd finally caught his breath, asked, "How far do you wager we get before their ships run us down?"

"We's already made it farther than anyone believed," Kylac reminded him. "And we has our Elementer. The greater folly might be to wager against us."

The others withheld any thoughts or appraisals of their own. Less a show of support, Kylac sensed, than a recognition of what little was to be won in arguing.

They might have revised their outlooks—Kylac alongside—had they known what they would find upon cresting the ship's rail: a hedgerow of Grenarr spears, ready to receive them. On the decks beyond, amid the familiar faces of their crew, an even larger pack of their dark-skinned enemies. Twenty, thirty . . . twoscore in all, Kylac estimated. Not enough to have overtaken their own crew by force, unless . . .

While his fellow boatmates were still gasping, fumbling for their blades, or stiffening with shock, Kylac found the members of Ledron's incursion party on their knees, subdued like the rest. Ambushed. The captain himself had been beaten to the deck. Temerius Seahammer loomed over him, sword in position to pierce the spine of his neck. The steward Barkavius towered over Nara, gripping her around the mouth, a dagger at her back. Thane . . . Thane had fallen to the mercy of none other than their own prisoner, Tormitius, somehow freed to put blade to the prince's chin.

"Resist, and we slaughter them all," the Shorecleaver promised with a cruel grin.

Sprung by his fellow Grenarr, Kylac determined. While he and Ledron had launched their night's rescue attempt, their adversaries had deftly executed one to match.

Only, he failed to imagine it. They'd have had to know the *Wail*'s location. Assembled a boarding party. Rowed out and scaled her hull without alerting the lookouts. Even bearing witness to the results, he found them difficult to fathom.

"Weapons down!" a familiar voice piped urgently. Pushing to the fore was the chief cook, Aythef. Unbound, Kylac observed. In no way threatened or cowed like the others. He even carried a longknife in his hand, the naked blade slick with blood.

Ah, thought Kylac, reassessing the situation as he and his companions sat paralyzed, swaying in their boat. The ambush had been sparked from within. That was how the other Grenarr had stolen aboard, despite their lesser numbers.

"Fine bit o' work," he allowed, smirking dangerously at the traitorous cook.

"Sheathe your weapons," Aythef begged again, "that there be no further bloodshed."

Though Kylac had yet to draw blade, Talon and Moh had. Sim and Jethmus beside them also looked as if they'd sooner loose their daggers and cut themselves free, if need be, than step into the snare awaiting them.

"None?" Kylac scoffed, eyeing the various positions of his allies and enemies, calculating what might happen should he unleash himself upon them.

"We have an arrangement," Aythef explained, standing boldly beside Tormitius.

"Festering fool," Ledron spat from his knees. "Even if our goodly Shorecleaver were to keep his word, he lacks the authority to—"

"Tormitius Shorecleaver is dead," Tormitius himself interjected, brimming with black amusement. "Slain in Kendarrion's cathedral."

A general confusion overtook the detained members of the *Wail's* crew, while the Grenarr among them grinned and snickered as if relishing a private jape. At Kylac's ear, Talon groped for a response. "Then who—"

"Grendavan." Kylac chuckled as he acknowledged the deception. "His name is Grendavan."

40

Kʏʟᴀᴄ ᴍᴀʀᴋᴇᴅ ᴛʜᴇ sᴜɴʀɪsᴇ from the darkness of his cage.

It shone brightest in a small splash upon the floor, raked by lines of shadow cast by the bars over the window vent. The same vent through which he'd first lain eyes upon Prince Dethaniel. Now, he sat shackled inside, where, until just a few hours ago, the captive prince had continued to reside—followed by the slain jailor left behind to impersonate him. Whistler, whose bloodstains marked the crude pallet in lingering accusation. A tinge of irony, the Grenarr must have thought, to imprison him in the very cell that had drawn him in the first place. The perfect hole in which to let him rot while reflecting on his crimes against them.

Which he might have, were his mind not engaged more thoroughly in retracing his steps, marveling now at his enemies' patience and cunning. At Grendavan's foresight in employing a decoy in Kendarrion's court, sending that man—the real Tormitius—to death in his stead. At the overlord's resolve in maintaining his own guise as a disposable lieutenant throughout their long voyage, so as to deprive them of the actual treasure held within their grasp. Great Grendavan the Eighth, whom Ledron had kept alive, shielded, all that time. Small wonder Temerius Seahammer and his ilk had been so intent on tracking them. For all the reasons they'd imagined—to forestall any attempt to rescue Thane, to retrieve Grendavan's flagship, to enact revenge against Kylac—they could add now the most urgent and obvious.

To liberate their kiros.

Had Ledron or any of their crew known, they might indeed have been able to arrange for a direct exchange, Grendavan for Thane, and thereby recover the abducted prince while sparing themselves incalculable effort and heartache.

Of course, at least one aboard *had* known. Aythef, it now appeared, as evidenced by his outright betrayal, had likely been working against them all along. Alone or aided by others, Kylac wouldn't be so bold as to say. For what cause or concern, he could only guess. But it was clear that the chief cook had stake in the matter hidden from them, to have volunteered his services and employed them to the enemy's benefit.

Guises and pretenses aside, Kylac had yet to discern how exactly they'd been able to best him, to execute the incursion that had eclipsed his. Its perfect timing suggested advance knowledge of his night's plan, carefully coordinated with Tormitius's release. But how? By what method had Aythef or his cohorts been able to communicate or signal to one another such precise information when Kylac's own strategy had been freshly hatched earlier that same day? How had Aythef come to learn all of the necessary details, for that matter, when the various elements of the plan had been shared with each crewmember only according to his specific role? The cook himself was to have played no integral part, and thus received no particular outline of events inasmuch as Kylac knew. How had he pieced it all together so quickly?

So many loose threads amid the unraveling of events. It was for this reason, as much as to preserve Nara's life—and Thane's, and those of his fellow shipmates—that Kylac had surrendered there atop the *Wail*'s decks. Though willing entrapment strained every shoot and fiber rooted at his personal core, he was tired of ploys and erroneous hunches and the overall whirlwind of subterfuge. Mayhap, if he gave himself over to their grasp, they might feel confident enough to share with him a measure of truth.

A futile hope, as of yet. The clutch of armed jailors stationed just

beyond his cell door had resisted any overtures to engage in conversation. As had the contingent prior, led by Barkavius, that had delivered
him here. He was discounting the taunts and jeers of those Grenarr
who'd welcomed his return to their stronghold, as these imparted
only an enthusiastic desire to inflict harm upon him, and nothing in
the way of information. For that, he still waited.

He presumed that, by now, Barkavius had long since returned to
the *Wail* with report of his successful incarceration. Tormitius—no,
Grendavan—had vowed that none of Kylac's shipmates would be
permitted to disembark for the relative safety of their own cages until
that report was delivered. Should the rogue suffer a change of heart
between ship and prison, his companions would depart instead as
ash and cinders, carried by the winds from the flaming deck of their
barbarian vessel.

Had he thought the threat worth testing, Kylac would have done
so before surrendering his blades and submitting to their bindings
and tethers. So he'd gone on to tolerate the insults and the prodding
and complied with their wishes. He really couldn't predict with any
certainty what might come next. Some form of torture, one might
expect. But Kylac didn't think so. Not without some further bartering
beforehand. With the revelation that he hadn't, in fact, murdered their
kiros, it stood to reason that they might seek or be willing to entertain
an arrangement more beneficial to both sides—his services, in some
manner, in exchange for his life. For if meaning to push forward
with colonizing a wild stretch of Addaranth—or Grenah, as they
called it—could they truly afford to put skills as rare as his to waste?

The answer to that, he supposed, would depend largely on just
how wroth Grendavan was with him for slaughtering the overlord's
crew, stabbing his foot and threatening his life, stealing his ship and
letting it be scuttled . . .

Mayhap retribution would indeed be deemed more valuable.

Parry or thrust, he anticipated at the very least an impassioned
gloating—that long-coveted moment in which his chief captor leered
at him face-to-face and exulted in having finally defeated him. Given
the intensity of the hatred Grendavan had shown him during their
brief encounters at sea, he was mildly surprised it hadn't happened

already.

An hour passed, and then another. He was provided no food, no drink, and no insight as to how long the silence might last. Mayhap they meant to soften him first. If so, it might be days before they visited him. Weeks.

He wondered about his shipmates. As of yet, none had been brought in to occupy any of the other cells in this wing. Thane and Nara would be treated well enough, he felt. At least in the short term. But what of Ledron or his crew of sailors and soldiers? The Head might serve prize for his intimate knowledge of Addaran affairs, but most of the rest would likely be relegated to slave labor, offered back to their families for a price none could afford, or disposed of. Their fears from the outset, fully realized in the end. Rendering all of their interim suffering meaningless.

Kylac did his best to keep that and other such sentiments from his mind. What purpose could they serve? Matters had yet to be fully settled. Despairing over the present setback wouldn't make it any easier to overcome.

The sun trekked dutifully overhead, waxing toward midday before waning in the afternoon. Its mark crept across the floor, morphing as it shifted positions. His watch contingent was relieved by another as tight-lipped as the last. He sought sleep for a time, but couldn't seem to stem the tide of restless recollections, compelling him to reevaluate his choices in the light of hindsight. Not something he was typically prone to. But then, seldom had he experienced such failure—fleeting or elsewise.

The blotch of sun on the floor had dimmed to a dull crimson when next he heard the outer door open. Another watch change, he supposed, until the footfalls told him elsewise. The steps were too light, and too few. He found himself straightening in anticipation, the chain of his neck collar clinking with the movement.

A pair of his jailors closed shoulder to shoulder beyond the bars of his cell.

"Stand aside," a voice demanded in response. *Thane?* "I've your lord's permission to speak with the prisoner."

The jailors parted. Kylac stood, stirred by curiosity.

Dethaniel greeted him with a vague, clean-shaven smile. Aythef stood at the prince's shoulder, frowning with mistrust, radiating disapproval. The sight of them triggered in Kylac a release of the disquiet he'd been carrying since the night of Thane's ill-fated rescue. Here at last, the source of his mysterious foreboding.

"Did they run short o' cells?" Kylac asked. He considered the treacherous cook before looking back at the prince. "Or mayhap ya'd be kind enough to share with me the nature o' your bargain with the Grenarr, that they should let ya roam free."

Thane's smile strained, laden with disappointment. Gripping Kylac with a bold gaze, he cocked his head to address Aythef. "Perhaps not as clever as you believe."

That simple goad, uttered with such smugness, spawned in Kylac a fresh suspicion. If the unchained prince hadn't reached some arrangement following ambush aboard the *Wail* . . .

Implausible as it seemed, the notion quickly unleashed a cascade of possibilities that flowed and churned, unleashing a warring mix of puzzlement and elucidation. Kylac's mind whirled, whipsawing amid a torrent of raw answers and rawer questions. He hadn't yet begun to sort through it all when Thane sighed and turned away, forcing Kylac to blurt his untempered theory.

"You're a willing partner. Only playing at prisoner."

Thane halted. Aythef scowled, clearly opposed to whatever purpose had brought them here. But those protests went unspoken as his lord prince turned back to the cell, grinning anew. "The latter upon your assumed arrival with the *Kraken's Reach*—when Temerius brought further word of events at sea, and of your likely attempt to steal away with my sister and I."

The threat to His Highness aboard the *Wail*—and long beforehand . . . all part of an ongoing ruse. "Accomplice to your own abduction."

"Architect."

The word echoed ominously in Kylac's ears. Desperate now for answers—not guesses—he resolved to learn what more the prince might confirm or reveal. "To what end?"

Thane tilted his head, almost pitying as he spread his hands in a gesture of supplication. "Peace."

"Ah, yes. A path o' roses we's laid, with our lies and shackles and killings."

Aythef looked as if he wished to intervene, but didn't dare. Whatever his objections, he'd voiced them already, and been overridden. He settled now for glancing disconsolately at the surrounding jailors, who, while maintaining their silence, couldn't help but attend to every word.

Thane himself would not be fazed. This was it. His moment of triumph. The *gloating* Kylac had anticipated, only from an unforeseen source.

"This standoff between my people and the Grenarr merits nothing but strife. I have long proposed a truce. Impart to the Grenarr a portion of land—unused by us—to call their own, in exchange for a fully partnered trade alliance. They partake of precious earthen resources, while we reclaim untrammeled access to the sea and its surrounding lands. An opportunity for mutual expansion, to the benefit of all. An end to the boundless bloodshed between us."

The accord. Much as Sabrynne, the Grenarr emissary back in Addaranth, had divulged it—only, without exposing Thane as the true mastermind. Kylac couldn't in that moment recall whether she'd merely omitted that fact, or deliberately concealed it. "Your royal father would describe it differently."

At this, the prince's features tightened with frustration. "My royal father is blinded by his personal grudge. To the point of dedicating the whole of our military strength to repelling the Grenarr against the slightest toehold, hoping that they should eventually die out."

"Some might forgive him his enmity, given the nature o' the affront."

"Even as a plague of monsters infests our shores? It is selfish and pigheaded. This ageless feud poses unnecessary costs with which we stifle our own prosperity. The world is ever expanding. Old grievances and blood debts must be set aside. The future must be built on trust, for we have seen what little hatred reaps."

An admirable view, Kylac supposed, if incongruous with man's nature. Others might deem it insensitive to disregard or downplay so many atrocities—including that committed against the prince's own mother. It caused Kylac to abruptly recall a brief conversation with the Blackfist Trajan that had taken place months ago, in their voyage from Pentania aboard *Denariel's Return*. A discussion in which the Tower had remarked on the crown prince's pragmatism. Kylac remembered judging those observations meaningless at the time.

Not so meaningless now.

Thane shook his head, frustration giving way to regret. "Despite endless entreaties, my father would agree only that, when I am king, I may rule as I see fit. Until then, I am to obey."

"But you decided not to wait." Though he believed he knew the rest of the story—the critical strands, at least—he wasn't going to pass up this opportunity to verify a matter or two. Not when so much he'd taken as obvious had proven elsewise. "To instead sell your sister for this so-called peace."

The prince's gaze narrowed. "I'll not deny that I first considered arranging for Nara to be abducted. But only because it was she who convinced me I could no longer afford delay."

"Oh? By what means did she do that?"

"Falling in thrall to a mutant."

The Ukinh. The one beloved of Nara. That which had attended her in her journey to Kuuria, and followed her back to Addaranth, hunting those who sought to return her to her father. Another thread in all of this that Kylac wished he'd been privy to earlier. "Ya knew o' this?"

"Sadly, my father's intolerance is reserved for the Grenarr, and not the abominations outside his door. He let them get too close, allowing his own daughter to be ensnared. It came to where she was pleading on behalf of the creatures, dulling my father's already slack interest in hunting them. When I came to suspect why—what had happened to lend such strength to her urgings—I determined something must be done to save my sister from herself, and to eradicate the creatures, for good and all."

Peace with the Grenarr, war with the Ukinha. Kylac couldn't immediately decide whether this secondary objective served to bolster or diminish the primary aim.

"Delivering my sister to the Grenarr seemed the surest way to sever the mutant's foul influence. But I feared suspicion for my part in making it happen. I knew also that there was a lesser chance of my father surrendering to ransom demands, since his greater love has ever been for me, his only trueborn child."

"So ya made yourself the bait."

Thane's proud grin returned. "Escaping any chance at blame, and ensuring my father would agree to terms. It required considerable effort to reach out to Grendavan, and greater still to convince him of my earnestness. So much mistrust. But my offer was sound. Possession of the land they crave, my sister to seal the pact long-term, and myself as collateral against artifice or treachery."

"And if'n your father found it within him to refuse?"

The prince's gaze slipped, betraying the slightest hint of uncertainty. "Then I was to facilitate his removal and assume the throne myself. I agreed, provided it be done without harm to him. A small allowance, given the unlikelihood of resistance once the terms of the accord were presented."

So it must have seemed. As Kylac had gathered from Sabrynne and others, the stretch of coastline to be imparted to the Grenarr lay upon Addaranth's northeast shore, separated from the king's own cities and settlements by a buffer of wilderness that would help to shield his people from any possible encroachment by land. This gift that would buy back his precious son would therefore cost Kendarrion next to nothing, save in pride.

"Thankfully, my wager was correct," Thane added, "and none of this need end my father's reign."

Only, His Majesty hadn't been the only one to have say in the matter. "A fair bit o' scheming. Pity your sister found the terms less to her liking."

Aythef's scowl became a glare, hot and piercing.

"My fierce, headstrong sister," Thane echoed, bridling his own resentment. "I knew she would balk at the perceived threat to our homeland. But I foolishly believed that she, too, bore me sufficient love to put aside her desires for the sake of my life."

"Did she not?" Kylac asked.

"Only after further . . . inducement," Thane said, raising his four-fingered right hand. A sure sign of his conviction, now that it was clear he'd *permitted* his captors to remove that finger—if he hadn't done it himself.

"Had she submitted from the first, my lord would not have been hurt," Aythef interjected, his voice sharp with rancor.

Thane reached back with his good left hand as if to tamp his friend's anger. Aythef took that hand in his, and used it to pull himself abreast of the prince, putting forth his other to clutch Thane tightly, intimately, about the forearm.

"*None* would have been hurt," Thane amended, unflinching at the cook's familiar touch. "How many of my father's Shadowguard had to die to bring Nara to heel, hmm? How many more of my devoted countrymen have perished on this ill-advised and unnecessary voyage of yours?"

Thane lowered his right hand and placed it—with its grisly re-minder—over Aythef's grip on his forearm, completing the embrace. Looking to his companion, he added soothingly, "But progress is seldom achieved without hardship. For our future, mine is a small price to pay."

And thus the impetus behind Aythef's machinations. As the prince's confidante, he'd have known that Thane was in no true danger while held by the Grenarr. He hadn't volunteered for the voyage to see his royal companion freed, but to offset whatever further harm Kylac might do to the prince's plans. To thwart and delay by whatever means possible, until the opportunity presented itself to betray his shipmates openly.

"Did ya has aid aboard the *Vengeance*?" Kylac asked. "Or was it you who loosed the shrike that drew Temerius?"

Aythef hefted his chin in unabashed affirmation.

"And poisoned Vorathus's Banshees, lest they reveal the location o' the Shards."

"From the first meal I prepared for them. My only regret is how many meals it took for the poison to work its course."

"Did ya not think to simply poison me?"

Aythef's satisfaction faltered beneath the weight of his returning scowl. "Grendavan desired elsewise."

"You were to be delivered whole," Thane clarified, "as a matter of appeasement for the wedding massacre. My fox's primary aim in your little journey was to look after Grendavan's treatment. To serve reassurance to him, and see to it that at no point did you fully evade pursuit. That you should eventually be brought to heel, and the accord fulfilled."

Kylac looked to the Grenarr jailors, who continued to stand silent watch, their own thoughts kept private.

"Then he took his time about it. Surely, a bolder man would have seized opportunities yours missed along the way. Say, Sanow?"

"An act of madness," Thane scoffed, "crude and careless. Unlike the grace with which my fox brought Nara aboard to begin with."

Aythef colored at the praise, then sneered at Kylac's questioning look. "Smuggled inside a barrel while provisioning the ship. The poor raven begged me to help her, and thought herself clever in overcoming my objections—reminding me of her value in any negotiations, and swearing to tell no man I aided her." The cook snorted. "As if I would risk the king's wrath on her word. No, I did it that I might use her at some point to placate our future allies, and gain leverage against you."

"Right up until Sanow tossed her overboard."

"A reckless situation, your voyage," Thane admitted. "A volatile brew into which he willfully plunged, despite all the unknown perils."

"Strikes me, you stand upon the wrong side of those bars to mete judgment." Aythef cocked his head, smug in his own rising confidence. "My plans were no less formed than your own. While some matters failed to unfurl as I'd hoped, I trusted in my lord prince's enduring belief—that patience fosters opportunity and breeds success."

Kylac wondered momentarily if he might have been able to deduce the cook's secret role had Nara shared with him the truth of how she'd gained access to the ship—or the truth of Aythef's and Thane's relationship, assuming she knew of it. But he quickly brushed the question aside, as one too far past to matter.

"And the ambush aboard the *Wail*?" he asked instead. While another event that couldn't be undone, it involved logistical mysteries that he feared might haunt him again, should he not educate himself now.

"How'd ya manage it?"

"You'd already told me you'd be coming, of course," Thane replied. "When my fox sent word, I finally learned how. We determined to let your incursion play out, knowing that the ship would be lightly guarded in your absence. Barkavius and his party swam out to the *Wail*, to board under the distraction of Grendavan's release—orchestrated masterfully by my crafty fox."

"Delivery of a meal, and a knife in the belly of an unsuspecting guard," Aythef added. "A simple matter, thereafter, to pose as hostage to an escaped prisoner long enough for the Grenarr to overtake our confused watch and set snare for the captain's return. And yours."

Kylac declined to point out that he'd deduced this much already. "A precious bond the two o' ya must share, to so know each other's minds. For how else to plot together over such distance, with nary a shrike aboard?"

Aythef's smile became wolfish, while Thane just eyed him with that condescending breed of pity.

"Shrikes serve admirably as long-range messengers," the prince explained, "but are limited to specific home roosts. For shorter distances, storm pegrils can be drawn by a smoky incense made from terinnel fruit, then set free to be enticed by another."

Lured readily enough, then, back and forth between two points. As soon as Aythef had gathered what details he needed of Kylac's rescue plan—a simple-enough task for a ship's cook actively seeking information—he could indeed have attracted one of these storm pegrils and affixed word. Thane would have long since advised his false captors of Kylac's secret visit, so Barkavius would have been anticipating such warning, and been burning this terinnel incense to lure whatever flocks he could. Once Aythef's message found its way to the designated rookery ashore Grenathrok, counter-plans could have been hatched and a return missive dispatched, advising Aythef to free Grendavan upon signal from Barkavius's incursion team.

Just one message each way, during the long daylight hours that the *Wail* had stood at lull, awaiting the fall of night. A single exchange that had undermined their carefully crafted rescue attempt, and cost Creyl his life.

"There is so much we can learn from our seabound adversaries," Thane enthused, in response to Kylac's lingering silence. "And so much we can teach."

"Is that why ya confess to me now? That I might marvel at your wisdom?"

Thane regarded him with an air of patient suffering. "That you would know I am not your enemy. There are matters yet to be settled. Exchanges yet to be made." An arch of his neck seemed to indicate the silent jailors serving backdrop to their discussion. "I know not what chance may exist to secure your pardon, but better from me, I think, than our new countrymen."

"Ah. That I might serve *you* in some manner?" The arrangement he'd anticipated, just not with whom he'd imagined.

"An honorless rogue, Aythef calls you. But the account he paints . . . strikes me you have served my sister honorably enough, in your own fashion. Perhaps you could continue to do so, in one form or another. For all the anguish you have caused, talents such as yours are not lightly squandered."

A token, he was to be. As he had been since the onset of this endeavor. If purchased, only on the chance that he might be later sold at a higher price. "Better odds o' that had ya been this forthcoming when first we met."

"And risk your anger? Unfettered? *Best* this, where I can trust my words may be duly considered, with time and opportunity to take root."

"We're to abide here, then?"

"Until the colony ships are ready. When our past and future brothers will load their families and embark on their voyage to Addaranth. Bearing us with them."

Kylac snickered, both rueful and mocking. "A weapon like me. O' what value to a purveyor o' peace?"

"Like any weapon, serving deterrent—a ward against the baser instincts of those who might elsewise seek to rekindle the conflict."

The justification felt skewed. Nonetheless, a viable hope, he supposed. After all he'd heard, Kylac remained impressed by the prince's aims, and the effort undertaken to see them through—even if he couldn't quite reconcile such idealism with what *he* knew of man's *baser instincts* and behaviors.

"My father has nothing more to barter with," Thane insisted, "no more games to play. Through no small effort, all that my sister and now you have jeopardized has been restored."

"And ya's no fear for her fate? After all the trouble she has and is certain to cause?"

"Harming her would be a poor means of ensuring my father's tolerance of a Grenarr presence upon our shores."

Kylac felt the stiffening indignation of the attending jailors. *Pretender*, they called him, this royal father. The prince would do better, he thought, to stop referring to the proposed accord as a magnanimous gesture, and more as a small overture of reparation—at least while in range of Grenarr ears.

"As that may be," Kylac pressed, "the stones o' your plot fit so cleanly, I can't help but wonder, did this professed desire to spare her from the Ukinh truly lend impetus? Or is it merely a means o' justifying to yourself her foul treatment?"

The shadow of a frown stole over Thane's smile, dimming his elation. "I've grown weary of defending my sister against her own vulgar impulses. She is guided more by her father's blood than her mother's. Truth unvarnished, she belongs with the Grenarr, and deserves whatever life her lord husband deems suitable for her. Should she wish to consort hereafter with mutants, and beg tolerance of them, let her pleas fall upon *his* ears, rather than my father's. For I intend that my own people shall be well rid of them."

"If'n I cannot agree to that?"

"You become Grendavan's trophy," Aythef huffed in impatient reminder, "to do with as he pleases."

"Given perhaps to Temerius," Thane added gravely, "in payment for his efforts to hunt you down, and to allay his grief over your murder of his father."

Tormitius.

"Or perhaps they shall each take half," Aythef posed darkly.

"What o' your countrymen?" Kylac asked. "Ledron and his shipmates?"

The prince waved aside his concern. "I see no reason they should come to harm. Held for now, against any misguided fervor. But I have every expectation of their release upon our return."

"I'll not see them suffer for my blindness," Kylac stated flatly. "Nor Her Highness enslaved for your aspirations—however well-intentioned."

"I would not expect you to condone the whole of my actions," Thane admitted. "No more than I would condone yours. And I make no assurances, only beg your pardon, that I might grant you mine."

Kylac searched their expressions, withholding further response. For all he'd learned, he felt distinctly dissatisfied, and couldn't say as to why. They'd answered all his questions, and more besides. That they'd done so from a position of perceived superiority left him no reason to doubt their words as truth—inasmuch as they viewed it. He might like to hear where Grendavan's view differed, but such a meeting would be up to the Grenarr overlord to impose.

Until then, he'd had his fill of the matter, and their company with it.

Seeming to realize this, Thane smiled wanly in parting. "Give ear to what we've shared, while I work toward some reckoning on your behalf."

Still clasping his companion's hand, the prince stepped back, drawing Aythef with him.

"And if'n Grendavan should make me better offer?" Kylac asked as they turned away. "Say, a chance to even the scales against *you*?"

The goad served to arrest their withdrawal—Thane stiffening, Aythef looking to his royal companion in alarm. In their reactions, Kylac recognized the truth. Thane hadn't come looking to recruit him as much as prevent the Grenarr from doing so. For all his pride and arrogance and royal magnanimity, it was *fear* that had truly motivated the prince in this parley.

With a gleam of unspoken anger, Thane set his gaze to probing the cell's walls and crevices, as if inspecting them for the first time. "A week I had to spend in here. Its comforts do not grow softer, I assure you."

He forced again a prim smile, then strode from view, drawing a glaring Aythef after. The Grenarr jailors did nothing to challenge their departure. Kylac waited for the outer door to close, then sat back down on his tattered pallet.

To watch a splash of moonlight begin its slow creep across his prison floor.

41

Chains clanked amid squeaking leathers as Kylac shuffled along the torchlit tunnel, staggering every so often upon the scabrous floor. His legs were sturdier than he'd feared after nearly two weeks' imprisonment, but he saw no need to inform his captors of this. They surrounded him now in an ironclad ring, six prodding spearmen serving escort to the four who drove him by way of poles affixed to the collars around his neck and waist. His arms were bound tightly behind him, his ankles cuffed in leg irons that permitted him only short, halting strides. A muzzle had been strapped over his mouth. A rampaging creature, he must have appeared, to warrant such treatment.

All part of the spectacle.

Or so he'd wagered while permitting himself to be bound and gagged in such extravagant fashion. The sneering jailor sent to oversee his transfer had revealed only that the time had come to embark— followed by an obligatory threat to deliver him in a chum bucket should he dare to resist. But the warning had carried little real menace, burning rather with fiendish elation. The zealous murmur of throngs gathering beyond the walls of his prison, down near the lagoon, brimmed with more of the same. Theirs were not the bloodthirsty cries of an execution gallery, but the cheers of revelers. Suggesting to Kylac an intent to parade him before the Grenarr populace not as a dead man, but as a trophy in some manner of celebration.

With what little concern he had for pride, he saw no reason to refuse the role.

However trussed and fettered, he was on the move again. Thirteen days had passed since his visitation from Dethaniel and Aythef. Thirteen days of forced solitude. He'd been held under constant watch ever since, day and night, but received no further callers. Either Grendavan had yet to determine what was to become of him, or the overlord was simply enjoying making him wait. He'd therefore been left to fritter away the hours in the mute company of his jailors and the privacy of his own thoughts. To exercise in what caged manner his shackles allowed, while watching sun and moon overtake each other in endless contest. Straining the fibers of his patience as seldom before.

Given that, he'd been only too eager to submit to his handlers' terms. Hopefully, he hadn't simply made his escape more difficult, should they in fact be leading him to slaughter.

The cries without intensified as the winding tunnel deposited him into the cavern serving foyer to the mountain stronghold. A spearman nicked the meat of his rib while directing him to the left. As if he hadn't determined yet where they were taking him. Kylac allowed the abuse to pass unchallenged. He'd done enough to earn it. Let them enjoy their petty cruelties while they could. He didn't intend that they have forever to do so.

His gaze narrowed reflexively as he ventured toward the wash of sunlight marking the cave mouth. The small pool illuminating his cell each day had been but a candle compared to this piercing brightness. But his escorts permitted no hesitation. So he closed his eyes to ease the sting, and trusted in his memory to guide him. His handlers would see to any missteps, he was certain.

An exultant roar greeted his emergence from the mountain, growling like an avalanche as more of the masses took note. Kylac didn't yet see them, but sensed their heavy presence, packed in dense waves along the roadway and down toward the lagoon. The heat of their gazes matched the red haze burning at his closed lids. Yet he continued to sense little real ire. Even as they rained curses and hurled insults, they did so from a place of euphoria. Whatever damage he may have inflicted, whatever trouble caused, he no longer served threat. Hatred could find only so much purchase against an enemy vanquished.

And what enemy was he, truly? A pale-skinned outlander who'd taken up cause with the Addaran landsnakes. Beyond that, he must have seemed to most of them a false hazard, more fool than menace. Kylac could only guess as to how many among the general Grenarr populace bore knowledge of the plotting between Grendavan and Dethaniel. But all knew by now that their kiros lived. That the resistance Kylac represented had been thwarted. A handful of brave warriors had fallen beneath his blades. A small price to pay, most among this hearty folk might have agreed, to have the Pretender's personal assassin pinned now like a worm on a hook.

There were some, of course, who genuinely despised him. Kylac felt their enmity like livid coals amid the ashes of a dying fire. Those whose friends or kin he'd maimed or killed, mayhap. Against whom he'd already committed unforgivable grievance. But what could they number? A hundred? Two? Scattered among the thousands present, they and all of their railing invective formed but stray gusts amid the gale.

Halfway to the lagoon, he opened his eyes. Having envisioned the assembly already, he nonetheless found it to be an impactful sight. The whole of the atoll's inhabitants, it seemed, had drawn together in a crush upon the lagoon shores, the inner banks become an amphitheater overlooking the central pier to which the *Kraken's Reach* had moored. Only, the *Reach* had been moved, anchored nearer the lagoon mouth, her berth given over to one of the gargantuan colony ships. The others remained in the shipyards to the south, at home in their slipways. The lagoon lacked sufficient dock space to house them all elsewise. This particular ship, she was special.

It took Kylac only a moment longer to discern why.

At the head of the pier, beneath the hulking shadow of the ship's bow, had gathered a sizable guard contingent in formal array. Within the cordon formed by their ranks, the erstwhile crewmembers of *Denariel's Wail* were tethered to one side. Unknown Grenarr filled the remainder of the area, engaged in lively ceremony. Colorful plumes of smoke wafted skyward from burning braziers, tended by half-robed

Grenarr who might have been priests. Around each brazier, Grenarr women danced, naked save for the chalky whorls and bands painted across their bodies. Attending musicians shook their rattles, whistled through flutes, and slapped their drums, else hummed or chanted alongside. A festive undertaking to enchant and delight the attentive crowds, even bearing as it all did a sense of overture. Judging by the palpable anticipation bestirred within the throng, the meat of the feast had yet to be served.

Time to embark, his jailor had announced upon arrival. Not merely from his cell, it now appeared, but from Grenathrok altogether.

A handful of stones flew at him as he pressed through the heart of the throngs. His handlers laughed. At pole's length, they were safe enough from the light barrage. Their mirth faded somewhat as Kylac ducked and dodged, avoiding the intended strikes. One overzealous spearmen went so far as to prick his ribs in response—the same who'd done so earlier. Kylac turned at that point, to memorize the Grenarrian's face. When the time came, he might not spare that one.

The volley of stones proved short-lived, as the crowd's attention was drawn back to the colony ship with another anxious cheer. A pack of figures atop the forecastle had approached the bow rail. These, Kylac recognized. Grendavan, with Barkavius at his heels, alongside Thane, with Aythef at his. The overlord's personal guard formed a wall at their backs. A pair to one side held a bound Denariel between them, her arms bent around a pole trussed to her back.

When Barkavius stepped forward, the cheers crescendoed. The steward waited, giving rein to the crowd. His gaze from the makeshift rampart fell upon Kylac, who'd reached the pier. Setting foot upon its planks served again to incite the masses. Women and children shouted and shook their fists alongside Grenarr men, praising their leaders or condemning Kylac and his ilk in equal measure.

Kylac weathered their venom and scorn like waterfowl under misty skies, with little notice and less concern. His fate, and those of his shipmates, would not be decided by this noisome brood, no matter how lusty its cries. His only worry was for Grendavan's state of mind—he who stood to pronounce judgment upon them all.

Barkavius watched and waited until Kylac had reached the head of the pier, where his handlers jostled him into a position near the remainder of his former companions—those who'd labored so hard to bring him here. Kylac surveyed their ranks quickly, assessing their condition. Haggard and hollow of cheek, some scraped and bruised, but elsewise unharmed. Had any gone missing since the ambush aboard the *Wail*, he didn't immediately identify them. Ledron, Ithrimir, Whitefists, Redfists . . . all seemed to be accounted for.

Offsetting his relief was the dire weight of their spirits. Some looked to him with pleading, some with accusation, some with derision. Others deigned not glance his way at all. Misplaced, their faith in him. Whatever the individual reaction to his presence, all could agree on that much.

And while the appraisal stung, he couldn't exactly refute it.

The music and dancing ceased, gazes peering up to where Barkavius had raised a hand to quiet the tumult. The nearest priest, if that's what he was, hissed gleefully at Kylac as he cast a pinch of powder into his brazier, before inhaling deeply of the resulting smoke. Through his muzzle, Kylac smelled only dank leather and his own stale breath.

"Grenarr!" the steward shouted from the towering forecastle. His voice echoed across the expanse, chasing after the expectant hush still rippling through the crowd. "All hail our kiros, Great Grendavan the Eighth!"

"Hail!" the crowd erupted in near unison. "Hail! Hail! Hail!"

The resounding cry rang from the lagoon shore like a drumbeat, pulsing again and again, in rhythm with a fist that Barkavius pumped repeatedly into the air. Kylac felt the reverberations of the hammering furor clear out at the head of the pier, in the vibrations of the planks at his feet.

For several moments it lasted, until finally the steward raised both of his palms in a gesture begging silence. Only after another round of cheers did that silence settle.

"Through our lord's foresight, our lord's cunning, this long-awaited day is at last upon us. The day in which we summon our friends, our families—all of us—to set forth for the homeland of our ancestors, the homeland of our progeny. First and forever, Grenah!"

"Grenah!" the throng roared with thunderous delight. "Grenah!

Grenah!"

As the new chant echoed skyward, Barkavius bowed and backed away, making way for Grendavan's advance. The crowd responded with a savage eruption of cheers. Such pride this people possessed, Kylac observed. Such fervor. The Grenarr around him—guards, revelers, his own handlers—were drunk with it. Unbound, blades in hand, he might have been able to sweep these docks clear before they realized their peril.

Alas, freeing himself and even Ledron's crew would do little to aid Nara above.

As Barkavius before him, Grendavan had to petition for silence before he could speak. More than once, he endeavored to do so, but the sound of his voice only ignited a fresh round of cheers. On the fourth attempt, his adulating audience finally permitted him to share his thoughts.

"You give honor with your praise. But one man, one woman, is not a nation. I implore you, honor yourselves. Your sufferings, your faith, the diligence of your labors. With these have you won the right—each among you—to take up your possessions and . . ."

A stunned and disapproving murmur of his people caused the overlord to trail off. Their attentions had shifted to Thane, who'd taken it upon himself to approach Grendavan's shoulder uninvited.

A brazen gesture, Kylac thought, still squinting against the sun's glare. No matter how deferential Thane's posture, to trammel such an address by the overlord to his people . . .

"My lord," the outland prince begged, "my lord, if I may."

A roar of boos rushed to refuse him. When Thane raised his palm, the outrage only grew. Barkavius took a step closer, as if to head off whatever the prince intended.

Grendavan himself assumed no outward sign of offense. Though clearly surprised, rounding to regard Thane as if oblivious of the prince's thinking, he raised his own hand to the crowd before beckoning the prince forward.

"You have declaration to share, lord prince?"

"With all humility, I do." Though undermined by the lingering jeers, Thane proceeded undeterred. "To the matter of your honor,

I feel *I* should be the one to pay tribute. For, with all respect, Great Grendavan, this day is not about your people, or mine, but a reconciliation of the two."

Another surge of disapproval. Yet the prince forged on. "Foresight, your good steward spoke of. Vision. Some of us are gifted with it, while others choose to remain blind. As a reminder, we need look no farther than my own sister"—he turned to gesture toward Nara—"or those who served her." With an expansive sweep of his arm, he indicated Kylac and his fellow captives below.

"And what has that made them?" he shouted, as the protests quieted—a greater number of listeners deciding like their overlord to hear him out. "Slaves! Slaves to moan and scrabble in the dark. For no cause save their refusal to accept the form true prosperity must take. A form derived not from self-glorification, but through honor and compassion toward others."

A fresh wave of groans and taunts overcame him momentarily, the Grenarr masses dismissing his words as drivel, or rejecting them as an affront. Only when he turned to Grendavan for help, and the overlord granted it by way of another calming gesture, did the objections subside.

"See with me, if you will, that there is honor aplenty. For individuals, and for nations. And let it be me, viewed heretofore as your enemy, to recognize the honor in you, my former and future brothers. You took my ancient forebears in, when they were lost and scattered by the seas. You gave them shelter, and shared with them the bounty of your lands. They treated you foully in return. They took to celebrating their own, burgeoning fortune, while forsaking those who had succored them in their hour of need."

Thane leaned forward upon the bow rail. "To this, I say, no more! I cannot undo the treachery shown you. But I *can* bestow upon us a new beginning. I can show you the future I envision. A tomorrow in which hatred and intolerance and struggle are at long last swept under a rising tide of peace. That a new and brighter era may buoy us all!"

As the prince waxed on, Kylac continued to measure the reactions of those giving ear. While some within the audience were beginning to turn toward bemused acceptance, most listened to the grandiose words with barely bridled disgust. It reminded him of the reception given by the Addaran people to Tormitius, serving decoy as Grendavan, upon his arrival at Avenell. The false overlord had on that momentous occasion sought to regale Thane's people with *his* vision of a similar future, yet won only ridicule and skepticism.

Much the same here.

Whatever sway words might have, the sort of forgiveness and goodwill of which Thane now spoke would take root only gradually over generations—if at all. To think one might overcome such deep-seated hostility with tongue alone struck Kylac as blithely arrogant.

"My people have a tradition," the prince admitted, flush with the exertion of making himself heard. "When a new ship is launched, we bless its future voyages with a sprinkle of duramond oil over the bowsprit. This precious oil is said to draw from the Fair Mother's winds the spirits of strength and unity, thus empowering the vessel in its endeavors."

Thane paused, beckoning to Aythef. The faithful consort, beaming with pride in his lord prince, advanced to deliver some small item. A wooden phial, it appeared, when presented by Thane to the watchful crowd.

"With your permission, Great Grendavan, I can conceive of no greater cause meriting this holy consecration, than the return of your people to Addaran shores by way of this mighty flagship."

With an exaggerated gesture, Thane unstoppered the phial and poured its contents out over the rail, onto the jutting bowsprit below.

Reaction was mixed. Recalcitrant jeers, a few half-hearted cheers, each uncertain amid the prevailing silence. As if most knew not what to make of it, and looked therefore to follow their overlord's lead.

Grendavan waited patiently on Thane, arms folded, head cocked to one side. At last, the prince pocketed his empty phial and stepped back, placing an arm around Aythef's waist. The other, he swept wide, as if to invite the overlord to continue.

"Eloquent words, lord prince. I've little to add. Save to thank you for your gracious sentiments, and offer that you bear witness now to the blessing of this ship in Grenarr tradition."

Kylac felt the darkening mood like a descending shroud. As Thane nodded amiably, Grendavan looked to Barkavius, who signaled to the attending guardsmen. A quartet detached from the main contingent. Two seized Thane by the meat of his arms, wresting him free of Aythef. The prince laughed in uneasy confusion. Aythef, wiser of the two, looked to pry at their grip, only to have the third soldier lock an arm around his throat.

"My lord?" the cook pleaded. "My lord!"

"What? Why do you—"

Thane's sputtering protest gave way to a pained yelp, as his arms were bent behind him to allow for the tail of a rope to be looped around his wrists by the fourth guardsman, binding him tight.

"No. No!" Nara cried, before being restrained.

With an outburst of cheers, weary spectators surged to their feet. Closer at hand, Ledron thrashed in his bindings—and promptly took the butt of a spear to his stomach. The Head doubled over, groping vainly for breath. Others among the captive Addaran crew hissed reflexive prayers or muttered startled oaths. Kylac felt a handful of expectant gazes turn his way.

His own was riveted upon the foolish prince above.

Thane continued to stammer, but his words were engulfed by the din. He still seemed to think it all a mistake. When the first pair of guards hauled him forward, he turned back toward Aythef, who squirmed frantically but couldn't break free. Only upon recognizing his consort's distress did the prince find it in him to fully resist, bucking and thrashing futilely as he was pressed backward over the bow rail.

Grendavan shouted, but his words, too, were lost. Clearer was his signal to Barkavius, who stepped forward with a curved longknife.

Nara shrieked. Aythef wailed. Neither stopped the slash of the blade across Thane's abdomen.

Ledron coughed and rasped, looking up in time to see the guardsmen heft the Addaran prince and hurl him over the rail. The Head's own roaring complaint was no more effective than those above. Thane fell until the rope around his wrists snapped taut, promptly wrenching his arms up over his back and tearing his shoulders from their sockets. Though his descent was arrested, his bowels continued to plummet, spilling from his eviscerated stomach. An organ splashed into the water below, along with the lower folds of his unraveling intestines.

There he hung at the ship's prow, mouth agape in a voiceless scream. The land shook beneath the thunder of the Grenarr nation, sending ripples across the lagoon. Their howling frenzy was more than sufficient to overwhelm Nara's angry weeping, Aythef's hysterical sobbing, Ledron's impotent growling, and whatever sounds of torment Thane might actually be mustering as he twisted eerily from the ruin of his shoulders, entrails dangling like strings of raw sausage. Where his innards raked the lagoon's surface, the waters began to thrash and foam. Fish. Schools of them. Come to feast on the fresh remains.

With each imagined bite, Kylac felt the sting of his own failure. *I will rescue your son the prince, or give my life in the attempt,* had been his promise to Kendarrion. This before knowing the prince's culpability in these affairs, yes. Yet his conscience wouldn't absolve him so easily. While every man wove strands within his own noose, could anything the prince have said or done merited such a grisly end?

Helpless questions such as this flailed Kylac where he stood. And slithering among them, the same one that had likely died on Thane's lips. Just what was Grendavan's aim if not the accord that he and the idealistic prince had agreed to?

"We embark for home!" the overlord trumpeted above the tumult. Though his words incited his people, his tamping gestures calmed their furor. "To Grenah!" He directed his gaze down at Thane. "You, my magnanimous worm, cannot bestow what was stolen to begin with. But that which is taken can be reclaimed!" He struck his own chest with a fist as he looked up again. "To that task, my brothers, my sisters, we commit ourselves this day. And to it now, that the morrow's sunrise may see us on our way!"

The throngs stomped and shouted. Few made any move to disperse. Grendavan didn't seem to fault them their zeal, standing patiently at the rail of his flagship, fist extended in acknowledgment. Kylac looked to the other colony ships. An impressive flotilla they would form. A floating city. An entire nation at sea. But an invasion force? Unlikely. Not populated primarily by a civilian populace. Not without the necessary arms and armaments. So what was the overlord's play?

A spear prick stole his attention. "Cargo on the move," his chief handler laughed.

Kylac looked back to the forecastle to find Grendavan peering down at him. *What now?* he wondered. For himself. For his fellow prisoners. For Nara and even Aythef above. While Thane's murder hadn't struck him as unexpected, it unleashed a host of fresh doubts about his enemy's intent. Could he still rely on Grendavan not to harm the princess? How long did he dare wait to find out?

A line of gangplanks descended from the hull of the flagship like the legs of an insect, to touch down along the length of the pier. Kylac found himself being herded toward the nearest opening. Cargo, his handler had called him. Then they didn't intend to kill him yet. He would have to trust that the same was true of Nara and the others. Thane's death . . . that had been a message. An assurance by Grendavan to his people that he wasn't, in fact, in league with the hated Addarans. A promise that the terms of their homecoming would be governed by *their* will, and not that of the Pretender.

The rest of them, Kylac reasoned—Nara and Aythef, Ledron and Ithrimir, the remainder of their enslaved crew—should be safe for now. For their deaths would fulfill no such purpose. Were it elsewise, they'd have served already a more integral part of the overlord's spectacle.

He still had time. To further his understanding of Grendavan's intent. To slip free of his enemy's clutches. To show Nara and everyone else that this game was not yet finished.

As his shackled foot touched the designated gangplank, he craned his neck for one last look at Thane. The cocksure prince with his earnest dream of peace. Set to swinging at the feet of his Grenarrian coconspirator, flesh-eating fish gnashing at his entrails, the merciless mockery of those he'd intended to aid roaring in his dead ears.

He'd believed *himself* safe, too.

Right up until he wasn't.

A haunting acknowledgment, which lingered well after the curve of the ship had stolen Thane's carcass from view. Kylac carried the morbid thought with him across the ramp's threshold, into the cavernous void of the vessel's forward hold.

Could well be a dragon's maw, he marveled, before shuffling deeper within.

42

A MONTH INTO HIS TENTH SPRING, Kylac had suffered the Winnowing.

An unofficial practice, but that's how his elder schoolmates whispered of it—those who dared make mention at all. Yanked from his billet in the dark of night by masked assailants. Bound and blinded and hauled through a series of dank tunnels that stank of the stew from a chamber pot. Imprisoned finally in a lightless cavern, ankles cuffed to the floor, wrists shackled overhead to an invisible ceiling. Provided no food, and only a steady drip of mineral-laden water from which to drink—a drip that elsewise pelted his skull with merciless repetition. No instructions, and no company, save for the rats and insects given to share his black burrow.

And there left to rot.

He remembered being unafraid, initially. By that time in his life— even at such an early age—he'd been well-versed in the consequences of fear and panic, and so denied them purchase. He didn't cry out. He didn't whimper or wail or even ask questions of his captors upon their departure. While his fear of confinement would have him beg release, he'd determined to accept and overcome this challenge as he did all others, confronting his circumstances rather than shirking them.

Admittedly, his courage stemmed in part from his understanding that it was just another exercise. Beyond the whispered reports of some of the older boys that had served notion of what to expect, he'd gathered clues as to the identities of his captors. The acrid thornwood smoke permeating Master Stromwell's lucky cloak. The sharp blend of sallowroot and gowermint tea that could belong only to Master Gorl. Master Vehn's crushing, callused grip. Xarius's hissing breath.

Friends, no. But it wasn't as if he'd been intruded upon by Menzo shadow-thieves. Were it elsewise, he'd have put forth more of a fight. But any resistance at that time would have surely resulted only in harsher struggle later. A student at Talonar wasn't permitted to simply dodge or beat his way clear of the Winnowing.

Nor did all survive it. A reminder that had seeped deeper into his mind as the ordeal had lengthened. Mayhap he'd been wrong not to fear. Mayhap he was intended to do more than just wait it out. By all accounts, that's what the Winnowing was, a test of endurance, a means of gauging one's physical and mental constitution. A candidate wasn't meant to escape, merely to persevere for as long as possible. To determine the bounds of one's tolerance for suffering.

As the days had passed, he'd come to wonder if he'd been forgotten. Or worse, intentionally forsaken. Had he displeased his father in some unforgivable fashion? He sensed in many ways that his father disapproved of him, but he hadn't yet come to learn of anything his father *did* approve of. Or mayhap his father no longer presided. He knew that some of the other masters chafed under his father's stern leadership and uncompromising vision. Mayhap they'd managed to depose him, and Kylac was merely a scrap of evidence to be discarded.

Such sinister possibilities had bored deeper into his heart and mind as the days mounted, his fearlessness giving way to forced calm and later to anger. If he'd mocked some of his father's lessons and exercises, it was only because they were too rudimentary. If he was prone to raising laughter at inopportune moments, it was only to counter the overwrought seriousness of his masters and schoolmates. He'd been endlessly instructed to guard his emotions, lest they induce disadvantage or weakness. But Kylac had been a fun-loving child, and wouldn't be made to feel shame for taking enjoyment—at no cost to others—where he could.

Mayhap it was that attitude that had sustained him through the weeks of standing there in the void, riddled with hunger, passing in and out of consciousness until time escaped him. If any looked in on him, they managed to do so without his knowing. Hope and despair warred within him in cycles—trust clashing with anxiety, acceptance with denial. To each he gave its fair due, never forgetting that, in the end, the trial would pass. Someone would come to retrieve him, or he would die. Freed from his shackles, either way.

He'd learned afterward that his time in that pit far outstripped any who'd gone before. There'd been questions as to his methods. To maintaining his silence. To keeping his mind's clarity. To preventing his body from wasting completely away. Kylac couldn't say. He'd walked out of that dungeon on his own feet, but knew not what nourished him. He'd felt no need to babble or moan as others did, and so couldn't speak to their madness. He knew only that, however unkindly, he'd been asked to wait, to demonstrate his patience. And so he had.

Only years later had his father confessed that he, too, lacked explanation for his son's unnatural stamina. His Winnowing hadn't been the first time it had been on display; nor would it be the last. But it defied logic and understanding by any of the natural laws of which his father was aware. A source of frustration for a man who believed he'd come to know the full capacity of the human form and all of its mechanical processes. For the answer would seem to border more on the mystical, in which his father put no stock.

While naturally curious, Kylac wouldn't be so troubled. He'd simply accepted the evidence of his physical gifts—whatever their source—and set about testing their limits.

If need be, he could do it all again.

Or so he assured himself as his latest pair of jailors removed his wrists from one set of cuffs only to clap them in another. The hard edges of the cold iron dug into his hands as the chains were drawn overhead through a ring hammered into the cabin ceiling. A pair of leg irons had been strung already through a ring at his feet. Leaving him in position to stand or sag—much as he had eleven years ago—for whatever interminable length of time his captors saw fit.

Given the distance to Addaranth, most likely measured in weeks.

When convinced that his chains were secure, the pair of jailors retreated to the cabin entryway and there took up watch. One on either side of the short ramp fronting the door in the aft corner, ahead to Kylac's right. Kylac didn't bother to attempt communication. Instead, he made a play of looking around, as if assessing the cabin's contents. He'd already done so upon entry. Little more than a supply closet, really, holding various sundries. Bolts of cloth and folded linens. Spare candles and sheaves of animal skin. Sacks stuffed with wool, feathers, or straw. No crates or jugs that could be broken into shards. Nothing that could readily be turned into a weapon.

As if he would require a weapon, should he decide to endure this treatment no longer.

The chamber wasn't entirely lightless. Though its lantern hooks hung empty, small holes drilled high upon the walls permitted thin rays of flame and sun to penetrate from the surrounding holds and halls. He knew not his precise location. Somewhere amid the stern-castle, he'd gathered. A deck or two above the ship's gunwale. While his captors hadn't exactly sketched him a map, they hadn't blindfolded him either. Nor would it have much mattered. His sense of direction was keen enough that, even winding and climbing as they had through the labyrinthine reaches of the ship's unfamiliar depths, he sensed well his general position.

Whether that setting might prove advantageous—or the opposite—remained to be seen. Mostly, he presumed it inconsequential. As with his childhood Winnowing, he had no designs of escape. Not without his companions, and not without his weapons. Neither of which he was likely to learn the placement of without further scouting, requiring greater range than he now possessed.

For now, patience.

No sooner had he assumed this mindset than a heavy tread of footsteps approached the door of the hold. His watchmen turned, readying their blades. Without knock, the portal slid open. The watchmen fell back. Grendavan himself ducked through the opening and descended the short ramp.

Deigning at last to pay Kylac visit.

He hadn't come alone. On his heels was Temerius, hand upon that precious, bone-handled blade. The overlord wore a vulture's smile. The Seahammer displayed only tight lips pressed over gritted teeth.

"Now here's a familiar scene," Grendavan extended in an oily tone. "The roles reversed, but the game the same, yes?"

Kylac glanced up at the ceiling, then down at his feet. "Less the comfort of a bed."

"For that, I must beg pardon. Berths aboard this vessel are precious—beds above all. With one spared our royal guest the princess, I'd hoped you'd settle for these accommodations over those in the bilge."

"The princess," Kylac echoed. "Serving what purpose that her brother did not?"

The twitch in Grendavan's smile seemed to congratulate him on the question behind the question. "For now, as my personal food taster, against threat of poison by our chief cook."

An evasion on the matter of Thane's murder. Kylac decided not to press. "Aythef. You spare *him*, as well?"

"Capable cooks are a rarity. Or do you feel I should relieve him of his misery?"

Meaning, the overlord had no intention of granting the distraught lad the mercy of death. Kylac shook his head. "I'll not presume to advise the captain on how to run his ship."

"*Captain*, is it now? Your tongue has softened, since last we spoke."

Kylac glanced at Temerius, son of Tormitius. The *real* Tormitius. Kylac wondered now how he could have been so daft as to overlook the many parallels, in name and bearing, that linked the two men. The Seahammer stared at him unblinking, tension in his shoulders and a hungry gleam in his eye.

"Do you recognize the manacles?" Grendavan asked. "I requested they be the same ones in which I was so long held."

"Is *that* the taint I smell?"

The overlord's smile widened. "Now that's nearer the tone I recall. And the words? Piercing, flaying, dismemberment. All the various ways to bleed a man. Was that not your threat?"

"Among others."

Grendavan leaned near, bending to meet Kylac eye-to-eye. "And here at sea, no one to hear you scream."

"True it was."

"And again now, in our new positions. Constraints and all."

"Constraints? You, who slew His Highness Dethaniel without stitch o' remorse?"

"Much as I would have my revenge, Temerius has staked claim to the same privilege," the overlord replied, again dodging talk of the crown prince. "And I cannot deny that he has earned it."

Kylac disregarded the Seahammer's sneer. Despite Grendavan's tone of false regret, this parley was with the so-called kiros, not any of his subordinates.

"Have you a preference?" the overlord asked.

"As to what?"

"To whose hand you would sooner perish by."

Kylac made a show of peering back and forth between the two, worrying an expression of diligent concern onto his brow. "I confess, death by any means holds little appeal to me."

"Yet so quick you are to kill others. Hypocrisy, some might name that."

"Way o' the world," Kylac remarked with a shrug, "as taught me by my father. A baker or cobbler or stone mason, I might has been. But my father was an assassin, and did his best to shape me in his image."

"It would seem much of it took."

"And I don't believe in wasting one's talents."

Grendavan's eyes glittered in the shadowy half-light. "I daresay I agree. And it may be that talents such as yours might yet be useful in the coming conflict. Forcing me to wonder, by what small chance might we come to some accord of our own?"

Temerius scowled. Had the fool earnestly believed that his overlord was considering turning Kylac over to him?

Kylac himself understood better. This was the negotiation he'd anticipated of Grendavan from the outset. The same that Thane had sought to head off. Because a leader as shrewd and patient as this kiros had proven didn't permit personal feelings—his or his advisors'—to supplant the potential for greater gain.

"In present light," Kylac allowed, "I'd be a dull blade to refuse such opportunity."

The overlord straightened, lifting a hand to his chin in affectation of thought. "Would you be willing to prove it? Would you, let us say, remove Denariel's head, to convince me that you no longer serve her, the Pretender, or any of their landsnake brood?"

"Would such act free me o' these manacles?"

"He lies," Temerius interjected, able to harness his disapproval no longer.

"Let us allow otherwise," said Grendavan, still feigning contemplation. "Let us believe for a moment that his survival instinct is strong enough to overrule any other loyalty."

Kylac nodded. "An honest man could stake no claim to the contrary."

The overlord's smile slipped. "And therein my difficulty. For any man who would turn so quickly against one master would as likely do so again."

Temerius eased, momentarily reassured by the verbal snare his lord had laid.

"For what opportunity?" Kylac asked. "Were I to murder the princess, I'd not be able to win Kendarrion's favor. And his princely son is dead, so I can't seek his. Who remains in this matter to extend a better offer?"

"He fences with us," Temerius huffed, renewing his objection. "He has professed before not to care for her, yet his actions belie his true devotion."

"Against that, I cannot disagree," said Grendavan, crossing his muscled arms before him. His pinched brow knotted in reflection. "Clearly he has fashioned some manner of bond with her. I wonder, might it be wiser to milk her value as hostage? Would he serve as commanded as long as we hold her life in our hands?"

"It would be wiser to slit his throat here and now," Temerius growled. "Wiser yet had we done so already."

Grendavan continued to stare only at Kylac, appraising him as a butcher might a slab of beef. Much as his own father used to regard him. "This ship I'd give for your certainty. Fickle are the ocean's currents, and fluid our needs. Time can erode any man's confidence, any man's aims. Who's to say what might become of our outlook—and his—in the weeks ahead?" He leaned again toward Kylac. "Perhaps, one way or another, we might find a way for the rogue to suitably demonstrate a new loyalty."

The dark hue of Temerius's skin deepened with rage. "You promised me—"

"Nothing!" Grendavan snapped, tongue cracking like a whip as he rounded on the Seahammer. "Nothing have I promised you. And I tell you now, I see no cause to act in haste." Slowly, he returned his gaze to Kylac. "I wish to think on the proper fate." With a predatory gleam, he added, "It may take me some time to do so."

Temerius stiffened, incensed. Kylac very nearly shouted an alarm in the heartbeat before the Seahammer drew his dagger.

But Grendavan required no such warning. Gaze narrowing, he whirled in time to sidestep Temerius's thrust and deftly catch the forearm driving behind it. A strike to the temple stunned the Seahammer, who stumbled to his knees while Grendavan pried the knife from his weakened grip.

By the time Temerius looked up again, he did so to find a pair of watchmen thrusting their spearheads around the sides of his neck.

"No!" Grendavan barked. The short, authoritative outburst froze the spearheads in place, preserving the Seahammer's life.

"Attempt that again," the overlord said, brandishing the stolen dagger, "and your skin will join that of the deceiver prince upon this vessel's masthead. Pared from your body with this very blade."

Temerius glared at his kiros, chest heaving, eyes enflamed with indignation.

"See him back to his ship," Grendavan ordered the watchmen. "He has preparations to make for our dawn departure."

The watchmen twisted their spears, bladed edges urging Temerius to his feet. He obliged them, rising slowly, before reaching forth an empty palm in request of his stolen dagger.

Grendavan considered the weapon before sheathing it at his own waist. "I believe I'll keep this for now. Until I know your reason has returned."

Kylac sensed little of reason emanating from the rigid Seahammer. Only murderous hatred and the promise of retribution. But the rebuked Grenarrian wisely bridled any protest as his escorts nudged him toward the exit at spear's length.

"Send me another pair to stand watch in your absence," Grendavan bade the sentries as they climbed from the hold. "Promptly."

"As instructed," one of the watchmen acknowledged.

"Constraints and all," the overlord reiterated, when he and Kylac were alone.

So it would be Ledron's former role that Grendavan played. Not only as commander of this new enterprise, but quite likely the only man aboard who wouldn't sooner see the prisoner tortured and discarded. Fortunate for Kylac, then—having stepped into the overlord's former shackles—that the Grenarrian's rule was absolute.

Kylac dipped his head. Message received. While far from making them allies, it served as a fair admonition to consider carefully before striking out against his chief captor.

The replacement watchmen entered in a rush.

"See to it he serves no disturbance," Grendavan commanded, still staring at Kylac. "Should he disobey, we'll find use for his corpse."

Only then did he break gazes and turn to take his leave, adding over his shoulder, "I'll have food sent. You've a hungry mien."

Kylac bowed again, though his adversary was ducking already through the portal.

Returning him to the solitude of his chains.

43

The great Grendavan made good on his promise of food, though it was nearly dusk, the Crow's Hour nipping at the Eagle's, before it arrived. Kylac's watchmen—the fourth pair in the day's rotation—rounded dutifully upon the knock at the portal, and gave ear to the muffled greeting from without. One barked a consent, though both remained at the ready until exchanging visual confirmation with those seeking entry.

Only then did they step aside to permit Aythef, hunched and haggard, to limp down the ramp into the hold, attended fore and aft by Grenarr escorts. At a glance, Kylac saw that the cook had been roundly beaten, his broken gait in keeping with his disconsolate air. He lugged beside him a cooking pot, tipping his shoulders sharply to the right. His head hung low, his gaze rooted to the planks at his feet. He winced with each scraping stride.

Upon final approach, the forward attendant stepped back and slapped Aythef's hamstring with the butt of his pike. The cook finally looked up. Kylac could have cringed at his former shipmate's battered face. At cheeks lacerated and bruised, teeth chipped and missing, eyes swollen and red-rimmed from tears.

"I'm to feed you," the cook mumbled, hissing from the wreckage of his mouth.

Kylac glanced at the pot full of stew, uneasy with the notion. Given the fury and accusation radiating from the cook's bloodshot gaze, it would seem unwise to eat anything Aythef had brought him.

And yet, hadn't Grendavan made it clear that he wasn't quite ready to kill Kylac? Even if the overlord were to change his mind, he wouldn't likely permit the pleasure to fall to a lowly Addaran slave—or utilize a method as subtle and undramatic as poisoning. Just as Kylac had been assigned constant handlers, he supposed Aythef's attendants—or others like them—had been with the cook throughout the stew's preparation.

All else aside, it smelled good, and Kylac was famished.

"To it," the lead escort urged. "Or he'll be lapping it up from the floorboards."

Aythef winced again as he set the stew down and withdrew a wooden spoon. His actions appeared limited to his right arm. He held his left protectively, favoring the elbow.

"Try not to choke on it," the cook snarled, full of venom as he thrust the first spoonful toward Kylac's mouth.

Kylac leaned forward to receive it, slurping at the spoon's contents. Fish, clams, carrots, potatoes, cabbage—no poison that he could immediately taste. Bland, unseasoned, but he wasn't about to complain. Herded back into a distant corner, his long-ignored hunger came growling to the fore.

"Suppose we fed him rat tails, he'd gulp it down the same?" the trailing escort snickered. His flat nose and high forehead lent his face a mashed appearance.

"Filth swilling filth," the lead said, idly scratching at an old scar raised upon his forearm. The mark of a burn, which gave that particular patch of flesh a scaly appearance. "Suck it down, swine. Time comes to relieve yourself, you'll get to wear it in your silken breeches."

"Or perhaps we should spare him a bucket," Mash-face suggested. "From which to dredge his next meal."

Unusually flippant, this pair. Kylac saw no reason to address their taunts. Whatever frivolity they might enjoy at his expense, he was content to provide, so long as they permitted Aythef to keep shoveling those spoonfuls of nourishment his way. For who knew how long they might starve him next?

"An asp, we're told," Scales observed, bending and squinting at Kylac. "More a mealworm, looks to me."

"Larval, at that."

"Think he's ever slain a man eye-to-eye? Or has it all been *thrusts from behind*?"

"Seems to be taking eagerly enough from this one," Mash snickered, indicating Aythef. "And we all saw how *he* wailed for his princeling."

Aythef stiffened, jaw clenching.

"Is that why you weep?" Scales asked, turning his invective upon the cook. "For fear you'll lack warmth in the night?"

Mash leered. "We can see that you don't."

"None touch the princess. Lord's command. But he ordered no such shield around you."

"Fret not the vast distance, my primrose. You'll know companionship night and day."

Kylac sensed less candor in their remarks than simpleminded malice. Whatever the measure of their sincerity, he didn't doubt that Aythef's unbearable distress would be the source of much cruel mirth for captain and crew during their voyage.

Justice, it might be said, for helping to land them in this predicament.

Aythef fought to ignore their mockery, focused intently on his task. But his pain and his fear were palpable, increasing steadily as his attendants dripped their foul scorn upon either ear.

"You'll learn there's no void that can't be filled."

"By the time we reach Grenah, you'll scarcely recall your prince's caress."

The cook's eyes threatened to water. His swollen lips trembled. Kylac felt a twinge of pity at the needless torment, followed by an urge to reach out and snap the pair of shark-fin-tattooed necks.

Shackled as he was, he looked instead to his present watchmen. They remained at the hold entry, silent observers evincing no concern. What might it take for them to intervene?

Either way, a protective impulse, Kylac realized. He looked back to Aythef, acknowledging the shift in his own feelings. His distaste of deception had made him bitter toward prince and cook alike. A misjudgment, to some extent. While not without fault for his own misery, Aythef had throughout his quest borne himself with unswerving intent. Not desiring that anyone come to harm, only that the person he cared for the most wasn't made to suffer.

He deserved better.

In the ravaged mirror of the cook's eyes, Kylac spied no such forgiveness. The intensity with which Aythef glared at him would seem to suggest that he alone was responsible for Thane's death and all subsequent suffering. Each thrust of that wooden spoon . . . another savage charge against him. As if the cook truly intended, by will alone, that he should choke on the contents.

Guarding against the possibility, Kylac very nearly spit out the shard of bone detected amid the fish and potatoes—before abruptly recognizing by the tang of iron, and then its shape, what it really was.

No bone, but a key.

He feigned a stifled cough to help mask his surprise, then used his tongue to tuck the key inside his cheek. Any suspicion that the implement's passing might have been an accident melted away as Aythef spared him an extra moment before feeding him his next bite.

With that simple gesture, a wordless understanding passed between them. Allies again, or so it would seem. To what purpose, remained uncertain. Mayhap he meant only to use Kylac as a weapon in the pursuit of personal revenge. But the mere act—marked surely by mortal risk—served to reinforce Kylac's faith in the cook's underlying nature.

"Enough, then," Scales decided. He shoved Aythef aside, knocking him over and slopping stew over both prisoners. "Alive, we're to keep you, not sated."

Mash laughed, then bent to retrieve the cook by the ear. At Aythef's yelp, the Grenarrian sneered, twisting harder.

"I don't suppose your master would let ya put his eyes out, too," Kylac said. "So I don't have to suffer his treacherous gaze while eating from his hand?"

A pair of frowns stole their laughter.

"It'd be *your* eyes I'd worry for," Scales hissed.

Kylac chuckled. "Did your master not mark me untouchable? Then it must be your fear that stays your hand."

Scales glanced at Mash, then whirled on Kylac with a sudden pike thrust. Kylac met the Grenarrian's gaze unflinchingly, even as the weapon's tip pressed to a halt against his throat.

"Gavrus!" one of the watchmen barked.

"A mere prick, I beg. To drain the venom from his veins."

"You?" Kylac asked. "Handler to a cook?"

"Gavrus . . ." the watchman echoed, his warning unmistakable.

"Untouchable," Kylac repeated softly. "For *your* sake, not mine."

Scales—Gavrus—leaned ever so slightly on his weapon haft. But the reins of his master held him in check. Forcing a smile, he withdrew. "Not worth the effort to wipe my blade."

"I thought not. But do feed your frustrations where ya can. See that traitor well coddled, yes?" He turned a narrowed gaze upon Aythef. "For me?"

With a look of disgust, Mash released his grip on the cook's ear. "Fetch your spoon," he huffed.

"And clear this hold," the vocal watchman urged.

Gavrus's false smile withered. Sneering dismissively, he turned heel for the exit. Kylac caught Aythef's eye once more—a parting glance—before the cook shuffled after. Mash followed, glaring, his hands to himself.

A minor victory, but it appeared he'd sapped their enthusiasm sufficiently enough to curb their abuse for now. He could only hope their taste for it wouldn't soon return.

Would that he were positioned to do more.

Better off than before, he reminded himself, observing as the watchmen ushered his feeding party from the hold and slid the portal shut. For the food, yes, but more so for the treasure delivered him. Though manacle locks and keys were among the simplest to be found, Aythef's gift would make freeing himself considerably easier. A trick it would be, under the unblinking surveillance of twin sentinels, to find a moment in which to utilize his newfound weapon. But a relief it was to be thus armed.

He wondered how the cook had obtained it, before quickly realizing that it was likely the same one used to spring Grendavan. These manacles . . . worn by the overlord in his role as Tormitius. Mayhap, with all that had transpired, the Grenarr simply hadn't thought to retrieve the key. As the cuffs were self-latching, why would they, until the time came for Kylac's release?

It scarcely mattered. Whether Aythef had been negligent in the key's return, or clever enough to obtain it anew, it belonged now to Kylac. The only remaining question of significance was when and how he might put it to use.

To put an end of *his* choosing to this second Winnowing.

Even in that, he had further cause to feel bolstered. *None touch the princess,* Gavrus had said. *Lord's command.* Suggesting no great urgency in slipping his shackles to see that she remained unharmed. Granting him additional time. To feign compliance. To see what more he might learn.

His jailors spared him a heated look as they returned to their posts. Kylac lowered his head, making no attempt to engage their thoughts. No need to risk overreaching for fortune's favor. Notwithstanding the discomfort of his chains, the stew spattered across his chest, and the lingering taste of iron in his mouth, he'd seldom been served better.

44

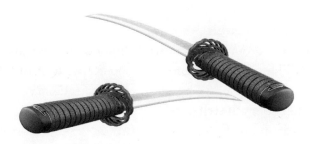

FORTUNE PROVED FICKLE with her favor.

The heat of her sudden ire flared in Kylac's stomach. He jerked from his slumber as if scalded, thinking it some form of torture—

He found himself untouched, the hold quiet save for the clank and rattle of his chains. His jailors eyed him from the hatchway, a pair of ebony statues limned now in the flickering half-light of a lone lantern suspended near the aft wall. Their strict frowns deepened at his sudden movements, gazes pricking him in silent reproach.

Poison. Mayhap Aythef had seen to it to poison him after all. But that, too, felt wrong. Already, the sensation was subsiding, cooling to a simmer as it climbed toward his throat. He was on his feet now. Physically, he'd suffered no harm. Merely a warning.

Not to be ignored.

He probed for the peril's source. They were still in port. The ship creaked softly in its moorings, rocking gently as if to a slumbering rhythm. The hour was late, well past midnight. The Shrike's, if forced to lay wager. Difficult to measure precisely in the absence of natural light, but his body told him roughly how long he'd slept, sagging there in his cuffs. A rust-tinged soreness in his cheek reassured him that the key to those cuffs remained in his possession. To what, then, might he attribute such dire foreboding?

A soft scuffle reverberated in the planks overhead, followed by a heavier thump. Kylac looked to his jailors. No reaction. Mayhap they hadn't heard it. Kylac himself had no reason to suspect anything untoward. The sounds were in no way discordant with the rest of the ship's mutterings—the myriad squeaks and groans, slaps and thuds, scrapes and rasps, that attended her restless jostling even now, in the dead of night.

Yet *something* was amiss.

An acrid scent touched his nostrils. Smoke. Just the faintest brush. Only after did his ears draw upon an echo of shouts. A muffled patter, distant, but undeniable. An assemblage of men, their voices raw and urgent. Their tones of strife.

The patter intensified to form a minor rumble. Indistinct, yet growing in fervor. His jailors heard it now. He saw it in the tightening of their necks, the shift of their eyes, orbs gleaming amid the shadows of their chiseled faces. The shorter one, marked by low-hanging earlobes, glanced at his companion. The other adjusted grip on the haft of his pike, fingers tightening like the body of a coiling adder.

Kylac cocked an ear to the elevated passageway outside, where a man's footfalls passed forward along the length of the hold. A steady pace. Purposeful, yet unhurried. Lobes craned his neck, tracking the approach to the portal at his back. Adder kept his gaze upon Kylac, lids narrowing in suspicion.

A moment's pause, before latches scratched in release. Whoever sought entry begged no permission. At a nudge from Adder, Lobes turned his pike upon the doorway, a muscled stride bracing him atop the ramp's lower lip.

"Announce," he demanded.

The hatch slid open. Lantern light flooded the portal in a concentrated stream. Lobes shied from the harshness of the sudden glare. He straightened quickly—

As a harpoon lanced down through the opening to pierce his gut.

A form hurtled in after. Long-limbed, lean-muscled, sable-skinned. Temerius. He flung his lantern at Adder, then reached with both hands to retrieve his harpoon. Setting a sandaled foot upon Lobes's head, he wrenched the weapon free.

The lantern splintered as it struck the floor, flames spreading quickly to consume the spilled oil. Adder back-stepped toward open ground, singed by the strike, but ready to defend himself. Lobes slumped, then toppled with scarcely more than a grunt, dropping his pike and gaping at the wellspring of his torn guts.

"Your lord is dead," Temerius declared. He glanced at Kylac, swollen with bloodthirst. "I claim command of this vessel."

Lobes sputtered, sprawled there at the ramp's base. With one hand clutching the ruin of his stomach, he reached out with the other in mindless desperation.

The descending Seahammer drove the butt of his harpoon into the dying watchman's face. Crushing his nose, cracking his cheek. Lobes gurgled and fell limp, eyes rolling and fluttering, blood bubbling from his mangled features.

Adder edged forward a half step, pike leading. Temerius snapped into a defensive crouch, brandishing his harpoon tip. Shreds of flesh still dangled from its barbs, flapping as the shaft twisted in its wielder's eager hands. Adder retreated, uncertain.

"You lie," the watchman said.

But as he crept into the globe of light cast by the lantern overhead, the Seahammer was revealed more fully—including the smears of fresh blood across his face, hands, and chest. None of which had been left by Lobes. At his waist was sheathed his bone-handled dagger. Retrieved from Grendavan, it would seem. And not likely given freely.

The distant furor still rumbled, the smell of smoke grown stronger. An ongoing diversion, Kylac realized, for the Seahammer's purpose. If he *had* slain Grendavan, then it was only to see to his greater desire, here in this hold.

Ever so slowly, Adder lowered the head of his pike . . . then lunged abruptly, aiming to empty the intruder's bowels. Temerius intercepted the thrust and pushed it aside. Snarling, he countered with a jab of his own, directed at the jailor's face. Adder stepped to his right, slashing at the Seahammer's ankle as he withdrew his weapon. A feeble effort, which Temerius dodged with a nimble leg lift, before pressing down the ramp onto level ground.

"Would you insist on serving a corpse?" the Seahammer taunted.

"Your allegiance is to me now."

Adder retreated another step, setting himself squarely between the Seahammer and his prize, not more than two paces in front of Kylac. "I'd sooner be lashed to the anchor."

Temerius grinned mirthlessly. "Let us spare you the trouble."

Kylac had seen enough. The moment the Seahammer initiated the next exchange, he reached high with his left hand, releasing enough chain length to bring the right down to his mouth. After fishing the key from his cheek, he brought his wrists back together overhead. Adder was battling dutifully, the close-quartered combat fast and fierce. But Kylac knew already how this contest was going to end.

He didn't want to be fettered when it did.

He worked mostly by feel. The Seahammer's discarded lantern had burned itself out. The lone light near the entry was largely blocked by the towering bodies thrashing and weaving before him, their ducked heads brushing the ceiling. Physically, the pair were an even match. Strong, swift, determined. But Temerius's bloodlust empowered him, lending reckless fury to his attacks. Accepting of damage that a wiser, more cautious man would have warded against, he pressed the pace, suffering and inflicting a host of lacerations in search of the killing blow.

Too long had he yearned for this moment. He would wait no longer.

Kylac was still scratching with his key at the cuff to his left wrist when the brutal flurry of strikes and counters came to an abrupt end. Adder seemed to have gained the advantage when a twist of his pike served to wrench the attacking harpoon from the Seahammer's grasp. But before it had finished clattering, Temerius spun, favorite dagger in hand, to plunge the smaller weapon into his opponent's kidney.

Adder arched in silent agony, gripped by a pain so intense as to deny his lungs the breath for a scream. A common target for an assassin seeking a quiet kill, though that seemed of scant concern and less satisfaction to the Seahammer. He savored the victory for only a moment, long enough to twist his blade and ensure the task was done. He then yanked the weapon free and stabbed up at Adder beneath the base of his skull, before shoving the limp body aside.

As he turned upon Kylac, his sneer gave way to a slack expression and dead eyes. He'd slain comrades and rejected orders—disloyalties that would see him outcast if not tortured for treason. He'd divorced himself from his people, his future. He'd shrugged aside all that he was or might have been, hollowing himself of everything but this single, desperate craving.

To avenge his murdered father.

Kylac felt a twinge of pity for the lad, even as he found and finally penetrated his cuff's lock. He gave the nestled key a twist.

The lock refused to turn.

Pity vanished, engulfed by dismay. Aythef's charity . . . A cruel jape?

Temerius looked up, and recognized his struggle. Only then did the Seahammer's expression regain its fire, lips curling with savage delight. He raised his bone-handled blade, lacquered in Adder's blood, and drove it at Kylac's heart.

Kylac lurched to his right, leaving the dagger to cleave only air. Better his adversary might have fared with a sidelong slash. To open a pocket beneath his entrails, or a smile across his throat. Either would have proved harder to avoid, anchored as he was top and bottom.

With the shift of his weight, the lock surrendered, clicking in release. As Temerius arrested his momentum and coiled for another strike, Kylac pulled his left hand free of the cuff and yanked down with his right, unthreading the chains from the iron ring overhead. He had to duck at the same time, to avoid a swipe meant to claim his head. Nonetheless, a surge of smug relief coursed through him.

Too late, he thought of the Seahammer's effort.

He whipped low with his manacles, wielding them as he would a flail. The free end wrapped around his assailant's calf. A wrenching tug pulled Temerius to the ground, the Grenarrian grunting a denial as the chains tore at the skin of his leg.

Scarcely a devastating injury. Yet it won Kylac the moment he needed to apply the key to his other wrist. When Temerius realized this, he kicked and thrashed—despite whatever pain—as if determined to pull Kylac's arm from his torso. But lying prostrate on his back put the Seahammer at a disadvantage. Down in a crouch, arm braced against his thigh, Kylac weathered the storm, tripping the lock just as a growling Temerius mustered the leverage required to jerk the chain away.

Like that, Kylac's hands were free.

His legs, however, remained shackled, preventing him from giving chase as Temerius scrabbled back to collect himself. When the Seahammer bent to unwind the length of chain from his leg, Kylac looked to the manacles binding his.

He thought better of the effort, and was glad he did, glancing up again as Temerius, hunched and heaving, cocked his throwing arm and let his dagger fly.

Instinct would have let the spinning blade pass, to stick somewhere amid the reams of canvas folded and stored at his back in the shadowy fore of the hold.

He decided instead to settle their dispute then and there.

Swift as thought, he reached up and snatched the dagger from the air, catching it by its polished handle. While he'd never before held the weapon, he'd heard the Seahammer hurl it enough times at the cabin wall to know its shape and heft. Before its owner could so much as blink in disbelief, Kylac flung the blade back at him, burying it in his heart.

Temerius froze. Stiff with shock, rigid with refusal. When his gaze tore at last from Kylac's, it fell upon the bone hilt protruding from his own chest. With curious detachment, he glanced up again, mouthing an unformed reply. Scowling, he reached for the dagger.

As soon as he touched it, his balance failed him. He fell back on crumbling legs, to land on his buttocks. His eyes rolled skyward, before regaining focus. He aimed them again at Kylac, with an expression that demanded explanation.

"Ya'd have done better to burn the ship to cinders," Kylac offered. He crouched anew, seeing to his leg irons, glancing warily between the cuffs and his defiant foe.

Temerius gasped as a shudder rolled through him. When the tremor had passed, he eyed his dagger once more, then peered back at Kylac.

And smiled.

"Nothing," he rasped. Against a choking spasm, he added, "This changes . . . nothing."

"Ya'll find it does," Kylac said, removing the first of his ankle cuffs. "As to what specifics ya may encounter, I cannot say."

"Your fate . . . is assured. They'll never allow you . . . or the other . . . *slaves* . . . to escape."

Kylac shed the remaining ankle cuff and approached his flagging enemy. "Your overlord is slain, remember? Given that, I'll wager very little is *assured*."

The Seahammer's smile broadened. "Grendavan lives."

Given the minimal amount of blood seeping from his chest, it may have been a pressure building on the lad's brain that had him confused. "By your own hand, ya said." Kylac tossed a glance at Adder. "His lord? Your claim to this ship?"

"Another . . . pretender. Arc captain . . . Yultus."

Kylac frowned. "Yultus. Posing as Grendavan. After posing as your father?"

"My sire . . ." Temerius began, before being wracked by another convulsion. It triggered muscles that caused him to buck forward, giving him the strength to clutch at Kylac. For a moment, it seemed he might attempt to strangle the rogue, then and there.

But as the convulsion passed, his strength faltered. He sagged back again, this time falling flat against the floor. "The real Grendavan," he said, his gravelly voice clearer and steadier than before, "is on Grenah. Executing her assault, while all of this . . . posturing unfurled."

"Her?"

"The Pretender is assassinated. Avenell . . . overrun. Whatever you believe . . . you've achieved, the Sundered Isle . . . is lost."

A sneering laugh caused him to gag. His eyes glazed, whites reddening with the rupture of vessels within.

"Tell your princess. Lest she find the grave before . . . before . . ."

He inhaled sharply, a stuttering wheeze. Once more, his body clenched, then finally relented. His last breath rattled an escape from his lungs. Bloodshot eyes drifted in their focus, peering sightlessly skyward into reaches beyond Kylac's vision. And all of it—his rage, his hatred, his obsession with his father's ghost—drifted away, spared the tethers of mortal concern.

Kylac waited, reluctant to let that be the matter's end. A favorable outcome, if measuring the blood upon the floor. But in the immediate aftermath, he felt distinctly dissatisfied. Cheated, even. Stripped of what small measure of certainty he thought he'd found. Burdened with fresh fears and chilling suspicions. Forced to reexamine yet again this snare he'd so willingly entered into.

To wonder if and when he might ever truly venture free.

45

"I should kill you now," Barkavius snarled, as his attending warriors inspected the integrity of Kylac's manacles. "I should slaughter your entire brood and be rid of your festering corpses."

The wiser course. The only means for the Grenarrian to curtail any unnecessary risk and bring about a certain resolution at this time. "But then, my brave jailors will have given their lives for nothing," Kylac observed. "The pair died to defend your master's desire that I be kept alive—for a time, at least."

The attending warriors stepped back, nodding smartly to Barkavius. The prisoner's chains were intact. Giving no indication that Kylac had at any time escaped his fetters within that closet hold.

Notwithstanding the three fresh corpses occupying it with him.

Barkavius scowled, keenly skeptical of the assessment. For it would seem to support the prisoner's account of Temerius's assault. How the embittered son of Tormitius Shorecleaver had taken it upon himself to see Kylac killed, murdering those faithful sentries whose duty it had been to prevent him from doing so.

The sum of which was true, enabling Kylac to meet the steward's discerning gaze now with a clear conscience and an unblinking eye. He'd merely withheld the fact that he'd positioned it to appear as if Adder and Temerius had killed each other—not so difficult, given

their very real attempt to do so—before locking himself in his shackles
again. All to appear a helpless onlooker, innocent of the entire affair.

"Should ya balk now at your master's decision, ya'd not be the
first," Kylac added, with a nod at Temerius.

The steward's expression curdled with disgust. He rounded momentarily, to regard again the bodies of the slain. To shine his lantern's
light over the carnage as he had upon entry, his emotions a roiling
mix of anger, sadness, and disbelief. But the scene hadn't changed,
and his contingent of warriors had thus far produced no evidence
contrary to Kylac's words.

With the Seahammer's blade in Adder's skull, and Adder's pike
through the Seahammer's heart, Kylac had seen to it that they wouldn't.

But even this—the pair's lethal, lasting embrace—provided only
supporting detail. The urgent haste with which Barkavius and his
warriors had stormed into the hold told Kylac that they'd suspected
already what they might find. Sweaty and breathless and in some cases
bearing cuts and scrapes, it was clear they'd arrived directly from some
prior conflict. Kylac could still smell the smoke of whatever distant
fires had been employed by the Seahammer's loyal crewmen—those
whose assault had paved the way for his own. By the sound of it, the
crew's effort to extinguish those blazes continued. Barkavius knew
already what had happened here—the nature of the infighting, and
its impetus. He just refused to accept it.

The steward eyed all three bodies again before letting his gaze rove
the hold—as if in search of some other witness. Failing at that, he settled finally on Kylac again. Nose wrinkling at the stink of deception,
he stepped forward to make personal study of Kylac's cuffs, inspecting
them in the light of his lantern. Wrists first, followed by the ankles.

"If'n I somehow slew them all, did I slay your master, too?"

Barkavius shot from his crouch. "What makes you think my master
is dead?"

"Our overwrought friend—with the pike in his chest—claimed
to have killed him. And your very presence here, if'n ya'll pardon
my presumption, would seem to suggest that none in a position o'
higher authority remain."

Grendavan's steward smoldered. Far short of the eruption Kylac might have expected if in fact his beloved kiros had been murdered. Seeming to suggest that either Temerius had lied about assassinating the Grenarr overlord, or, more likely, that the man revealed to Kylac as Grendavan—whom the Seahammer *had* slain—was yet another imposter as Temerius had claimed.

"Your attempt at cleverness displeases me," Barkavius admitted. "As does your insolent tongue. Perhaps, rather than ferry you in comfort, I might educate you in matters of conduct over the course of our voyage."

A toothless threat. Serving only to support Kylac's theory that the steward served now as the highest-ranking member of their convoy, and reinforcing his confidence that he and his shipmates would be kept safe—at least until their return to Addaranth. For if Barkavius truly meant to kill him, or Denariel, or any of the remaining prisoners, the steward would do so now, before going through the trouble and expense of feeding them or hauling their bodies across the seas. As Grendavan—or Yultus, as it might have been—had remarked, space aboard any vessel—even one as large as this—was too precious to be wasted on useless cargo.

That they'd been imprisoned in the first place, rather than slaughtered alongside Prince Dethaniel, had clearly indicated a desire to keep them alive. If not by Yultus's command, why not that of yet another Grendavan, back on Addaranth? Either way, Barkavius had never made secret of the fact that he was beholden to the will of another. It was this person, however well cloaked in deceit, who would personally decide Kylac's fate. And the steward, whatever his sphere of influence, wasn't in a position to belay or countermand those orders.

That had been the logic and intuition with which Kylac had voluntarily returned to his shackles. A gamble, yes, but one that seemed to have paid as expected. Regardless, he had the comfort of knowing that, if need be, he could free himself again at any time. The Grenarr were headed back to Addaranth. Why fight them? Why relive the chaotic struggle that had marked their quest to find Thane among the Blackmoon Shards?

The westward voyage would not be comfortable, but he could tolerate discomfort. As could his former shipmates. The alternative had struck him as untenable. Slaughter countless Grenarr. Rescue his fellow prisoners—scattered as they were among the various ships—without any being harmed or killed. Commandeer a vessel and—with a shorthanded crew—race back to the Sundered Isle with a swarm of bloodthirsty pursuers fore and aft.

Perilous work.

Instead, his enemies would now do him the favor of returning him unimpeded, unharried, to his desired destination, while giving him time to determine how best to act upon arrival.

The latter being difficult to predict, so long as he remained blind to what he might find.

"Is it true?" Kylac asked, and watched the steward's brow pinch in question. "That Kendarrion is dead? Avenell fallen?"

The Sundered Isle lost, as Temerius had put it. But how would that be possible? After innumerable invasion attempts in the past, what might have turned the tides? Was it not the Grenarr's inability to overcome the Addaran people by force that had led to their acceptance of Dethaniel's proposed accord?

It may as likely have been no more than a last-gasp fiction concocted by the Seahammer to cripple Kylac's hopes—mayhap even trigger some reckless reaction that might get the rogue or his precious royal charge killed sooner rather than later. *Tell your princess . . .*

Barkavius clung to his expression, guarding against potential revelation. Impressively so. A more emotional man would have been unable to keep from Kylac some clue as to his feelings. Some minor flicker or twinge, one way or the other, that might confirm or deny the rumor. If Temerius's claims were true, the steward evinced no particular excitement or anticipation. If false, no disappointment.

But there was also a decided lack of curiosity, no spark of confusion. An unfavorable sign.

"Know this," Barkavius said. "I'm having your princess moved to another ship. Should I discover you've escaped, or in any way attempted to do so, retribution—against her, and against the other slaves—will be swift and severe."

"So long as she remains unharmed," Kylac agreed. If those in command were respecting another's ranking wishes regarding his own condition, he expected the same would hold true of Denariel's. But it couldn't hurt to press the point. "Ya might inform your underlings, should they violate her in any way, they'll wish they hadn't."

The stone-faced steward let the challenge pass unanswered. Patient, this one. Not easily riled. Clearly willing to wait until they reached Addaranth to see what would become of Kylac and the other captives, whatever his personal discomfort in transporting them.

"Clear out the bodies," he commanded. "Add a third hand to the hold's watch, mirrored in the passageway without."

He stared unblinking at Kylac for another long, lingering moment, before rounding and striding toward the exit, disdaining this time to consider his dead comrades. His attending pair of warriors followed him out, leaving the rest to carry out his bidding.

After he'd gone, a few turned their gazes upon Kylac. Their black visages reflected bitter malice and sneering derision in equal measure, the balance revealing no more than Kylac had learned already. A pity, as further inquiry wouldn't only be futile, but would risk betraying a level of concern that he would do better to hide. However insistent and troublesome the many issues demanding resolution, it seemed wiser that he forbear seeking answers just yet.

As to the fate of Kendarrion and the Addaran people . . .

The larger significance, if any, of Dethaniel's slaying . . .

The true identity, if such existed, of this elusive overlord, Great Grendavan the Eighth . . .

Of all the terrible uncertainties, the latter haunted him the most deeply. Not because it bore the greatest import, but because, deep within his core, where intuition was conceived and no lie could live, he believed he already knew. *On Grenah, executing her assault,* Temerius had said. Kylac had no other evidence, only a cold, cruel inkling. But if his assumption was correct, then he'd twice held the overlord's life at the edge of his blade.

And as many times set her free.

If Denariel had hated him *before* . . .

But the sunrise lay hours hence, and with it their planned embarkation—provided the ship had escaped substantial damage. Once underway, their crossing of the seas would require weeks. Plenty of time in which matters might turn, in one direction or another. Given the winding, haphazard path of his most recent journey, it might be foolish to assume—or even accept—much of anything.

So he did his best to bridle his suspicions and quiet the tempest of his thoughts while watching the body of Temerius Seahammer be hauled from the hold. Standing there in the callous grip of his chains. Steadying himself for the voyage ahead.

And whatever lay in wait at ocean's end.

Here ends Book Two of the *WARDER* trilogy.
The adventure concludes in Book Three:
The Sundered Isle